Alan Fleet's first novel 'Woollyback' was selected for a tutored adaptation into a feature film by the UK Film Council at the prestigious Bournemouth Film School. This in turn led to Alan, after a long career in the international oil exploration industry, completing a Masters in Screenwriting in 2006.

He now has two scripted feature films, with a third in development, a short film 'Giri' playing on the festival circuits, and a third novel waiting in the wings.

Alan is currently adapting 'North Sea Tigers' into a six-part TV drama.

He lives with his wife and family in Cheshire, England.

NORTH SEA TIGERS

Alan Fleet

NORTH SEA TIGERS

Vanguard Press

VANGUARD PAPERBACK

A CIP catalogue record for this title is available from the British Library.

ISBN 978 1 84386 493 6

Vanguard Press is an imprint of Pegasus Elliot MacKenzie Publishers Ltd.

www.pegasuspublishers.com

First Published in 2009

Vanguard Press
Sheraton House Castle Park
Cambridge England

Printed & Bound in Great Britain

Dedication

For my wife, Doreen.

Acknowledgement

With many thanks to my son, Adam Fleet,
for designing the cover for this book

CHAPTER 1

1987

Rabat, Malta,

Paolo Caruana always tried his best to park as near to the kerb as he could, but tonight he was having a difficult time of it. Martha, merry widow, and next door neighbour for the past fifteen years, hadn't left him enough room to reverse into his allotted space outside his terraced house in the side street. Her car was definitely overlapping. He sighed, reversed, drove into the space again, reversed, moved forward, sighed, reversed, and gave up. He wouldn't have a word with her tomorrow because at eighty-five he didn't think that it was worth the effort. He slowly got out of his car, closed the door without a sound, shook his head at his parking, and opened the door to his house. He didn't turn at the sound of the speeding car up the street, and neither did he notice the door slam shut behind him. Through her open window Martha heard it all. She quietly cursed deaf old Paolo as she rolled over, broke wind and tried to get back to sleep.

The loss of control had started imperceptibly yet within seconds Edward Grayson was fighting to keep the car in a straight line down the narrow street lined with double-parked cars. His blurred vision made the over-steering worse and as he sideswiped the first vehicle his coordination seemed to desert him completely. With each swerve he bounced from car to car at an ever increasing speed because his alcohol-laden senses were not aware that he was pressing on the accelerator instead of the brake pedal. The more he wanted to stop, the harder he pressed, and the faster the car went. The scraping of metal on metal and the tearing of silver trims from their mountings shattered the still of the beautiful Maltese evening.

Paolo's treasured Ford Anglia finally ended the carnage. The tail end was at least two feet from the kerb, presenting a perfect buffer stop for Edward's snaking car. After shattering the Anglia's tail-lights and flattening the offside wing, his car slewed to a halt. Inside, Edward's nose broke painlessly against the steering wheel before he was thrown against the driver's door. His head continued to spin after the car stopped and the door handle was just a blur as he forced it open and spilled out onto the road, throwing up where he lay. In the next few days his body would ache and swell, and fortunately, apart from his nose, his injuries were all superficial, courtesy of the relaxing effect of the local beer. But now he had to move; he had to get to the company villa fast. There Dog would hide him, Dog would sort it out, Dog was his friend; Dog also worked for his father.

At that very moment, Dr. Godfrey 'Dog' Tate was giving an internal to a local prostitute. However, because Dog was a doctor of marine geotechnics and not medicine, he was using the end of his penis for the inspection, and he had no idea that coitus interruptus would shortly be hammering on the door of the villa. Still, for the next ten minutes he continued in his attempt to break the woman's back, knowing from previous encounters that she could take it all night and still sit on top of him in the morning.

Tonight she was already winning the race to the first orgasm and Dog was having difficulty holding back. The price for the night was always set by whoever came first. If she came first, it was half price. If she made him lose control, it was double. With the first resounding bang on the villa door Dog jerked and the woman smiled.

He cursed and lifted himself up onto his knees, the woman's legs still locked behind his back. She shook her head, grinning as he reached behind his back to uncross her legs, her smile turning to a mock frown as he withdrew from her.

"This won't take long," Dog promised as he hurriedly pulled on his trousers and shirt, leaving her lying on the bed, her dress round her hips and her blouse undone to the waist, the material firmly kept apart by her substantial bosom. He ran down the stairs, concentrating on maintaining his fading erection, and opened the door. Edward fell in.

"Brilliant! Absolutely brilliant! Do you know what you've just interrupted, you selfish little shit?" Dog yelled.

"You've got to help me," Edward slurred, "serious mess!"

"I can see that!"

"No, listen," Edward said as he climbed up the wall and leaned against it, "I'm in trouble, and it's bad."

"I'm still waiting," the woman shouted from the bedroom.

"He's leaving now," Dog replied but Edward put his hand out to stop Dog pushing him out of the door.

"No, wait! It'll stop the survey. You have to help."

Dog went cold. "What will stop the survey?"

"The car crash I've just had."

The last remnants of Dog's erection completely faded.

"I'm hot and wet, and I need to come as well," the woman pleaded.

"Then do it yourself," Dog said dismissively while Edward glanced up the stairs, wide-eyed and curious. His head turned abruptly back as Dog's hands clamped either side of his face. "Look at me, you moron! Tell me quickly. What crash? Where?"

“Bang, bang, bang, all down the street,” Edward replied, miming the turning of a steering wheel and grinning.

“Which street? How many cars?” Dog shouted, his hands not moving from Edward’s face.

“The street with the Cuckoo’s Nest Tavern. I don’t know the name, and I don’t know how many fucking cars, so let go of my face.” His head jerked, and Dog let Edward go, allowing him to slide down the wall.

“Don’t you leave this fucking villa. Understand! I’m going to see.”

“Is she really..?” Edward asked, raising his eyebrows.

“Go and watch if you want, but don’t leave.”

“Okay,” he said scrambling to his feet as only a drunk could.

“Someone’s coming to watch,” Dog yelled up the stairs as he grabbed his shoes and left the villa.

“He’d better make it fast,” the strained, husky voice replied.

Twenty minutes later, Dog was back at the villa and on the phone to Great Yarmouth in England. “That’s right Mr. Grayson, he hit eleven cars and his own hire car is a write-off. It’s only a matter of time before the hire car is traced to Edward, Edward to the vessel, and the vessel to Britannia Surveys.”

“What do you think?” Aldred Grayson, owner of Britannia Surveys and father of Edward, asked.

“It could hold us up if the authorities get nasty, and Edward could easily see the inside of a gaol cell for this.”

“We can’t allow that. The survey has to start on time. Any delays mean penalty clauses, and potential loss of contract.”

"Then you'll have to pay for the damage and fast, with extra money as a sweetener to keep quiet. Most of the cars aren't new, so £50,000 should do it."

Aldred said nothing as the cost of bailing his son out of trouble again sank in.

"And it will have to be here tonight," Dog added.

"Impossible! I'll never make it."

"You have to. If I go to the owners now we can stop it going any further. Otherwise the police will be involved. You have to come out here tonight with the money." Dog heard the heavy sigh on the other end of the line.

"I'll call you back as soon as I have my flight details. Where is he now?" Aldred asked.

"With me."

"Keep him there." The phone went dead.

Dog slammed the receiver down and went up the stairs three at a time to find the woman on the bed, straddling Edward. Dog looked, shook his head with indifference, and walked out. She really was a credit to her profession.

"Keep him here," he ordered.

"No problem," she replied.

Later that night Aldred Grayson pressed the recline button on the armrest and eased back into his seat. At least now he could relax for a few hours during the flight from Heathrow to Malta. The briefcase he had carried onboard was now beneath the seat in front of him, held firmly in place by both feet. If he fell asleep the briefcase would be safe. It had to be. He had pulled so many strings to obtain the contents in the short space of time since the phone call earlier that evening.

Dog was waiting at Luqa airport when Aldred's flight got in, and the two were soon driving across the island to Rabat.

"What was the response, Dog?" Aldred asked.

"Initially very angry as you would expect, but the money is good. We have until 10 a.m. to distribute it. It will cover the residents' cars, Edward's hire car, and ensure complete memory loss."

"We're going there straight away?"

"Right now."

"Where is he?"

"At the company villa in Rabat, being looked after while he sobers up." Dog didn't mention the prostitute who had been given orders to leave when she had fucked Edward to sleep.

———

Shortly before noon the following day Aldred Grayson, Dog and Edward took their seats in the meeting room of the shipping agent's office in Valetta. At the head of the table was Willie Dimech, the owner. Willie had been taken into confidence seeing as how he was bound to find out anyway; whatever happened on Malta was his business.

"The vessel? She sails tomorrow?" Willie asked.

"Yes, the mobilisation trials are over, and the work really begins at last," Dog replied.

"Big contract for you, eh?"

"Yes, it's good for Britannia," Aldred said, "especially with the North European market tightening up."

"Trans-Med Pipeline Survey is the biggest contract for years. You have done well to win it. And to keep it after last night." Willie's eyes bore into Edward's as he spoke. "You're lucky. Many fathers leave boys like you in shit to teach a lesson."

"I'm twenty-two years old, not a boy!" Edward snapped at the old man, "and let me tell you, he did this for his company, not me!"

"Excuse me," Willie said politely to Aldred, "May I?" He motioned to Edward. Aldred nodded. The head of the largest shipping agents on Malta rose purposely from his chair, his powerful shoulders keeping his head erect as he walked around the table. Edward averted his eyes from the man's stare.

"Look at me," he ordered. The young man's bloodshot eyes slowly turned upwards as he raised his head to look at Willie and receive a resounding slap to the side of his face.

"On Malta we show respect to our parents." Edward moved as if to stand up, but the old man's strong hand gripped his shoulder, pushing him down. "You break your father's heart and mine." Willie then let him go, and watched him leave the room. "He needs some time by himself to ease his embarrassment, but he will be fine. Tonight, Aldred, I have booked a table at the Birdcage Restaurant beside the churchyard in Rabat. Your son will be brought to dine with you. It is now up to you to make your peace." Willie resumed his seat and sighed. "Now back to business. Who is shore controller for the first month?"

"Dog here," Aldred answered, "you already know him."

"Good. He keeps things in order. Your wife will be coming?" Willie asked Dog.

"Yes, in two days time."

"Good. You look after her and have holiday as well. You are lucky to mix business and pleasure. What about the second month? Who will be replacement shore controller?"

Aldred looked at Dog who had arranged the personnel for the six-month survey.

"Alexander Haines. He's a freelance geophysicist."

"A geo?" Aldred asked, "Is that wise? Most of them are useless when it comes to organisation, and they can't make a decision to save their lives! All they ever say is 'maybe', 'possibly' or 'probably'!"

"Hey, thanks a bundle Aldred!" Dog laughed.

"You excluded, of course, but you know what I mean."

"Possibly," Dog replied, grinning. "Anyway, this one's different. He's got a good reputation for being straight to the point. Plus he's not afraid to stand his ground by all accounts. Don't worry, Aldred, he'll be good."

"I hope so," Aldred said as he stood up. "Gentlemen, I must get some rest before this evening; it has been a very long night. Willie, I must thank you for having a word with Edward, and although he might not appreciate it right now, I'm sure it will have an effect on him."

"Don't thank me," Willie replied, "Dog said that he needed a good slap, said that you spoiled him too much."

Aldred turned to Dog who shrugged his shoulders and smiled.

"Perhaps you're right, but isn't that what fathers do? Anyway, I owe you, Dog."

Southern Sicily, 6 months later

The van pulled slowly off the small, island ferry, watched intently by the young man leaning back against the unobtrusive white Fiat. The man stared at the driver as the van passed by and instantly knew that the trouble would come from him. The heavily ringed eyes, set in the baggy face of the forty-year old power drinker were hostile. Six months in the sun on the Mediterranean island of Pantelleria had done nothing but age the man, helped considerably by his habitual alcoholic excesses, and now that his company hadn't come up with the last two pay cheques the man's mood was as ugly as his face. He was out to get even. If he had known that the young man watching him was the shore controller, the trouble would have started there and then, but he didn't. Jeff Gayle only knew the name but not the face of Alex Haines, and drove past with just his habitual scowl he had for everyone, cursing to himself as the heavy rain started.

Alex smiled and quickly got into his Fiat out of the rain. For the next half an hour he followed the van through the heavy storm along the winding coastal road until it finally came to a halt at the entrance to the old, family-run hotel. Jeff Gayle turned the van through the gates only to be stopped by two of the four sons of the owner. Alex flashed his lights twice to signal to the men that this was the vehicle and one of their guests for the night. The two Sicilians did not flinch as they stood in the pouring rain, their soaked white shirts picked out in the headlights of the van, and despite the protestations of the bad-tempered Yorkshireman, he was escorted down the drive to the hotel, suitcase in hand, by one of the brothers whilst the other reversed the van out of the drive and followed Alex to Nico Santini's farm, where the large truck was waiting.

Within half an hour all of the equipment from the van had been transferred to the truck, just as the other two vanloads had been earlier in the day. Alex and the brother then left the farm, leaving Nico Santini to guard the three-quarters full truck overnight. Only one part of the cargo was now outstanding and that was already on the island of Sicily. In fact it was just one field away, standing in the same position it had occupied during the whole of the summer. This had been Ben Small's station, and it was Ben who had been the first of the NeptuScan surveyors taken to the family hotel this morning. With the arrival of Jeff Gayle, all four surveyors were now safely at the hotel.

Earlier that day Magnus Tuck had arrived on the mid-morning ferry from Malta and his van and equipment had been taken from him at the docks. He had been surprised when Alex had met him, but said nothing during the drive to the remote coastal hotel that had been purposely picked for its out of town position and the fact that the four brothers would soon quell any rowdiness. Magnus didn't know that by the time he arrived at the hotel, the equipment he had brought over from Malta was already safely loaded onto the truck, one-quarter of the cargo being quickly accounted for.

Phillipe Ronez had arrived from the island of Lampedusa at two in the afternoon, and had received the same treatment.

The Trans-Med Pipeline Survey from Sicily to Libya was now completed and the four huge Argo towers that had provided navigation signals for the survey vessel from the picturesque Mediterranean islands were now redundant and were being shipped back to England along with other associated pieces of equipment. Alex Haines, back as the shore controller for the demobilisation, had the task of ensuring that all the equipment was exported through Sicily in accordance with the original importation documents. A security bond of £75,000 was resting on his successful completion and exportation within the last remaining days of November.

Ordinarily there would have been no problem, but NeptuScan, the company who provided the manpower to service the Argo stations all through the summer survey, had run into financial difficulties and the men from the islands had not been paid. It had been like telling Wild West cowboys that they would not be paid after the round-up. Trouble was expected when they arrived from the islands and that was why Alex had arranged for each of the vans to be met at different times. This had ensured that the equipment would be taken from them when they least expected it, and most importantly, before they met each other. Jeff Gayle had a reputation for trouble and the other three men, who were all in their late twenties, were easily swayed.

Up until now, Ben had been the most reasonable of the surveyors, and Alex had told him that Britannia Surveys, the main contractor for the survey, was already holding back part-payment to NeptuScan until it paid the men what they were owed. Alex had kept quiet about the bond on the equipment, and had purposely not dismantled the last tower before the others arrived for fear that they would do something to their own equipment before they arrived on Sicily. He gambled on them behaving while they knew that one tower remained, and he hoped that once that had been dismantled and loaded he would be able to deal with any problems. What Alex didn't know was that Ben, now fluent in Italian after six months in Sicily, had overheard the customs officers discussing the bond arrangements.

During the summer, when Alex had done his first stint as shore controller based on Malta, he had had little dealings with the men on the islands, but Magnus had told him their backgrounds, especially that of Jeff Gayle. Alex hoped against hope that the prostitutes, drinks and banquet laid on for them tonight would keep them sweet.

The following morning, as arranged, all four men were waiting when Alex turned up at the hotel at 10 o'clock. They looked the worse for wear; one due to all-night drinking; the other three because of some drink and all-night sex. Alex had expected the trouble to start there and then, but it didn't. Ben gave a last tonsil-licking kiss to his bed-partner, much to the derision of Jeff, and then joined the others in the car.

"About fucking time!" Jeff sneered as Ben slammed the front passenger door behind him, causing Jeff to wince as his head vibrated with the noise.

"Piss off and play with yourself. Drink get your dick, did it?"

"You obviously had a good night lads," Alex said in a mock friendly tone, while watching Jeff through the rear view mirror for any warning signs.

"Not for everyone it seems," Ben replied.

"You do what you want, and I'll do what I want," Jeff rounded.

"Fucking queer!"

The slap to the back of Ben's head surprised Alex, but it didn't seem to surprise the others, and instead of turning round to have a go at Jeff, Ben just laughed. Something was definitely wrong. The slap was too hard not to react to, unless you were purposely not reacting that is. The arguments continued all the way to Nico's field where Alex had left the truck one hour earlier. Next to the truck, standing over forty feet high, was the remaining Argo station.

Ben was the first out, "Right, let's get this baby packed away and back to the bar. Job done."

The others didn't argue and within two hours the aluminium tower and all the equipment was dismantled and stowed away; the truck load was now complete. With one short drive to Catania, the manifest could be checked and the £75,000 bond released.

"You've done a good job lads," said Alex as he walked over to the cockpit of the truck and reached beneath the driver's seat to take out an eighteen-inch long cane. With the cane he checked and twisted a couple of the canvas ties tighter on the bundles of equipment.

“Slow down, Mr. ‘Shore Controller’,” said Jeff, and on this sign the three other men walked apart, spreading in a semi-circle around Alex who was still facing the side of the truck. He turned to see Jeff swaggering forward, the slow walk purposely aggressive. Jeff stopped about six feet away, but even at that distance Alex could smell the acrid odour of alcohol and sweat of an unwashed body. Jeff wiped his forehead and looked at the ground before speaking.

“This will be…” Alex started to say.

“Shut your fucking mouth and listen,” snapped Jeff. The other three moved closer and Alex’s eyes darted to each one, measuring the distances. The attack was coming.

“This truck is going nowhere until we get paid. Got that?”

“The bond is not your concern. Ben, you know what’s happening from Britannia to help you get paid, tell him,” tried Alex, his arms by his side, the cane now hidden from view beside his leg. Out of sight, out of mind.

“I said ‘Shut it!’ He’s already told us, and I say it’s not enough. This truck is now ours, so out of the fucking way!” The lunge at Alex followed quickly, but even faster was the upward swing of the rattan cane that broke Jeff’s jaw, leaving him crying in pain at Alex’s feet.

Ben moved next with a rapid step forward and a kick that he would regret all his life, beginning with the pain as his kneecap shattered under the force of the returning downward strike of the cane. Phillipe was already within punching distance to the right of Alex’s head when the bottom end of the cane, protruding slightly below Alex’s fist, slammed into his mouth, causing months of remedial dental treatment to be arranged once the swelling had died down.

Only Magnus had the sense to back down.

———

CHAPTER 2

Present Day

Tarporley, Cheshire.

As Alex walked into the conservatory, his normally easy, confident movement seemed heavy, his shoulders unnaturally rounded. He carried the chilled bottle of Sicilian Regaleali in one hand, and the two wine glasses he held in the other were gently ringing in time with his footsteps in the stillness of the evening. His wife, Sarah, already waiting in the semi-darkness, turned to look as the soothing sound announced his approach. The lanterns outside were positioned to show off his Japanese garden to beautiful effect and the flickering flames brought movement that was impossible with electrical lighting. Alex was the first to admit that it was but a simple first effort at such a garden, but every few months he created a new feature, and over the past few years his garden was slowly taking the shape he wanted. He knew it would never be finished, because it would change as he changed. That was the pleasure of keeping the garden.

"Are the children tucked in now?" Sarah asked, as he set the glasses down on the bamboo table, and the sound of glugging wine replaced the earlier ringing.

"Yes, in a few minutes they will be fast asleep. The hot bath has made them very relaxed," he replied, taking his wine and sitting opposite her.

"What about Carrie? How is she?"

“She’s upset,” Alex replied, his voice tinged with sadness and resignation. “I think she had forgotten what it was like.”

“Don’t worry about her. She’ll be fine in a day or two,” Sarah said, sensing how her husband was now feeling. “We know it’s not for long.”

“I know, but to an eight-year-old, four weeks is an awful long time to be away.” He turned his gaze to the garden, his eyes fixed on the acer with the burning red leaves. Sarah watched him in his silence, allowing his thoughts and emotions to clear without interruption. He would begin talking soon. It was always like this the night before he went away.

“Why do you have to go away to work, Dad?” Carrie had asked as he patted the duvet into place around her arms and neck.

“It’s just my job. It’s what I do,” he replied, trying to sound neither happy nor sad.

“But I thought you had stopped that? It’s been such a long time since you stayed away, that I couldn’t remember when it was. I don’t want you to go away,” and then the tears came. He put his arms round her and hugged her, feeling such enormous guilt at upsetting his daughter. She was beautiful, and to see her cry was breaking his heart. He didn’t want to go away any more than she wanted him to, but this job had been forced on him.

“Hey, Carrie, don’t cry, you know other dads work away too. Sian’s dad does.”

“Yes, but he doesn’t go away for four weeks.”

“I know, but the time will soon pass.”

“No, it won’t,” she said looking into his eyes.

“No, you’re right. It goes slowly doesn’t it?” he replied, unable to lie to her.

“I love you, Dad.”

"And I love you too." He hugged her once more and she lay back on her pillow.

"Will you kiss me goodbye before you leave in the morning, Dad?"

"Of course I will. Time to sleep. Goodnight, Carrie."

"Goodnight, Dad," she replied.

"Goodnight, Dad," said the voice from the next bedroom.

Alex walked quietly into his son's room. "I thought you had fallen asleep."

"I was waiting for you as well. I heard what you were saying to Carrie. Do you think jobs like this could always keep coming up?"

"Come on, Andrew, it's been over a year since the last offshore work. But no, I won't do it forever," he replied, saying the words he knew his son wanted to hear.

"But what will you do if you leave the oil industry?"

"Maybe I won't leave the oil industry. Maybe the plans I have mean that I can carry on without having to work away."

"Have you got plans like that, Dad? It would be great if they worked."

"Yes, I have got plans, but these things take time to organise. Then maybe I will be able to quit the offshore side for good."

"That would be great!" Andrew's eyes told his dad just how much it meant to him. "Because it's not much fun when you're away."

"You still do things with Mum."

"I know, but she misses you as well, so it's not as good for all of us."

"I know what you mean. It's not much fun for me by myself either."

"I just want you here all the time," Andrew said, his eyes now glassy as he tried to stop the tears rolling down his cheeks. Alex wiped his son's tears away and kissed him on his cheek. Andrew wrapped his arms around his dad's neck and squeezed tight, as if he didn't want to let him go.

"Hey, hey," Alex said gently, "I'll be back soon, now you be a big boy while I'm away. Okay?"

"Okay," Andrew managed to say.

"See you when I get back, and before you ask, yes, I'll call when I can."

"See you, Dad. Love you."

"And I love you, too."

Alex sipped the Regaleali, and his gaze turned from the acer to his wife.

"Don't feel sad," Sarah offered.

He smiled. "You would think after all this time, I would be used to it."

"Why? I'm not. I don't think it is something you get used to. It's just something you have to accept."

"But, I don't want to accept it anymore. And I don't understand why it has to be me on this particular job. To take me off the Delta Mex contract in London after twelve months just stinks. Carl must have found out something or it wouldn't have happened. I'm one of the key personnel on the project and it will run for at least another two years. To take me off must mean that he is worried, and he wants me out of the way for a while. Vietnam is just the place to do that as well. I couldn't be sent much further away."

“How could he know? So far all that has been agreed upon is the coastal surveys operations. He can’t possibly know that some of his freelancers are going to take consultancy work through you, or can he?”

“What if he knows that we have already bid for some of the oil company contracts, including the Delta Mex work?”

“How could he know? Who have you told?”

“I haven’t told anyone yet. The curriculum vitae of the proposed personnel do not have to be submitted for the pre-qualification, so no one can know. All that he could know is that I have gone into partnership in a coastal survey company. It’s just too much of a coincidence, though. The Delta Mex work only involves two days in London each week, and the two other days needed to complete the reports can be done from an office anywhere. I’ll bet he thinks I’m going to take the work from his company, and this is his way of keeping me out of the way.”

“Well, if he thinks that, he’s right anyway,” said Sarah, smiling. “You intend to take as much work away from him as possible, don’t you?”

“Yes, I certainly hope so. He has made enough money out of me over the years.”

“Then don’t expect him to give it up without a fight. I would probably send you to the other side of the world to protect my business as well.”

“So, we know whose side you’re on.”

“Yes, the side that keeps you in bed with me every night.”

“I will bear that in mind during my lonely nights in Vietnam.”

“Good, you do that. Then when you get back you can tell Carl what to do with his freelance work with Oceansearch, and concentrate on winning the contracts for your own company.”

“I will, Mrs. Haines.”

“Now, stop thinking about tomorrow, and concentrate on me,” she said as she put down her glass, and went over to share the large armchair with him.

“I know all the things you say are right, Sarah, and you do make me feel better, but I still don’t like the idea of going away tomorrow. I really am travelled out; perhaps having such a long spell of office work has spoiled me for offshore work now. I feel I miss out on so much when I am away. Not the main things, but the little things about home life, the things that mean you are always around. Taking the kids to school, helping with homework, training with you. Just being there. That’s it, being there, that’s what counts. It’s as if life carries on without you when you are away, and on bad days you wonder just how much you are missed.”

“Look, whatever you might think you miss, you more than make up for in the time you are at home. Our children have always seen more of you than other children see their dads. Look at Michael and Jane. Their dad leaves home at seven each morning and only gets home at six-thirty in the evening, and he does that for forty-eight weeks of the year. He also plays squash three evenings a week. You tell me who the lucky kids are! You have only ever worked a hundred days each year, and when you are at home, you are here all day and every day. We have more of your time than any other families have of the man in their house, and the best thing of all is that you want to be with us. You know the project you are going on tomorrow is not your regular type of work anymore, and with any luck, it will be your last offshore trip.”

“I hope so.”

“You don’t sound so certain. Are you sure that everything is still going according to plan for your new company, Alex?”

“Yes, it’s not that.”

"Then why do you feel this way? You've been to Vietnam before, and you liked it, so it's not the country. Do you think this job will be a particularly bad one? Is that it?"

"No. It's not straightforward, but no worse than any of the others."

She put her arm round his neck and kissed him. "Don't worry about the job. I know you will cope with it, and we'll still be here when you get back."

He squeezed her closer to him. I know you'll be here for me, he thought. He wanted to tell his wife more, but it would only cause her to worry. Oceansearch had changed almost beyond recognition since the early days when Alex had first started to take freelance representative work through them. With Carl now the managing director, coming out on top at any cost was all that mattered. As a result, each job seemed to be more confrontational than the last. The money from this job would give Alex extra cash reserves to help through the first few months of his new company's life, but he was determined that this would be his last job for Oceansearch.

"Will you have time to call us after your meeting?" Sarah asked.

"Of course I'll call. I'm meeting the American engineer for a late meal at eleven, so with the time difference, I can call you after the meal and it will still be early evening here."

CHAPTER 3

Ho Chi Minh City, Vietnam.

As Fletcher looked out from his fourth floor window, the huge warrior seemed to be pointing directly at him, as if choosing him; he smiled at the irony of the view. His suitcase was still by the door. Unpacking could wait until after a shower but it was too early in the day to sleep, even though it had been more than twenty-six hours since he had last slept. The daytime flight from London to Singapore had taken over twelve hours, and he had read most of the way. Who could sleep on those flights anyway, even in Business Class? His first shower of the day had been in the Raffles Executive lounge at Changi airport while he waited for the flight to Vietnam. Two hours later he had arrived at Ho Chi Minh City, a place that would forever be known as Saigon to the people who lived there.

The view across Hero Square from his room at the Saigon Floating Hotel was impressive, although he did wonder why the semi-circular park with the statue of the thirteenth-century Vietnamese warrior Tran Hung Dao in the centre was called a square. The statue's base was about forty feet high and white, whilst the warrior, at least twenty feet high and in full, ancient battledress, was completely black. Was he dirty or not? It was difficult to tell with this city. Half of what Fletcher saw from the window was falling down and the other half was being erected. Six enormous cranes dotted the skyline. Saigon was being rebuilt, but how long would it be before another country shat on it again he thought?

The warrior's arm was extended, pointing to the enemy, a leader's signal for his troops to attack. The sculptor had captured the pose perfectly, except now the hand was pointing directly at the blond-haired Englishman. Oh no, he thought, as if talking to the statue, I'm not the enemy; you will like what I am here to do. You will be pleased with me. And then he realised that the statue already knew, he was pointing to him as a reminder to do the job well.

At 4 p.m. after a long, cold shower and two cups of black coffee, Fletcher left the hotel on the Saigon River, ignored the taxis waiting by the entrance and took his life into his hands as he started to walk across the road. From dawn until dusk the streets of Saigon teemed with 50cc motorcycles, bicycles and cyclos. No one ever stopped to let people cross, but no one ever seemed to get run down either. The rules were walk at the same pace, never slow down, and never start to run. If you did that, they would all swerve round you. Well, that was what he had been told anyway. He kept walking even though the riders' faces were impassive as they bore down on him, tempting him to run, but breaking into smiles as they swerved round him. Some game of chicken!

He reached the sanctuary of the small park and stood beneath the warrior. At least the traffic only moved one way around the semi-circle. How could it be as bad from here he thought? But it was. Not everybody wanted to go one way.

"Hey, you first time here?"

He looked at the man with the laughing smile who had stopped next to the pavement causing others to swerve round him. "Maybe."

"Maybe definitely."

"You know that, do you?"

"Sure look that way when you cross road."

"Thanks."

"You welcome. You want cyclo?"

"No, thank you."

"Why not? Safer than walking. Good cyclo. Very fast."

The cyclo, a remnant from the French days of Indochina, looked anything but fast. This 'modern' replacement of the rickshaw must have been built in the forties or fifties, and had probably never been painted or had oil on its chain since.

"Fastest cyclo in Saigon!" said the young man. "Come, you take. I show you Saigon very well. Where you go? Want whore?"

"It's four in the afternoon!"

"So? Why not? You ill?"

Fletcher began to cross the next road. The man and his cyclo followed, straight across the flow of traffic. Riders and drivers blew their horns and swerved; a quick smile as they missed. Fletcher started to walk along the pavement, the cyclo slowly moving alongside him on the road.

"You kangaroo?"

"No."

"Kiwi?"

"No."

"What then?"

"English."

"You sure?"

"Yes."

"Not American?"

"No, definitely not American. I take it you don't like them."

"No, not that, just charge them more. They stupid. Big head, big mouth, big wallet," he grinned, "but little dick."

"You sure?" Fletcher laughed.

"Sure. I know good whorehouse, we go, they tell you same thing."

"No!" still laughing.

"Where you go? I take you. One U.S. dollah."

"Anywhere?"

"Anywhere, one U.S. dollah."

He relented. "OK. Buffalo Blue bar on Nguyen Du. You know it?"

"Yes, know everywhere in Saigon, I tell you. But how you know Buffalo Blue if first time here?"

"I don't. My friend has been. He said it was a good bar."

"Him right. Get in, we go Buffalo Blue first, then go whorehouse."

Fletcher climbed onto the cyclo, sat back in the single seat, and became a colonial settler. It was like going back in time. The young Vietnamese man sat up high on the seat behind him, pedalling the fixed gear carriage, the work made harder because of the missing pedal and the flip-flops he wore.

Going with the flow of traffic was quite enjoyable despite the pitted roads, but turning corners was nerve-racking. There seemed to be an unwritten rule that due to their weight, cyclos started off first at traffic lights, which really meant before the lights changed. They were allowed to cut the corner, and yet they still ended up in the opposite flow of traffic. To turn a corner only to see masses of motorcycles heading straight for you is truly not a sight for the faint of heart, and yet after the third road junction Fletcher stopped worrying and began to ignore the incessant blowing of horns. No one else seemed concerned by them, so why should he?

"I take you down Dong Khoi. Many nice shops. You want see?"

"No. We go straight to the bar. Maybe stop later."

The cyclo man smiled. He knew now that he would be hired for the next few hours, and the English were always a soft touch when it came to tipping.

Going to the bar now was important. Fletcher wanted to get a feel for the surroundings so that he would be in a more relaxed frame of mind ready for the evening's work. He hated walking into somewhere cold, and although some jobs could be carried out on the spur of the moment, he much preferred at least some idea of what was possible. The American would be arriving at the Caravelle Hotel in the centre of town at six o'clock and allowing another hour while he showered and changed, it meant that there was just less than three hours before they would hit the bars. Plenty of time. He smiled as he leaned back and enjoyed the bumpy ride.

After twenty minutes the man pulled on the rear wheel brake using the single metal rod with a loop at the left of his seat. The cyclo jerked to a halt.

"OK. We here."

Fletcher looked around, but couldn't see the bar, or any sign.

"Look, look. Through there," the cyclo man pointed, "through gate into garden. Buffalo Blue."

Fletcher stepped down from the cyclo causing it to creak and groan. The young Vietnamese pulled it up onto the pavement, parked it against the wall, and then sat back in the seat in the shade. "Go! I wait long as you like."

Straightening his trousers and easing the damp shirt from his back, he walked through the gate into the garden. At the top of four steps, almost hidden from the road was the entrance to the bar. As he stepped through the door, his eyes took a few seconds to adjust to the darkness, but he liked what he saw as the images took shape. The bar was immediately in front of him. It was a rectangle, which grew from the right hand wall of the room, bar stools on three sides, with the fourth side recessed into the wall. It was from there she appeared.

"Yes please. What you like?" she asked smiling.

"Singha."

"Why you want Thai beer? You no like Vietnamese beer?" she asked still smiling.

"I don't know, it's my first visit."

"Okay. You try Baa Baa Baa. See if you like."

Fletcher nodded, and she turned and walked down the bar. His eyes followed her petite body as she reached for the chilled bottles and poured his beer, her smile never once fading as she served him. Was her manner genuine, or just business? He didn't care. She looked good and the beer was cold. He took a seat at the end of the bar, as if sitting at the head of a table. To his right was the door he had just entered, to his left was a group of young men playing bar billiards, and directly ahead of him stood the woman.

"You here holiday or business?"

"Business."

The men at the table looked up. No emotions or feeling in their eyes.

"What business?" she asked.

"Oil."

"You not American?"

"No, English."

"That good."

At this the men turned away and ignored him. That's the spirit, you just ignore me, treat me like I'm nothing, he thought, as he took a drink from his glass.

"You alone? No friends with you?" she asked, her smile still present.

"Later. I come here to see bar. Maybe we come tonight." As soon as he spoke he realised he was copying her speech. It sounded condescending. He stopped.

"Have you seen bar upstairs? Come, I show you."

Before he had time to decline, she had walked round the bar and taken his hand. She was tiny compared to him, barely five foot tall, but her curves were eye-catching. She walked to the stairs beyond the men playing billiards, and he was oblivious to their stares as his eyes followed the hypnotic swaying of her slender hips.

"English," she said as they passed the men.

"No problem," said one and they turned back to their game.

None at all, Fletcher thought; just as long as you mind your own business.

Upstairs was more like a club than a bar. The long bar on the right with foot rail and stools allowed for general drinking, and through the two archways were two rooms with secluded seating. A third arch linked the rooms, and at the head of the largest room was a small stage. Above the stage was a buffalo head, mounted on a trophy shield, the back wall was coloured blue of course. Directly across from the long bar was a balcony that looked down over two pool tables, which were set on an intermediate floor. The only entrance to the room was down a narrow set of stairs to the left of the archway to the smaller room.

"You like?"

"Yes, very much. What about music?" he asked.

"Live band every night. Very good. Girls also. No need look anywhere else. You come back tonight?"

"Will you be here?"

"Of course. I wait for you."

"With a friend?"

"You want both of us?"

"No, one for my friend!"

"Okay, we be here."

He knew she wouldn't wait. If other punters came in before them, the girls would be off like a shot. Her smile was probably the same for every customer who came through the door, but she had 'fuck-me' eyes and he hoped her friend was the same. The bar couldn't be better for the American to loosen up in, and the girls would add to his entertainment and encourage him to drink more.

"We will come back tonight," he said.

"Come, finish beer while still cold." She talked about anything she could find enough words for while he drank, but she could not persuade him to have a second beer. "I look forward see you later," she said as he finally left, her smile permanent as ever.

The cyclo was ready to go as soon as he stepped out of the door. "Ready for whore now?"

“No,” Fletcher laughed, “now we go to Apocalypse Bar.”

“How you know Apocalypse Bar?”

“I told you, my friend has been here.” Actually his friend was Carl Moston, head of Oceansearch Associates. He was the man who had hired him, and had recommended the bar as a prime choice for the job.

The cyclo man finally gave up on taking Fletcher to a whorehouse, and said little as they made their way back to the river. It took twenty minutes, almost as long as the first ride, which was to be expected because from the bar entrance on Dong Du Fletcher could see the warrior in Hero Square. It was almost six o’clock and the Apocalypse Bar was getting ready for the night-time. Two Vietnamese youths were playing pool while four men were loading up the shelves with bottles of beer. More crates of beer were stacked up on the pavement on the main street, which was a good sign because it probably meant that the back of the building had restricted access or no access at all.

Fletcher paid off the cyclo and went inside for a beer. There was no entrance as such to the single-roomed bar, it was more like a garage where the two large sliding doors had been pulled aside to reveal a war-time bunker. He looked round and shook his head in disbelief. The walls were dark red, the ceiling was black, and the D.J.’s turntable in the far left corner was surrounded by sandbags as if it were a machine-gun post. The bar he stood at extended two-thirds the way along the right hand wall, and pinned up on the wall were posters from the film *Apocalypse Now*; the faces of Marlon Brando and Martin Sheen stared eerily over the room. Only someone who was sick in the head could have dreamed up this place. It was like stepping into a bar from hell, and Fletcher knew the American would love it!

He drank the first beer slowly, and then ordered a second. No glasses here, bottles only; the American way! The men carried on stacking the shelves, and packed more crates behind the bar when the shelves were full, obviously expecting a busy night.

In the centre of the back wall, over an arched doorway, was the sign for the toilets. Fletcher walked across the room and down the dimly lit passageway. Following the arrow to the right when he came to the far wall he could see the equally dark corridor ended at a bolted doorway. The toilet was half way down on the right hand side and was about as basic as they come. There was only one cubicle with half a door. The gap at the bottom was about eighteen inches and the top was only five foot high. It was like an army latrine for both men and women. A small hand basin was on one wall and a mop and bucket stood in the corner. No expense had been spared! It was perfect. Fletcher knew immediately how he would carry out the task at hand.

He quickly took one of the spare toilet rolls from the back of the latrine, squashed it as flat as he could, and forced it down the toilet bowl, jamming it round the bend. The whole place stank of urine and he was glad to get his hand out of the water. He undid his flies and relieved himself; careful not to touch himself with his wet hand, splashing as noisily as possible so that anyone who wanted to hear could hear, and then held his breath as he flushed the toilet. He watched the water begin to rise, almost reaching the top before it slowly drained away. Excellent! In a few more minutes the toilet roll would finish expanding and the toilet would be blocked. He washed his hands, but left them wet. The only towel was filthy, and he would probably pick up more germs from the towel than he had just washed off.

When he returned to the bar the stacking of the crates was nearly over. He took one gulp of beer then left for the hotel. As he walked out Fletcher felt as if Marlon was looking at him from the poster on the wall, hatred in his eyes, as if he knew what was going on. Fuck you, Marlon, it's only business!

"…but I thought we were meeting later for a meal. I have the details here. Shi-it, where did I put that paper? Damn…"

"Well, that's what the companies arranged, but I prefer to hit the bars. How about you?"

"Sure. Thank fuck fer that. I had a piss-poor meal on the plane, but its drinkin' time now. I was thinkin' I was going to have to go on a pussy hunt by myself."

"How soon will you be ready?"

"Just as soon as you get here."

"I'll be at the hotel in ten minutes."

"You bet!"

Fletcher put the phone down and picked up the drinking straw he had taken from the mini-bar. He cut it in half and discarded one piece in the waste bin. With the other half he twisted one end a few times and folded it over. He then took the two sachets of salt from his travel bag and tore one corner off each of them. Very carefully he poured the salt into the straw. When it was nearly full he twisted the other end and folded it over, preventing the salt from pouring out, and placed the straw in his shirt pocket. From the telephone table he took the note pad and tore off a sheet. Placing it on the glass coffee table he neatly printed a short message, and put the note in the side of his wallet. He then removed the business cards bearing the name Christopher Fletcher from his wallet and replaced them with cards having the same Oceansearch logo, but the name Alex Haines instead. Fletcher then stood, took a quick look at himself in the long mirror on the back of the door and smiled. His mind was clear and calm, and it was now time for work.

During the short walk to the Caravelle Hotel in the centre of Saigon, he was propositioned twice by prostitutes and asked to buy all sorts of souvenirs from postcards and T-shirts to fake

G.I. dog tags. Such was the new capitalist society in Vietnam! He shrugged his shoulders – at least everyone smiled, and above all, they were polite.

An involuntary shudder passed over him as he entered the air-conditioned foyer of the hotel, and he heard the American before he saw him. The man was huge, about six-five and twenty stone, and was complaining loudly to the reception staff about the half-stocked mini-bar in his room.

"Hell, there weren't but eight beers in the fridge. That ain't enough to quench a boy's thirst! Anyhows, they're all gone now, and I expect…"

"Clayton Bika?" The American was cut off in mid-sentence and turned to see who had dared to interrupt him. "How do you do, I'm Alexander Haines. Pleased to meet you," said Fletcher, extending his hand.

"I do real good, thank you," he replied in his brash Texan drawl. "So you're Haines? Well so much for the description I got of you. I was expecting dark hair and taller, but hey, good to see you. We all set?"

"Whenever you're ready."

"Okay, we'll scoot." He turned back to the young man behind the reception desk. "You see it gets filled now."

"Yes, Mr. Bika," he replied, whilst the woman just stared at the big man, clearly surprised at his brash manner.

"C'mon, time to hit downtown Saigon. Say, Alexander is a hell of a mouthful, how 'bout I call you Alex? Sounds friendlier, don't it?"

"That's fine by me." Fletcher smiled to the woman apologetically, and she nodded, obviously sorry that he had to spend the evening in the company of such an animal.

"How far to the first bar? All this flyin's made me damn thirsty."

"Ten minutes, but we'll take cyclos. You'll like them!" Fletcher grinned as he said it.

"What the hell is a 'see-clo'?" Clayton asked.

"You'll see, come on," he said as they went through the doors and out into the sultry evening heat. Two cyclos appeared as if from nowhere and the men climbed onboard. Clayton never stopped talking or shouting the whole way. He was like a boy seeing the fairground for the first time, but his booming voice and American accent brought some bad stares, especially from the few older men on the streets. He was still full of it when they arrived at the bar.

"The Buffalo Blue. Hell, you see, we did influence them."

"If you think this is a sign of influence wait until you see the next bar."

"Why, how's that?" asked Clayton.

"Oh, you'll see later. It's a surprise."

"Okay. You're the leader."

They got down from the cyclos, told the riders to wait for them and walked through the garden into the bar. She wasn't at the downstairs bar. Two men were serving and locals took all the seats. No one smiled as they walked by.

"The upstairs bar is bigger, and that's where the women serve at night."

"Upstairs it is. Let's go."

They took two stools at the long bar, and ordered two beers. The place was already half-full. Nights start early and finish late in Saigon. The band's first set was about to start, and the tables were nearly all taken. Within a few minutes Fletcher realised that getting Clayton drunk was going to cost; his first beer was already gone.

"Tell you what," said Clayton, "I think it's best if I order two to your one, otherwise it might just put a dampener on the evening."

"Whatever you want. I'm certainly not going to try and keep up with someone your size." The stupid American smiled at what he thought was a compliment and ordered more beer.

"Say, do we have an early start tomorrow or what?" asked Clayton as he laid into his second beer.

"No. If we check out at 08:00 we should be in Vung Tao by 10:30. Is that time enough for you?"

"You say the seismic boat is alongside?"

"She'll clear customs at 10:00, so we can go onboard as soon as we arrive. How sure are you of fixing the DFS V?"

"Pretty damn sure! I designed most of the original circuitry for the Digital Field Systems, and I've come across this type of problem before. But the DFS V's ain't common now, and most of the new engineers won't have worked on these old systems. If the fault's where I think it is, the survey engineers would be chasing their tails for days trying to find it, and even if they did, I doubt if they'd carry enough spares to fix it. That's why they sent me, but it must be costing a packet to get me here all the way from Houston. I'm surprised they were prepared to pay it!"

"The survey company has no options. They've been on downtime for four days already. If they don't become operational by midnight tomorrow, they lose the survey contract, which is worth US $5million. Four months work!"

"Shi-iit! No wonder they don't mind paying. Anyway, no sweat. I'll have them up and running by four in the afternoon, you see if I don't." Clayton turned to the bar. "We'll have three more beers over here," he half said, half shouted, undressing the waitress with his stare. “Damn, these ladies sure are cute. Such tight little asses! I’ll have to have some of that before I leave.”

“The band isn’t too bad either,” the Englishman said, turning to look at the small stage. The lead singer, a Vietnamese man in his mid-fifties with a surprisingly good voice, was now singing ‘Stand By Me’.

“I bet he learned the words to that song when we were here in the sixties,” Clayton said, “but I sure hope he ain’t gonna sing black music all night long, white folk came to ‘Nam as well, you know.” He took another long swig of his beer, and belched. “Hell Alex, just look at that kid in the band on the left. Look,” he nudged, “the dumb kid is playing the fuckin’ guitar upside down. Well that beats all. What a fuckin’ nation.” Clayton laughed and turned back to the bar, starting on his second bottle.

Fletcher looked at the ‘kid’ in the band whom Clayton had laughed at. The man’s face was half Asian and half Caucasian, a child of the war; but he wasn’t a kid. He was probably in his mid-thirties and it was true, he played the guitar upside down; he was also left-handed. The odds were that the only thing his American father had left him when he went back home after the fall of Saigon was his guitar, and as a youngster it would have been natural for him to strum the guitar with his favoured hand. Did it matter to him that the guitar was upside down, and who could have showed him how to re-string it anyway? As a boy he must have practised for hours to teach himself, and look at him now, playing a reverse strung guitar with such ease and talent, and all the American could do was ridicule. He shook his head at Clayton, who, typically, thought he was agreeing with him about the guitarist.

“Shit Alex, it sure takes some beating, don’t it,” Clayton said, laughing again.

A thin smile of disbelief crossed Fletcher’s lips as he stared at the American, wondering how he had managed to live so long with such an attitude. He then turned to look over the pool tables and immediately spotted the girl he had met in the afternoon. She was standing next to the cue rack, but she wasn't dressed as a waitress tonight. She was dressed in white, the silk top and mini-skirt left her midriff bare, her olive skin adding to the allure. Her friend was wearing identical clothes and was racking up the balls on one of the pool tables. As she stretched across the table the skirt pulled tight over her hips and buttocks, leaving no one in any doubt that the only clothes she was wearing were the ones you could see.

"Jesus H. Christ! There's no wonder you went quiet," said Clayton. "Hell that ass could raise the dead! I think we'd better go shoot some pool."

"I'm with you all the way."

The first effects of the beer were evident as Clayton stepped off the barstool and stumbled against the bar. The alcohol and jet lag were beginning to take their toll, and he made his way unsteadily down the stairs to the pool tables.

The first girl glanced across at the two men walking down the open stairway and her delight at the arrival of Fletcher was clear in her eyes. Now at least one of her fucks tonight would be with a good-looking man. She nudged her friend, whilst also feeling sorry for her, but still, business is business, and she knew her friend would give the tall, old man with the beer belly a good time regardless.

The two girls walked over, and Clayton couldn't believe his luck when the girl he had been lusting after only minutes before linked his arm.

"Welcome to Saigon, Clayton."

"You bet, Alex," he said, as the other girl linked arms. "Looks like we are both set for the night. Girls, I'm Clayton, and this little fella is Alex. Hell, Alex, did you arrange this?"

"I certainly did. Do you mind?"

"Shit no! I can see me and you are going to get on just fine and I think this pretty little thing and me should play as a pair. She looks like she might need some coaching, and I would certainly like to give her some. Say Miss Saigon, why don't you rack up the balls like you did before?" Clayton made no attempt to conceal the bulge at the front of his pants when she had finished setting up the table, and he insisted on letting her break, assisted of course by him pressing against her rear, his arms surrounding her body giving the grotesque impression of a grizzly bear trying to copulate with a squirrel.

The girls flirted with both men throughout the games, touching and rubbing against them as often as possible, while making sure that neither of them ever had an empty glass. The American lost most of the games because he found it hard to aim with a raging hard-on, and never noticed that for all the other girl's urging, Fletcher's hand stayed firmly around her waist, never once groping her. He let the girl play the come-on game, pushing her hips against his thigh, her hands wandering over him, feeling his hard muscles.

"You no like me?" she asked.

"Of course I do. I think you are very attractive."

"Then why you no touch back like your friend does? Maybe I better off with him."

"If that's what you think, be my guest," Fletcher replied, motioning towards Clayton, whose cheeks had just puffed out through trying to suppress his belching.

"No," she said, shaking her head, "I think I stay with you even if you don't like me." She squeezed his thigh tighter between her legs. "Maybe you like me much more later on. I not give up yet."

The three men at the upper bar had been watching Clayton's display first of all, but the man in the muscle-filled T-shirt was now watching Fletcher.

"He's queer, I tell you."

"Bullshit, you're just jealous," said Flowered Shirt.

"By this time last night I had her up against the wall outside. Look at her, she's asking to be fucked," Muscles replied.

"So? What does it matter to you?" asked Lacoste.

"I just don't like queers, that's all."

"Then don't ask him out," quipped Lacoste sarcastically.

Muscles ignored his remark. "She's wasting her time on him. Hell, she's almost rubbing herself off on his thigh and he hasn't even got a hard-on."

"Leave it out. C'mon, let's go somewhere else," said Flowered Shirt.

"No, I fancy fucking her again now that I've seen her." Muscles knocked his drink back and made for the stairs.

Lacoste grabbed his shoulder to stop him. "This is stupid. Why go looking for trouble when there are so many girls to pick up?"

"Because I want that girl, and that queer isn't going to be any trouble."

"Maybe not, but his friend could be. Look at the fucking size of him."

"Well you know what they say, 'the bigger they are, the harder they fall'."

"Yes, but first you have to hit them!" Flowered Shirt said, shaking his head. Muscles ignored him. He was already part way down the half-flight of stairs.

"Aw fuck, here we go," Lacoste said, "we'd better follow him." Their quick movements to catch up caught Fletcher's attention, alerting him to the approach of Muscles, whose manner of walk spelled trouble.

He was right. Muscles walked right up to the girl as if he wasn't there.

"Hi, recognise me?" Muscles said, flexing his arms and puffing out his chest. The girl shook her head and lowered her eyes. "Sure you do, take another look," he said lifting her chin. She looked again and shook her head. "Oh I know what it is, maybe you should kneel down and look up at me and then you would recognise me, because you sure looked up at me long enough last night. How much are you charging tonight? I'll double it and we'll leave now."

"I not whore. Don't know you," she said holding tighter to Fletcher's arm.

"The fuck you don't," said Muscles as he grabbed her arm and pulled her away.

"Alex…" she cried, her arm hurting from the hard grip. He didn't move, instead he stayed still, pleased with this development because it meant his arms were now free and he could pick his moment. However, Clayton had other ideas.

"Well fer fuck's sake, now I seen it all," the big American shouted as he threw down his pool cue and started to walk over, bumping into the corner of the table on the way. "Where I come from we look after our ladies, and if you chicken-shit English wimp ain't gonna do it, then I suppose I'll have to."

"Fucking great," complained Lacoste, his eyes darting between Muscles and Clayton, "I told you he would start, but oh no, you wouldn't listen."

"Shut it!" snapped Muscles, "the big bastard's drunk, look at his eyes."

"Stay out of it, Clayton," Fletcher shouted, whilst never once taking his eyes off the three men as he took the slightest of movements forward, centring the weight of his body over his right foot.

"At last, the queer speaks," scoffed Muscles. "This whore is coming with me. Any objections?"

"Not whore," the girl said again, "you hurt arm, let go!"

"Too fucking right you're a whore, and a good one! Not that this queer would notice."

"Now why did you have to insult her again? I was prepared to let it go the first time, but now I think you should apologise to the lady before you leave."

"Before I leave? I'm not going anywhere, queer, especially not without the girl. Hold her," Muscles said to the others as he roughly jerked her to one side, "and fuck you!" The swinging right fist would have felled an ox if it had connected, but Fletcher moved inside with lightning speed, his left hand easily deflecting the punch while his right hand delivered a snap punch to the man's solar plexus, driving all the air from his lungs, dropping him like a stone. The short economical movements ended the fight before it had even started.

"Now, would anyone else like to try?" Fletcher asked politely as he took the woman's arm. Flowered Shirt and Lacoste said nothing as they stooped to help their retching comrade in the now puke-stained T-shirt. "You okay?" he asked the girl.

"Yes, okay."

"Well shit, Alex, you sure suckered him. That was poetry in motion. I think I should buy extra drinks to celebrate," said Clayton.

Fletcher shook his head. "Not here. I think maybe we should move on now. Anyway, there's another bar across town I want to show you. You'll love it, believe me."

"But I already love it here," Clayton replied, clutching the second girl's tight little ass.

"She'll still be here when we get back. Anyway, the atmosphere in here has taken a bad turn and I think we would be wise to move on for a while. No-one likes trouble in their bar, whoever starts it." Clayton looked up to the row of faces staring over the iron rail into the pool table area. Even his unfocussed eyes could see they were not friendly. Fletcher knew it was the faces of the men who had been playing bar billiards downstairs earlier in the day, only now it looked like there was a problem! "We'll give it a couple of hours and then come back if you like."

"If I like? You bet I like," Clayton replied, pulling the girl closer. "Say now, see you're still here when I get back."

"No need to go, no trouble now."

"My guide wants to show me a new bar, and I think he's right, we oughta make ourselves scarce for a while," he slurred.

"You no come back, I know."

"You bet I'll come back. Look, here's $40 that says I'll be back. Okay?"

Her eyes widened at the money. "Okay." It was easy money because even if he did come back she knew he wouldn't be able to get it up.

"Hey, pardner, c'mon my kung-phooey friend, let's git moving 'cos I got a thirst coming on," Clayton said as he started up the stairs, "just give her a kiss and a hug and $40 and she'll wait forever."

"Where you go to?" she asked.

"I have to take Clayton to the Apocalypse Bar."

"That place bad. Many drugs, too much fighting. Anyway, why take M.I.A. anywhere? Stay with me."

"M.I.A.?"

"Mouth In Ass. All Americans talk through ass."

He laughed as he looked at Clayton. "A good description."

She smiled at him and brushed her hand over his face. "You have nice face. Thank you for what you did. I not forget you, but I know you not come back."

The warm air hit them like a wall as they stepped out from the air-conditioned bar. So did the torrential rain.

"Aww fuck! Is this bar far away?" moaned Clayton. "Are you sure we can't stay here?"

"Don't worry. Look," said Fletcher pointing to the cyclos waiting on the pavement with their canopies up. The men walked quickly through the garden, and stepped up into the cyclos.

At the same time Clayton and Fletcher settled into their cyclos once more, a taxi pulled up outside the Continental Hotel. A man quickly got out and rushed through the pouring rain to the hotel entrance. The taxi driver hurried behind carrying a suitcase.

Inside the foyer the receptionist smiled as the man wiped the rain from his face.

"Good evening, sir."

"Good evening. I have a room booked for one night."

"And the name, sir?"

"Alex Haines."

"Is this civilised or what?" Clayton shouted above the sound of the rain, his head peering round the side of the canopy. Hell, Vietnam ain't so bad after all! Perhaps I should've come the first time round instead of dodging the draft. Tell you what, how about a race?" he shouted to the two cyclo riders. "First to the Apocalypse Bar gets $10." They both nodded. "Okay boys, off you go!"

They pedalled like there was no tomorrow. $10 for one journey was a hell of a lot of money when you consider that they only earned about $5 per day. Horns blared as they simply refused to stop at any of the road junctions.

"Hey Alex, c'mon, cheer your man on." But he wasn't looking. He kept his face down as the traffic swerved to avoid them. 'Faster, faster' was all he could hear as the other cyclo pulled ahead, followed by hoots of laughter.

The race was over in just ten minutes. Clayton won, and gave the man $10. Fletcher came last, as Clayton put it, and also paid $10 to his cyclo man.

"American asshole," Fletcher's cyclo man said in the direction of Clayton and the other cyclo. "This bar bad. You careful. Okay?"

"Yes, okay."

"I wait for you?"

"No, last stop. Goodnight." He turned to the front of the bar and went to find Clayton, who had already pushed through the crowds and was ordering the beer. Half of the first bottle was already gone in the short time it took Fletcher to get alongside the American.

"This place is Fuckin' A!" boomed Clayton, "Fuckin' A!" His eyes were wide with delight as he looked round the bar.

"You looked at the ceiling yet?" Fletcher asked.

Clayton tilted his head back to look, spilling beer on his shirt as he did so. "Outta this world!" He loved it. The warped mind that had dreamed up such a place had even painted helicopters round the ceiling fans. The swirling fans now looked like the rotors on the infamous Huey choppers that had caused so much pain and suffering in this country.

"I love this place! Fuck, I should never have missed out before. And just look at the pussy over there." He signalled to the young girls over by the D.J.'s sandbagged bunker. They were all lined up, waiting to be picked for the night.

"Still think you're up to two of them?"

"You bet, but first I reckon it's time to show Charlie how to shoot pool since we invented the fuckin' game." He drained his bottle and passed it to Fletcher. "Get 'em in, buddy. Watch this!" Unsteadily, he started to push his way to the table, second bottle of beer in hand. "Who wants to play me for twenty bucks?" he shouted, slapping the note down in the middle of the table, spoiling the game already in play.

While his 'buddy' stayed back against the bar and ordered three beers, Clayton's challenge was taken up by the older of the two Vietnamese men whose winning play he had just ruined. Clayton was swaying as he eyed up the white ball, but his break was good, downing a stripe and following up with two more. He swung his cue like he was Tom Cruise in *The Color of Money*, and he looked up at Marlon and Martin on the wall. "Fuck, but we boys are good!" he said, giving his best Ronald Reagan salute.

The man cleared the table without Clayton taking another shot.

“Flukey little bastard, ain’t ya? Double or quits!”

While all the attention was on the pool table, Fletcher lifted one of Clayton’s beers from the bar, swallowed a mouthful, and took the straw from his pocket. Holding the bottle in front of his stomach he carefully twisted open one end of the salt-filled straw and poured the contents into the bottle. He swirled the beer a few times before replacing it on the bar.

One of the bar girls racked up the balls, and Clayton rubbed his hand up the back of her legs and beneath her short skirt as she leaned over the table. Wolfman Jack couldn’t have howled better as his hand touched pussy. “Hell, doesn’t anyone wear panties in Saigon?” She turned, smiling, and grabbed at his crotch. “Mmm mmh! This is my kinda bar, honey. Now you see the small, white guy at the bar holding up those beers? You go get me one quick like, and come back here to bring me luck.”

Fletcher passed the girl a bottle of beer, and followed her back holding the other two bottles, the doctored bottle in his right hand. Clayton greedily snatched the bottle from the girl and took a long pull before wiping his mouth with the back of his hand.

Clayton lost the next game on the black ball. “Well fuck, Charlie, I mean luck like that ain’t gonna hold! Say, where’s the goddam fuckin’ chalk,” he said looking at the worn cue tip. “I’m sure we must have left more than one block after we kicked your asses when we was here last.” The few westerners in the crowd were now losing interest in the big drunk, but the Saigonese were watching it all. They loved seeing the American lose, but a small group were definitely not enjoying the American’s line of insults.

“You on for a $100 game?” goaded Clayton, as if he had only been hustling.

"$200." The man replied, his face devoid of emotion.

"Boy, you got it."

While the bargirl did her stuff flashing herself around and over the sides of the pool table, Fletcher went to check on the latrine. The blockage was working perfectly. He walked quickly back into the bar, passed the doctored bottle of beer to the girl indicating it was for Clayton, then stayed on the edge of the circle of people so that when the time came he would be able to follow close behind.

Clayton finished the good bottle and stepped forward to break. "Prepare to die, little man," he said cockily as the white ball slammed into the pack. The game was close and when the Vietnamese doubled the black into the centre pocket, the locals roared and clapped. The man's eyes looked at Clayton with a hatred born years ago.

"You lucky sonovabitch gook! Hey fuck, Marlon, how come you didn't help me?" Clayton said to the poster. He took the beer from the girl and started to gulp. He stopped to belch but realised immediately it was more than wind coming up from his stomach. He staggered away from the table, clamping his hand over his mouth, the locals now laughing and pointing at him as he lurched to the toilet. He slammed open the latrine door and threw up into the bowl which was already full to the brim with shit, piss and water. The mixture splashed his trousers and shoes as it overflowed.

"Shit, fucking mess!" was all he could say before his stomach went into another violent cramp, dropping him to his knees as another stream of puke burst from his mouth and nose.

Fletcher had started to follow but the five young Vietnamese men standing at the back wall had moved quickly into the passageway at the signal of the man who had just won the pool games against the American. Halfway down the dimly lit passage, Fletcher's path was blocked by one of the men. He made as if to walk past, but his action was met by the arcing of the switchblade, its shiny edge catching what light there was. The man said nothing, leaving the blade to give the message as it gently waved in front of his face, in a way that an adult would admonish a child by waving the index finger. The man raised his eyes and his head in a small movement that unmistakably said turn round and walk away. Fletcher did so, to the sound of retching coming from the latrine. He hadn't planned for this, but this was all Clayton's doing, and there was not a chance in hell that he was going to fight in a place like this. Fletcher walked straight past the pool table and Clayton's opponent, who was now moving towards the passageway. Their eyes met briefly and the man drew a single finger across his neck and smiled, his Asian face showing the faint Caucasian features that made him stand out from the other Vietnamese. That and his eyes, dead pools that showed no emotion. Fletcher left while he still could, not wanting to be associated with the American in any way.

The man with the dead eyes walked slowly from the bar down the passageway, the men moving aside as he kicked open the latrine door to find Clayton with his head over the bowl. He said nothing, as he stood close behind the kneeling figure. He waited for the next cramp to hit as Clayton's stomach convulsed, sending another stream of puke on its way. When the American's head involuntarily went down, the man struck. Using the palm of his hand he pushed with all of his weight at the back of Clayton's head, ramming his forehead into the rim of the ceramic bowl, knocking him unconscious. The body slumped over the bowl, face down in the foul mixture. The man lit a cigarette and calmly smoked it down to the filter as he waited

"Fucking asshole. Drink too much and drown in shit! Is there any wonder you lost? Only when you learn some manners can there be a future for your kind here. Take him and dump him in the Saigon River," he said to the other men.

The door marked 'Private' at the end of the dark corridor was quickly opened and three of the young men moved swiftly to the latrine. Two other men were lighting cigarettes in the passageway, carefully blocking the way. The big American was dragged out the back way and the door closed; it was as if he had never been there. Outside in the heavy rain the men hauled the body into the boot of an old car, slammed the lid closed and quickly jumped into the car. Within seconds it was gone.

Outside, at the front of the bar, Fletcher walked to the first of four cyclos who were waiting with their canopies up. Although things had not gone exactly as planned, he still had to finish what he had started. "You know Vietnam House Restaurant?" he said to the cyclo man, his nerves showing in his voice.

"Sure, know everywhere in Saigon."

"Good," he said reaching for his wallet. "I want you to take this note to the restaurant and give it to the waitress in the bar. Tell her it is from the American."

"How much?"

"Five dollars."

"Ten dollah."

"Okay."

The cyclo set off on its jerky ride and Fletcher went to the second cyclo.

"You follow him slowly."

"Where to?"

"Just follow."

"How much?"

"Ten dollars."

"Fifteen dollah."

"For fuck's sake."

"Him nearly gone," the rider said looking down the street, eyebrows raised.

"Okay, fifteen dollars, but stay back when he stops at the restaurant."

Fletcher sat back beneath the canopy, keeping his head from view. His mind was racing. His plan had been simple. All he had wanted to do was push the American's head into the toilet just once. That would have necessitated a hospital visit, possibly a stomach pump, and guaranteed that he would not have got to Vung Tao to carry out the DFS V repairs. At least he would still be alive, because Fletcher didn't doubt for one minute what the pool player with the dead eyes had intended to do. None of the jobs were ever meant to go this far. They were all only basic sabotage of personnel movements to prevent work from being carried out. He was now out of his depth by a long way. He shuddered, and it took all of his willpower to stop throwing up himself.

He prayed that the rain continued while they made their way through the streets even though the canopy only covered so much; from the knees down, his trousers were very wet. Still, a cyclo with the canopy up in the pouring rain meant that the occupant's face would not be seen. His movements from the Apocalypse Bar would be difficult to trace, even if anyone did remember he had arrived with Clayton. He prayed that the man with the dead eyes would ignore him. Christ, how could tonight have gone so wrong? Fucking American. Why did he have to have been so loud?

It took about ten minutes to reach the restaurant, and they stopped about fifty yards back down the street. Fletcher watched the first cyclo rider go to the restaurant door and saw him pass the note without going inside.

"Okay," Fletcher said, his head out in the rain once more. "That's it. Take me to the Floating Hotel."

"Five dollah more."

"All right, five fucking dollah more. Just go, but not past the restaurant." The cyclo slowly turned and went down a side road.

Fifteen minutes earlier, Alex Haines had himself rushed to the front door of the restaurant in order to get out of the rain, and had been greeted by the same waitress.

"Good evening. I have a table booked for two at eleven. I am Alex Haines and a Mr. Clayton Bika will be arriving shortly. I am a little early." The waitress smiled and checked the list. He admired her attire that was traditional Vietnamese, as you would expect from a restaurant calling itself Vietnam House. The peacock blue silk top with mandarin collar, long sleeves, and long body reached below her knees, but was split high to the waist on both sides to show off the wide, brilliant white, silk trousers. The effect was both attractive and demure.

"I'm afraid your table is not yet ready, sir," she said apologetically, "perhaps you would like to wait in the bar." He nodded his agreement. "I will show you. This way please." She held out her hand to direct him, and he chose a table near the window. The young man playing at the white grand piano nodded politely, as Alex took a seat and looked around.

Now, before he had even finished his glass of beer the waitress reappeared; this time she was holding a piece of paper.

"Excuse me, Mr. Haines, this has been delivered for you." She bowed and left. Before she reached the door Alex had read the note saying that Clayton Bika would not be making it for a meal, and that he would make his own way to Vung Tao in the morning. Alex just looked and stared. There was no reason given.

"Of all the …"

The waitress turned at the expression in his voice. "Sir, is something wrong?"

"Well, my dinner guest has just cancelled, so first of all could I change the booking for just myself?"

"Of course, sir, that is not a problem."

"And could I use your phone to make a quick call to the Caravelle Hotel where he is supposed to be staying?"

"Certainly. But I will call them for you if you like."

"Yes, if you don't mind. Could you ask if Mr. Bika is there?"

The waitress was gone only a few minutes. "I am afraid that he is out. They said a man called for him and they went to the bars earlier tonight."

"But I didn't realise he knew anyone here? I was supposed to be his contact."

The waitress just looked at Alex, unsure what to say.

"Did they describe the man? Vietnamese, American, anything?"

"White, Englishman."

"What? Are you sure?"

"That's what they said."

"That's very odd." Alex shook his head and looked at the note again.

"I should not worry, sir, they said he was drunk already. Maybe your meal will be better alone." She smiled.

"Yes, perhaps it will. Is it possible to go up to the restaurant now?"

"Of course, sir. Follow me."

Upstairs in the restaurant, the three-piece ensemble was playing Vietnamese music on a slightly elevated stage, surrounded by lush potted plants and carefully arranged bonsai. The pitch and intensity of the music was perfect, designed to be heard but not interfere with conversation. Not that Alex had anyone to talk to as he enjoyed his seafood meal, but the music was such that it did not disturb his thoughts either. He couldn't understand why the American would have cancelled the meal, which was also to have been an informal meeting to discuss the details for tomorrow. But by the time he had finished the food Alex wasn't really bothered. Perhaps Mr. Clayton Bika had heard some friend was in town, and had just taken off. Anyway, Alex was now looking forward to his call home.

Back in his room at the Continental Hotel, Alex stripped and showered, washing away the clammy sweat of the evening, and then he called home. Due to the time difference it was still only six o'clock in the evening in England, and his daughter answered the phone.

"Hello, Carrie, it's Dad."

"Hi Dad, quick, Mum, Andrew, it's Dad on the phone," he heard her shout. "When will you be coming home?" she asked.

"In a few more days, the work hasn't even started yet!" As he talked to his family in turn, Alex yearned to be with them and when the call ended, he lay on the bed in the darkened room, his eyes closed. The first night away was always the worst. Tomorrow he would have the full impact of the problems to consider and deal with, and time would pass more quickly as the job progressed. What he couldn't have foreseen was the additional problems about to unfold. His last thought before sleep took him was for Clayton Bika. He hoped the American made it to Vung Tao on time.

———

The *Tethyan Explorer* was tied up alongside the V.T.S.C. Marine Base in Vung Tao when Alex arrived the next morning. The journey from Saigon had taken a little over two hours, and when he stepped down from the air-conditioned Land Rover the overhead sun began to burn immediately. A small man in a white shirt and light trousers greeted him.

"I am Mr. Tran, the V.T.S.C. superintendent. Pleased to meet you."

"Alex Haines," he replied, shaking his hand.

"You are alone?" the puzzled look turning to one of concern as Tran glanced at the Land Rover.

"Yes."

"But where is Mr. Bika? He should be with you."

"I have no idea. I was due to have a meal with him last night in Saigon, but he never showed. He sent a note that he would be making his own way here. I expected him to be here already."

"This is not good," said Tran, shaking his head as he motioned Alex towards the office entrance. "No, not good at all."

Once inside the conference room, Tran closed the door, so that they would not be overheard. "This is very serious. If the repairs are not carried out today, then I am afraid that Eastern Surveying Services will lose the contract to their British rivals, Britannia Surveys, who were the next cheapest bidders for the work. The *Tethyan Explorer* will be stood down in favour of the *Pacific Challenger*, who is anchored off Vung Tao at this very moment, waiting like a vulture!"

Alex smiled, "You can't help but admire them can you? Anyhow, I thought you were their agents also. You won't lose out."

"No, that is true, but Easterns have a large penalty clause in their contract, and at midnight tonight the company will go bust if it can't get the digital system working. Please, you must excuse me; I must try to contact Mr. Bika in Saigon. He stayed at the Caravelle Hotel?"

Alex nodded.

"Okay. I will also have to contact his company in Houston to let them know what is happening. Then I will have to break the news to the Party Chief of the survey crew that their engineer has not turned up yet. You say you did not see him last night?"

"That's right. We were supposed to have a meal together, but he didn't turn up at the restaurant. I heard from the hotel that he had met up with a friend and hit the bars. Maybe he struck lucky and got laid," Alex replied.

"Americans are assholes. All the same. Too much beer, too much pussy. He's probably still at it now."

"Who knows? Maybe he will show up later."

He didn't. The journey by river would take a few more days.

At midnight an emergency meeting was called in the conference room at the V.T.S.C. Marine Base. Four people were in attendance, plus a secretary taking minutes.

"Gentlemen, this meeting has been convened because of the non-compliance of Eastern Surveying Services to meet the five-day breakdown clause, set out in the contract for the regional high resolution seismic surveys in the Vietnamese sector of the South China Sea.

"In accordance with Section VIII (3) of the agreement, their contract is now terminated and the penalty clause invoked. The contract passes to Britannia Surveys Ltd. using their vessel *Pacific Challenger*, which I believe is now alongside in Vung Tao, awaiting sailing instructions.

"Before we proceed with all the finer details and data handover, I would like you all to announce your name and company position so that they can be entered into the minutes, and form part of the legally binding document."

"Mr. Tran, V.T.S.C. Marine Superintendent. Ship's chandlers."

"Charles Fallow, Far East Operations Manager, Eastern Surveying Services."

"Alistair Singleton, Asian Operations Manager, Britannia Surveys Ltd."

"And this meeting is chaired by me, Alex Haines of Oceansearch Associates Ltd., representing the client, Nautilus Oil International, in all aspects of this project!"

As if on cue, the door to the conference room opened. The secretary looked up as the four men turned to see who had entered without knocking. The greatest surprise was written on the face of Alex.

"Come on, Alex, why the look?" Fletcher said. "After all, we do work for the same company."

"Fletcher, what are you doing here?" was all Alex could manage, as his mind raced through the possibilities.

"Well, there has to be a safety audit before the *Pacific Challenger* can be accepted for the work. Surely you know that?"

"Of course, I know that, but how does that concern you?"

"I'm here to do the audit."

"Really?"

"Yes, really."

"Gentlemen," Alex said to the others present, "perhaps you would permit us to have a word in private." There was an awkward silence as Alex followed Fletcher out of the room.

In the corridor Alex grabbed Fletcher's shoulder and spun him round. "What are you playing at? You are not an auditor."

"Shut it, Alex, and listen," the threat very clear in Fletcher's voice. "You know as well as I do that the vessel cannot be accepted until the safety audit has been carried out. I will do it in the morning, and the vessel will pass. We both know that the vessel is really good anyway. What's the problem?"

"How could you have known to be here? If Clayton had arrived, the *Tethyan Explorer* would probably still be on the job."

"Well he didn't, did he?" Fletcher smiled as the words left his lips.

"Take that smug look off your face." Alex paused as the realisation hit him. "It was you; you were in Saigon last night, weren't you? You met Clayton Bika."

Fletcher put his face close to Alex's. "Watch the tone of your voice when you speak to me. Now once, and once only, *forget Clayton Bika.* All you need to know is that I am here at the suggestion of Carl Moston, because he was wise enough to foresee this situation. He spoke with Nautilus Oil International yesterday and they agreed that it was a sensible fallback option. Satisfied?"

"No, I'm not satisfied, and don't even think of threatening me, Fletcher, your posturing means nothing. I knew something was wrong with me being put on this job. I knew it!" Alex shook his head. "Where is Bika? Oh Christ, the note! I should have realised. He never sent it, did he?"

"Don't give it another thought, Alex, otherwise you will be in it deeper than you could ever realise." From his wallet Fletcher took some business cards. "Oh, almost forgot, Carl asked me to give you some of your business cards in case you were running low."

Alex grabbed Fletcher by the throat, and then pushed him hard against the wall. "If you have done anything that incriminates me…"

"What? What will you do?" Fletcher said, rubbing his throat. "We have three guys inside wondering what is going on out here, and this meeting has to go ahead or we are all in the shit. Now back off, and get this meeting moving."

"You as a safety auditor?"

"Got it in one."

"When did you arrive?" Alex asked.

"It doesn't matter. I'm here; you need a safety audit, and my curriculum vitae now says that I am a qualified auditor. Problem solved."

"You met him."

"Let it go, Alex. Now, I suggest we go back inside and you explain my position very carefully. Just make it clear that Oceansearch Associates Ltd. wanted to cover all eventualities and that's why I am here. Now finish this meeting."

Fletcher, smiling, followed Alex back into the room. Once they were seated Alex again rose to continue the meeting, this time adding the name of Christopher Fletcher to the minutes.

CHAPTER 4

Great Yarmouth, Norfolk.

The midnight blue XJ6 glided effortlessly through the bustle of the morning traffic going over the town bridge to Gorleston. Aldred Grayson relaxed in the back, thinking about the morning meeting he had just chaired. He'd called the meeting at 8 a.m., two hours earlier than usual, which he knew had caused a minor panic in his project managers. He allowed himself a smile at the thought of them rushing around to get all the details of the six vessels on time, but his smile was short-lived, the situation of his company was the worst he had ever faced and it would take all of his skills to turn it around this time.

Dave, his driver, suddenly swerved, the sound of the blaring horn slicing through Aldred's thoughts as the white Golf GTi cut in front of the Jaguar. Dave glared at the young man driving the car, but did nothing in response as the man laughingly stuck two fingers up to him, and then to Aldred. His hands never left the wheel as he calmly straightened the car up and headed down the south side of the river Yare. Aldred shook his head at the stupidity of the driver, so much energy wasted in anger, and why? Was it the car the young man hated, or the fact that he wasn't driving it? He couldn't hate Aldred, because he didn't know him. If he had known him, he would certainly never have cut him up like that.

"Did you get the number, Dave?" he asked casually, as if it was a nuisance he could do without.

Dave recited the number.

"Good, perhaps you could deal with it? Nothing serious, but I think he should be pulled over and have his car checked a few times, just to let him feel like he's being watched. He needs to calm down before he hurts someone."

"It'll do him good. I'll get on to it tonight after we get back," replied Dave.

Aldred relaxed again, it was as good as done. Dave had been with him for nearly thirty years, long before Aldred ever entered the survey industry and Dave's apparent familiarity with his boss was perfectly understandable when you considered they were brothers.

"Pull over by the lighthouse; I want to walk around for a while before we leave. You wait here."

Dave nodded and Aldred got out. Turning his collar up to keep out the fine September rain drifting in from the sea he sighed, thrust his hands into his overcoat pockets and walked slowly along the jetty. Deep in thought he gazed across the harbour entrance to the Great Yarmouth side of the river. His side. He loved this place, had done since he was a child on holiday. He remembered when his parents had said that they were leaving London to live in Great Yarmouth; it had been a dream come true. They had bought a guesthouse after the war and all Aldred's childhood memories hinged on this river, and the beaches of Great Yarmouth and Gorleston. He'd loved his parents dearly, and from them learned the meaning of respect and loyalty. As they had grown old he had looked after them well, forever grateful for his perfect childhood.

When Aldred left school at sixteen to take a job as a mechanic, they could not have been more pleased.

"I thought you would have been disappointed about me not staying on at school to take 'A' levels," he'd said to his father.

"Nothing of the sort. I hated the thought of you maybe going to college or university. I just couldn't bear having a son and not seeing him every day," his father had said. "Selfish, isn't it?" At the self-conscious age of sixteen when most young men shy away from showing their feelings, Aldred had hugged his father.

After he had qualified as a mechanic, his mother and father had helped him to set up his own small garage, using one of the old buildings on the riverside. His reputation for doing a good job on time soon spread, and he rented out more space to expand. The declining fishing industry had meant that land along the river was very cheap to rent, and he set up a car breaker's yard next to his garage. Not one to turn away business, he soon started taking any metal, and within a few years he had become one of the most successful scrap dealers in East Anglia.

During the sixties, as Aldred's fortunes grew and grew, the face of Great Yarmouth began to change dramatically as the Spanish package holidays hit the holiday trade, and the fishing fleet declined making way for the new oil and gas industry which had decided to make Great Yarmouth the base for the southern North Sea fields. Aldred's break into the survey world came completely by chance, purely because survey vessels were in short supply.

He had been negotiating the purchase of two small cargo ships on the scrap value alone, with a third, an old lightship, thrown into the deal. The cargo company had gone into receivership and Aldred eventually bought all three as a job lot, but he didn't scrap them. He moored them at his frontage on the river next to his scrap yard, and over the following three months he hired out-of-work ships' engineers to cobble together two working ships out of the three. When this was done he broke up the third one for scrap, and put the former lightship up for hire as a survey vessel for charter on the spot market. Within two months of the first job, he also had the other cargo boat out on hire as well. He knew nothing about oil or gas exploration, but he had two working ships, and all he needed was to hire the right equipment and people.

He renamed the vessels *North Sea Tiger* and *Baltic Challenger*, and the company he set up to run them was Britannia Marine Ltd. He hit the market at the end of the sixties, and within two working seasons had carved himself a solid niche in the market. At the start of the third season, he bought enough basic analogue equipment to equip both vessels, and from that day on he never hired any more equipment. He nursed his new venture along by ploughing the first four seasons profits back into the vessels, living solely on his garage and scrap metal business. At the beginning of 1974, his fifth surveying season, Aldred stopped hiring out his vessels and equipment to other surveying companies, and applied directly to the oil companies to be placed on their tender lists as an independent surveying company. Britannia Surveys joined the race for North Sea oil and gas!

Owning his own vessels had meant that Aldred could undercut his competitors on daily rates, and at the end of 1974 Aldred bought a third survey vessel. There appeared to be no end to the oil boom, and the 70s and early 80s made Aldred a very wealthy man. Other companies were formed and joined in the fray, but Britannia Surveys led the field with Aldred pulling the strings. He surrounded himself with experts in acoustic engineering, surveying and marine geophysics, without whose recommendations and expertise Britannia Surveys couldn't progress, but he never allowed financial decisions to be made by anyone else but himself. It was his company and his money, and no one was ever in any doubt as to who had the final say.

It had been Aldred who had first looked to West Africa in the early 80s for additional work, riding in the face of opposition from his managers who wanted to stay only with the North Sea fields.

"It's not worth it; the rates are too low. If we take a vessel out of the North Sea, then we give work to our competitors. For what? Less money, even if we win the African work. It doesn't make sense."

"Ian's right, Aldred. We would be playing into their hands. You know what the oil companies are like, if you don't bid for North Sea work when they ask you to, then they don't ask you again. We can't afford to risk it."

"Then bid too high, Clive, so that we don't win it," replied Aldred, "at least we stay on the tender lists that way. Anyway, we have five vessels in the North Sea, and for the last four months it seems to me that one or another of them has always been tied up somewhere, and not on charter. If there is so much work around, why weren't they all working? Clive? Ian? Anyone?"

Silence. Not one of the project managers for the five vessels wanted to go head to head with Aldred on this. Whoever did would have their vessel's work rate looked at with a magnifying glass, and not one of them would come out completely clean. The industry wasn't that simple. Aldred looked at them all, one by one, and as each turned away from his gaze they knew that one vessel would be going to Africa, and its project manager's workload, in terms of logistics, was going to increase tenfold.

"The North Sea is good right now, we all know that, but if anything in life is certain, it is that nothing lasts forever. We need to look at other markets now, while things are good, because when things get bad everyone will be looking, and those who already have a foothold will take centre stage. That crowd from Manchester, the ones that rose out of the ashes of Sea-scan…"

"Sci-Tec?"

"Yes, Sci-Tec Surveys. They have already started working out of Pointe Noire in the Congo. They chartered an old fishing boat, put a DFS III onboard, and they're now winning work. It's the same in Egypt with Ocean-Engineering, they're hiring in supply boats and putting a container onboard that is kitted out like a lab, and they're winning work all around the Gulf of Suez and the Red Sea. If rag-tag-and-bobtail outfits like them can do it, then we can do it better."

"Simon," Aldred said, the authority in his voice causing Simon to involuntarily sit up straight, as if he were a schoolboy, "*Atlantic Challenger* is going to West Africa, and so are you. You leave on Thursday to find suitable agents in the Congo and Nigeria." Simon nodded, there was little else to do. The others sighed inwardly with relief, but Aldred continued, "and Chris, at the end of September, *Pacific Challenger* will be sailing to Egypt. We're going to hit Africa from two sides. This is a market we have to force our way into. No holds barred."

Four years later, in 1985, whilst the rest of Britain was thriving in the 'Thatcher Years', a recession hit the oil industry with a ferocity few could have imagined. For two years oil prices hit rock bottom and exploration work virtually ground to a halt. Survey company after survey company went to the wall; Palmers, Comap, Huntings, Fairfield Aquatronics, Sci-Tec, Cosag, all fell by the wayside. At the beginning of 1987, Britannia Surveys was the only wholly British survey company operating in Great Britain, its survival attributable to rock bottom tender bids at home and overseas, together with generous subsidies from the scrap metal business.

"We really must be going soon, Aldred," said Dave, who had walked over from the waiting car, "we need to allow at least four hours for the drive to Guildford."

Aldred turned, drawn out of his memories by Dave's interruption. "I'll be along in a minute." Dave nodded and returned to the car. There would be no more reminders; the old man would come when he was ready.

Aldred stared up the river to the Britannia Holdings yard. The scrap metal business was still there, but what saddened him was the sight of three of his survey vessels tied up alongside the quay, all without work. They had been idle for most of the season. Each vessel needed to work one hundred days per year to break even, and not one of them had reached that target this year. Only his three vessels overseas were now making money. His eyes narrowed and his stare became cold and hard as the reasons for his problems once again flashed into his mind to torment him. Here he was, the last of the British owner-operated survey companies, and yet the Norwegians and the Danes who had come to prominence in the last few years were forcing him out of his home market. They had opened offices in Aberdeen and Great Yarmouth, parading under a 50% British owned tag to satisfy the British Government and the oil companies' requirements on foreign interests. These so-called 'British' companies were wholly financed indirectly by the Norwegian and Danish governments, and were designed to corner the European market. They had unlimited resources, and Aldred was fighting a losing battle against them. Christ, he couldn't get a look-in at the work in the Norwegian sector of the North Sea, even if his bids were more competitive. Other governments would not allow foreign companies to carry out work in their sectors of the North Sea if a company existed in their own country capable of doing the work, irrespective of the price. Why didn't the British Government help him the same way?

He could feel his anger rising as he looked out across the mist-shrouded North Sea. "I survived the mid-eighties crash, and I'll damn well survive this. Fucking Vikings: you'd better stand with your backs to the wall and clench real tight, because I am going to stick those horned helmets of yours so far up your arses you'll wish that you had never heard of Britain. This is my country, and my industry!"

Turning towards the waiting car, Aldred thought of the morning meeting and the news from Vietnam. The *Pacific Challenger* was now four weeks into its survey for Nautilus Oil. Everything was going well onboard. The offshore client representative, Alex Haines, was very pleased with the progress made to date and the quality of the data collected. It now seemed likely that Britannia Surveys would win the Australian work for Nautilus Oil when it came up in the New Year. Aldred had, of course, known Alex for many years, having once employed him directly on the Trans-Med Pipeline Surveys. Now he was a very experienced client representative, and they had talked professionally many times, but he had been surprised when he had heard that Alex had been assigned to this job. Aldred felt sure that Alex had never been aware of some of the other activities of the Oceansearch representatives, so it seemed odd that he had been close to this one. But there again, Alex had once dealt with four men himself in a field in Sicily. Aldred now wondered about Alex. Did he know? Maybe he did, and maybe he didn't.

Fletcher certainly did, and had won the day; but Aldred was bothered by him. The American engineer had disappeared without a trace and although he made it a rule not to ask for details of how the special jobs would be carried out, this was a departure from the norm that he needed to know more about; he decided he would bring the matter up that afternoon when he met Carl.

The rain began to fall more heavily. He looked up at the cloud-filled skies and hunched his shoulders in an attempt to keep his neck dry. "What a day to have to go to a funeral," he said under his breath, as he carefully avoided the puddles rapidly forming around him.

CHAPTER 5

Guildford, Surrey.

The journey to Guildford was uneventful, as was the funeral service. The rain never stopped all the way from Great Yarmouth, and it was still raining as they stood at the graveside. There were only a few mourners, work colleagues mostly, and employees who had been told to attend to make the numbers look respectable. When the coffin was lowered into the ground, the first handful of earth was scattered by Carl Moston, partner of the deceased, and now sole shareholder in Oceansearch Associates Ltd. Dr. Godfrey Michael Tate would have been forty-four next birthday had he lived to see it, and as he had requested, the plaque on the coffin was inscribed with his nickname, Dog.

Aldred Grayson threw the next handful of earth, and walked off beside Carl, as the other 'mourners' paid their last respects. There was no immediate family present; Dog's parents had both died more than ten years ago, and his ex-wife and daughter had not been contacted. Any other relatives had stayed away as a final protest against his lifestyle and its consequences.

Dog had died of Aids, contracted in Africa in the early 80s before the world ever knew it existed. He had always been partial to 'a bit of the local' as he called it, and if any irritating rashes or weeping occurred, he had merely dosed up on penicillin. He had once passed on a dose of V.D. to his wife, who, to her eternal regret, had forgiven him and stayed with him. But the gift he had taken home after one trip to West Africa had remained undetected for six years. In 1988 the world began to recognise the enormous danger of the HIV virus, and sensationalism via the media brought massive panic reactions towards sufferers. Dog's condition only came to light after he had routine blood tests for a Norwegian medical certificate, two years after the birth of his daughter. He was declared unfit for work and his offshore days were over. As a consequence he set up his own consultancy business using freelance personnel for offshore projects, whilst keeping the U.K. office consultancy work for himself. It marked the birth of Oceansearch Associates.

The results of the two additional blood tests carried out after Dog's condition was known, brought with them the most devastating blow possible. Both Dog's wife and daughter tested HIV positive. Through his own weakness and infidelity, he had passed a death sentence onto his family. His wife left him immediately, taking their daughter, never to make contact again. Carl had never heard if they were still alive, and the instructions from Dog's solicitor upon his death made it clear that no contact should be attempted.

"He hung on a long time," said Aldred, as they walked between the gravestones towards the cemetery gate.

"Well, it was a long time before the HIV turned to Aids, if that's what you mean, but he wasted away in a matter of months when it finally blew up," Carl replied.

"Such a waste, and all for what? A quick leg-over with a cheap prostitute? Hardly the stuff of erotic dreams, is it?"

"I agree with you, Aldred, but we both know damn well that he could never keep it in his pocket. It was as if every woman was a challenge."

"Prostitutes aren't a challenge, they're nothing! He had a good-looking wife as well. Why play away? Senseless!" Aldred said, shaking his head at the thought of the wasted lives.

"Everyone doesn't think like you, Aldred, you're from the old school."

"Rubbish, Carl, there's nothing old about my values. It's a matter of loyalty and fidelity. It isn't hard you know. Try it and you might enjoy it."

"Hey, you're preaching to the converted," Carl lied, "but you can't make everyone act like yourself."

"Yes, I know," he sighed, "I know. It's just that families seem to be so easily forgotten in this industry, as if they don't matter. But they do. By Christ, they do!"

Carl let Aldred say his piece, knowing full well that his outburst was linked to his own son's untimely death just as much as it was to Dog's. Aldred had come to the funeral because of the old friendship between his son, Edward, and Dog. A friendship born out of the car crash in Malta many years ago, where only the quick thinking of Dog had saved Edward from prison, and from which had began Aldred's real connection with Dog. Carl could see from the distant look on Aldred's face that his memories were flooding back as they walked in the rain. The day after the crash had been a day of truth for Aldred and his son, a day which had finally brought them together, if only for a few short years. Aldred had never forgotten Dog and the debt he owed him.

"Such a waste," Aldred muttered to himself.

"Sorry, Aldred…?" Carl said, not quite hearing.

"Nothing. It was nothing," he quickly replied, jogging himself out of his memories and back to the present. "We need to talk about problems at hand. Serious problems. Get someone else to take your car back to the office, Carl, I want you to come with me so that we can talk on the way."

"Sure, no problem," replied Carl as he quickly spoke to one of the office girls and gave her his keys.

No problem! thought Aldred. You couldn't be more wrong.

"You remember your way to the office, Dave?" asked Carl, as he stepped into the Jaguar.

"If you're still by the railway station."

"We're still there."

Aldred hung his damp overcoat on the stand by the door, and sat in the armchair across from Carl's desk. When his eyes met Carl's, the younger man was taken aback by the sudden change of mood.

"So what happened in Vietnam? Where in Christ's name did the American disappear to? Talk about drawing attention to ourselves."

"He brought it on himself by all accounts."

"*By all accounts!* What on earth does that mean? How many people know?"

"No, I don't mean that. I mean our representative said that he brought it on himself."

"Look, Carl, I wanted the American to miss the work the following day, that was all. I did not want him to disappear off the face of the earth."

"He went too far, that's all."

"Who? The rep?"

"No, the American. My man had a plan all worked out, and it was going well until Bika started playing pool and upset the locals."

"That seems to be the understatement of the year. Why couldn't your man have helped him out?"

"Oh yes, good idea. Then they would both have disappeared."

"So he just left him?"

"Yes, he just left him, as you put it. The alternative was to deal with the knife that was being waved in his face."

"So the American is probably dead."

"I would say so, wouldn't you?"

"That is not what I wanted."

"You wanted him out of the way."

"This is no better than murder."

"Don't go over the top. You paid for the job, and it was carried out. Not as planned, I grant you, but carried out all the same. We are all in it together."

"Yes we are, but I want more control on the next one."

"Well, you take some beating. First you come on with the 'holier than thou' approach, and in the next breath you need another job doing." Carl laughed and leaned back in his chair, hands behind his head.

"That's right, you enjoy it while you can. Your time will come, and when you are about to lose your business, it will be interesting to see what lengths you will go to in order to save it." The tone in Aldred's voice was icy; the effect instantaneous.

"That bad?" Carl asked, his smile gone, and his chair upright.

"Yes, that bad. The Danes and the Norwegians are hitting us hard. They have so many subsidies and grants available to them from their governments that they can afford to bid jobs at a loss in order to win them. Any shortfalls are then made up to them so that they break even. If I don't break even, I go under.

They're trying to squeeze me out, and once they do, they'll go for one another. It's madness."

"What about the oil companies? Surely they don't want to see only one contractor bidding for the work? The surviving contractor would be able to set its prices at any level if there is no competition, and take the oil companies for a ride every time."

"We both know that, Carl, but at the moment all the oil companies see is 'healthy' competition forcing prices down. They think that they are on to a good thing, without giving a thought to the consequences. Almost like Dog in a way."

"Cutbacks and streamlining measures are affecting them all, and a price war between contractors helps the departmental heads when things are tight. All it does is solve immediate problems."

"I know," said Aldred, "but where does it leave me? And where will it leave the Danes? I find their stupidity overwhelming. They are no match for the Norwegian outfit, so when the time comes and the Noggies turn on them, the Danes will go down as well. They don't stand a chance."

"It seems to me that neither of you do, unless you start to fight back. I suppose this is where we come in."

"I can't see any other way. Two long-term contracts come up for renewal in the next three months, and I need both of them to survive and fight off the Scandinavian parasites. I can only do so much legitimately to win the work, which I am already doing, but I'm afraid it will take additional help to secure the contracts."

"Are we talking about help on one, Aldred?" Carl asked.

"No, both."

"Inside three months? That's too much, too soon. We have to let the dust settle after Vietnam, otherwise it won't be long before someone links our representatives to these coincidences where you just *happen* to step in at the right time and take over."

"Do you think I'm not aware of that? That's why I'm fuming about the American going missing. Of course I know the risk, but I'm damned if I'm letting go this easily." The anger in Aldred's voice rose at the frustration he felt.

"Okay, okay! Give me more details. Let's talk it through before we jump to conclusions. Maybe we can find a way to deal with them in a much lower key. Who are the clients?"

"Delta Mex Oil and National Petroleum."

"Ye gods, Aldred, you don't ask for much! You want both of them? Hell, you know what their safety records are like. They'll come down on us like a ton of bricks if they even get a whiff of foul play."

"Well in that case, they won't have to, will they?" replied Aldred, his eyes hard as steel. "If these high-minded companies gave me a fair shot it wouldn't come to this. I've always believed that someone in Delta Mex got backhanders for giving the Danes the annual contract but I can't prove it. It already stinks as far as I'm concerned; I'm no worse than they are. Anyway, I know that you can do the work because you have people working in-house for these companies, and you can ensure that you put out the geophysical representatives you choose for both companies."

"No! It's not possible. We simply can't do too many specials close together. I will not break that rule."

"This time will have to be an exception, because the first job needs to be hit next week!"

"Absolutely not! It's too soon. I can't take the chance."

"You will take the chance, Carl, because believe me, if you refuse to help me and I go down, I'll take you with me. I'll shop you on every special job you've done for me over the past eight years. See if I don't. If it wasn't for me this company wouldn't exist, and you know it. You owe me."

"I owe you nothing, old man," shouted Carl as he stood up and slammed his hand on the desktop. "You paid and we delivered. Simple. So don't you threaten me. Maybe your time is over!"

"Sit down, son," Aldred said, his clear blue eyes never flickering as he glared at Carl. "Sit down, I said!" he repeated, the authority in his voice adding a chilling edge to the stare. "I put up the money to help Dog set up this consultancy in 1988, long before you ever came along because I owed him a favour. He paid me back, and that was the end it. When you came along a few years later with your cowboy tales and shady deals, I didn't approve of Dog's choice of partner, but it was his business and his decision. As it was, things turned out okay, and your inner circle of special representatives proved useful to me. I don't like you or your mercenary outlook on life, but I do need the services you can provide and I have always paid well for them."

"You hypocrite! You criticise my outlook and then ask me to help you. Where do you get off, Aldred? You're no different from me."

"Believe me, we are worlds apart. I do these things because it is necessary to survive in business. You do it for fun. Now that Dog is dead, I have no affinity with this company. Refuse and I will take you down." Aldred paused to let the threat sink in. "But I also realise the risk. Therefore, I am willing to pay double the standard rate for you to carry out these jobs. The choice is yours."

"Two hits at £150,000 each? That's what you're saying?"

"Correct."

“£400,000 for the two and you’re on; but no more for at least twelve months.”

“Deal,” Aldred agreed, inwardly smiling at the greed of Carl’s mercenary ways. “The first has to go down next week. Delta Mex has awarded site surveys and 2-D exploration work to the Danes and their vessel, *Bon Chance*, will be mobilising in Pointe Noire in seven days time. If the 2-D work is successful it will lead to future contracts worldwide with Delta Mex, including the North Sea. My own vessel, the *Atlantic Challenger*, is currently in Walvis Bay in Namibia and it will take her six days to sail to Pointe Noire. I want something to go wrong on the *Bon Chance*, so that the *Atlantic Challenger* picks up the work. It is then up to us to make it go well. If it does then the Danes will be out of the running for the Delta Mex contract.”

“Even in the North Sea?” asked Carl.

“Even in the North Sea! The next Delta Mex contract will run for five years worldwide; I have to have it. Here,” Aldred said as he took the white envelope from his inside jacket pocket, “you’ll find basic details of the work together with the personnel list. You will find it interesting reading.”

Carl took the envelope without opening it. “What about the Norwegians? How will you deal with them, and I thought you said National Petroleum came into it?”

“They do, but that job is not for two months, and it is in the North Sea.”

“Two months! You just said three! That’s just too soon for the two reps I normally use. Look, I can cover the West African work next week,” he said, without really knowing that he could, “but the N.P. work isn’t on.”

“Yes, it is,” Aldred said adamantly. “My problem is your problem. Just find another representative to do the work.”

“Oh, you think it’s that easy do you? Do you suggest I run an advertisement in Thursday’s Daily Telegraph? Perhaps it should read ‘Opportunities in the Oil Industry, saboteurs needed for personnel based projects!” Carl said sarcastically. “I’m sure there would be a queue at the door. Headed by the police no doubt!”

Aldred wasn’t amused. “You’ll find a way for the money I’m paying though, won’t you, Carl?”

“Anyway, how do you know it’s two months off? What is the project?”

“I know it is two months off because N.P. have already awarded the contract to the Noggies using their vessel *Odin*, and I also know that the *Odin* will be working for the Norwegian government for the next eight weeks. N.P. is next on the list. The project is west of the Shetland Isles, on the Atlantic Frontiers program, and I want an incident which will blacken the name of the Norwegian company and personnel record throughout the North Sea.”

“How on earth can I guarantee an incident like that without being able to use my two best people?”

“You must have at least forty other people who rep for you.”

“Yes, but they don’t do special jobs. They’re just bog-standard honest representatives who wouldn’t have a clue how to carry out the sort of thing you’re asking for. All they are is a perfect cover for our special operations, which bring in the real money. You damn well know that!”

“Then do it yourself. How about it Carl? Or have you been behind a desk too long?”

Aldred’s parting shot stung as it was meant to do. He stood, and put on his overcoat. “I’ll speak to you after the African work has been successfully completed, and perhaps then we can go over one or two points concerning N.P. and the Noggies nearer the time."

"I'll look forward to it," Carl replied, inwardly fuming that the old man had dared to threaten him. Aldred had been too close to Dog and now there was no tie left to Oceansearch. Carl didn't doubt for one minute that Aldred would break him if it came down to it. Could he fight him, or should he just take the money and smile? He smiled. After all, £400,000 for two jobs was a hell of a payday, and he who fights and runs away, gets to retire!

"Straight back to Great Yarmouth, Aldred?"

"Yes please, Dave, that's enough business for one day. We will make it back in time for the lodge practise tonight, won't we?"

"Easily."

"Good. It will nice to be in the chair again for another year. I'm looking forward to it. It was a shame about George not being able to go up the ladder, but I must admit that I was pleased when they asked me to be Master for a second time."

"I'm sure you were. It seems such a lot to remember though, I wonder if I'll ever get that far myself."

"Of course you will. It's only practise. How are you getting on so far this year?"

"Well this year is easy because the Junior Deacon is straightforward enough."

"They all are, if you put the time into learning the ceremonies."

"I'll take your word for it."

Aldred smiled, and then a thought crossed his mind. "Before I forget, Dave," he said sitting forward, "you'll be able to get the Golf driver's name and address from Stuart Tomlinson, the speed cop. He'll be at the lodge tonight, and he can use his in-car computer to flash up the driver's details."

"Don't worry, Aldred, it's all in hand. I spoke to Stuart while you were at the funeral. I have the name and address written down here already. I've arranged for the driver to be pulled over and his car checked every time he's seen on the roads for the next few weeks."

"Nice work, Dave," Aldred said as he settled back for the journey home.

CHAPTER 6

Tarporley, Cheshire.

Alex looked out from the bay window at the front of his house into the small secluded close. His daughter Carrie and her two small friends were having races down the sloping drive on their silver, micro-wheeled scooters; all three girls wore identical T-shirts with Vietnamese ladies in national costume on the front, and Vung Tao written in stylised letters on the back. As he watched, the 'Dragon' gang roared past on their mountain bikes; different coloured shirts for the boys but all with the same Saigon dragon. Those were the souvenirs they had asked for; the only difficulty now would be getting them to wear something different!

His wife's present had been an exquisitely embroidered blue silk dressing gown that he had seen in a small tailor's shop along one of the run-down streets of Vung Tao. She too had worn it on each of the three evenings since he had been back, and he hoped she would wear it again tonight after the children had gone to bed, but at the moment things were rather tense.

Sarah was worried about how this job had affected Alex. He had been unusually quiet since his return, and although he generally took a few days to unwind, he seemed pre-occupied and wouldn't talk about it.

"Why are you having second thoughts now?" Sarah asked, causing Alex to turn away from the window. "Is there ever going to be a perfect time to break away?"

"Probably not," he said, surprised by her bluntness at carrying on the conversation from over three hours ago when he had refused to answer her questions.

"Then it has to be now. You can't carry on this way, and I don't want you to either. Nor do the kids for that matter."

"Leave them out of it; this has to be a rational decision," said Alex.

"Why does it? Isn't it pulling you apart being away from them, away from me? You don't seem to be able to rationalise that aspect do you?" Silence. "So why expect to rationalise anything else?"

"Because it has to be at the right time."

"God, not again!" Sarah said, exasperation in her voice. "Stop it, Alex, you have to stop it! You are going over the same points again and again. You know that the others will go with you if you split."

"Maybe…"

"Alex!" she shouted.

"Okay, okay." He held up his hands.

"Make the break, Alex. These long jobs are too much for you, and for us, anymore."

Alex sat next to her on the sofa, taking her hand in his. "Look how this last job has left you," she said, stroking his hair. "Quit the offshore side and just do office work. Between the coastal survey work and the oil companies surely there's enough around? And what about the environmental management systems?" He smiled a weak smile, surprised she had even remembered. "See, I do listen. In fact I've done nothing but listen for the past three years while you've been doing that blasted M.Sc. with the Open University. To be honest, I'm glad you've finished it." Now they both smiled, knowing that at times he had been fed up to the back teeth with some of the tutor-marked assessments and stupid comments. “You’re one of the first group to graduate from the Environmental Decision Making course, surely you are not going to let Oceansearch benefit from your knowledge? Why not bring the clients needing this knowledge to your own company? Break away, before Oceansearch start their own marketing. You know that the bulk of the work can be done from your office here; and without anyone taking a cut; you need fewer days per year to earn the same money. Quit now, Alex, before it affects your health. And another thing, you should have said no to going to London tomorrow. Christ knows, you’ve only had three days at home after four weeks away and they’re calling on you again!”

“It’s too late.”

“What, how can it be too late?”

“Oceansearch have already started their marketing for the environmental management systems. That’s why I am going to London tomorrow.” She turned away. “Look, it’s only one day, and I’ll be back tomorrow night. Anyway, I had agreed to do this presentation the first week I got back, so it’s not as if it is something new.”

“But it’s something for Oceansearch again, when you could be doing it for your own company. If your presentation is good, you will win them another contract. Oh, and why does Carl want you to ‘call by the office’ in the morning? As if Guildford is ‘calling by’ when you are going to London from Cheshire! He’s just putting on you again. The truth is, he can’t cope without you.”

“Yes he can, and he will if myself and the others leave. We can’t simply forget about him, because he certainly won’t forget us.”

“Well, if you’re frightened of him, then of course you can never leave. It’s as simple as that!” The finality in her voice said that she had given up. This time it was her turn to walk out, leaving Alex alone with his thoughts once more.

Before the work in Vietnam, Alex had no doubts about breaking away, but the events in Saigon had brought another dimension into the situation. Somehow he knew that Carl was behind the disappearance of Clayton Bika, but why would he want Britannia Surveys to win work? Oceansearch Associates were independent consultants, or so he had thought. During his time away Alex had been thinking about any other jobs where 'odd' things had happened. He had remembered two for certain during the past ten years, one in Italy and one in the North Sea. The Italian work had suffered numerous hydraulic failures with the gun deployment rams, and the North Sea job had electrical failures so obscure that the chief engineer joked about a saboteur being onboard. Both companies had ultimately been thrown off the jobs due to the failures. Alex had never connected the two before now, but he now recognised a common denominator; on both jobs there were two representatives from Oceansearch. Nothing really odd about that, except that on both jobs one of the representatives had been Chris Fletcher, the Englishman who had turned up as the safety representative and threatened Alex in Vung Tao.

If Alex were wrong about the coincidences, then Carl would just be pissed off, but if Alex's fears were right, what then if he took work from Oceansearch? What would Carl do to protect his company? Alex thought he had every right to be frightened of Carl.

The next morning, Alex caught the eight-thirty train from Crewe to London Euston, and by eleven he had made the connection from Waterloo to Guildford. The two-hour journey to London had passed quickly, due entirely to his thoughts being on his family. He and Sarah had not spoken again about setting up his own company. There was nothing more that could be said, and neither of them wanted to argue any more. Besides, they now had nine weeks where he would be at home every night, and a lot of things could happen in that time.

"I'm glad you're back Dad, but you know you are going to the office tomorrow…"

"Yes," Alex said, looking at Andrew, whom he could see was leading into something.

"Well, will you be coming home tomorrow night, or is this really another job you are going on?" The boy's eyes looked down as he said it, as if this action would shield him from the expected answer.

"Of course I will be back tomorrow night. I won't be going away for a long time yet."

"Sure?"

"Positive. I told you, I'm having three weeks at home, and then I am going to do office work for six weeks, but I will be home every night, and I won't be working at weekends."

His son hugged him. "I hope so, Dad."

"Hey, don't you believe me?" Alex asked, holding him so that he could see his face. Andrew looked down again.

"Yes, I believe you, but things change, don't they?"

This caught Alex off guard, and he could feel the pressure build up in his chest, brought on by what his son had said. Andrew really didn't believe him! His son was eleven years old, but was already distrustful of the industry. It was another example of the underlying effects of working away. He knew clearly how it affected himself, but did he really know the full effects it had on his family?

"Andrew, believe me, what I have just said is how it will be. Nothing will change it, I promise."

Andrew smiled. “Okay, I believe you.”

“Good, now what about the weekend. What shall we do? Any ideas?”

“Well, yes, but you might not want to do it.”

“Try me.”

“Alton Towers.”

“Are you sure?” Alex said, surprise in his voice. “You know what that means.”

“Nemesis!” Andrew replied, nodding his head.

“When we were there in the spring, there was no way you were going on the ride.”

“I know, but I said I would ride it the next time we went.”

“I remember. So what’s changed your mind?”

“Nothing’s changed it. I’ve just decided I want to go on it.” But it was obviously not the truth, and Alex stayed silent. “Really, that’s all,” Andrew added.

“Okay, I believe you. We’ll go on Sunday, and we’ll make it early so that we beat the queues.”

“Great.”

“Dad?” the voice came from the next bedroom, “I won’t have to go on Nemesis will I?” Carrie asked, her eyes wide with worry.

“No, you’re still not big enough,” Alex said as he walked into her bedroom.

“Thank goodness for that!”

“Yes, but even if you were big enough, you wouldn’t have to go on it if you didn’t want to. It’s your choice. Just like Andrew has now decided he wants to have a go.”

"Oh, okay. But I still want to go on Air with you, like we did last time," she smiled, and held his hand. "It was great, wasn't it? Do you think we will get Mum on it this time?"

"I doubt it. I think she will stick to the log flume and the rapids." Carrie laughed, remembering just how wet her mum had been after the last ride on the rapids. "It'll be great fun."

"Now you get to sleep. Just one more day at school."

"And then the weekend! I'm looking forward to Sunday already."

"So am I." Alex kissed his daughter goodnight, and was two steps down the stairs when Andrew called him.

"Dad?"

"What is it now, Andrew? You need to get to sleep, otherwise you will be really tired at school in the morning."

"Just one thing, Dad. You know I said I had changed my mind about Nemesis?"

"Yes," Alex replied, standing in the doorway.

"Well, it's not quite true."

"Go on," he said, now moving to sit on the edge of the bed. Alex could see that his son felt awkward, so he gave him time to pick his words.

"I'm still scared of Nemesis, Dad, but I have to go on it."

"No, you don't. Forget about what you said the last time. Wait until you are ready."

"I think I'll always be scared before I first ride it. If I keep waiting, I will never do it. But anyway it's not just that. I'm the only boy in my class who has been to Alton Towers and not rode Nemesis. I have to go on it, Dad." Alex saw the look in his son's eyes and he knew exactly what he meant. Was there any man who hadn't been through a similar thing when they had been young?

"Okay, we'll sit together. It'll be good fun."

"Sure?"

"Sure!"

"Definitely Sunday?"

"Yes, definitely!"

"Great! I love you, Dad."

"And I love you. Goodnight."

Alex walked slowly down the stairs knowing that everyone had trials and tests at different times in their lives. Who was to say which of the tests was the hardest to face?

———

CHAPTER 7

Guildford, Surrey.

"He's here now," the voice said.

"Send him up straight away."

"I'm afraid he's already on his way, Mr. Moston. He didn't stop to ask if you were free."

Carl's door swung open without even a knock, and it didn't take any special instinct to tell that Alex was not pleased about coming to the office. Carl rose from his seat and moved round the desk, hand extended. "You're looking well Alex, the tan suits you."

Alex shook hands quickly, without any sense of greeting. "A sun tan from work generally mean one of two things, either there hasn't been anything to do, or that you have been there too long. Guess which this was."

Carl inwardly cursed Alex's mood, but swallowed and carried on with his polite facade. "It could have been worse, it could have been the northern North Sea! And who wants that?" He gave his best 'been there, done that, know what you're thinking' smile, and saw Alex shrug his shoulders. Was that a good sign? He couldn't tell. "Take a seat, Alex," he said gesturing with his open hand and returning to his own chair behind the desk. "Coffee?"

"No. Whatever it is, it has to be quick. I'm due at the Bicentrol offices at two this afternoon, and this 'quick' call at the office is a pain in the arse."

Obviously it hadn't been a good sign. Carl decided to jump in with both feet. "We have a problem and I need you to solve it. No, let me re-phrase that, *only* you can solve it."

Alex shook his head in anticipation of what was coming next.

"Hold on, hold on. At least let me tell you…"

"Forget it, Carl. Whatever you are going to say next, don't."

"Alex…"

"No, let me tell you my plans. I have been away for four weeks, and I have been at home for three days. I intend to make the presentation to Bicentrol this afternoon, and then I shall be having three weeks off. After that, there is the first of the six-week desk studies in Delta Mex Oil on the Strand, which means Monday and Thursday in London and two other days working from home. All together that means I will be home every night for the next nine weeks. Got that? That's what I told my family, and that is what will happen."

"Hey, Alex, we all know that with the best will in the world we can't tell our families exactly what we will be doing from one week to the next, let alone that far ahead."

"I already have, and I intend to stick to it."

"What if I put someone else on the office work?"

"Try it!" Alex snapped. "I proposed these desk studies and had them accepted by the various departments in Delta Mex. The projects are mine."

At this, Carl leaned forward, forearms and hands flat on the desk, clearly irritated. "Now let's get one thing straight, Alex, the projects belong to Oceansearch Associates, my company! Not you! We have the contract to supply freelance consultants to Delta Mex Oil, and if I decide that you are not available, that's the way it is!" He stared at Alex for a moment or two before sitting back once again, pleased at the way he had made his point.

Alex ignored Carl's posturing and stood up. "Well, if that is all, I will be off to Bicentrol to win another contract."

Carl was amazed, and again leaned forward. "No, it fucking well isn't all! I'm the one who runs the show. You will do what I say."

"I'm freelance, don't forget."

"Then don't you forget whose contracts they are."

"Listen, Carl, the desk studies are my project. Delta Mex won't let anyone else do them."

"Wrong!"

"What do you mean, *wrong*? I've been working in their London offices off and on for the past two years. I know what I am talking about."

"Not this time. This time Delta Mex International have put their foot down, and London has had to agree."

"What on earth does the International side have to do with this work?" Alex asked, surprised at this piece of news.

"You see, you don't know everything after all, do you? Why don't you just sit down and listen?" Alex sat.

"Your reputation in Delta Mex is obviously very good, so much so, in fact, that the International section is insisting on having you as their representative on the vessel for this project in West Africa, otherwise we don't get the work."

"So that's it! International has forced their will on the London office. Why didn't you say that I wasn't available? You knew I wanted the London work," Alex asked, his temper rising.

“Simple! It is easier to cover the London office work rather than the African project.”

“Don’t give me that! What’s wrong with some of the other reps? They’ve done similar jobs in the past? I don’t believe Delta Mex International won’t take one of them. What about Andy? He’s onshore right now, he could do it.”

“No, he can’t. Delta Mex wants you. They want your West African experience, but something else has changed as well. The seismic programme has been extended.”

“So what? Lots of jobs get extended. There’s nothing special about that.”

“Not like this. Listen, you know how the cost of 3-D surveys have rocketed over the past few years?”

“Yes, but how does that affect us? We only do rig site surveys, not exploration!”

“For God’s sake, Alex, shut up and listen!” shouted Carl, “then perhaps you’ll understand. Delta Mex has increased the scope of work by including 2-D exploration in the project. They believe that the *Bon Chance* is capable of shooting 120 channel 2-D data at a fraction of the cost of a conventional 3-D seismic vessel.”

“But 2-D data is history in terms of exploration. No-one has shot 2-D for years!” said Alex, very much surprised at this development.

“I know, but that has been more a result of the excellent marketing programmes of the 3-D seismic companies than anything else, and to keep pace, all the old 2-D vessels were converted to 3-D spreads. Now there aren’t any 2-D vessels left. This has left the door open and Scandi-Seis, the Danish shallow seismic company, have sold Delta Mex the promise of a site survey vessel capable of shooting 48 channel hazard surveys and then reconfiguring the TTS digital recording system and streamer to 120 channels to collect 2-D data down to four seconds penetration."

"What about the source?" asked Alex, intrigued by this approach.

"They propose to change the air gun array to 640 cu ins guns giving 24 bar metres. Simple enough really!"

"Yes, it sounds it, but what is the shot point interval and the gun timing? Can the compressors cope?"

"Scandi-Seis say they can, and the guns passed the sea trials last week. It seems that the pulse signature can be maintained under survey conditions. If this spread really can be reconfigured to collect good data then Scandi-Seis are on to a winner worldwide with Delta Mex." Carl now felt good; Alex was asking all the right questions; his interest was piqued. Carl had him, but then the bombshell dropped.

"Good for them," Alex said, easing back in his chair, "but I'm not interested in another project right now. And now I know the specifications, I also know that any one of us can cope with this work, and you know it as well, Carl."

"Jesus Christ! No, I don't know it! It's you who has the most West African experience in this company; you know the old French colonies better than any of us, and you speak French dammit! I want someone on this job that I can trust. Look Alex, this project is very important to us as a group because of long-term considerations. We want to win the repping work for all of the Delta Mex International projects like this, and you can create the right impression from the beginning. Regardless of how Scandi-Seis cope with the set-up, I want it to look good for Oceansearch. I know you are the person to see it through."

Alex laughed, shaking his head in disbelief. "Don't give me that sales crap, Carl, I've just had four weeks working in

Vietnam, and I need some rest. Get someone else to go this time, and put me back on the London work."

"The client wants you as their representative, otherwise we don't get the work, it's as simple as that," Carl replied, lying again.

"Are you really saying that Delta Mex won't accept any of the others? Rubbish! Why me?"

"Hey, if you want to know the truth, I don't know either. As far as I'm concerned you are all the same. I can't see any reason to insist on you, is that what you want to hear?"

Alex shrugged. "I'm not available, I'm taking some time off. It's only the end of September and I've already done over one hundred days this year. You know how I feel about this. I'm only doing more days because it's office work and I'll be at home."

"You really don't understand, do you Alex? I am the boss, and I have already said that you are available."

"You've what!" shouted Alex, the anger in his voice coupled with disbelief at what he had just heard.

Carl pushed the manila folder over the desk. "There are your air tickets and visa. You leave on Sunday morning for Pointe Noire."

Sunday! The day Andrew was going to ride Nemesis. His son was prepared to face up to things and he was not going to let him down. Now it was Alex's turn. His hands gripped the side of the chair as he tried to control his temper. "You're a chancer, Carl! Where do you get off?" He stood up and walked to the window, needing to move to try and dissipate his anger. He glanced at Carl, seeing him leaning back in his chair, loving every minute of the situation. He strode to the table, picked up the manila folder and took out his second passport, put it in his pocket, and flicked the folder across the table. "And you can take that smug 'Burt Reynolds' grin off your face. I'm not available! Not now, not on Sunday, not ever! I quit taking work through Oceansearch!"

"Really! And what will pay the bills, Alex? It certainly won't be that two-bit coastal survey company you've gone partners in."

"It will be better than putting up with this shit from you."

"You'll be bust within a year."

"Don't bet on it."

"Well this is a tough guy stance you're taking. Tell me, why shouldn't I bet on it?" asked Carl, not liking the certainty in Alex's tone of voice.

"Don't try and draw me out; save it for the likes of Chris Fletcher. I'm sure he will rise to the occasion. It certainly seemed like he did in Vietnam."

Carl said nothing.

"Well, that took the cat's tongue, didn't it?"

"You know fuck all, Alex."

"Don't I? Well look at this." He took the note from his wallet, the same note that had been given to him by the waitress in the Vietnam House Restaurant. "Notice anything odd about it?"

Carl took it, read it, and let it fall dismissively onto the table. "It says you have been stood up."

"Oh, very droll. Yes, it does indeed. But have another look at the paper. Look beyond the writing. Anything?"

"Fuck all."

"Well done. That's exactly what Chris Fletcher must have thought. Look at the watermark, you cretin, it says *SFH*, and that does not stand for The Caravelle does it? No, it stands for Saigon Floating Hotel. So don't tell me that I don't know anything, because I know it was Fletcher who met Clayton Bika that night."

"Oh, so you know it all, do you Alex?"

"Enough to walk away from you."

"Well, walk away then, but just be careful what you say to people."

"Don't threaten me."

"Then don't push."

The door slammed loudly behind him, leaving Carl staring at the manila folder. Shit! He hadn't expected him to quit taking work, but he wasn't going to chase after him. No, once you know someone feels that way, let him go. After all, he was just another rep who had gotten too cocky, too full of his own self-importance. Carl shrugged his shoulders, but he knew he was only kidding himself. Alex was excellent, and this really did fuck things up! Talk about overreacting. Where did the quit come from? Carl had no intention of sending Alex to Africa; it had been a bluff to see if Alex would say anything about the Vietnam incident. Christ, and he did, didn't he!

"Okay, Chris, you can come in now," Carl shouted at the door to the adjoining office. Chris Fletcher walked in, looking less than happy. "Well for fuck's sake, Chris, that was almost perfect wasn't it? You really topped yourself with the note, didn't you?"

"Big deal," was all Chris offered as he sat in the chair.

"Hey, it is a big deal, if you hadn't been sloppy Alex wouldn't have had any idea."

"I wasn't sloppy. You weren't there, and you have no idea how it was."

“Oh stop being so fucking melodramatic and listen. You heard the blurb I gave to Alex about this work in Africa…”

“Yes.”

“Well this job requires a particularly well experienced Party Chief to control all this work, wouldn’t you say?”

“Of course, otherwise Scandi-Seis will be well and truly stuffed.”

“Nicely put! Any ideas who it might be?”

“No, because I know they haven’t got anyone in-house with that experience, so they must be hiring someone in for the work.”

“Nearly right, but not quite. Delta Mex won’t allow freelance survey crew on this project, so Scandi-Seis have just employed a new Party Chief who was given a considerable lump sum to join them.”

“So? Why is he of such great interest to you?”

“The project has a special element to it as far as we are concerned, which Delta Mex International know nothing about, and we believe that the Party Chief is central to the issue.”

“Definitely not! No more special jobs for quite a while! That last one was too close for me.” Chris shook his head, his eyes hard and his voice cold.

“Oh, you’ll get over it.”

“Maybe I will.”

“See you’re feeling better already.”

“Definitely no.”

“Look, the Party Chief is Richard Peterson, an old shit I once worked for when I first started out in this business,” said

Carl, "arrogant, overbearing, and the most two-faced bastard I have ever come across."

"You obviously learned a lot from him."

"Having a good time?" Carl asked, trying to ignore the remark. "Believe me, the man is a lizard. He has tried to stab me in the back so many times. You would be doing the industry a favour by getting rid of him."

"And you, by the sound of it."

"Yes, and me! There's nothing I would like better than to see him go. The job has an extra £10,000 on top of the standard £30,000, purely because I hate him."

"Well, well. He really must have got under your skin for you to give money away," said Chris, now delighting at the turn of events, "but it seems to me that you are the perfect man for the job. All that hatred! Surely it would be a pleasure for you to deal with him? And as I said, definitely no."

"Is that final?"

"Final. Besides, it's only a few years ago that the fighting in Brazzaville spread down to Pointe Noire and people were lying dead in the streets. Or are you conveniently forgetting about that?"

"For Christ's sake, Chris, you know what Africa is like. It's all blown out of proportion."

"Bollocks to that. It's worse than it ever was."

"Oh fuck off then, and be a wimp. Go on, get out."

Chris stood, reached for the manila envelope and pulled out the tickets. "Well you cheeky bastard! You really did think I would go, didn't you? Looks like you will have to change the name on these tickets. It's a good job Alex didn't see my name, or your game of bluff would certainly have backfired."

"I think it backfired anyway. I told you, Alex was never going. He just overreacted."

"But he threatened you, didn't he?"

"Did he fuck. That was just hot air. Let him go and play at coastal surveys. As long as he doesn't get in my way, what do I care? There are plenty of others who want to be reps."

"He's got to you, hasn't he?"

"Look, I hate long goodbyes. Now are you going to fuck off, or not?"

"Okay. If you're going to be miserable. But come on, where's my passport?" Carl opened the top left-hand drawer, took out the passport and handed it to Chris. He flicked through and saw the new visa. "I hope you remembered to get one for yourself."

"I said *fuck off*, and close the door after you."

The African project starting Sunday was worth £200,000 to Oceansearch, and had to be done well. Perhaps he should do it himself, just as Chris had suggested. Why shouldn't the Managing Director still do occasional jobs? Let Mick Jones, his Operations Manager, sit in the driving seat for a while. He was paid enough, and was also completely unaware of the other activities Oceansearch were involved in. He was a perfect choice, naive and truthful, a wonderful combination! Besides, what other options did he have? None. He picked up the phone.

"Theresa, could you change the bookings to Pointe Noire on Sunday? Yes, that's right, Chris won't be going. In fact, I will, and could you also speak to Delta Mex International to ask for their agents in the Congo to arrange for a visa to be ready for me when I arrive? Thank you. Oh, and could you tell Mick to come and see me immediately?"

As he replaced the receiver, Carl smiled. Actually it would be nice to see the Congo again after all these years, and especially good to see Richard Peterson, the Party Chief.

———

Alex walked briskly to the station, his mind racing at the implications of his actions. He had done it, finally done it, and the catalyst had been the promise to his son about a ride in a park. The thought of breaking that promise had been the final straw, and now he felt relieved. Relieved that when the decision had been forced on him, he had not backed down. He was now looking forward to taking the work from Carl.

By the time his train arrived at Waterloo Station, Alex's first plan of action was clear in his mind.

———

CHAPTER 8

Trafalgar Square, London.

"Gentlemen, I would like to thank you for the opportunity to present our company and its services to you this afternoon. I feel certain that during the next two hours you will see the benefit of using a consultancy such as ours."

Alex Haines had been educated at his local grammar school, and afterwards had scraped a second-class degree from the marine sciences department at Bangor University. Hardly an impressive education, but he had gained his experience the hard way and had become a well-respected consultant over the years. Plus he was a hell of a presenter and organiser. He had fronted meetings like these countless times before, and it was generally acknowledged that the broad client base that Oceansearch Associates enjoyed was due very much to the impressive introductions of Alex. He was the one who got the foot in the door; after that, the expertise of the consultants in the group had always carried the work through.

"I shall cover a brief history of our company, its aims, and most importantly, the expertise it carries, which is directly applicable to yourselves in the shallow seismic oil industry."

The four managers attending the presentation were in no doubt about how precarious their positions in Bicentrol Oil were; their departments were seriously undermanned due to imposed job cuts, but crucially, the expertise amongst those remaining was threadbare. All the best people, those with years of experience behind them, had been the first to be made redundant because their salaries had been the highest. It had made fiscal sense to the bean counters, and in the beginning did not seem to have any great impact.

They found themselves in this position through no fault of their own but they could see that their own futures were at risk if the problem was not addressed urgently. They had inherited this problem from their predecessors, managers who had wholeheartedly embraced the concept of Total Quality Management (TQM) and ISO 9000, the buzzwords of the 90s. It was a simple concept; if there were quality assured processes in place, then a quality product would be produced. Those older managers had used TQM as a career stepping stone, and had implemented the policies with great gusto and almost religious fervour. For training and implementation companies it was a time of plenty, but more importantly it allowed Bicentrol to achieve a 25% redundancy target and still have the expertise in place to run the business, albeit in written procedures rather than experienced human form. Having gained accreditation themselves, with the all-important Lloyd's seal of approval, they then insisted that all contracting companies must also have accreditation.

The logical outcome of this, the managers argued, was that the oil company could now be sure that the contractors would do the work properly, and there would be no real need for the oil company to have in-house expertise to check that the work was done thoroughly; it therefore followed that further redundancies could be made without compromising operations! But those original managers, the career TQM men, had now moved on, promoted or retired, safe in the knowledge that they had taken the company to a new level of operation; they never saw the cracks begin to appear, or if they did, they quickly glossed over them before they moved on.

TQM was flawed from the outset. ISO 9000 was merely the European equivalent of BS5750, which had always been intended for use in manufacturing, not an exploration environment. To develop a European quality system had been an idealistic pipedream of ambitious managers, eager to promote a new initiative where they would be the protagonists; a perfect career opportunity for high flyers into the unknown. Manufacturing was benefiting from the uniformism, but in the world of oil and gas where assessments and interpretations of data relate to hazards in exploration, there could never be such clear-cut processes, and the four managers now present at this meeting realised this; the Emperor was in fact naked!

The contracting companies simply couldn't be trusted not to cut corners; reports were being produced by individuals with between two and three years' experience, and mistakes were being made. The marine survey industry was a harsh environment and careers were often short-lived, few ever lasted more than five years, and career progression had always been to the oil companies, the very companies where redundancies were now the order of the day. ISO 9000 would ultimately ensure that there would be no senior personnel in the oil industry. But as if that wasn't bad enough, environmental awareness was around every corner, and ISO14001, Environmental Management Systems, direct from the European Union, was now required to be put into place by the senior oil company executives. The few middle managers left had only previously paid lip service to environmental concerns, and now they were being ordered to implement their own systems. Outside expertise was their only solution.

"Oceansearch Associates was set up in 1988 as a direct response to the offshore industry pulling itself out of the drastic slump of '85 to '87 when many survey companies went bust. As the price of oil started to rise and the industry began once again to increase its exploration activities, equipment and vessels were easy to find, but experienced personnel were not. No new people had been recruited into the industry since 1984, and many people quit the industry when their companies went bust, never to return. The only real experience left lay with the people from the 70s who had ridden the lean years as freelancers. They were the only ones with more than five years' experience to offer."

"We formed our consultancy using these people on a freelance basis to run the surveys for the oil companies, to act as their representatives offshore. We effectively cornered the market within two years, providing client representatives to surveying and geophysical departments in many major oil companies. As you know, a large number of oil companies actively recruited many of their own staff straight from university, but they rarely sent them offshore, and consequently these people had little or no practical experience to call on. The United Kingdom Offshore Operators Association (U.K.O.O.A.) laid down guidelines for the hazard surveys to be carried out prior to an exploration well being drilled, and the new men followed these guidelines to the letter. But they were only guidelines after all, and with no experience to call on, they could never question or deviate from those guidelines without the help of the representative. Gradually, the oil company personnel had enough knowledge to complete basic report checks, but then, in the search for the Holy Grail of TQM they were made redundant; just as they were becoming useful, you got rid of them!"

Alex took a drink from his glass of water as he let the fact sink in, not that they weren't already aware of it! In fact, if Alex's group couldn't help, then all four of them would be going down, a charge of mis-management firmly stamped on their CV's.

"If it's any consolation, I can tell you that you are not alone," Alex resumed, "in fact, you are a long way behind Delta Mex Oil and National Petroleum in discovering the flaws with TQM."

"But they have been praising the whole system, still insisting that all companies contracting to them have accreditation," interrupted one of the managers.

“That’s true, but you tell me what else they could have done, having walked so far down the path.”

“Do you know for sure about these difficulties?” Roger Southerland, the head of site surveys, asked.

“Absolutely.”

“But why has it taken longer for us to become aware of the problem?”

“For two unrelated reasons as I see it. Delta Mex was also a victim of its expatriate culture. They have a quota of local staff at any of its world-wide locations, and the remainder of the personnel are all expatriates who move from location to location every three years, always moving to a slightly different position so as to increase the individual’s experience for ultimate management positions. It sounds good, doesn’t it? But in practice, it means that every three years, someone who has become capable is transferred, and a new person arrives needing training. If a department is made up of 75% expatriates, you can see the problems this will cause. TQM. compounded the problems to an extent no one could have foreseen.”

“And National Petroleum?” Roger asked.

“A different problem altogether; it was a victim of its own success. The exploration of the Atlantic Frontiers, west of the Shetland Isles, located massive oilfields, larger than anything found in the North Sea. They shot blanket coverage surveys over the whole fields of Uther and Mordred, and ordered dozens of site survey reports for specific locations from the surveys. The quality-assured processes of the contractors did not work. Interpretations were wrong, shallow gas pockets were missed during hazard assessments; buried channels were omitted. It was a nightmare and N.P. simply could not cope in-house any longer with the report checks and corrections.”

“And you stepped in? How?”

“We had always provided the offshore representatives to the oil companies, and they simply came to us to provide highly experienced, office-based consultants to cope with the problems. Where else could they go? We have the only group of professionals with over fifteen years of experience in the site survey industry. Our consultants now run the site survey departments in Delta Mex and N.P. on behalf of the ‘management’. We deal with all tender documents; we put together the scope of work for every project, assess the tender bids, and choose the contractor to carry out the work. We have one of our offshore representatives on the vessel for the site work, and when the contractor completes the interpretation and report, our people in the oil company’s office check it before we issue it internally. Basically we run the show in the absence of in-house expertise, and we cost less.”

“I would have to question that last statement,” said Gordon Letty, the area manager in charge of the three departments, “experience costs, we know that!”

“I agree,” replied Alex, “if the individuals are employed on a staff basis. Your overheads include a salary commensurate with experience, share options, bonuses, annual holidays, bank holidays, pension scheme, private health insurance, sickness payments, and redundancy payments. The cost to you of a man with fifteen years’ experience would be in the region of £1,500 per working day, five days per week, every week of the year.”

Gordon Letty nodded in agreement at the figure. He knew only too well the costs involved. “And what would it cost to have you working for us?” he asked.

“£900 per day. You can hire us on a daily, weekly or monthly basis, and you can call off the hire with only 24 hours notice if the workload changes. This arrangement is working with Delta Mex and N.P., and there is no reason why it shouldn’t work for you gentlemen.”

“What about the individuals? How are they linked to you? Do you guarantee them so many days work per year? Are they shareholders?”

“Oceansearch offers them work as it comes to us, there is no guarantee of work, and they are not shareholders. No overheads are the golden rule. Just like you, we would only pay them when we have work. All the individuals are freelance professionals with a minimum of fifteen years’ offshore experience. They are the best available.”

“But not shareholders. Why not?”

“No shares are available. All shares are held by the remaining director.”

“And what is the company cut of the £900 charged?”

“33% in every case.”

“The consultants are happy about that?”

“They accept that as the going rate. Their daily rate is £603, which isn’t bad, don’t you think?”

“What’s to keep them from leaving?”

“As I said, we don’t employ them, they work for themselves, and there isn’t anything to leave. But if you mean why don’t they work through some other company, there isn’t one to compete with us. We have virtually secured the market.”

“Do you think you win work as a company identity, or simply on the backs of the fifteen year CVs?”

“The company.”

“And you’re in no doubt?”

“No. Anyway, the people are loyal to us. We have good working relationships with our consultants.”

"As long as they are happy with the 33% deduction. Do you ever worry that some of them might decide to kick-off on their own?"

"That is always a possibility, but the uncertainty of earnings while they make a name for themselves would be enough to deter them. Is this something which greatly concerns you?" Alex asked Gordon.

"We would be concerned about anything which would affect continuity with key personnel should we decide to take up your services. We are deep enough in the shit as it is. I'm sure you understand."

Alex reached into his briefcase and withdrew five particular curriculum vitae. "These consultants are proposed for you to consider. Why should they leave now? No, gentlemen, these individuals benefit from the arrangement with us as much as we benefit from them. All of us," he outstretched his arms, "benefit from this arrangement."

The four managers looked across at each other, silently nodding, as if they had already made up their minds about the outcome prior to the meeting. Gordon Letty was the one to speak.

"We are in agreement that there is no doubt we need your services on a long-term basis. Perhaps we could now move on to a more specific presentation of your capabilities, starting with the exploration side, and then moving specifically to your own environmental expertise, where we have definite long-term office requirements for the right person."

"Of course." Alex allowed himself an inward smile, but his face remained impassive, and his voice coolly professional. That would be the last time he would make this presentation on behalf of someone else's company. "But before I do, I must make it perfectly clear that I have now ended the Oceansearch presentation, and my final obligation to that company."

Three of the managers looked at each other; only Gordon Letty was not surprised at the announcement.

Alex continued. "I need to make a number of things clear regarding the five individuals whose CVs you are now holding. The first is that as of today, none of them are associated in any way with Oceansearch Associates (a white lie, but justified considering the circumstances). As a direct response to the 33% profit taken from the daily rates by Oceansearch, I have formed my own company, which will, among other things, provide senior consultants to the survey industry. In terms of cost, we will charge exactly the same amount, £900 per day, for exactly the same services you have just agreed you need, but the company cut will be 20% thereby allowing the consultants to earn £720 per day; a substantial increase on their former pay at Oceansearch."

"I did not set out from home this morning with this ending in mind, but circumstances have precipitated today's developments. The choice is now yours as whether to proceed or not, but be assured, my colleagues and I are no longer part of Oceansearch Associates."

It was Gordon Letty who spoke. "Gentlemen, I have to be open with you and tell you that I had prior warning of this announcement," he nodded to Alex, and raised his hands to stifle any questions, "and I agreed that Alex should make the formal presentation on behalf of Oceansearch as arranged. That way there can be no comeback on any of us, and no comments to the effect that we showed any undue bias. My own view is that it is indeed Alex and his colleagues that we need, not just a list of names from a company. Alex, I would like you to continue the presentation on behalf of your own company."

CHAPTER 9

Pointe Noire, Congo-Brazzaville

Carl Moston was weary. Anyone who said that they enjoyed flying obviously didn't fly enough. His third flight in less than twenty-four hours was almost over, and from his aisle seat he could just see the sunrise of another African dawn. As the treetops of the Congo gave way to the West African coastline, the plane circled and lined up for its approach to the airport at Pointe Noire.

This short flight from neighbouring Gabon hadn't been too bad, but the flight from Paris Charles De Gaulle to Port-Gentil had been five hours of discomfort. All the window seats had been taken by the time he checked in, and it had been his misfortune to have to sit next to a very overweight Frenchman who had kept the hostesses busy throughout the flight topping up his glass of chardonnay. After the man's third visit to the toilet it had become obvious that sleep was out of the question because the leg room did not allow for the passage of such a bulk without disturbing the person in the aisle seat. When the plane had landed at Port-Gentil, the Frenchman had immediately unbuckled his seat belt and stood up, wanting to be one of the first to disembark, but Carl had remained seated, much to the man's annoyance. With typical Gallic charm, he'd tried to push past, but Carl would not move his legs, leaving the man half-standing, half-crouching with his head bent sideways under the overhead locker. When the plane had taxied to a halt, Carl unbuckled his belt, stood and allowed other passengers to remove their belongings from the lockers first in an overt display of English manners, whilst firmly blocking in the Frenchman who had continued to tut and blow during the whole five minute wait. When most of the other passengers had moved along, Carl had stepped into the aisle without even a glance at the man whose urgency had made no sense at all because they would soon be joining another queue to get their transit tickets and a seat for the short flight to the Congo.

The airport at Pointe Noire had barely changed since Carl's last visit almost ten years ago and he walked to the same dusty entrance hall to queue before one of the two makeshift wooden booths where the immigration officers stood and deliberated over each passport and visa. Voices were raised as some passports with valid visas were not stamped and the owners directed to wait outside at the back of the queue in the rapidly warming African sun. Carl calmly waited knowing full well that he did not even have a visa and would have to persuade the officer that the Delta Mex agent would be waiting for him, visa in hand. When it was his turn he passed his passport to the officer.

"Delta Mex…"

"Yellow Fever?" the immigration officer interrupted.

Carl quickly flicked to the vaccination stamps attached to his passport.

"No Yellow Fever, no get in."

The man looked, nodded and pointed to a desk further down the passageway. "Pay visa there." He looked away dismissively.

The baggage desk was on the left immediately after the immigration booths and was surrounded by local porters who swamped those arriving, demanding their baggage tickets. Carl gave his ticket to the man who spoke the clearest French, then stood back against the wall as the man elbowed his way to the desk to claim the suitcase. The noise of all the porters shouting in their local dialect was deafening, and yet within minutes the man was pushing backwards through the crowd, pulling Carl's suitcase with complete disregard for the knees and shins it was hitting.

As they moved towards the visa desk Carl's attention was drawn to the loud argument behind them at the passport booth. He turned to see the fat Frenchman being escorted to the back of the queue, passport being waved in his face by the soldier's comrade. You stupid fat man, thought Carl, your government may support the Congo-Brazzaville economy but these people do not welcome expatriates with open arms. They see you as being wealthy and exploitable, and the more you argue, the more it will cost. The only thing cheap here is life.

After paying for his visa Carl walked to the taxi stand and bartered over the price to the Novotel. The price was soon agreed when the driver realised that Carl spoke some French, and after paying the porter 10,000CFA, the taxi bounced along the main road to Pointe Noire.

The Novotel was like an oasis sent from the first world, perfectly placed in the centre of Pointe Noire, just off the Boulevard Charles De Gaulle, the one and only main road in the town.

The message waiting for Carl at reception was curt and to the point, a style he immediately recognised:

Vessel taking bunkers, will move to timber wharf later.

Briefing onboard 14:00 hrs tomorrow (Thursday).

ALL personnel to attend.

Estimated Time of Departure 1800 hrs. same day.

You are invited to dinner @ Chez Paulette, 20:00 hrs this evening.

Regards,

Richard Peterson.

Carl looked at the flamboyant signature and printed name at the bottom of the note. Excellent, the bastard was here!

The room at the Novotel was bright and clean, and most importantly, cool. It was still only nine a.m. and after quickly hanging up two shirts and two pairs of trousers, Carl closed the curtains and took off all his creased and sweat-stained clothes, leaving them on the floor where they fell. Within five minutes he was fast asleep on the bed, the alarm set for two in the afternoon.

Like the airport, Pointe Noire town hadn't changed at all. There were no new buildings and no old ones had gone. Maybe a few of the bars had changed hands, but nothing that made any difference. In an odd way it was comforting, and as he walked down the Boulevard Charles De Gaulle, Carl did not feel at all like a stranger.

Approaching the square he could see that one side was lined with local stallholders, all selling malachite carvings and chess sets, just as they always had. They beckoned to him, each one claiming to have the best prices, but all of them probably working for the same boss. There were eight large stalls set out in the shade of the building behind, each full of beautiful carvings of all types of African animals, with the most ornate chess sets carved out of stone standing behind. The exquisite shades of green in the malachite would make the most fervent critics of the game of chess want one of these sets, and although Carl ignored the stallholders and carried on walking, he knew he would be back shortly to haggle over the prices because he had already decided to buy one for his office. He didn't stop for two reasons, the first was because in terms of bartering, the traders would be very pleased when he returned and the prices would start lower, and secondly he wanted to see if the art students still displayed their oil paintings outside the old colonial style railway station at the end of the boulevard.

He walked, unhurried, enjoying the afternoon sun and made his way to the old railway station with its bright red terracotta roof atop sandy coloured walls. It was one of the few buildings to retain any hint of their former glory, and gave an impressive burst of colour to the otherwise run-down street. The students were still there, but even by the West African standards they were lazy, not even bothering to get up from their prone positions in the shade as he looked at the paintings. There were two he liked and would have bought, if only the young man had stood up. This display of apathy towards life was inexcusable and Carl's eyes momentarily flashed with hatred for the man. But there was no response from the man's blank stare; seemingly nothing was more important than to lie there.

Carl turned and headed back to the malachite stallholders, now looking forward to haggling. They would try to rob him, all the while pleading with him that they were giving the best deal, saying that they were making so little money already that a further discount was not possible. They would tell him that they had families to feed and had to charge such prices. But at least they had a passion for life, even if it was a passion to rip him off! And in the end who was ripping off whom? The starting price for a chess set was £50, and Carl would eventually pay £30, yet the value in England was over £300! These men had stalls full of malachite carvings worth thousands upon thousands of pounds in Europe, but they would only get a few hundred pounds for the goods in Africa. Was colonialism really over, or was it now simply present in different forms?

Carl glanced briefly at the beautiful chess pieces once more before closing the door behind him. His second change of clothes of the day felt cool and fresh as he walked down the corridor to the foyer where the taxi was waiting outside to take him to Chez Paulette.

Ten minutes later he was standing at the bar ordering his customary *kir normal*. Paulette still looked the same, even though she must now be in her late seventies, and he smiled at her typical French expatriate manner that the years had not softened. The bar had its own charm, and was still one of the few places where you could sit, drink and eat without being pestered by hawkers or prostitutes, courtesy of Paulette's rules, administered with a rod of iron. Here was the meeting place for the Pointe Noire oil industry. No-one visited the town without at least one night at her bar where the walls were adorned with life-belts from the various ships and supply boats of her customers, and the continual squawking and talking of the African Grey parrots on their tree-stands in the corner of the lounge threatened to drown out the conversations.

Carl was half an hour early on purpose because he wanted to see his old boss arrive with his minions in tow; he was not disappointed, but he had to admit to being surprised at the age of the survey crew. Most could barely be out of college from the look of them! Either that or he was forgetting how old he must look himself.

"Well Carl, it has been a long time, hasn't it?" The condescending smile on Richard's face was as irritating as it had been all those years ago, bringing the memories of his backstabbing nature surging back. Carl shook Richard's thin white hand, loathing every second of the touch.

"It certainly has, thirteen years to be exact, with an awful lot of water passing under this particular bridge."

The drongos making up the survey crew were introduced in turn. Carl made no effort to remember their names.

"We are old friends," said Richard to the drongos, "isn't that right, Carl?"

"We worked together in the past, if that's what you mean."

"Actually, you worked for me if I remember correctly. Isn't that right?" added Richard, playing to his crew.

"Yes, it certainly is, and now after all this time, you are the party chief and I am the client's representative with my own consultancy company. So who has come off the best?"

"Who can tell, Carl, and does it really matter? I think not."

"Really? It sounds to me like it matters a great deal, even after all this time. How about saying it all to my face now, you know, like you did behind my back, or don't you have the balls?" Carl's threat was unmistakable; the drongos went quiet.

"Carl, Carl," came the patronising reply, "you really should relax more. Don't take everything to heart. Surely you haven't been bearing a grudge all this time? C'mon, let me get the drinks in. Lads, what are you having?" Richard put his hand around Carl's shoulder and they turned to face the bar.

"I still feel the same fucking way about you," said Richard, seething at the way he had been insulted in front of the others, "you were never good enough to be a rep and I've not heard anything to change my mind."

"I'm glad you've just said that, because it removes any doubts I might have had that you really did try to stitch me up."

"Oh, don't ever be in any doubt about it, my friend. Why do you think that Oceansearch don't work in America? Because of you, that's why. Your name is shit in America, because over there they listened to me and believed me. Any consultancy you are linked with is blacklisted. Good, isn't it?"

"Keep talking, Richard. That's what you've always been good at, even if it's garbage that's coming out. The Americans were bound to love you."

“I knew we were going to have a nice time here, I said so to Scandi-Seis when they told me who the rep was going to be. It’s going to be like old times, you’ll see.”

“Oh, it’s going to be fun all right,” replied Carl, “but I think you should get the drinks in before your drongos begin to think we don’t like each other.”

“Of course, we can’t have that at the start of such an important job, can we?”

The food and the service were excellent, but the atmosphere between Richard and Carl was decidedly cool, and not helped by the immature, although lively, conversation between the crew, that came mostly from Dr. Death and Orville. They were really Julian and Sean, but they seemed to prefer their nicknames. Dr. Death was the marine geophysicist with a PhD. in acoustic sources, a head for trivia and a memory for disgusting jokes. Apparently he was also seasick on every job, hence the name. Orville was a twenty-three year old engineer who had to be the only man in the world to resemble a ventriloquist’s duck. His voice had never completely broken and he had a forehead so high that even before his red hair had started to recede it would have had no chance of covering it, plus his ears stuck out! It therefore came as no surprise to anyone that during the meal Orville admitted to still being a virgin.

“I’ve come ‘ere to come,” Orville announced in his high-pitched, Yorkshire accent, giggling at his own stupidity. “I want a black woman to initiate me into the pleasures of the night.”

“How can anyone be a virgin at twenty-three?” asked Chicken George, the Jamaican engineer.

“Perhaps in Yorkshire they didn’t go around fucking the schoolgirls behind the hen coops like you did,” Shed said.

“There’s nothing wrong with that,” Chicken George replied.

“At ten years old there is,” added Slug.

“It’s only jealousy I’m hearing, just because yours was still soft and squidgy at that age.”

“Better than being black.”

“I wouldn’t mind mine being black if it was that big,” butted in Razor.

“Don’t pander to the slave, for fuck’s sake,” replied Slug, “it’s only a myth.”

“It didn’t look like a myth to me,” Razor replied.

“Have you been peeking or are you close friends? Richard, I am definitely not sharing a cabin with either of these two on this trip,” laughed Shed.

Carl was amazed. It was like sitting with a bunch of school kids who were in their twenties! “Well you really have surrounded yourself with a winning team this time Richard,” he said, dropping his napkin onto his unfinished meal. “What a shower of idiots. Is this the best you can do? You don’t seem to have progressed at all.”

“You and me both, Carl. You’re sitting at the table as well, remember.”

“At least I have the consolation of being paid more for putting up with this shit.”

“Oh, I wouldn’t be so sure of that! Without me, Scandi-Seis can’t pull off this work, and believe me, I don’t come cheaply.”

“Tell me, Richard, who did you stab in the back so you could get this job?”

“Merit, Carl, merit. I’m the best available. You should know that, I taught you all you know.”

“Now who’s kidding who? You had no digital experience when you set up your company, you just bullshitted your way through. You did it back then and got away with it, but I’m going to see to it that you don’t do it this time.”

“Really? And how will you know? I would have thought that a person would need some sort of relevant experience to do that,” Richard said grinning.

“Keep talking, Richard.”

“It’s what we both do, so cut the crap. We’re here to make money, and we have to work together. I don’t like it either, you know, but I can stick it out for the cash.” Richard turned to speak quietly, “And if it means wet-nursing these kids, then I’ll do it and so will you. We’re not so very different, Carl, we’ve simply taken different paths.”

“You’re wrong, there’s a world of difference between us. You make my skin crawl, you two-faced bastard!” Carl said, suddenly standing up.

“There you go again! Always one for the dramatics. Stop overreacting Carl, you don’t have to impress the kids!”

Carl seemed to ignore him as he placed his chair under the table, but as he walked past he leant down to whisper in Richard’s ear. “Say one more word to me and I will split your fucking face wide open.” He drew his face back and nodded at Richard, as if to confirm what he had just said, then walked out of the room to the adjoining bar.

The drongos looked at Richard, but he dismissed it. “I think he’s having period pains,” he said, and as all good drongos should, they laughed out loud at their leader’s joke, every one of them now looking towards Carl at the bar.

Richard shrugged to the others, laughing it off as best he could, but knowing full well that Carl would have carried out his threat had he said more. The conversation started up again as if there had been no break, with the release of Orville from the prison of virginity fast becoming the priority of the night.

"I think, in all fairness to Orville," said Richard as the last one finished eating, "that we should retire from this bar to one of lesser repute, where the ladies of the night will continually fondle and molest us until we agree to inject them with whitesnake." His own groin began to stir at the thought of having some cute little thing up against the wall. "Let us adjourn to the Atlantic Bar."

"The Atlantic Bar," they all toasted, "and the end of a man's torment."

Within fifteen minutes they were all standing on the terrace of the Atlantic Bar on Boulevard Charles De Gaulle. Perhaps terrace was too grand a title for the roughly tiled front garden of the bar, but by the third bottle of West African beer, with all its added chemicals, they were beyond caring. Even Carl was loosening up as the alcohol took effect. No one sat inside, it was simply too hot, and besides the lights were off, permanently. All activity centred on the terrace, with its small wooden bar in the corner of the garden, and the cheap ghetto blaster providing the music.

The crowd was split roughly fifty-fifty, half drinkers, half prostitutes, with the occasional hawker selling malachite bangles and necklaces. Orville thought he was in paradise, a black one. He had never had so much interest shown in him, and the two women rubbing up against him were promising all kinds of delights if he took the two of them together. Tonight was going to be like a porn film, and he was going to be the star!

Razor and Slug ordered more beers while Richard took the youngest of the prostitutes through the darkened bar to the room at the back.

"Not there, not safe," she said in broken English.

"Pourquois pas?" Why not, he asked.

"Sometimes pimps wait in the shadows and watch," she replied in French, "you might be attacked. Steal your wallet. It is better to stay in the corridor where the light is on. No-one will care."

He lifted her skirt and fucked her against the wall. She was right, no one interrupted them.

"That was quick," Orville shouted across the terrace as Richard walked back a few minutes later. "What's the matter? Couldn't get it up?"

"That's the one," Richard said to the prostitute, "he's the virgin."

Her eyes opened wide, the whiteness made all the more striking by her black skin. Richard thought how pretty she was. Pity she was a whore.

"You sure he's a virgin?" she asked, "I don't think so."

"Orville, are you a virgin?" Richard shouted.

"Not for much longer," came the reply. "Why, does she want something bigger than you can manage?" The others all laughed at Richard's expense, especially when Orville raised his little finger towards him.

"Very good, Orville," said Richard, laughing sarcastically as he turned to the woman. At that point Carl walked over and joined the two of them.

"I think it's time for the virgin to be sacrificed, don't you, before he has too much to drink and brewer's droop sets in? I don't think I could go through this again tomorrow night," Carl said.

"I couldn't agree more," Richard replied. "Listen," he said to the prostitute, "tell four of your friends to wait round the back, then you take him to them. How much for all of you to fuck him? Let's give him a good send off shall we, Carl?"

"25,000CFA," she said quickly, knowing the man would never manage five of them. It was easy money. He would probably come in the first few minutes.

"I'll pay that," said Carl, "it will be worth it just to shut him up. Break him in and give him a show. Okay?" She nodded. "Go and tell your friends, then come over to us."

Carl and Richard walked over to the table where the beers were quickly mounting up, and told the others what had been arranged.

"Are you sure you don't want us to share the cost?" Slug asked.

"Not at all," Carl said, "after having had to listen to him during the meal, I feel it is my duty to release this man from his torment. It is my pleasure."

"It sounds like the pleasure is going to be all Orville's," laughed Chicken George.

The prostitute whispered to the others and they went over to the bar, but before she could approach Orville, a strong hand grabbed her arm, turning her roughly. The look in the pimp's eyes terrified her.

"What's the score with the whiteys?" he asked, squeezing her arm tight. She told him exactly, too frightened to even lie about the price. "Very good. Take him to the back room. Understand!" She nodded; the fear in her bright eyes told him that she would obey.

"See you later, Orville," they all shouted as he disappeared inside with the prostitute. "Okay, whose round is it?"

“I’m going, I’m going,” said Dr. Death, “and I’ll get one for Orville as well. He’ll probably come as soon as he sees a black pussy. I’m telling you, it was a waste of money.”

“He might be gone for some time,” Chicken George said in a deep, serious voice, emulating a famous explorer.

“I hope Orville can still get it stiff after all that beer,” Slug said, shaking his head.

“Don’t worry,” Chicken George replied, “we black people have voodoo and can raise the dead. A dick won’t be any problem to these women.”

It wasn’t.

Orville was already naked on the floor, held spread-eagled by the four women, while the fifth kneeled over him rapidly rubbing the head of his erect penis against her clitoris. In the dim light he could see the beads of sweat breaking out on her skin at the exertion, and he felt her muscles tighten in her thighs as she quickly came. She held him tight, smearing her slickness over him before forcing down on him in one strong movement, his virginity lost with one thrust of her hips. She rode him quickly for ten strokes, each counted out by the giggling women holding him down.

After ten, the woman eased off him, careful to hold the condom in place, and the women changed places, it now being the turn of the second woman to repeat the process. Each woman was careful not to go too far. They had been paid for five fucks, and that was what he was going to get. By the turn of the last woman Orville was so hard and swollen that he could not hold it any longer, coming on her first push, his body shuddering with the feeling. His eyes closed in ecstasy as he thrust upwards, giving way to his orgasm, causing the fifth whore to scream involuntarily.

It was as though the scream was a signal, because as Orville felt the pulsing in his groin, he also felt the grips changing on his arms and legs. His eyes shot open, only to see the gag being pushed over his mouth. The hands now holding him were no longer smooth and feminine, but rough and strong. He felt his penis slip out of the woman and slap on his stomach just before he was violently turned over to lie face down with his legs spread wide. The fear shot through him in an instant as he realised what was about to happen. His stomach knotted and his buttocks clenched tight in a feeble attempt to protect himself.

"So, little white boy, you want to lose your virginity, do you? You think our women are just black whores?" the deep voice asked.

Orville struggled, tried to say no, only to feel a large hand slap the back of his head, forcing his face down to the floor, breaking his glasses and splitting his nose. He heard the man spit into his hand while the others holding him laughed, and in one horrible instant he realised that the man was smearing the saliva over his penis as lubrication. Orville was completely overpowered and screamed in pain as his rectum tore under the force of the first thrust. The man laughed as he viciously raped Orville. When the man shuddered tears ran from Orville's eyes as he realised the man had orgasmed inside him. But it was not over until all five men had had their turn. When the last man stood up, Orville curled up into a foetal position. The men laughed and threw his underpants at him but kept his money and clothes. Orville pulled on his underpants as he was dragged to the back entrance of the bar.

"One shout and you die," the biggest man said, sneering down at Orville, waving the knife in his face.

Orville said nothing; he just lay there, bent double, clutching himself and sobbing.

After two more beers the drongos realised that Orville still hadn't come back. "Perhaps he has more staying power than we imagined," Carl said. "The whores aren't back yet anyway. Leave him to it."

"I'm going to have a quick look," said Chicken George.

"Pervert!"

"I'm going anyway." Chicken George went across the terrace and down the corridor. Two minutes later he was back. "No sign of him. He's pissed off. Gone!"

"You sure?"

"Of course I'm bloody sure."

"Well, there's gratitude for you," Carl said, "not even a thank you. Fuck it, I'm not waiting for him if he's playing humpy all night."

"I don't think we should leave without him," slurred Slug.

"He left without us! I'm getting a taxi, anyone else? He could be anywhere by now. He'll turn up at the ship when he's had enough," Carl said, glad that the evening was finally over.

Chicken George had checked Orville's cabin at first light, and when he found it was still empty he woke the Party Chief to report it.

"He's probably still humping, who cares where he is? Now that he knows what to do with it, there'll be no stopping him. Close the door and let me sleep off this hangover."

Chicken George slammed the door in disgust, and went to sit on the ship's bridge to keep a lookout. After two hours and three cups of tea, he saw a naked figure stumbling towards the boat. No! He wasn't naked, he had white shreddies on, that was all. When he first saw him, Chicken George laughed.

"Who the fuck's plucked your feathers?" he called out to Orville, but as he stumbled closer, Chicken George could see that things were not okay. He ran down the gangway and caught hold of Orville, who was on the verge of collapsing. Tears fell from Orville's squinting eyes when he realised it was Chicken George.

"For fuck's sake, man, what happened?" but from the blood on his split nose, and on his legs and shreddies, Chicken George had already guessed.

The agent was called and Orville was taken to the hospital for a check-up with strict instructions to have no injections, but it was probably too late, the chances of Orville being contaminated were very high. If the prostitutes hadn't got him, the men almost certainly had. Arrangements were made for Orville to be returned to England for blood tests, which, if they proved positive, would end his career in the industry, but would he really care about a career if his life expectancy had just been practically decimated?

"It was you who said that you couldn't be bothered to wait," Richard shouted at Carl, "you were the one who said he'll probably be at it all night, and in any case we checked where he was and he'd gone. What's the big deal? We'll have a twenty-four hour delay while a replacement is sent out, that's all."

"You callous bastard. The kid could have been killed. As it is he probably has a death sentence over him, and all you can think about is a short delay, you're not fit to be the Party Chief. It was his first time in Africa, he was an innocent abroad."

"He was a twenty-three year old man, that's what he was!"

"Yes, but he'd never been outside of the U.K. before, you had a responsibility towards him. You should have raised the alarm when you found he wasn't on the boat when you got back last night."

"I cannot be everyone's dad, and neither do I want to be. It was his decision to go with the whores, and don't forget who egged him on and who fucking well paid for it. You are not Snow White in this matter, so don't even think about trying to lay all the blame at my feet. Now if you don't mind, we have a briefing to get on with, instrument tests have to be carried out, and I'm an engineer short until tomorrow."

"And that's it?"

"What else can it be? Orville was a fucking idiot anyway. I would never have hired him for this type of work because of his lack of experience, but on top of that he wasn't a particularly good engineer from all accounts."

"But you're prepared to mean mouth him without even knowing? That's just your style isn't it? Call someone behind their back."

"Ah, get stuffed. I've got work to do."

Watching him walk to the lab, Carl realised that Richard hadn't changed in the slightest during the past thirteen years. Just as he had slandered Carl and his ability after leaving his company, he was now starting to do the same to Orville, despite what had happened to him. Carl was convinced that only good could come from ridding the industry of this vindictive bastard.

When the end came, it came quickly and easily, and like so many opportunities, it simply presented itself. The two site surveys had been completed off the Congo in only ten days and the vessel sailed south for forty hours into Angolan waters in preparation for the 2-D exploration work. The work was expected to take up to four weeks once the configuration had been changed, and after two days of supervising the changeover, Richard was still up and about seeing that everything was running smoothly as the vessel shot the first 2-D line.

The airgun array was deployed from the stern on the port side of the old supply boat, and the security camera to the lab was trained on the streamer winch, which was deployed directly mid-ships over the stern. Richard had been pleased with the deployment of the equipment and was having a final look before turning in. In his tiredness, he didn't notice that Carl had walked to the stern on the blind side of the camera, but when he saw him standing there he couldn't help walking over to boast about how well it was all going with him as Party Chief.

The surveyor and engineer on watch in the lab saw Richard walk out of the camera shot, but they never saw the lightning fast uppercut that lifted Richard off his feet, leaving him hanging backwards on the safety chain over the stern of the ship.

"Goodbye, arsehole," said Carl as he lifted Richard's legs and watched him roll backwards into the Atlantic.

Richard sank beneath the water, and the coldness shocked him into full consciousness. Realising the danger he kicked frantically for the surface, desperate to get his head above the water, but he was not fast enough. The air guns fired again, and a pulse of 8000 psi was discharged below the sea surface immediately bursting Richard's eardrums; his brain reeled from the shock. In his pain he forgot to kick and lost all orientation, but with the next cyclical firing of the guns his brain seemed to explode and he lost consciousness.

Carl couldn't see if the body had surfaced in the wake of the vessel, and neither did he care. He walked away from the stern on the blind side of the camera and retired to his cabin for the evening. When Richard was reported missing tomorrow, the job would be delayed indefinitely while an investigation was held. The man went overboard in Angolan waters and the vessel would have to sail into Luanda to report it, and because of the political unrest and instability, it could very likely stay for up to two months. During that time Carl would have to advise Delta Mex to relieve Scandi-Seis of the contract and recommend

Britannia Surveys, who coincidentally had one of their vessels standing by alongside Walvis Bay in Namibia.

Chicken George stayed in the shadows at the rear of the upper deck for another hour before daring to move. He couldn't believe what he had just witnessed, and he didn't think anyone else would either.

CHAPTER 10

Great Yarmouth, Norfolk.

On the third floor of the Britannia House building, Aldred Grayson was reading through the morning emails while he waited for Darren to arrive for their meeting regarding the progress of the *Atlantic Challenger* on the Delta Mex project in West Africa. It was now almost three weeks since Britannia Surveys had moved in to take the work from the Danes, and so far the reports had been good. The project file holding all the specific information lay open before him on the desk, but Aldred always preferred to speak directly with his project managers about the vessels. Only that way did he feel he really knew what was going on.

The last memo to be sent to the vessel was concerning an Aids update for West Africa. The old man shook his head at the enormity of the problem, and the figures for infected prostitutes was staggering, almost 75% tested positive. Christ, he thought, surely the men working for him were not using these women when they hit port? One surprising fact caught his eye in the medical update which stated that some prostitutes, who had initially tested positive, showed to be negative when re-tested some weeks later. It was as though the Aids virus had disappeared. Further testing at a later date had showed that many had been re-infected with the disease, but again in the future they had once again tested negative. Somehow their bodies were fighting off the Aids virus, and now some sections of the medical research world believed that the ultimate cure for Aids might eventually come from the very prostitutes who had done so much to spread the disease!

The closing paragraph of the memo was typical of Gordon Shaw, the Britannia Surveys Operations Manager.

> "In summary, m'lud, I would like to say that a hand has never yet been cited as a co-respondent in divorce proceedings, has never failed to please, is completely trustworthy, and the silence of said hand is absolute. Could there be any greater recommendation for its use in leisure pursuits for offshore personnel?"

Aldred sighed as he thought of Dog's recent funeral and wondered about his wife and daughter. Maybe he should try to trace them, help in some way…

"Come in, Darren," he said in response to the two heavy knocks on the door. The tall, thin man walked in and sat down in the chair opposite to Aldred.

"Morning, Mr. Grayson. You received the project file, I see."

"Yes, I've just gone through the main points. It seems that the work is progressing extremely well. Delta Mex is obviously very pleased. So much so, in fact, that the scope of work has already been increased. We will be receiving confirmation of the additional lines to be shot later today, but the work has already been verbally confirmed to me this morning. It's quite a substantial increase, I might add."

"That's excellent news. The crew have worked very hard to meet the tight shooting specifications. It's not been easy."

"If it was easy, Scandi-Seis would never have made such a mess of it."

"Of course not," replied Darren, not daring to say that other events had come into play as well.

"In fact I've heard, and I know it to be true, that the Danish backers of Scandi-Seis are about to pull the plug on their U.K. operations now that they are effectively out of the running for the Delta Mex five-year service contract. Fifty per cent of their people have been given redundancy notices; it will be announced formally next week."

"That can only be good for us." Darren wanted to ask how he knew, but thought better of it.

"But we still have the Norwegians to contend with, and that's why we must really go to town and impress Delta Mex in Africa. Getting back to the *Atlantic Challenger*, I want to know more about the general feeling on the vessel because it will be two months before we can carry out a crew change."

"Two months!" said a surprised Darren, "but they're due to change out in three weeks. Most of the crew were onboard when the vessel left Namibia, before the work even started."

"I know, but I want to keep the same people onboard for continuity, I can't over-emphasise how important it is to win the Delta Mex service contract, and this work looks like it could do just that for us."

"But we don't know if we will beat the Norwegians even if this job is the best Delta Mex ever have done for them!" Darren said, still thinking about the reaction that was bound to come if there wasn't a crew change soon.

"You let me worry about the Norwegians, and you worry about your project."

"Some of the crew won't stand for it, they'll insist on getting off. It wouldn't be half as bad if the boats weren't dry."

"But they are now, and there's nothing I can do about that. Ten years ago all the ships had a bond onboard, but one by one the oil companies changed; health, safety and total fucked-up quality management! They now treat grown men as children who cannot be trusted with a few cans of beer even after a twelve-hour shift. I personally don't agree with it, but that's the way things have changed. Anyone found drinking on board will be sacked. Make sure the older hands know it applies to them as well; no gins and tonics with the captain anymore!"

"They know," replied Darren.

"Good. What I am prepared to do is pay double the sea allowance for every day over the normal crew change date. I think that is generous enough. Anyone not accepting this will be dismissed from the company!" The tone in Aldred's voice made it perfectly clear that it was non-negotiable.

"I understand. Let's just hope the bonus will be sufficient to persuade them. I'll leave out the bit about sacking unless it becomes absolutely necessary."

"Deal with it however you think best Darren, and bear in mind that your job rests entirely on the success of this project. That will be all."

Darren stood to leave, not in the least surprised by Aldred's final comment. Ah, what the fuck, he thought, the bonus was good enough to keep the people onboard, and once he let them know that Scandi-Seis was making 50% of its people redundant, they wouldn't be shouting too loud about what's fair and what's not. At least they still had a job! As he closed the heavy panelled door behind him, he gave a sigh of relief; today's meeting hadn't been too bad at all.

At the same time that Darren Thompson walked out of Aldred's office, the phone rang on the desk of Terry Manning, Operations Manager of Scandi-Seis. "Dr. O'Neil from Delta

Mex Oil has finished collating the data to be transferred to Britannia Surveys and is waiting to see you, Terry."

"Thanks, Lyn, I'll be right down, and could you arrange for some coffee to be sent up immediately we get back into my office?" Dr. O'Neil was exactly on time. Manning just hoped that there would be no recriminations or a shouting match; he didn't think that he could handle that. Too much had already gone wrong without adding a domestic problem to his list. He patted the few long strands of hair into place across his bald head, and went down to the geophysical department.

"Dr. O'Neil," Terry said, holding out his hand.

"Thank you for seeing me at such short notice, but it seemed like the most economical use of my time."

"Not at all. Shall we go to my office, where we can talk more privately?"

"First of all," Dr. O'Neil said as Manning closed the door to his office, "I have been asked by my mother to thank you and your company for all its help since my brother's death."

"It was the least we could do. Orville, I'm sorry, Sean, was a well-respected member of our staff, and it is a tragic waste of life. We only wish that we could have done more for him after the attack. Perhaps if we had monitored him more closely, we might have seen more signs of his true state of mind."

The knock on the door caused the conversation to cease, and the two sat in silence as the coffee was brought in.

"I don't think any of us could have guessed how it had affected his mind," continued Dr. O'Neil. "Apart from the physical side of the attack, I'm sure it was the three month wait for the results of the blood tests which finally caused him to lose it."

"Yes, there's no doubt you're right. I don't know how anyone would cope with that. But if only he'd waited, he may have been clear. He might have been lucky."

"Lucky! Can you imagine the stigma attached to being gang-raped when you are a twenty-three year old man? Even if he hadn't got the Aids virus, it was a hell of a burden for him to carry!"

"What can I say? I totally agree with you. The attack is the most serious that has ever happened to any of our personnel since we began operating in 1987. We are completely reviewing our safety guidelines for overseas projects as a result of this."

"Spare me the boardroom bullshit. I said I had been asked to thank you on behalf of my mother, but that does not include me. You know he should never have been left alone, don't you? He was too inexperienced. Why did your people leave him at the bar?"

"Dr. O'Neil, we have interviewed everyone about that night," Manning said quickly, "and they all say the same thing. Sean had paid for the prostitutes and hadn't wanted to leave the bar when the others left. You have to appreciate that these are grown men, and you can't make them do things if they don't want to. They make their own choices, just like Sean did."

"And Sean is now dead, with a suicide verdict for my mother to cope with. That's a hell of a price to pay!"

"He still made up his own mind and refused to leave. I agree that they should never have split up, but Sean should have followed them. It was an seven-to-one decision."

"The Party Chief should have made him go and you know it. It's a pity he can't answer for his actions."

"Christ Almighty! He's dead, dammit. Lost overboard. Isn't that answer enough?" shouted Manning. "Don't you think that I would like to know what really happened?"

"Your own management is firmly to blame. If you can't appoint people to lead, then you have no place working in such parts of the world."

"Well we won't be anymore, will we? Delta Mex have put paid to that, and I wouldn't be at all surprised if you didn't have something to do with it," Manning snapped back.

"Oh, believe me, I had a lot to do with it. I have done my absolute damnedest to see that you never work for Delta Mex again. A male gang-rape and a man lost overboard! Hardly a good safety record is it?"

"Is that why you pulled your rep so quickly? Amazing what you can do, isn't it, when you don't want to be associated with a company any longer. We were delayed for fourteen days before we could take people off, but you had your man off within twenty-four hours."

"He was needed back in Europe to give his input to high level safety meetings regarding your company. The incident was your concern, and you lost the work because you couldn't carry on without the Party Chief. It seems there was not enough technical competence assigned to the project."

"Are you sure that was the reason, or was it because you did not want to be a associated with a safety incident for longer than was necessary? Brush it under the carpet, isn't that the approach, or is it to find someone else to blame as quickly as possible? The more distance Delta Mex could put between themselves and us, the quicker it would be forgotten."

"I really don't care how you see it," O'Neil said.

"Of course you don't. Why should I expect you to? People like you sit in your ivory towers and pass judgement, safe in your own security, insulated from the real world of harsh decisions and tight budgets. What do you care about all the people we are about to make redundant? Your time is up,

Doctor, forget about the coffee, it's time for you to leave." Manning stood up and opened the door, not even looking as his guest left.

O'Neil had been wrong about Manning. He did care, and it was obvious that he felt the Party Chief could have thrown some light onto Sean's attack, but Manning was wrong about life in Delta Mex Oil. No one was ever as secure or as valuable as they might think.

Chicken George quickly followed O'Neil across the car park, and deftly passed a business card into O'Neil's hand as he passed by. The message on the back read 'The Dolphin, Atlas Quay, at 14:00 hrs, I know about Orville'. O'Neil's eyes flashed up to see the man's face, but Chicken George was already walking away.

The run-down Dolphin pub on the dockside road still had a few lunchtime drinkers dotted around when O'Neil walked in at two o'clock. Chicken George was already at the bar, had been for about an hour, and being the only black man in the place, O'Neil walked straight to him.

"I'm…"

"You're Chicken George," O'Neil said.

"I'm actually Barclay Simpson III," he said, smiling at the use of his nickname, "but my grandparents do still have the chicken farm in Jamaica."

"Okay, Barclay, you said you know something about Sean. What?"

"I know that I wish I had stayed with Orville. We all do."

"That doesn't help any, does it? What do you know? Anything, or are you wasting my time?"

"He was set up to go with the prostitutes. Orville never paid. It..."

"His name was Sean," O'Neil interrupted.

"Sorry, Sean didn't pay for the prostitutes, the client representative did."

"What! Carl Moston paid? Why on earth did he do that?"

"You know Carl?"

"Of course I do. I've known him for almost six years, ever since Oceansearch first started to supply people to Delta Mex, and I met him at the safety debriefing for this job only a few days ago. I can't believe he would have done that."

"He said he felt sorry that a man should be a virgin at the age of twenty-three. It was a big joke. Sean thought so too."

"Okay, okay! But why did you leave him?"

"He'd been gone for a while, and after half an hour, I went to look for him, but he wasn't there. He must have left the back way, not wanting to see us. The attack must have taken place while we were drinking. We never left the bar, but we never heard him shout or anything. We thought he was with the prostitutes."

"Oh God! So it took place only a few yards from where you were?"

"It was a joke that went badly wrong, but what I don't understand is why the whores took Orville, sorry, Sean, into a room where men would be waiting. They must have been paid to do it."

"Do you think it was Carl Moston who paid for that as well?"

"That I don't know. It makes no sense. I don't know why the attack happened; I just want you to know that we didn't leave him. He was our friend and we all feel bad about this."

"You think that Carl was behind it, don't you?"

"I really don't know, but if I were you I wouldn't push this anymore."

"Why on earth not? If he set my brother up, I want to know, and I want to get even!"

"No, you don't want to know, and you don't want to cross Carl Moston. He's not what he appears to be. He's very dangerous. The Party Chief wasn't just lost over the side, Carl pushed him, and I saw him do it! Carl killed Richard Peterson and caused us to lose the work. Now you tell me, is that the work of a normal representative? There is something bad about the whole project, and all I know is that it's best not to get involved."

"But you are involved."

"My involvement ends today, and so does my debt to Orville." As Barclay continued to speak his manner became more nervous, his hands fidgeted, and perspiration broke out on his brow. O'Neil could see the tension the man was under, and the fear he felt. There was no doubt the man was telling the truth and that he was genuinely scared, but even that did not prepare O'Neil for the next few words.

"I have been told to inform you that an inner group of industrial saboteurs operates within Oceansearch Associates, headed by Carl Moston, the client representative on this particular job. I can quote recent jobs that prove this to be true. The attack on Orville caused a delay, and the loss of the Party Chief was enough to have Delta Mex throw Scandi-Seis off the job. You yourself were instrumental in that. Your reaction was calculated, and you performed as expected."

"Who told you this?" demanded O'Neil who was careful to disguise any hint of shock at these revelations, and determined to keep a level head whatever was said.

"I cannot say, and I will never repeat what I have just said. If you ask me again, I will deny any knowledge of this conversation. This information has been passed to you because of the disgust at the rape of your brother and the involvement of the representative. What you do now is entirely up to you. I have never met you, now please excuse me." Barclay took his pint and sat down at the table in the corner, watching O'Neil slowly leave the bar.

For an hour Barclay waited, as he had been instructed to do, and then left by the back entrance. Within five minutes of leaving the Dolphin, he was at the offices of Britannia Surveys, where he was immediately shown to the offices of Aldred Grayson.

"Sit down Barclay," Aldred said as soon as his secretary had closed the door, "how was Dr. O'Neil?"

"Angry about Orville. Certainly blamed the Party Chief at first, but now seems convinced that Carl Moston was behind it all, and wants to get even with him! The idea of Oceansearch being a cover for industrial sabotage was an obvious surprise, but it certainly fit with this particular job, especially as I had witnessed Carl's actions. There weren't any questions about other jobs. O'Neil is looking for someone to blame for Orville, and Oceansearch are now the prime suspects. But the real swinger was the thought of having been used personally to have Scandi-Seis thrown off the job, which, of course, O'Neil had pushed for because of the two safety incidents. Believe me, Carl Moston had better watch his back."

"Well it will be interesting to see how our Dr. O'Neil tackles the problem, because someone must have paid Oceansearch to do the work, and I would say that the paymasters present the greatest danger to anyone," Aldred said with great feeling and a certain amount of trepidation for the benefit of Barclay. "I certainly wouldn't want to cross them. How about you?"

"Absolutely not, Mr. Grayson. It's sad about Orville, but these are dangerous people."

"I couldn't agree more, and thank God you came to tell me about what you saw. I've always had my doubts about Oceansearch in the past, and the last thing I want is for my company to be remotely connected in any way to such things. We got the work afterwards because we were lucky, in the right place at the right time, simple as that. I am in your debt for telling me what you saw, and so is Dr. O'Neil, but I think for both our sakes, I must have your absolute word that you have not spoken, and will not speak, of this to anyone else. Your new position as an engineer with us depends on your silence, Barclay."

"And my family depends on me to provide for them. I'm very grateful for the job, and I know that the information I gave you about the Scandi-Seis redundancies will remain a secret until next week."

"Of course, Barclay, we all have our secrets to keep. We both know that Carl Moston needs to be dealt with, and I am sure we can now leave it in Dr. O'Neil's capable hands."

"Thanks again, Mr. Grayson," Barclay said as he rose from the chair, extending his sweating hand to Aldred, "I won't let you down."

"I know, Barclay, I know." They shook hands and Barclay left. Aldred stared at the door long after it was shut. That man had taken one hell of a gamble coming here to tell Aldred what he had seen, hoping it would win him a job, all for the sake of his family. Men with that type of commitment deserve to be helped, and Aldred knew he would never talk about it again. The man was safe and Aldred had now set the ball in motion for the removal of Carl.

Picking up the phone he pressed the auto-dial for Oceansearch Associates. “Put me through to Carl Moston.”

“I’m afraid he’s on a call at the moment. Can anyone else help you?” the young girl replied.

“No! Interrupt him. Tell him its Aldred Grayson. I assure you he will take it.”

“Hold on sir, I’ll try,” the voice said, not at all sure it was a good idea. In less than twenty seconds he was through.

“Afternoon Aldred, what can I do for you?” asked Carl, sounding pleased with himself.

“Sharpen up your act for a start,” came the curt reply, instantly spoiling Carl’s good mood. “Someone saw what you did in Africa.”

“Impossible! I…”

“Never mind impossible. You were seen. I know it for a fact.”

Carl didn’t doubt that Aldred was telling the truth from the anger in his voice. “What needs to be done?” he asked, unsure of where Aldred was leading him.

“Nothing this time. I’ve been able to deal with it, but it seems to me that you are losing your edge, Carl.”

“I resent that!”

“Resent it all you like,” Aldred said, “it’s still true! This could have ruined us both. I’ve decided to hold payment until the second job goes through.”

“Like fuck you will!” Carl shouted.

"Oh? And how do you intend to force me to pay? No, son, I will pay the full amount when the National Petroleum job has been executed to my satisfaction. Perhaps holding back the money will focus your mind. I don't want another potential cock-up, do you understand? We were lucky this time, but no-one's luck lasts forever. Put someone good on the next one!"

"You got the work, didn't you?" said Carl, bridling at the insult.

"There can be no room for error in this work, I want someone good on the N.P. job," Aldred said, still pushing his point home.

"Let me spell it out for you. *It is too soon*! The men are tired and need time off!"

"Well then, if your regular men are tired, get in someone fresh. You only have two more weeks before the vessel sails. Make sure it goes well. Goodbye, Carl." The line went dead.

"And goodbye to you too, you old fuck!" Carl shouted as he slammed down the phone. He was stuck; he needed someone new, but from where? People like that just don't knock at the door and ask for a job.

Two days later someone did just that.

Aldred merely sighed after he replaced the receiver. Perhaps he shouldn't wind Carl up so much, but it was too easy, he couldn't resist it. Carl took the bait every time.

The last memo on Aldred's desk was about the vessel *North Sea Tiger*. The news wasn't good. The old lady was in a bad way, and the estimated costs of repairs to her port engine, coupled with the costs of the refit, did not make financial sense. She simply wasn't worth repairing. He felt sad that the ship he had started off with was ready for the breaker's yard. Still, that was where she had been headed over thirty years ago when he had first rescued her, but now she was beyond rescue. He reached for his note pad, at the top wrote the name of the vessel and underlined it. The vessel was synonymous with his company, and the crews that worked on her had always had the nickname 'North Sea Tigers', but it had gone beyond his own company. The North Sea was one of the most hostile environments in which to work anywhere in the world, and anyone who trained there had now become known as a North Sea Tiger. It had become a byword for the best in the industry and was known worldwide.

He felt sad as his pen moved over the paper. He drafted a note requesting a full inventory of equipment onboard the vessel, with market values attached, details of all certificates and insurances which were still current, and finally added that the vessel should not be regarded as a member of the fleet any longer. A skeleton crew was to remain onboard for safety reasons, but the remaining regular crew was to be laid off immediately. Signed Aldred Grayson.

The young man pulled up alongside one of the taxis waiting at the rank outside of the Star Hotel. He looked round, saw there was no queue and decided to double park while he ran to the cash point at the Nat West Bank. In the minute or so it took him to draw out his cash, the police car had pulled up behind his Golf GTi and the officer was already stepping out of his car as the young man ran back.

"Double parking at the taxi rank, engine still running. Not really supposed to happen, is it son? I'd better see your licence, and check your documents."

"You must be joking. I have been stopped so many times in the past few weeks that I expect birthday cards from you lot."

"Now, now. Sarcasm can get you into trouble."

"But why am I being stopped all the time?"

"Because you are being naughty, son, and until you learn to drive like a sensible adult, we will keep stopping you. Now, documents!"

He handed them over. "Thank you. Now, that wasn't difficult was it?" He slowly checked the name and dates, then handed them back. "Thank you. Everything seems to be in order."

"Of course they are, you only saw them yesterday."

"Actually, it was last week. You were speeding down Admiralty Road, weren't you?"

"If you call 35 speeding."

"Well, in a 30mph zone that is speeding, you know."

"Can I go now?"

"Oh no, not yet. I need to give you a ticket for double parking and leaving a running car unattended."

"You must be joking. Come on, give me a break."

"Excuse me, sir? Are you suggesting that I should be an accomplice to you breaking the law? Are you trying to subvert the course of justice?"

"Jesus Christ! Why is this happening? Why have you got it in for me?"

"Sir, surely you are not suggesting that this is victimisation? I take that as a serious affront to my integrity. Are you aware of how serious an allegation that is?"

"Okay, okay," he said, holding both hands up, "it was a slip of the tongue. I'm sorry."

"Well, thank goodness for that. At least I won't have to sue you for defamation of character."

The look on the young man's face was one of total disbelief. Was this really happening?

"You shouldn't be surprised, sir. One of the lessons you have to learn in life is how to behave properly, and show respect to others. That includes when you drive your car. Show more consideration, and I am sure we will not have any reason to pull you over. Until then, see you soon. Oh, and here's your ticket."

He looked at the ticket, and then at the police officer walking back to his car. He now had collected three tickets in four weeks. If he wasn't careful he could be banned from driving. He shook his head in disbelief.

"Don't worry son, it's not the end of the world. Be a nice driver, that's all," the officer said before driving away.

CHAPTER 11

Covent Garden, London.

Her squats were perfect, just like her well-honed body. Heels flat on the ground, thighs pointing out at the same angle as her feet, back straight as she balanced the Olympic bar across her shoulders. Sixty kilo full squats, none of the cheating parallel squats for her, all the way down until she was almost sitting on her heels. Feeling the full stretch in her glutes she pushed hard, the quadriceps in the front of her thighs straining as she stood straight up, finally pushing her hips and abdomen forward as she squeezed her glutes tight together. That was the only way to have a high tight ass when you were thirty-four. It was no secret, it was simply hard work.

She tackled all of the muscle groups the same way; perfect style for perfect results. Three times a week she came to the Jubilee Hall in Covent Garden, to push herself and maintain the figure she had created through her own determination. She admitted that God had helped her with a good bust and curvy hips when she was sixteen, but the rest was down to her. She knew that she looked better now than when she was a teenager, unlike the masses of women who flower for only a summer or two, before swiftly sinking into the shape of middle-age which they would carry to the grave.

The gym, packed with free weights and machines, was full as usual, but if you knew what you were doing there was never any reason to wait for a piece of equipment; that is, unless you wanted to. Morgan had no time for the dozy bitches in their skimpy leotards and the steroid-bloated action men who didn't mind how long they waited because there were always mirrors to keep their minds active. For her, this was a place to work, and sweat, and finish in fifty minutes; posing was for at work and at night. The Jubilee Hall attracted the *beautiful* people who were trying to make it and needed to look good. Tonight as she looked around she saw a poorly endowed former male Gladiator, recognised only because of repeats on UKTV Gold, a familiar looking games show hostess, great bust, skinny legs, and one of the androgynous Saturday morning TV presenters. Perhaps others looked at her and wondered why the women with the fiery red hair and green eyes was so obsessive about her training; to Morgan it didn't matter one jot. In this place everyone was fair game for passing comments, complimentary or otherwise.

After finishing her workout she left the weights hall through the smoked glass doors into the dividing corridor. In the facing room she could see the escrima class practising with their rattan canes. Pretentious fools, she thought, they've just seen one martial arts film too many, and look at the idiot in the front row. Good old Alex Haines; typical of him to train at such a 'different' type of sport. Poser! She watched his well-muscled arms swing the canes, and just for a moment wished that she could have bedded him. His loss, she thought, as she turned away, heading down the corridor to the changing rooms.

Leaving her sweat-soaked training pants and vest in a heap next to her locker, she walked naked to the showers, eager to feel the refreshing spray over her tired and glistening body. Her pure white skin and red hair stood out in stark contrast to the others in the communal showers; not for her the white bum and boobs look of the bikini suntan crowd. Morgan ignored the hushed comments and defiantly held their gaze as she enjoyed the feel of the cool shower. Only the woman with the superb figure and almost jet-black skin nodded to her. Morgan nodded back, an acknowledgement of type. They were poles apart to look at, and yet the same.

She dried her hair and dressed quickly, her work clothes left to one side as she pulled out the stretch dress, stockings and high heels from the bottom of her bag. Dressing quickly was easy when that was all you were wearing, but her 'no make-up' make-up took time.

At seven o'clock she was walking towards the exit between the smoked glass walls separating the weights room from the step class, her tight dress attracting the looks she wanted. As she went down the stairs and out of the large double doors, she briefly looked back, wondering if she would train there again. Who knows and who cares, she thought, turning to walk across Covent Garden in the direction of the Lamb and Flag pub, where her colleagues from Delta Mex Oil were organising a farewell drink for her. Well, they were colleagues up to 5 p.m., at which time she had been made redundant after ten years as a site investigation geophysicist.

The early evening office drinkers were spilling out onto the pavement at the front of the Lamb and Flag, and as Morgan turned right into the narrow street, many of the heads turned, conversations forgotten, to look in the direction of the sound of high heeled shoes, their eyes not disappointed by the figure in the clinging green dress. She loved the looks; it was what made the weight training worthwhile. Without hesitation she walked straight through the groups of men into the small alleyway to the side door, which lead up the old wooden stairs to the first floor bar where they would be waiting for her.

At the sight of her red hair a loud cheer erupted. Turning to her right she saw a banner proclaiming *Morgan's Area* hanging from the ceiling over the far end of the room. Most of her old colleagues had called to have a farewell drink with her, a number of whom must have started early from the look of their glassy eyes. She was quickly herded into the midst of the throng and given two drinks to contend with. Everyone was saying how they would miss her, it shouldn't have happened, what would they do without her, what would she do now - all the usual crap! She nodded, shrugged her shoulders, but evaded questions like a professional. Some of the people she genuinely did like, but most were so two-faced that she really had to try hard to be polite to them. Just like it had been at work really.

"Excuse me, but don't I know you?" asked a familiar voice. Morgan smiled, knowing who it was before she even turned around.

"Hi, Carl. You made it then; thank God. Now at least there's someone here I like," she lied convincingly.

"Now, now!" he admonished mockingly, "these are your friends."

"Like hell they are! Most have only come here because Delta Mex is paying for the drinks. They don't give a damn who's leaving."

"Yes they do. Who else is going to look as good walking down the corridors?" he said, eyeing her up and down.

So that's how he wants to play it, she thought, not even a hint of our talk two days ago; we are still to be business contacts with a flirtatious relationship. Okay that's fine by me, just so long as it keeps me close to you. She played the game. "Stop that!" she laughed, "I'm more than just a piece of skirt!"

"I know!" Another up and down stare.

"You'll be in trouble if you carry on like that," she said, feigning annoyance.

"Okay, okay. Let's broaden the scope of this conversation," he said, raising both hands in submission. "Let me introduce you to two of our reps who I don't think you've met." Carl signalled to Vince and Chris to come over and join them.

"More drinks?" shouted Lawrence as he thrust a pint and a glass of wine at Morgan, "take your pick." He obviously thought the joke was hilarious from his laughter. Carl took the white wine and soda for her, and Lawrence moved away. Chris was the first to make it through the crowded bar.

"Chris, I'd like to introduce you to Dr. O'Neil."

"It's Morgan. Ignore him," she said holding out her hand. "Pleased to meet you."

"It says 'Dr. O'Neil' on your business cards," said Carl, interrupting.

"Will you stop it!" she said laughing.

"A PhD. and a figure like that! Talk about the luck of the Irish…" was all Chris could say as he looked at her tight dress before being pushed out of the way by Vince.

"Pleased to meet you, Morgan, I'm Vince Grange, and do ignore my exceptionally coarse associate. I'm afraid he's been out in the bush too long."

"He's a smooth bastard! Christopher Fletcher at your service, and be careful Doctor, my friend is only trying to get into your knickers," Chris said in a mockingly serious voice, as both men vied for her attention.

"Is he really? Well, I can assure you he will be disappointed," she replied, answering Chris but looking at Carl. The look was unmistakable and in that fraction of a second her eyes had told Carl that he wouldn't have to try very hard at all! And then the look was gone. "Surely these two aren't part of your group?" she asked Carl.

He hesitated slightly before replying. Had he really imagined her look? It had been two years since their affair had ended, and although they had continued to do business together, she had refused to resume their relationship, even after his wife had finally left him. He couldn't believe his luck, especially after how their meeting on Tuesday had ended. "The best!" he managed to say, raising his eyebrows. She burst out laughing.

"Then why haven't I seen them in the Delta Mex offices?"

"We're too good for Delta Mex! Simple as that," butted in Chris.

Just then the door opened and in walked Alex, hair wet and still sweating from his late training session. Carl spotted him immediately.

"Well, if it isn't Alex 'I-couldn't-hack-it' Haines," Carl said, both surprised and irritated that he of all people should have turned up.

"Enjoy Africa?" Alex replied sarcastically. Carl said yes, and Morgan went cold.

"Nice hair, Alex," said Vince in an effeminate hairdresser type of voice.

"Kiss it, ape man!" Alex said, now ignoring Carl completely. He nodded hello to Morgan, then moved through the crowd to meet James and Lawrence at the bar.

"What's he doing in London?" asked Carl in a tone not at all friendly.

"Delta Mex meeting," said Morgan.

"Really! And what would that be about?" Carl's eyes bored into the back of Alex's head, as if trying to read his mind. What was he doing in Delta Mex? He needed to find out and quickly.

"Carl, you don't think I want to talk about the company who has just made me redundant, do you?"

"Sorry, Morgan. You're absolutely right. What were we talking about?"

"Me," said Chris.

"Actually, I think it was you who was saying how good you both are!" Morgan said grinning. "But I thought you associates go on any type of job, depending on who is available?"

"Definitely not. Alex used to be one of us, but he lost it, and James is certainly not in the same league as us," added Vince. "Isn't that right, Carl?"

"I hate to admit it, but it's true. These are my special reps; I save all the difficult jobs for these two. Those you see in Delta Mex can only cope with straightforward projects because of their restricted outlooks on life."

"Are you winding me up?" she asked, not sure whether to take him seriously or not.

"Of course he is," said Vince, "we just don't like office work. Overseas and challenged is where we want to be."

"Why haven't you got an Irish accent, Dr. O'Neil?" queried Chris, completely changing the subject.

"Because I'm from Harrogate."

"Oh, okay. Carry on," he said, but the puzzled look was still on his face.

"Do you mind!" mocked Carl, "we're having a nearly serious conversation here."

"It's just that she looks Irish, and O'Neil is an Irish name, I believe," Chris said, sarcasm creeping into his voice.

"My grandparents. Okay!" she laughed.

"That's fine by me," he said, holding his hand up. "I'm happy now, but we need some more drinks." They smiled as he made his way to the bar.

"So, any plans yet? Or is it too soon?" Vince asked Morgan.

"She's joining us," said Carl, "as an offshore representative."

Vince's eyes flashed momentarily at Carl, then it was gone.

"Surprised?" asked Morgan.

"Delighted is more like it," Vince said. "I just hope that they need two offshore reps for some of the jobs! I'd love to work closely with you."

"Your special reps certainly don't waste time do they?" Morgan said, grinning at Carl.

"What have I missed now?" charged in Chris, clutching at four drinks.

"I'd like you to meet my new Associate, Dr. Morgan O'Neil," Vince announced, putting his arm around her shoulders.

"Really? That's excellent news. Just promise me that I can walk up the office stairs after you. Please, just once," Chris begged.

Carl had to admit he was impressed at Chris' ability to act surprised at the news he was already aware of. "You'll enjoy it with us," said Carl, "this industry doesn't have to be all back-biting and the 'me! me! me!' attitude."

I certainly will, she thought, but you, Carl, will have to watch me like a hawk, because when the time is right I'll have you for what you did.

"Ladies and Gentlemen," shouted Lawrence, followed by three loud raps on the table, "I think we should now say a few words of thanks to Morgan, and carry on with the presentation." All the people in *Morgan's Area* fell quiet, while the rest of the bar carried on without let. "Morgan, come over here to me. Come on! I know you're not the shy type," grinned Lawrence, his eyes looking her up and down as if the dress had fallen away.

She dutifully walked over to stand with Lawrence in front of the old fireplace, her colleagues forming a semi-circle around them in anticipation of the leaving speech. He was over twenty years her senior, and he put his arm around her waist to give a fatherly hug. That's what it looked like to the crowd, but both of them knew it was a last grab! The action brought a cheer and a few ribald comments, and both laughed outwardly.

"As usual," he began, "it comes down to me as leader of you worthless parasites to be the chief mourner and thanksgiver as we kick out the only member of the team that was any good!"

The comments were greeted by light-hearted boos and jeers from the crowd. "Get on with it," shouted someone.

"Patience, patience, my worthless ingrates," Lawrence continued, "the right attitude is everything, and I think a story about attitude is fitting at the present time. I remember when Morgan first came to this department…"

As he spoke, Morgan felt the slight pressure in his hand and arm, pulling her against him very gently, softly releasing the pressure and then pulling once again. Seductive in its rhythm. She looked at him as he told his joke, laughing along with the others, but her mind was elsewhere. She had been in Seabed Services, the geophysical arm of Delta Mex exploration, for six years when Lawrence had been transferred from Rotterdam to become the head of the department, putting him in charge of all shallow seismic and engineering survey projects. He had been attracted to her from the start, paying her extra attention through little comments at first, but slowly moving to casual touches and seemingly innocent brushes against her. She had played it for all that it was worth, egging the old fool along, until it became too serious and she succumbed in a moment of recklessness. Four months out of her last relationship she had been at a low ebb and her physical urges were driving her crazy. It began in the office, and it never went further.

She remembered how they had both been working late to finish the final report for a new exploration well, and the blatant pass had come from behind. In an all or nothing shot, Lawrence had pushed his groin against her buttocks as she laid out the final copies of the report on his desk. She hadn't pushed him away, and he'd wasted no time. Neither had said a word as he'd lifted her skirt, eased her thong aside and spread her legs. Even now she went wet at the thought of how fast he had made her come with his fingers. The first thrust of his penis had made her gasp and her tightness from not having a man for so long added to his excitement. When he finally entered her, she let out a deep moan and held onto the desk as he pounded her from behind, his hands gripping the inside of her thighs and forcing them further apart with each thrust. There was no emotion, just lust, two animals rutting and she had loved it. Within minutes it was over, and she lay motionless over the desk, her thighs bruised from his grip, and her insides aching from his thickness. She had never thought that he would have given it so hard!

They kept their relationship strictly for the office, every third Tuesday Lawrence would work late, and Morgan would bend over the desk. No kissing, no emotion; she didn't need that side of the relationship. Within twelve months she had been promoted to Senior Geophysicist, and within two years she could expect to become the Team Leader of Seabed Services. That's what should have happened, but the bastard didn't deliver, and she didn't bend over the desk again.

"That post was mine. I earned it, and I'm capable of running this team," she screamed at Lawrence.

"I know, I know, but it's out of my hands," he replied, his hands held out like the Madonna.

"How can it be? It's your department. You're lying!"

"No, I'm not! I wanted you for the job. I know you are the person who should take over, but it's not your turn."

"Not my turn! What on earth does that mean?"

"You have to wait. You're only thirty-four, and your time will come. The post has been given to a senior geologist who has waited seven years for a Team Leader's position to come up. It's his turn."

"But that's patently stupid!"

"I know it, and you know it, but that is the way of Delta Mex. He is being given a sideways promotion."

"A geologist? What the fuck does he know about marine data acquisition?"

"He is deemed capable of learning, and his previous experience means that he can cope with the administration side."

"So we have to carry him, do we?"

"Yes, I'm afraid so. I don't want him any more than you do."

"Then count me out! I want redundancy."

"You won't get it."

"Why not? Packages were announced months ago."

"I won't recommend it."

"You're joking, you can't do that to me!" The shock in her voice showing total disbelief.

"I need you to look after the new Team Leader and cover for him."

"I won't do it!"

"I'm afraid that you have no choice," Lawrence said flatly.

Each day after the argument Lawrence had been round her, touching, complimenting, testing the water again, but Morgan refused his advances. The following Monday had been no different until the phone rang at 6 p.m. and Morgan answered. Monday night was always theatre night for Lawrence and his wife, she would come to the Delta Mex offices on the Strand at 6:30 p.m. prompt, and security would call Lawrence's office for permission for her to enter the building. Tonight his wife was early.

"Of course, just sign her down to Dr. O'Neil."

She replaced the receiver and walked straight into Lawrence's office. He was on the phone, as she had suspected, and he was surprised at her entering without knocking, but even more surprised as she closed the door, and bent over his desk, lifting her skirt as she did so.

"I have to call you back," Lawrence managed to say, "something very urgent has just come up." He said nothing else as he moved round the desk; his trousers open as he spread her legs. Within two thrusts he was deep into her, laughing at her stupidity, his brain controlled by the feeling in his groin so much that he never heard the office door open, or his wife walk in.

The recommendation for her redundancy was put forward the next day, due entirely to the ultimatum from his wife that either Morgan went or she did.

The loud laughter as Lawrence finished his joke broke her thoughts, and she was immediately back in the Lamb and Flag being presented with a beautiful cut glass decanter and wine glasses. The case of wine would be delivered to her home, she was told. She thanked everyone for their kindness and generosity, as was expected.

"Well come on, tell us where you will be working next," a voice shouted.

"I can't, not just yet. It's not finalised," she replied.

"Oh, I think it's very much in the bag, don't you?" said Carl, walking forwards much to the surprise of Lawrence.

"Morgan is joining Oceansearch Associates. She will be the first woman client representative in the North Sea," Carl announced to a surprised audience. But the surprise was the greatest between Alex Haines and James Price. They looked at each other without saying a word, both acutely aware of how this could affect the timing of their plans.

The buzz of conversation resumed after the initial surprise but Carl raised his hands again. “If I could just say one more thing. Oceansearch have a banquet booked for 9 p.m. at the Rickshaw restaurant in Covent Garden, which I’m sure most of you know, and you are all welcome to attend. It is our way of welcoming Morgan to Oceansearch.”

As expected, a number of the drinkers made their excuses and headed off home, leaving sixteen to make their way to the Rickshaw to carry on the evening. A large table had been reserved for twenty-four people, but it was quickly re-arranged for the reduced numbers, and eight bottles of house wine were immediately opened and placed round the table. Menus were placed in front of the diners, but by a rapid consensus of opinion, coupled with the desire to continue drinking, it was unanimously decided that the chef should be allowed to present his own selection of dishes.

“Everyone can dip into whichever dish they like,” said Carl. “No objections? No? No?” he asked, looking round from his position at the head of the table. “Good. A toast. To Morgan’s new career with Oceansearch.” They all raised their glasses and Morgan acknowledged their toast.

“May the serious drinking now begin,” said Chris, “all this being nice stuff makes me feel pukey.”

“Just like when you’re offshore, eh, Chris? They call him the Martian, because he’s always green for the first few days.”

“And what would you know about it, James? You’ve been office based for so long you wouldn’t know what a survey boat looks like anymore!”

“At least I know what good data is though!” came the immediate reply.

"Oh! Bitchy, bitchy! You've been working with the girls too long. "

"Beware the North Sea Tiger who bares his claws," piped up Vince.

"North Sea Tiger? North Sea Pussycat more like. Isn't that right, James?" asked Chris, raising his glass and his finger towards James.

"Well, well! The Associates are restless tonight! Too much testosterone in the northern blood. That's what it is you know!" joined in Jeremy, Essex man without the hair.

"I wasn't aware that Chester was in the North, were you Vince?" asked Chris.

"Not at all. But if it is, I wonder where he thinks Harrogate is," he replied, laughing along with Morgan.

"It's all North if it's not Home Counties – don't you provincials know anything of geography and the ruling classes of this country. We're the 'upstairs' and you are the 'downstairs'. So it was and so shall it ever be," concluded Jeremy, as though finishing a Sunday morning sermon.

It had no effect on Chris. "Personally, I think this insecurity Jeremy so obviously feels is down to his overwhelming desire to be a rep," he said in his most condescending tone whilst looking round the table for agreement.

"Dream on," was all Jeremy could say.

"You see it's true!" Chris continued. "He wants to be like us really, but unfortunately he isn't good enough, alas he is but a simple surveyor who works for Delta Mex. A grunt, in fact. Tell us, Jeremy, how many times has Carl knocked back your application to join Oceansearch?"

"None at all. It doesn't interest me."

"Bollocks, it doesn't!"

“What a quaint phrase, Chris! Will you be sharing more with us later? I do hope so. And I thought it was going to be such a boring evening,” said Jeremy, looking at Barry from the drafting department for support.

“Are they always like this when they’re together?” laughed Barry, “we should have made sure more full-time Delta Mex people came to combat them.”

“There’s nine from Delta Mex as it is,” said Morgan. “Surely your feeling of superiority isn’t wearing thin?”

“Well, you changed sides quickly enough, I must say!” Erik, the expat Dutchman, said.

“Delta Mex made me redundant, remember.”

The chatter slowed as the first course was delivered to the table, but the consumption of wine certainly didn’t. Various conversations struck up after the initial flurry of insults died away. Morgan had hoped that Jeremy would have been one of those to go home after the Lamb and Flag, but unfortunately the carte blanche invitation for a free meal was too much for him to resist. She hated the little shit, had done from the day she had joined Delta Mex Oil. He knew it, and that’s why he always criticised northerners when she was around. It was the only way he could get any reaction from her. What she hadn’t realised until now was that the three other Associates here tonight, James, Chris and Vince (plus Alex who had now gone his own way), were all from the north. She hoped to God that Jeremy left soon, because she wasn’t sure how they would take Jeremy’s digs, especially Chris and Vince.

She looked down the table to Alex and James. It had been obvious that they had been surprised about the announcement that she would be joining Oceansearch. Their private game would soon be out in the open and they knew it from the way they were talking. Still, it’s their own fault, she had wanted to join them but they had turned her down. Or rather Alex wouldn't have her, either in his new group or in bed. Not that she would have wanted it now, not since Sean died. She had other, more important things to deal with. But she had never had her sexual favours turned down before, so revenge on Alex would be sweet. Yes, Mr. Haines, soon you will be regretting passing me over, and the way I've done it has got me even closer to Carl. Two birds with one stone!

"Alex," Carl asked, as if he had just read Morgan's mind, "glad you could make it for one last meal. By the way, what do you think of your replacement?" He wanted to draw Alex into the conversation because in the four weeks since he'd quit, Carl had heard nothing about him, save what Morgan had told him two days ago.

"Well she is a damn sight better to look at than those two suntanned gorillas next to you."

"Here pussy, pussy, ch, ch, ch," mocked Vince, rubbing his thumb and two fingers together, causing the whole table to laugh.

"Seriously, I think she'll do well. You're lucky to get her, because I'm sure other companies would have jumped at the chance of her joining them if they had known."

"Thanks very much, Alex, it's good of you to say that," Morgan said, raising her glass in acknowledgement of the way that he had just lied through his back teeth.

"What about your plans, Alex?" Carl added. "Time off still?"

"As much as I want," he replied, refusing to rise to the bait.

For the next forty-five minutes the dishes just never stopped coming, and extra white wine was ordered to cool the burning palates from some of the hotter preparations on offer.

"Do you think Morgan going to Oceansearch will give us any problems?" James quietly asked Alex.

“Hard to tell. It will just come out a bit sooner than we expected, that’s all. She’s bound to tell Carl, now that she’s in.”

“Maybe not.”

“I’m willing to bet he knows already. Just look at the smug look on his face. He thinks he’s playing it cool, but I’ll bet she’s told him. When she saw our tender go in she approached me about joining us. She tried a direct business approach, and a not so direct approach. I turned her down, as you know. She wasn’t amused. If it wasn’t for Lawrence’s invitation, you can bet I wouldn’t be here tonight.”

The look on James’s face was one of amazement. “I can understand not wanting a woman in the group, but I would have given her one and then said no. You must be mad not to want to jump that body.”

“Do you just think with your dick? I’m not interested in playing away,” Alex said, pointing to his wedding ring.

“Well, you’re a damn rarity if that’s the truth.”

“Why should I lie? I have nothing to hide.”

“Jesus Christ, you sound like Superman.”

“Don’t criticise me for being loyal.”

“Well it doesn’t sound very loyal what we’re about to do to Oceansearch, wouldn’t you say?”

“That’s business. I’m talking about family loyalty.”

“Oh, excuse me, I wasn’t making a distinction. But anyway, I would have had her if it was offered,” James said, a wry smile on his face.

“You’re just a male tart,” laughed Alex.

“Eee, that were reet grand!” mocked Jeremy loudly as he sat back patting his stomach. “Isn’t that what they say in ‘Arrogate after a good meal?”

"Give it a rest, Jeremy," said Morgan, stifling a yawn, "it does become boring after a while."

"Yeah, fuck off Jeremy," added Vince.

"No, let me guess! Manchester isn't it? I'd recognise that delightful Lowry lilt anywhere."

"Just ignore him Vince, he's going through the male menopause and being bald isn't helping him," Morgan said.

Carl was watching Morgan's reaction to Jeremy, and he was intrigued to see how she was really going to stop the clown spoiling the night with his comments. He nudged Vince with his leg and gave enough eye contact to tell him not to intervene.

"Talking of hair, my flame-haired friend, is it really true or merely another piece of Irish folklore?" asked Jeremy, his tongue now getting the better of him. Chris's eyes flashed at this remark, but Morgan was more than ready.

"Is what true?" she asked, the slight shake of her head in disbelief betraying the fact that she already knew what he meant.

"About redheads, you know," he answered, nodding downwards.

"I wouldn't spend too much time wondering about it, because you'll never find out."

"I bet Lawrence knows," Jeremy said, tapping the side of his nose.

It was exactly what Lawrence had feared. He had been half-listening to Jeremy whilst he had been talking to Alex and James, but his face flushed with embarrassment at being dragged into this bickering.

"That's too far!" said Vince. "Just shut …"

"Keep out of it!" Morgan shouted, "I'll deal with this wimp."

"Really! How? Are you going to beat me with your manly biceps? How typically northern of you," goaded Jeremy, but his smile soon disappeared as she stood up and walked round the table. "My, my, I do like a woman on heat," he said seconds before her fist slammed into his mouth, splitting his lips and knocking him backwards.

"Oh, yes! Now that has my vote!" cheered Chris, as Carl and Vince grinned to each other.

"I told you she was good, didn't I?" said Carl.

"I think she handled it like a complete wanker," said Barry, to the utter amazement of everyone. "That's not the way for rational adults to behave."

"Sorry, what's your name?" asked Vince, as Morgan returned to her seat.

"Barry," he replied, the smugness in his voice wonderful to behold.

"Well, Barry, I think that sometimes in the real world, real solutions to problems have to be found which are immediately effective. I would call that effective, wouldn't you?"

"If you agree with that course of action, then I don't think that people like you are fit to represent Delta Mex at all."

"Barry, what do you do for a living?" asked Vince with such condescension that it would have been funny, but for the fact that his face showed he was deadly serious.

"I'm the Team Leader in charge of drafting in Seabed Services, and if you think her actions were correct, then you are obviously a wanker, too."

Carl glanced quickly at Vince and shook his head. "Barry, Vince is one of our best representatives who works worldwide in some very remote and dangerous places. I think that you are ill-advised to call him a wanker, and for your own safety I think that you should shut the fuck up and leave, taking that sorry mess," looking at Jeremy, "with you."

"This is ridicul…"

"GO!" snapped Carl. No one said a word as they left, but the glasses were held up in salute to Morgan once again for a neat piece of work.

"You can hit me like that anytime," laughed Vince.

"And me," agreed Carl.

"Who knows, maybe I will," she replied, looking directly at Carl.

"Well, that little scene has to be good news for us," James said. Alex nodded in agreement.

"Before we leave, there is one more presentation to make, and then those who are able can proceed to the Road House for more drinks," said Carl.

"Oh God! Not more presentations," sighed Chris.

"The last, I promise you." Carl held up a new leather briefcase and handed it to Morgan. "A new briefcase for a new job. Be careful, it's heavy." He bent to kiss her cheek, whispering, "£10,000 inside in cash for services rendered over the past year. You deserve it for the contracts you put our way." She smiled and held up the briefcase, things were working out perfectly. "I hope this is the start of a long relationship within our special group at Oceansearch."

The use of the word special caused Chris to glance at Carl. He returned his look and shrugged his shoulders slightly, the simple movement conveying the message 'what else could I do?'

CHAPTER 12

Tarporley, Cheshire.

The 17:45 Intercity Pullman eased slowly out of Euston station, packed as always on a Friday, even in the first class compartments, carrying a mixture of weekend travellers, day trippers, and businessmen returning home to the peace of the country after another hectic day, or week, in the city. There seemed to be no limit to commuter travel anymore, and in terms of time, it was simply a matter of cost; plane, train or car.

Alex was a perfect example of the long distance commuter when he was working in London. Before the Vietnamese work he had been working a four-day week for Delta Mex, and every Monday and Thursday morning he had caught the 06:00 train at Crewe, arriving at Euston at 08:10. The four stops on the underground to Charing Cross usually took between five and ten minutes, and after a brisk walk up the Strand, he would be at the Delta Mex offices before eight-thirty, invariably beating the Network SouthEast commuters to the office.

The quality of life in Cheshire was superb, and his children were thriving on it. During his own childhood he had never regarded a particular place as home, due entirely to his father being in the Air Force. He and his brother had seemed to be constantly on the move, no sooner had they settled in one country before they were moving again. The longest Alex had ever stayed in one place had been the Far East, in Singapore, from the age of twelve to sixteen, and it was here that his interest in escrima had developed. Not because he had ever been interested in fighting, but because as a fourteen year old, he had once been severely beaten up by a gang of boys the same age. He had tried to defend himself, but they all fought with short canes. He had stood no chance against them, and when his father saw the state he was in after the beating, he had immediately taken Alex to enrol for lessons at the local club, surprising some of the gang who already trained there. Alex never had another fight until Malta, and neither did he stop training with the rattan canes.

By the time Alex was accepted at University in England, his parents were back in Europe, but by his third year they were in Cyprus. Perhaps it was his nomadic parents and their continual desire for new countries that made the international oil industry seem attractive to Alex. He had never envisaged wanting to be in one place all the time, but his visits to Cheshire with his girlfriend Sarah, when she came home to see her parents, began to change his outlook. He hadn't realised how beautiful a place could be, and there was no doubt in Sarah's mind that she would eventually return to live in Cheshire.

After graduation they had married and moved to the granite city of Aberdeen, taken there by Alex's first position as a geophysicist in the seismic survey industry. Both had hated the bleakness of north-east Scotland, the cold winds and stinging rain ever present, but they had stuck it out for three years while Alex built up enough experience to enable him to move on.

He had toyed with the idea of becoming a freelance geo, but when does anyone ever have enough experience to stand on their own? Being freelance meant that there wouldn't be any restriction on where in the country he could live, because at that time all the work was offshore, and as long as he lived within one hour of an airport, he would be okay. But, as always, the freedom had a price, and in this case it was the uncertainty of work. Would he get enough days per year to survive? This had been the sticking point that had held them back, until the company he worked for relieved Alex and his wife of the problem. In order to be competitive, the company had decided to change its policy of thirty days offshore to ninety days on any one trip. This would, the company strongly believed, promote greater continuity on the long-term projects they were hoping to win, and by having fewer crew changes, it would reduce overheads, thereby making them more competitive in the marketplace. It also signalled the immediate resignation of three offshore staff that resolutely refused to do ninety days away from home. Alex was one of them. The two electronic engineers quit the industry for good, totally disillusioned, and Alex became a freelance geo.

Within six months, he and his wife had moved to the Cheshire village of Tarporley, where the view from their garden was one of rolling fields, with the two castles of Beeston and Peckforton in the distance. Sarah's work as a child psychologist continued with a new post in Chester, and there was never any lapse in his work as a freelancer. Alex only worked one hundred days each year, and his freelance lifestyle gave him the best of both worlds. He could travel internationally, but he could also enjoy the countryside and the feeling of having a real home base to come back to. Sarah's parents were delighted with their move to Cheshire and played the doting grandparents, until fate dealt Sarah a tragic blow when both her parents died within six months of each other shortly after Carrie was born.

Gradually Alex's offshore work had begun to change from that of an offshore geo, to offshore client representative, with office-based consultancy work occasionally. It was a natural progression for those with the confidence to take the step, and like many things, it was a case of being in the right place at the right time. For Alex, being in the right place had been the Trans-Med pipeline survey, and when Dog Tate was looking for new people to go out as representatives after the bad slump of the mid-eighties, he had remembered the shore controller from Sicily and how he had dealt with the problem of the four surveyors. The chance presented to Alex was simple: if it went well, there would be more work, if it didn't, there wouldn't. It went well.

At first the representative work offered more of a challenge, but it was the continual travel that eventually took its toll. To combat this Alex had pushed to get more and more office work in London, and desk studies that could be done from his office at home started to become more frequent. For the past year he had been making plans for a company of his own, specialising in office based consultancy work, with more emphasis on the environmental approach in line with his newly acquired skills. He wanted to offer freelance representatives as well, obviously at a more competitive rate than Oceansearch, but financing it all himself had been the greatest drawback. His breakthrough came when a struggling coastal survey company approached him to join them as a partner. Their expertise lay in surveying and civil engineering, and after researching the market they could see the potential for a company specialising in inshore engineering surveys using dedicated vessels. They had some exposure on the new offshore wind farms that were rapidly cropping up around the UK coast, but they needed much greater geophysical expertise, preferably in the form of a third partner with cash to invest. With the ideas Alex brought to the table, together with the desperately need cash injection, they could all see the benefits of a joint venture using the same offices. It cost them 51% of the company but for that Alex would oversee the geophysical side of the business, and his consultancy operations, providing his own expertise and freelance representatives to the oil companies, would provide additional turnover allowing further investment in a second inshore vessel.

The coastal side of things was already ticking over; it was the timing of Alex's contract work that was the problem. Somehow he needed a way to get round the January start for the new contracts, otherwise he would have to lose out on work until then. In that respect he was still at the mercy of

Oceansearch, and had to go where the work was; Vietnam had underlined that for him. Carl had forced the project on him. In no uncertain terms had he been told to do it. Either he carried out the work, or he would be out, no more office work, no more offshore work. His livelihood had been threatened and he'd had no choice. The job had been worse than he could ever have imagined and when Carl had threatened again over Africa, it had been the final straw. Stopping the work through Oceansearch had been forced on him, and Nemesis had to be faced.

It had now been four weeks since his first meeting with Bicentrol, and his meeting again with them today had brought the news he had waited for expectantly. His new company had won the contract to supply personnel. All Alex had to do now was convince the other four to take work through him. He smiled as he thought of his economy with the truth when he had made the presentation to Bicentrol, but he had gambled on them not contacting Carl at Oceansearch to check, and his gamble had now paid off. Carl would be informed on Monday that he hadn't won the work, and then when he asked who had, the shit would hit the fan. That's if it hadn't already done so, courtesy of Morgan.

"What's so amusing?" asked James Price, fellow passenger, geophysical consultant, co-worker in Delta Mex Oil and would-be freelancer with Alex.

"I was just thinking of last night's spectacle in the Rickshaw, what did you think of it?" asked Alex.

"Certainly entertaining, if nothing else. He deserved it anyway. I'm only surprised it hadn't happened before now. Jeremy is such a prat with his north - south divide attitude."

"I didn't think she would have punched him though."

"Neither did Jeremy," laughed James, "it must be the Irish temper in her! Carl obviously loved it."

"I'm not too sure about that."

"Well he seemed to be taking her side."

"Maybe." Alex wasn't sure. "I think that could have damaged the Oceansearch image with Delta Mex, don't you?"

"I doubt it, she's only just joined them."

"But that was another surprise as well. Carl had never said a word about her ."

"Do you think he should have taken her on?"

"Technically she's good enough, but as a woman, there's no place for her offshore. That's one of the reasons she was no good to us."

"Well, that's a hell of a sexist statement. I bet you don't say that at any company meetings!"

"Of course not, it's not what the politically correct oil companies want to hear, but that doesn't mean it isn't true. Woman cause problems offshore, you know it, I know it, and every man who works offshore knows it. The only ones who would disagree are the ones who want a bit of something on the side, and the idiots in oil company offices who don't know any better."

"I actually agree with you. I've seen it myself with the contracting companies. They can't pull their weight on the back deck, which means more work for the rest of the survey crew, and if you give a woman a bollocking there will always be someone with a soft spot for her who will take her side. Before you know it, you have a split in the crew."

"Carl knows that as well. None of the survey companies are going to take a woman rep seriously. He must have other plans for her. It must be office work somewhere. I hope he wasn't thinking of Bicentrol."

"Well if he was, he's in for a surprise," James said grinning. "She'll never get work in Delta Mex though. They never take back people they have just made redundant."

"Well, whatever he's up to, it means we have to come to a final decision at the meeting tomorrow about who is in and who isn't, otherwise we are going to miss the deadlines for submittals. I know the five of us can make a go of it, we are so well placed already."

"I agree, Alex. You know I'm with you all the way. Anything I can do to reduce time away from home will be a bonus. I'm sure we'll get the other three onboard."

"I hope you're right. Geoff is the key. If he comes in, Roger will follow straight away, and with the four of us moving at once, I just know that Tom won't want to be left behind."

Their conversation faded away as the two men thought about the meeting planned for tomorrow at Conwy. It had been arranged two weeks ago when it was confirmed about the crew changes affecting Tom and Roger. Geoff was doing similar work to Alex and James with National Petroleum in Aberdeen, except that his commuting was a flight from Manchester each Monday, and returning on Friday afternoon. The three men, along with James, lived in the North West; two in Manchester, one in Cheshire and one in North Wales. All were well placed to take advantage of Alex's proposals.

At a quarter to eight Alex pulled onto his drive, to be met by his two children and the dog. A game of hide and seek was being played by all the children in the close, but a two minute break was called while Alex put the car in the garage.

"Mum said we could play until half past eight," his son called out.

“Okay, but only in the close. It’s too dark for the woods,” Alex replied.

“I’m going in now that Dad’s back,” Carrie said.

“You can play out a bit longer if you want to.”

“No, I want to come in,” she said putting her arm round him.

“Dad, don’t forget the frog hunt later!” Andrew shouted as he ran off to play again.

“I won’t,” Alex said, smiling as he walked to the door with his daughter.

Friday evenings were very special for Alex; they were family nights that were always spent together. He would cook the meal, lately wearing the striped chef’s apron that the children had bought for his birthday, and the large kitchen would become the focus of the house for the next few hours. The first bottle of wine would be drunk while he prepared all the ingredients, placing them on separate plates as a professional chef would do, while his wife would sit and watch him, the two of them constantly chatting, catching up on the week’s events and making plans for the weekend.

Alex insisted that the first music to be played was *The Ventures Golden Greats*, the twangy guitar sounds of the sixties that The Shadows had imitated but never bettered. All the kids in the close could now tell you that *Walk Don’t Run* was the greatest hit the American group ever had, even though their parents probably didn’t know who The Ventures were. Loud was the only way to hear their music, and when *Hawaii 5-O* came on, the game of hide and seek was halted, and ten kids were pretending to surf on the patio. After The Ventures, it was the turn of his wife, and then the children, to choose the music.

The food preparation always took a long time because of the lively atmosphere and constant interruptions, but it was as much a part of the evening as anything else. When the food was finally ready at about 10 p.m., Alex and his wife would sit down to eat the main meal and the children would join them, sharing a plate of crispy wantons which they would dip into the variety of sauces he had specially prepared for them. This was an extra treat for them, having already eaten at six o'clock, but they wanted to share the conversation and feel part of the evening.

After the table had been cleared, the games would start; conversational games where the players had to repeat something and either a word or an action was the key to getting it right. Carrie generally had to be helped, but they always included some funny ones which she could do the best, her ability to mimic voices and accents beating them all, even at the tender age of eight.

Tonight there was an additional item on the agenda; the frog hunt. Sarah and Carrie stayed in the conservatory to watch as Alex and Andrew walked slowly over the rock path towards the pond, the security light now illuminating the whole garden, and creating long shadows from the two silent figures. There was a very fine rain which was good, because it always encouraged the frogs to leave the pond in search of insects. Tonight the two hunters were not disappointed, four frogs were already sitting on the path by the trees. Alex and Andrew split up in a sort of pincer movement but the frogs were having none of it and frantically hopped away from the two crouching humans creeping barefoot in the rain.

"Look at the size of him, Dad!" said Andrew, pointing to the stone garden.

"See if you can catch him."

"Not on your life. He looks like he would swallow my hand."

"Let me get closer," Alex said, moving towards the staring, monster frog. Sarah and Carrie could see the two of them leaning towards the stones, and saw Alex reach out. Suddenly the frog made an almighty leap to escape. Andrew shouted, Alex jumped back in surprise and Sarah and Carrie burst out laughing as the frog hit Andrew in the chest and he fell backwards onto the wet grass. Andrew's shock turned to laughter as the frog bounded into the pond in two great leaps.

Alex picked him up, tears in his eyes from laughing. "Want to search for more?"

"I will if you will."

After another fifteen minutes they were both inside drying out.

"The kids love Fridays, you know, it's all they talk of all week," said Sarah.

"I wish every night was a Friday," he replied. The music in the background was a soft tango, and they sat holding hands across the table, looking out at the garden, both children now fast asleep.

"Do you think the meeting will go well tomorrow?" she asked.

"I really don't know, but it will be madness if they don't take the chance now."

"If it works, it will perhaps cut out you working away altogether. I want that more than anything."

"So do I. The others all want to cut down their time away as well. I have to play on that aspect tomorrow, it is the one thing that we all agree on."

She squeezed his hand as she stood up. "I love you so much, more than ever," she said, holding his hand and leading him out of the room, towards the stairs. "Come on, it's our turn to play now."

CHAPTER 13

Conwy Marina, North Wales

At 11 a.m. five men walked from the car park, past the entrance to The Mulberry pub and along the path to the marina.

"Are we not even having a swift half?" asked Roger.

"It's best not to," replied Alex, looking at the flags blowing in the wind before punching in the code to open the security gate.

"North Sea Pussycats," Roger smirked.

"Keep talking Roger, you never did much small boat work did you?"

They walked down the ramp and headed towards the waiting survey vessel *Loki*, a white, fifteen-metre long catamaran. Onboard stood the skipper Gary, a Liverpool import from Rhyl almost as wide as he was tall, whilst his deckhand Geraint, a dyed-in-the-wool local from Conwy, stood on the wooden pontoon holding life vests.

"Morning Alex, lads," said Gary as he nodded to Geraint to hand out the vests to each of them.

"For fuck's sake, we don't have to wear these, do we?" asked Roger.

"If you don't, you don't come aboard, simple as that," replied Gary.

Alex and the others put on the vests and climbed aboard using the rear outboard deployment platform.

“I’m not a child.”

“Then stop acting like one and put it on,” said Geoff.

“Listen pal,” Gary said, “I’ve never seen you before and your safety is my responsibility, so until I know what you’re going to be like on here, you wear it.”

“Just put it on, Roger, so we can get going,” Alex said as he walked into the wheelhouse.

Roger shrugged, clicked the life vest and adjusted the tension.

“There, that wasn’t too hard was it?” smiled Gary. “Okay Geraint, bow line first.” Gary went into the wheelhouse, fired up the engines, and Geraint let the lines slip. *Loki* slowly moved away from the mooring pontoon and headed out to sea.

The wheelhouse was well laid out with a small galley on the left, a long line of benches and racking for equipment on the right, a central chart table with seating on two sides, and three mounted seats for’ard; with the central one at the helm for the skipper.

Alex took the seat to the left of Gary, Geraint took the one to the right, and the four men sat at the table.

“Whenever you’re ready, Gary,” said Alex.

“Hold on lads, this might be a bit bumpy for the next hour,” Gary said, smiling as he opened up the throttle. *Loki* surged forward. “Oh, and you can take the life vests off now that you are all inside.” Roger was the first to comply.

“But straight back on if you want to go on the back deck for anything.”

“Aye, aye, captain,” Roger said sarcastically.

“And you want to work with him?” Gary asked Alex.

"He's actually very good offshore, but he doesn't take direction too well."

"Now there's an understatement," added James.

"This is just a 'jolly' for you lot, but I spend most of my time offshore not in offices, and I really don't want to be spending my free time on small boats. I don't see why we couldn't have met up at a hotel like we originally planned."

"We're here because I want you to see close-up what the windfarms are like," said Alex, " to get an idea of the scale, and remember that North Hoyle has only thirty turbines. Gwynt-y-Mor, which will be installed exactly where we are now, will have over two hundred, and Triton Knoll off the east coast near the Wash will be even bigger."

"It's still peanuts compared to oil, and you know it," said Roger.

"Of course I do, but I'm not going to miss a chance of getting in at the beginning, and remember that it gives a good safety net for what we are planning."

"For you maybe…"

"All of us, but we'll talk about that when we get to North Hoyle. Just sit back and enjoy the ride." Alex looked at Gary. "What's the speed now?"

"Just touching twenty-two knots."

For the next forty minutes the men all sat in silence as the wind turbines on the North Hoyle Bank loomed closer. As expected Gary did not enter the exclusion zone, but they were near enough to get a feel for the sheer size of each turbine.

"Okay lads, tea, coffee anyone, before we put the rods in?"

"Surely we're not fishing as well?" asked Roger.

"Not you, mate; me and Geraint. You've got a business meeting to hold."

Geraint made the drinks and then he and Gary went onto the back deck.

"We'll just bob here and fish while you have your meeting, Alex; there's nothing about to bother us," Gary said before closing the sliding door to the wheelhouse.

Alex moved to sit at the table with the others.

"Okay, I brought you out here to give you an idea of what I have bought into. It's only a small part of my plans as you all know, but it is still a risk, just like our plans for going it alone without Oceansearch are."

"The windfarms are an 'as well as' risk, not an 'instead of' risk that we'll be taking by going up against Oceansearch; it's not the same thing," said Roger, taking his jacket and sweater off.

"It is a financial risk just like all business ventures; nothing is for certain, and to balance that risk, we must look at ourselves and put things into perspective. We are all geophysical client representatives with over eighty years cumulative work experience in seismic surveying around this table. This is where our strength lies and is the reason why none of us need Oceansearch Associates any longer. Each of us has widespread national and international experience, concentrating in some areas more than others, which again is to our advantage. Between us we have represented the interests of over fifty oil companies worldwide. I believe that we can bid for, and win, most of the service contracts coming up for renewal."

"Very impressive, Alex, but the bottom line for all of us is how many days can we expect to win in the first twelve months?" asked Geoff.

“I agree,” added Roger who was rapidly breaking out into a sweat, “also, my position is probably the weakest of the five of us because I’ve only been a rep for three years, and in that time I have only worked for five clients.”

“Yes, but doesn’t that tell you how safe it is for you?” asked Alex. “Those companies ask for you by name; it’s you they want. Oceansearch is merely the company they can hire you from.”

“Are you sure about that? We are five out of how many reps, forty, fifty? Oceansearch could easily put someone else out onto the work,” said Geoff.

“Oceansearch has about fifty reps it finds regular work for, but they cover all aspects of the industry. We are five geophysicists, and we know that there are only eleven regular geo reps. When all those are working, Oceansearch has to ring round freelancers they don’t often use, just so that they don’t turn the work away.”

“If we leave, then the other six will have a field day. They will be able to do as much work as they like, and we will be struggling.”

“You know that isn’t the case, Geoff,” answered Alex. “You have been based at National Petroleum for over twelve months, and there is no way that you would be replaced. Your own mother could hire you out to N.P. and they would take you.” His joke eased the tension slightly, but he hadn’t won them over yet. “It’s the same with James and myself at Delta Mex. James, you have been there three days a week for two years. Does it look like it will stop?”

“No. Not at all, especially now that Morgan has left and the new team leader is in place.”

“Exactly, and I must have done almost one hundred days each year for them over the past four years. Believe me, we are in a strong position.”

“Yes, you three may be, but not us,” said Roger. “Tom and I are the only two of us who regularly go offshore. We don’t have office work like you. What about us?”

“All my work isn’t office work either, I’ve just had to go to Vietnam,” Alex replied. “That’s why I want to get out. But look, who calls Oceansearch for reps from N.P.? Geoff does. Who arranges reps for Delta Mex? James does, now that Morgan is no longer there. Who do you think he would recommend for the work in the future? You would be as safe, if not safer, if we stick together.”

“Alex, you are asking us to work for you when in fact you don’t have any work. We have work where we are, why should we quit working through Oceansearch?”

“Because you know you are being ripped off, that’s why, Roger, and we all know that we cannot bid for work as one-man limited companies. We have to have a group of us for our bid to be taken seriously.”

“Then we have to win the contracts,” Geoff said.

“Do you think I don’t know that? But it’s the same for Oceansearch; it still has to win the contracts as well. No one is ever guaranteed any work with Oceansearch. How will it be so different?”

“A hell of a lot different! You would be presenting a new company to sell our services, going in against Oceansearch and others who have been around quite some time; they have a proven track record.”

“Yes, Geoff, but whose track record is it?” asked James.

“Exactly!” said Alex. “That’s the point. We are the people who actually do the work and it’s *our* track record that wins the work. I know that Oceansearch gets the contracts because of the personnel it can provide, not because it is Oceansearch!"

"*How* do you know? Oceansearch win the work because of their reputation and standing in the industry," Geoff continued.

"Yes, a reputation and standing based on the personnel it provides, and we in this room are the core personnel of the geophysical group. Without us they cannot claim that standing. I know I am right, Geoff, because *we* have just won the Bicentrol contract. Not Oceansearch, but us! Four weeks ago I presented our services to their managers, and yesterday they accepted our bid. We already have our first contract."

Alex had timed the announcement perfectly. By holding the information back at the beginning of the meeting, he had been able to use its full weight to drive the point home.

"You did what?" broke in Roger, angry at what he had just heard.

"Roger, are you alright?" asked Geoff, concerned over his change in pallor.

"Yes," he snapped, irritated by the interruption.

"I reckon you're feeling seasick," Geoff continued.

"Am I bollocks."

"There's no shame in that; she is rolling a lot."

"Geoff would you just leave it and let me make my point?"

Geoff shrugged.

"Alex, are you saying that you told Bicentrol we were no longer taking work from Oceansearch before even asking us?" Roger, still annoyed, finally asked.

"I asked you months ago, and you said you were interested, and also less than two minutes ago you were saying that I hadn't got any work for you. Well now I'm telling you I have. Which way do you want it, Roger, because you can't have it both ways? You are either in or out."

"Is that an ultimatum?"

"Yes. We all know the score. Any one of us could have set up on his own and we all would have gone along. But who could be bothered? Who wants to have the responsibility of a company? Well I have made the break, and I have neither the time nor patience for indecision at this stage."

"Yes, well you also have the coastal surveys to fall back on."

"Roger, if it wasn't for this company and this boat, none of us would probably be here. The fact that a joint office can cover both sets of operations and enquiries is a major factor in this getting off the ground. In or out?"

"Don't know." Roger had barely said the words when he clamped his hand over his mouth and quickly stood.

"Then it's out," Alex said, "and stay on the back deck after you've finished throwing up."

Roger shook his head in protest, but dared not open his mouth. He angrily jerked the door open and ran to the side of the boat to throw up.

"Hey, I told you life vests on the back deck," shouted Gary.

Roger ignored him as he heaved again. After wiping his mouth, Roger glared at Gary then walked back inside and picked up his life vest and jacket from the seat.

"We have a meeting to get on with, and you're holding us up," Geoff said. "The set-up is the same; nothing is new except the good news about Bicentrol."

"Get stuffed," was all Roger said as he went back out on deck and jerked the door closed. Through the window he glanced at the others; their faces were impassive.

“Let me show you some figures I have come up with,” Alex said as he reached for the folder on the table, and passed two sheets to each of them. “It will only take a few minutes to see that our risk is only small, even though the step may be large.”

“Let’s look at Delta Mex Oil first. In the office James already does one hundred and fifty days per year and I do one hundred. They always have one vessel working for five months between May to September, so that’s another one hundred and fifty days offshore. A total of four hundred days and we all know that there is often a second vessel on hire during June to August, which would provide another ninety days. But let’s just use James and one hundred and fifty days for this example. James, we know that Oceansearch charge £900 per day for your services, but you only receive £603 of that, 67%. I will pay £720 per day, which gives you an extra £17,550 for exactly the same number of days.” Alex paused to let the figure sink in.

“Geoff, how many days do you get out of National Petroleum each year?” Alex asked, although he already knew the figures.

“About two hundred and twenty.”

“And how many days does N.P. employ offshore reps?”

“About one hundred and fifty, but that’s only the North Sea. With the additional work in Angola, Egypt and the Caspian that could easily double over the next two years.”

“Okay, let’s just use your two hundred and twenty days for a similar example. Oceansearch charge £850 per day to N.P., and you receive £569.50 per day. I would pay £680 per day, giving you an extra £24,310 for the same number of days.”

“I’m up for that.”

"And what about all the other companies who need reps? We haven't even mentioned those, and remember, Bicentrol is already ours," Alex added.

"It sounds very easy. So why hasn't anyone else done it before?" asked Tom.

"Do you want the hassle? I know I don't. I just want a couple of hundred days work each year at the best possible rate, and if Alex offers the best rates then I'm with him."

"Same here," added James, before Alex had a chance to speak.

"Hey, I'm all for that," said Tom, "I just wonder how many contracts we can expect to win."

"Who knows?" answered Alex. "But if we don't bid, we'll never know. I bid the Bicentrol work at £900 per day and won the contract because I told them that anyone taking Bicentrol work would receive £720 per day. I will always work on a 20% profit margin, which all of us in the past have said we would accept. Why would the other oil companies turn down the same rates? They would be getting the same people, but more importantly, the people get a big increase in pay."

"Okay, Alex. So say we enter a bid, or bids, and we're successful. What about the jobs we can't cover when we're all working and more come in? We don't have a list of other reps to call on like Oceansearch. That would certainly put us at a disadvantage if we couldn't cover all the work."

"That would be a nice problem to have."

"But a problem, nonetheless. We would lose our credibility very quickly. The oil companies expect you to have people when they want them."

"When the word gets round that we have contracts in place, people will contact us. That is only what we have done in the past when Oceansearch was tight for work. And we all know there are people itching to become reps and get the higher rates of pay."

"I know there are people waiting for the chance. Everyone feels that they can do the reps job," Geoff replied, "and you can bet that they have already been in touch with Carl at Oceansearch. If we quit, what will stop him contacting those people and using them?"

"Then I'll just have to do it faster," said Alex. "Remember we have an advantage because we know how many of them are actually good enough to be reps, and we could put new reps with certain clients. Take Bicentrol Oil for example. They are desperate for help. We could take an experienced geo with one of us and lead them in gradually until that person becomes the Bicentrol man. Let's build a new group with us at the head."

"And you become Carl," said Tom.

"If you think that, the door is over there. Walk through it and set up on your own."

"Tom, don't make the same mistake that Roger just made. This is an easy deal for us. Shut up and make more money, like Geoff and I intend to," said James, shaking his head.

"Okay, okay! I haven't worked through Oceansearch as long as you three have and I do have a little bit of doubt about it. I've had a decent amount of work out of them, and what we are doing doesn't seem very loyal."

"We owe them nothing," said James. "They have made a profit on us for every day we worked. Loyalty doesn't come into it. If they had wanted to keep us close, keep us loyal as you put it, then a shareholding scheme should have been brought in, where we would have had a share of the profits at the end of the year. That would have kept me loyal, and probably the rest of you as well. But it never happened and it never will."

"Since the death of Dog, Carl is now the only shareholder, and that's the way it will stay," Alex added, "and the rates will always reflect a 33% take off the top for Carl."

"If we don't make a break now," James continued, "we will be working like this, for Carl, for the rest of our lives. I want to cut down on my time away from home, and this is a way of doing it while still earning the same amount of money each year."

"You're right, sod the loyalty, I'm in," said Tom.

"How long do we have to put our bids together?" asked Geoff.

"It varies with each client, but roughly four weeks to the closing dates," Alex replied.

"So we have four weeks before Carl finds out?"

"I'm afraid not. I expect he already knows."

"How can he know? We haven't agreed anything yet," Geoff said surprise evident in his voice.

"The Delta Mex list closed last week, and I entered a bid before the deadline. I couldn't risk missing it."

"But how will Carl know?" asked Geoff again. "He won't have seen the bids sent to Delta Mex."

"No, you're right," replied James, "but Morgan O'Neil probably did, and on Thursday night Carl announced that she was joining Oceansearch as a new representative. I'm willing to bet she will let him know about our bid in order to get on the right side of him. Besides which Bicentrol will be informing him he hasn't won their contract sometime next week as well. No, we have to assume that as of now, Carl knows."

"James is probably right," Alex agreed. "He may not know about you two, but he almost certainly knows about us. We no longer have a choice. James and I have made the break. The choice is now with you. Are you in?"

"I've already said I'm in," said Tom.

"Count me in too," said Geoff. "Pity about Roger."

"He just didn't think things through. When he calls me, he'll get work," Alex said. "Although not on small boats!" They all laughed.

CHAPTER 14

Harrogate, Yorkshire.

Dr. Morgan O'Neil had also travelled home that weekend, and at the same time that the *Loki* cast off from Conwy marina, Morgan was walking through the lych gate of the old church in the village where she was born. The path to the church doors weaved through the graveyard, and was itself made up of gravestones of people long forgotten, whose descendants had moved away or had themselves passed over. The fallen autumn leaves rustled at her feet as she followed the fork in the path to the right, passing underneath the great oak tree and up the small rise to the new part of the graveyard.

She carried with her a bunch of twenty-three carnations, one for each year of her brother Sean's short life. Her mother had declined to come with her, still finding the loss of her only son difficult to bear. As Morgan neared the grave, her swirling emotions threatened to take away her dignity, and try as she might, she could not hold back the tears. She stopped walking as the tears turned to sobs, her shoulders heaving with the strain of trying to suppress her feelings. The pain she felt in her chest was the pain of grief for her lost brother, and also the pain at the loss of her innocence.

She stood for a few moments by the wooden bench at the crest of the rise, waiting for her sobs to subside. Looking round she could see beyond the graveyard and over the fields towards the distant hills. She had only been here once before, for Sean's funeral, and on that day she hadn't seen how beautiful the view was. Then her mind had been focussed on the open family grave, and although she refused to read the headstone upon which her brother's name would be engraved, it was as though the very stone itself was willing her to read it. She had resisted, maintaining her fixed stare into the open grave until the coffin was slowly lowered. When it was over, she had turned her back and walked away without once looking at the headstone.

Now, as her tears finally stopped, she walked towards the grave. This time she would make herself read the inscriptions. With each footstep her heartbeat increased, just as it had done every time the abuse had been about to start. The pain she felt now was just as intense as the pain she had felt when her father had first raped her, and every week afterwards for the next five years! How could her mother have not known? Why hadn't she stopped it? She was a little girl who knew that every Sunday evening when her mother went to church, it would happen. There was no God, Morgan had known that from the age of eleven, and as a teenager her blossoming figure only made things worse, so much so that by the age of sixteen there seemed to be nothing she hadn't had done to her, or that she hadn't had to do to him. Sex meant nothing to her except control.

The happiest day of her teenage life was when news of the farming accident reached their house. She had cried with her mother and five-year-old brother, but for Morgan they were tears of joy over her father's death. That day her abuse had finally ended and she never used the name Morgana again. She had refused to go to his funeral and had vowed never to go to his grave, but how could she have foreseen Sean's death?

Now she knelt and placed the flowers in the vase, her tears flowing freely for her brother. She didn't say a prayer. Who was there to listen? No one had listened when she had prayed for help as a young girl. Instead she read her father's name, and felt the hatred surge through her. She remembered the pain, the anguish, and the feeling of complete abandonment. Morgan knew what Sean must have suffered, and she let her own hatred for her father pour into the poison chalice of revenge she had already crafted for Carl Moston. She would see that Carl drank deeply from the cup; that was her graveside promise to her brother.

Morgan sat on the bench in the graveyard for a while, not wanting to go back to her pitiful mother just yet. She waited, and watched the autumn sun slowly sinking, bathing everything in its red light. Morgan's own hair looked even more fiery than normal, creating an artist's dream-like quality. She closed her eyes, and became part of the portrait. All except her mind, which was re-living her clash with Carl Moston from earlier in the week, a clash that put into motion the vehicle with which she would take her revenge.

The Tuesday morning she had taken the train to Guildford had been bright and cold, a typical English autumn start to the day. Morgan had walked the short distance to the Oceansearch offices to be greeted by Carl, who was checking the overnight emails as he always did when he first arrived.

"Excellent timing, the coffee is just filtering. How do you like it?"

"White, no sugar, just as before."

"Just checking, times change."

"So do lots of things, it seems."

"Such as?" he asked, wondering at the cryptic comment.

"It can wait."

He poured the coffee, and they went upstairs to his office. She took the chair facing his desk, in preference to those over by the coffee table that were used for more informal discussions.

"Nice chess set."

"Yes, I thought it would add a little colour."

"African?"

"Yes."

Her gaze stayed on the chess set until he spoke again.

"Morgan, I would like to think that this was a social call," he said, watching her cross her legs, the skirt purposely short enough to distract, "however, something tells me it isn't. Am I right?"

"First time. Strictly business, as it has been for over two years now."

"It didn't have to end, you know. We could have worked things out."

"You chose your wife, remember, and with what I know now, I realise I was a fool to trust you the way I did."

"Meaning?" he asked, now seated behind the desk.

"I'll come to it. First things first. I want a job, a repping job."

"You're leaving Delta Mex Oil?" Carl asked, sitting forward in his chair, surprised by her statement. "What on earth for?"

"Simple. I'm being made redundant."

"But why? You're the only one left with any experience."

"It doesn't matter why. I'm out, that's all there is to it, and I want work. I'm good enough and you owe me."

This was a serious blow to Carl and Oceansearch. Over the years it had been Morgan who had helped to get so many of their people accepted to rep for Delta Mex. Carl had initially started their affair with that sole reason in mind, and he had subsequently made good money out of Morgan's position of trust. What he hadn't bargained for was her falling in love with him.

"You say I owe you. How?"

"Contracts, bringing people in, always asking for an Oceansearch man. You know the score."

"I've always paid you well for that, and you know it."

"This year's payment is late."

"It's being seen to."

"Good," then she dropped the bombshell. "I want to be a *special* rep." Carl nearly choked on his coffee trying to hide his surprise. "Yes, it was a surprise to me as well when I found out about some of the real operations Oceansearch get up to," she continued.

"I don't know what you mean."

"Don't insult me, Carl. I deserve better than that. I guess it was going on even when we were together, wasn't it? What else did you keep from me, you lying bastard?"

"I'll say it once more, I don't know what you are talking about."

"You, West Africa, death of Party Chief. That's the most recent job I believe. Shall I name others?" she bluffed.

"How did you find out?" he said, realising it was pointless to deny it.

"It doesn't matter. What does matter is that I want in. I'm good enough to be a rep, and I want the extra buzz and money from the special jobs. I take it that extra money is involved?"

"So it really all comes down to money?"

"What's wrong with that? You do it for cash, don't you? I will be losing payments to me because of Delta Mex making me redundant, and I want to replace it. Do a few jobs and quit. Get out of this shitty industry."

"Don't we all?" He finished his coffee and sat back, looking at the striking woman sitting across from him. They might still have been together if she hadn't been so pushy for him to leave his wife straight away. His marriage had failed anyway, but Morgan had to have all or nothing right from the start. She was obsessive about commitment and she ended up without him. "There's certainly repping work here for you, but not on the special jobs. You're not the right type for it."

Her green eyes blazed at him as soon as the words left his lips. "I obviously didn't make myself completely clear, or perhaps I forgot to mention about my letters to the oil companies and relevant authorities regarding your activities, but I do expect to be given a job."

"Are you threatening me?"

"Of course I am, Carl. If I don't get work, I will blow the Oceansearch cover wide open."

"You are playing a dangerous game, lady. Don't you think it would be an easy matter to have you dealt with?"

"Maybe it would, but by doing that, you would ensure that my solicitor mails the letters on report of my death or absence, and their receipt, coupled with my disappearance, would really be good for you, wouldn't it?"

He looked at her and smiled. She was still as hotheaded and daring as she had ever been. He wanted her back, and this could be the way of getting her.

"Far be it from me to bow down to blackmail but…"

"But you are about to," she interrupted.

"…there is a special job due to start soon, which you may be able to handle. Maybe I should let you do it. I've got no-one else to put on it, in any case."

"Thank you for the confidence in me," she said sarcastically.

"Shut up, and listen," he snapped, "these jobs are dangerous and are not to be taken light-heartedly. This work is urgent and success is vital. You would have to land running if I say yes to you doing it."

"Then say yes. Give me the details and the plans. It will go well, I know it will."

"What do you think this is? Some kind of planning department in Delta Mex Oil? We don't write things down, our plans are made up as we go along. The only thing we know for sure is what the outcome must be; the way it is brought about could change any number of times during the job. Are you sure you still want in?" he asked again, now warming to the idea of putting Morgan on the National Petroleum job. If it worked, he would satisfy Aldred, collect the £400,000, and be a step nearer to getting Morgan back in his bed. Basically he had no other option anyhow.

"Yes I am, but isn't there any guidance you can give me?"

"Give it time, get a feel for the vessel, the crew, and the project. Somewhere along the way, a method will present itself. Until you are actually on the job it is impossible to know for sure how it can be done. Some jobs are easily thought out beforehand because we can target a certain individual who is crucial to the project. Other times, we have to play it by ear. Just like this one. You will have to decide who to use."

"I can do that," she said.

"Good, because this is the real world, Morgan, and the pay is £30,000 for this special operation. For that kind of money I expect you to work on your own. For our safety and for yours, I do not want to know how you intend to carry out the job, and you cannot expect me to tell you how to do it. Now do you still want in? Remember, a few minutes ago you came here doing all the pushing to join us. You wanted more than being just a rep. Well here it is, and the stakes are high."

"Yes, I want it."

"The only guidance I can give you is that we never use equipment to sabotage a job. We did that in the past when companies didn't carry as many spares but now it is too easily replaced. Always go for personnel, they are the weakest link in any project. Target the right individual and you can break a job; and pull the company down with it."

"And the choice is mine?"

"All the way."

"What about timing?" she asked.

"The cruise is scheduled for four weeks on the Atlantic Frontiers programme. It is an extension to the Uther and Mordred blanket surveys. If it goes well, the contractor will be favourite to complete the full oilfield development during the next four years, a multi-million pound deal. Our client wants the Norwegian contractor to lose the deal. The survey must fail in the second or third week, and it must have far-reaching consequences."

"Christ, you don't want much do you?"

"For £30,000 I expect a great deal. If it goes well you can expect more work, if it doesn't, you're out for good. No second chances."

"So all the work I put your way from Delta Mex Oil counts for nothing?" asked Morgan.

"You were paid for that, and paid well. That's all in the past. Listen, are you up to this or not?" The edge in Carl's voice all too clear. "Or are you now looking for a way to back down?"

"I can deal with it," she snapped back, realising what a truly hard bastard Carl was. She would have to be extremely careful about how she played this man in her search for revenge.

"When do you leave Delta Mex?"

"This Thursday. Why?"

"Because the vessel will start mobilisation trials a week from next Saturday. Is your survival certificate up to date?"

"No. Expires soon."

"Okay. I'll need to get you onto a three-day refresher course next Monday. Are you having a leaving celebration on Thursday?"

"Only drinks at The Lamb and Flag."

"Then I'll see you on Thursday night. You did just invite me, didn't you?"

"I guess so," she said as she picked up her briefcase.

"Good. Thursday it is."

"One last thing, Carl."

"What's that?"

"You have trouble brewing with Alex Haines."

"Alex? What's he going to do that will cause me trouble?" Carl said dismissively.

"Well, his coastal survey company have just put in a bid for the Delta Mex service contract. It seems that he has more planned than just wind farm surveys."

"You are joking, of course."

"Never been more serious. He's competing against Oceansearch and his chances are very good."

"What? It's not possible! We both know they won't entertain a one-man band."

"He's not by himself. It seems that he has persuaded a few of your regulars to bid with him."

"How do you know that?" Carl asked, totally stunned that Alex would have the nerve to make such a move.

"Lawrence showed me the bids."

"The two-faced shit. I'll break his fucking neck!"

"Perhaps something a little more subtle might actually achieve more. Anyway, I just thought you should be aware of what your other reps are up to."

"Yes, thanks for the tip-off. Sneaky bastard. I wondered what he had been doing since he quit. He knows all the contracts we have. I will have to move damn fast on this."

"Don't see me out," Morgan had said as she walked to the door. Instead, watch my tight ass and wish, was what she was thinking.

———

As the sun finally disappeared behind the hills, Morgan became aware of the chill wind now blowing through the churchyard, and the creeping twilight added a dimension to the gravestones that she didn't altogether like. She stood and turned to leave, giving one last look in the direction of the grave. She wouldn't be coming back.

———

On that Tuesday morning two men had actually been watching Morgan's tight ass and wishing as she left the building and crossed the car park after her meeting. She hadn't seen them because she hadn't glanced back; her mind had been racing at the thought of what type of game she was now playing. Chris Fletcher turned away first.

"Big mistake, Carl," said Chris, walking away from the window.

"I'm not so sure about that," Carl muttered, still watching her. "Look at her… mmh! And those legs. They're in the wrong place, though."

"What?"

"They should be round my neck," grinned Carl. He moved behind his desk. "So tell me, why have I made a mistake, Chris?"

"She's been pampered for too long. She's institutionalised. She believes she's as good as Delta Mex says she is. You know what they do to their people, it's just one step away from indoctrination, and it's dangerous. She's like a stick of Blackpool rock; bite her head off and you'll see Delta Mex written in her neck!"

"Fuck off, Chris, you've been in the sun too long," said Carl.

"It's true, her arrogance will be our downfall, and we should never have taken her on."

"We didn't, Chris, I did! I still run this company, remember. We need her, and more like her if we are to carry on."

"And what is that supposed to mean?"

"Exactly what I said, that's what. We've got trouble brewing at a time when we have more special requests than we can handle," Carl replied.

"But giving her a special job straight off is dodgy. One of us should have taken it."

"Christ, that is rich coming from you. It only seems a few weeks since you were saying that you couldn't do another job."

"I know, but I was just tired, that's all. This is different, she's..."

"Chris, shut up. It's not that simple. When I tell you this, only the two of us will be fully aware of the facts. Sit down. We have three problems as I see it," continued Carl, "the first is that we have another special project very close behind the Vietnam and Congo jobs. Britannia Surveys need to win both the long-term contracts with Delta Mex Oil and National Petroleum. Thanks to yours truly, the parent company in Denmark are withdrawing their backing from Scandi-Seis, so the Danes are out, but it still leaves the Norwegians to be dealt with. The next National Petroleum survey of the Atlantic Frontiers is the best opportunity this winter to fuck the Norwegians. You are not available, so what choice do I have?"

"Why am I not available?" asked Chris.

"You're just not. As I said, other projects are coming in, and in ten days you leave for Brazil."

"And that's why you took on Morgan. Well, okay, that's fine by me. Look out Ipanema!" His concern for Morgan now completely forgotten as images of all those thong bikinis came to mind.

"Wait, let me finish, Chris, for fuck's sake. Our second problem is right on our doorstep. Some of our geo reps are banding together to bid for work themselves. Alex is the ringleader, and if it goes ahead, it will undermine our positions in the oil companies, as well as hitting our profits."

"How do you know that?"

"Morgan just told me."

"So what? There's nothing you can do to stop him, its only business. People change jobs. You knew he was setting up his own coastal group, and that didn't bother you."

"Of course it didn't fucking bother me when I thought that's all it was. Coastal work is more trouble than it is worth. But this is something different. Christ, he can do us serious damage if he starts to win some of the contracts."

"It was bound to happen with someone sooner or later."

"Oh, so you're on his side, are you?" The look in Carl's eyes was cold, threatening.

"No, I'm fucking not, and don't give me a look like that unless you want to back it up. All I'm saying is that if he wants to go his own way, we can't stop him. Not legally anyway."

"Exactly," said Carl, "but perhaps we can frighten him off, persuade him it would not be a good idea."

"You won't scare him off. He might not be the best boat rider in the world," Chris added, "but he doesn't back down. He's stuck his neck out loads of times when he thought he was right, and I haven't seen him quit at anything. We were lucky in Vietnam, and when I tried to threaten him, he had me by the throat against the wall. Carl, you should know that better than anyone what he is like. Dog told us about the Sicily job when Alex was the shore controller, and about the NeptuScan people when they came off the islands. That's why Dog gave him his first job."

"So what, he was lucky."

"Are you really quite that stupid, Carl?" asked Chris. "Don't you think that this seems to be the kind of man who *won't* be frightened off?"

"I would have agreed with you at the time Chris, but all things change."

"Do they? I wonder. If he could fight like that once, he could still do it now. Okay, he might have been lucky against those four, but it's the fact that he was prepared to have a go that is the disturbing part. I wouldn't take on four men, would you?"

"No, but he wasn't married with children then," said Carl. "Now he has a weakness. His family."

"Oh, no," said Chris shaking his head in refusal, "you can count me out. You touch his family and the gentle rep will disappear. You mark my words."

"Perhaps, perhaps not. It only has to be a warning."

"I'm out of this. We're turning against our own if we do this; he's still an offshore man. His family should be left out of it. There has to be another way of dealing with this problem."

"If that's the way you feel Chris, then there's nothing I can do to change your mind," said Carl, not even trying.

"Nothing at all, just make sure that I stay in Brazil for a few months," Chris replied as he left the room, slamming the door behind him.

Carl never got to say what the third problem was. He walked to the coffee table and sat in one of the easy chairs, idly picking up one of the pieces from the malachite chess set, hoping it would give him some inspiration. Morgan was risky for a special job, he agreed with that, but he had no choice other than to put her on it. Somehow she knew he had taken out Richard Peterson in Africa, but how on earth had she found out about the inner group and the special jobs? That was the question he really needed to answer.

CHAPTER 15

The Strand, London.

The following Monday morning, Alex was back at the Delta Mex offices on the Strand, to be met, as soon as he entered the department, by Lawrence Taylor who had been waiting for him to arrive.

"Morning, Alex. I'm glad you could come down at such short notice. I do hate calling people over the weekends, though."

"Don't worry about it. The oil industry can never operate on a nine-to-five routine, no matter how much we may want it to."

"Very true. I had to bring you in early because it's the only time I have free all day, and we need to discuss matters that cannot wait. Let's get some coffee and start right away, shall we?" No reply was needed, and both headed for the coffee machine. Once inside Lawrence's office, they changed the door sign to *Meeting in Progress*, and for the next hour shut themselves off from the department.

Alex remained quiet as Lawrence mentally arranged his priorities. At fifty-three, Lawrence was in good shape, and his hair, although grey, was as thick as a twenty-year-old's. The only real indication of his age came from the deeply furrowed brow, and heavy dark rings under his eyes, both the result of nervous tension. The job gave him headaches and was now taking its toll.

"This industry," Lawrence began, "is constantly changing, updating, expanding in some areas, streamlining in others, and it seems to me more and more these days that Delta Mex Oil has to be seen to lead the field. Yet in doing so, we seem to create as many problems as the changes are meant to solve." Lawrence's eyes were watching Alex, then darting to the desk, to the wall, to the door, back to Alex. The man was very much on edge, as if the ability to relax had been taken from him.

"My own department is a perfect example," he continued, heavily massaging his forehead and temples. "Basically I have too much to control and not enough people. Last week I lost Morgan, the last of our in-house people with any real experience, and later today the new Team Leader joins us; he will need to be watched like a hawk. The only consolation about him is that he is an excellent contracts man and negotiator. Ultimately I will be passing him on to you, because I have decided that the job of nursing him will fall on your shoulders, Alex. You will have to guide him through the department, and I will have to ask you to check all of the reports he writes and signs off initially. It shouldn't be like this, having to depend on external reps so much, but there is no other option available."

"You seem to be forgetting that I can't work here any longer, now that I've quit taking work with Oceansearch," Alex interrupted.

"I'll get to that in a minute, please allow me to continue," he said, virtually ignoring Alex's comments, "you are now the most experienced geophysicist in Seabed Services."

"I was before Morgan left anyway," Alex added wryly. Lawrence smiled briefly in agreement.

"Yes. Of course, you're right. We all knew it was a game really. Part of the stupidity of the TQM system that Morgan should have held superiority over you."

"I'm not bothered. I choose to work as a freelancer."

“Indeed, and this brings us to a very serious point,” Lawrence said in all earnest, as if it should have been the first thing he dealt with. “Late on Friday afternoon I was called by Carl, requesting a meeting later this morning to discuss next year’s contract for Oceansearch Associates to supply personnel to Delta Mex Oil. It seems he wants to change some of the nominated personnel he originally submitted in the tender document.”

“Then it means he knows about our new group,” replied Alex, totally unmoved. “Morgan must have told him last week.”

“That’s my guess as well, but it means you’re now out in the open. Are your plans finalised?”

“Yes, they are. Four of us are making the break, it was agreed on Saturday, and we will wait to see if any more approach us.”

Carl will go wild if Oceansearch lose the Delta Mex contract, you know, especially if it goes to a group he considers to be his own people.”

“Let him. He’s made a lot of money out of us up to now, but no longer. It’s time for him to find some others to ride.”

“I’m afraid that *some others* as you put it, won’t be acceptable to Delta Mex. If we cannot have the same people, then Oceansearch Associates are out of the running.”

Alex realised what had just been said to him, but remained silent, waiting for Lawrence to continue.

“I cannot possibly lose any more people from this department. I have recommended that Delta Mex Oil accept your new company’s bid to provide personnel for the next two years provisionally, with a virtual guarantee of another three years after that. UK and International.”

“International as well?” Alex blurted out, his mind now racing.

"Yes, the international department, currently based in Rotterdam, will re-locate to London next year when Charles Coultas, the current head, retires. I will run the whole show. You and James are essential over the next few years. Believe me, you couldn't have picked a better time to go it alone."

"And to think we all had reservations of some kinds. Are you sure we will get the contract?"

"You already have. Heads of departments were informed last Friday, and it will be announced officially two weeks from today. Carl's meeting today will be too late, and his shit will hit your fan."

"What on earth can he do about it?" asked Alex. "He can't change things."

"No, he can't, the agreements have been signed. But be on your guard. He has a tough reputation, and he will not take kindly to you taking his people and setting up against him."

"Thanks for the warning, but I am capable of looking after myself."

"I hope so, because Carl has moved fast, and I have a problem already."

"What sort of problem?" asked Alex, suddenly on his guard.

"James is currently working here on the Oceansearch Associates contract, and Carl informed me on Friday afternoon that he is no longer available through Oceansearch!"

"Did he really?"

"Yes he did, and he enforced the 24 hour call-off clause in James' working contract, which means that we cannot use his services under that contract any longer. Basically we cannot hire him. That's why he is not here now. I had to phone him at home yesterday to tell him not to come in."

"So that's two of us you can't use now."

"Exactly. It leaves me up to my neck in it. I need you both, and find I cannot hire either one!"

"Carl's existing contract runs until the end of the year, so even though we win the next contract, we still have to wait," said Alex resignedly, "no way round it."

"That was my first reaction, but after his call on Friday, I contacted the Seabed Services contracts manager at home over the weekend to see what could be done. There is so much work on at the moment that I had no choice but to pull as many strings as possible; anyway, we have a solution. As I said, two weeks from today, the service contracts for next year will be announced, and because of the pressure on this department, I have obtained special dispensation for your company to be able to supply people as from that day. Basically you will only be unemployable for this week and next, then both of you will be back in. It's the best I could do," Lawrence said, almost apologetically.

"Don't say it like that, it's excellent news! In fact, for us it is better than having to wait until the end of the year. I know James will be happy about it."

"Good, but I don't want Carl knowing about it today. If you see him, please resist from telling him, no matter how tempting it might be."

"That's a pity, but yes, I understand."

"I knew you would, the least amount of aggravation I get, the better I like it. However, the situation does still cause problems for the next two weeks, and I have been forced to accept another rep for the next three days."

"Really? And who might that be?" Alex asked, surprised. He had to give Carl credit, he had certainly been quick off the mark.

"Christopher Fletcher."

"That animal? He's only one step away from a jungle life-form."

"I take it you don't approve?" asked a worried Lawrence, not really wanting an answer.

"He's too unpredictable. My own opinion is that he has spent too much time overseas in third world countries, and he just feels he can bulldozer his way through any situation."

"But his CV certainly is good."

"Oh, it reads very well indeed. What it doesn't mention is his explosive and unpredictable temper. His mood changes at the flick of a switch. You know, you did actually see him on Thursday night at the Lamb and Flag and again at the Rickshaw. He was at Morgan's leaving party."

"Oh, not one of those two who were sitting with Carl?"

"Yes, that's right."

"Christ, I thought we were getting someone good," Lawrence said, now very worried by his agreeing to the man coming in to his department. I wish I had called you at home to check on him! Carl highly recommended him."

"He would do. They are old friends from university, both studied geophysics at Liverpool, for what that's worth."

"So he should be able to cope with the interpretation we need doing?"

"Yes, in all fairness, I don't see why not. He's just normally offshore, that's all."

"Well, he will have to cope! The 210/12-f well spud date has been brought forward, and the drilling hazard summary report has to be issued by Friday of this week. After it has been issued, the rig will be on location anytime in the following ten days. Morgan didn't finish the report before she left, lazy bitch, and I was going to get James to do it, but that's now out because of Carl's actions. Our illustrious new Team Leader won't be able to do it, so it now falls to this Christopher Fletcher to write it. He starts this afternoon. I take it you two don't get on?"

"No, never have done," replied Alex.

"As for you, Alex," Lawrence continued, briefly looking at his wristwatch to check how he was for time, "the first of the data from West Africa will be processed next week, and I want you to go to Britannia Surveys to check it over on the first Monday I can hire you again."

"The African work? But what about Rotterdam, isn't it their concern?"

"They want us to do it. They are testing us, would you believe, ready for next year."

"That's a bit unfortunate. The kids will be off school for half-term that week, and I had planned to spend time with them."

"Take them with you. At least you would see them in the evenings, and I expect your wife would enjoy dining out a few nights, courtesy of Delta Mex Oil. I'm sure we pay enough overnight allowance to cover her as well!"

"Actually, that's not such a bad idea. The kids have never seen any survey ships, or Great Yarmouth for that matter."

"Well, they probably won't be too impressed by Great Yarmouth, but at least they'll be having a few days holiday. Britannia Surveys will be expecting you there at 2 p.m., two weeks from today. I already said you would be driving down."

Alex smiled at Lawrence, sometimes he seemed out of his depth, and yet other times, he really seemed to be on the ball. Alex would have bet that Lawrence already knew it was half term before he had mentioned it to him.

“I’m afraid our hour is up,” said Lawrence studying his watch with an almost worried look, as if time was his constant enemy. “I have another meeting before Carl arrives. Once again, thanks for coming down at short notice.”

“No, it’s definitely me who should be thanking you for the service contract,” said Alex as he rose from the chair.

“Not at all. If you weren’t good enough, you wouldn’t get it. Catch you later.”

The meeting was over. Alex wanted to shout at the top of his voice as he walked past his usual desk in the open plan office. Instead he settled for a quiet call to his wife to tell her the good news, and about their half-term break in Norfolk.

CHAPTER 16

Nautical College, Fleetwood

At the same time Alex was phoning his wife, Morgan O'Neil was fastening her seat belt at the back of the helicopter. Her all-in-one suit was zipped up to her neck, and even though it was labelled small, it must have been at least two sizes too big. Beneath it her heart was pounding with the fear she now felt. She was certain she would have a panic attack as the claustrophobia started to play with her mind. The two men either side of her were hemming her in, if only she had a window seat it wouldn't be so bad, but they were always reserved for non-swimmers or poor swimmers. She silently cursed herself for opening her big mouth when they had asked for any good swimmers to come forward. All it had done for her was to get a white helmet and a middle seat. An elbow nudged her left side.

"Soon be over, love," said one of the men in the red helmets, "this will be my last time. I retire in three years; perhaps I'll learn to swim in my spare time; an interest, you know." He was laughing. The old fool couldn't swim, and he was laughing!

"Okay, knock it off," the instructor shouted. "Nose clips on, ready with the re-breather. You all know what to do."

Morgan didn't reply she just concentrated on keeping in the correct position. Hold the front of the seat between your legs with one hand, and re-breather mouthpiece with the other. The helicopter suddenly lurched as the descent on the chains began. Slowly, the water started to rise round her feet, her calves, then her knees, until her hand was submerged. Relentlessly the water crept up her stomach and reached her chest. She wished she were taller. She would be under the water before these two big things either side of her, and her air would have to last longer. 'Take one last deep breath when the water reaches your chest', the instructor had said, 'pop the re-breather mouthpiece, grab the seatbelt clasp and then sit still; the helicopter has to be completely submerged before it turns upside down.'

She sat still, her eyes open, the helicopter now full to the roof. Quarter tilt, half way, at three-quarters she began to lose her orientation, finally upside down. The helicopter rocked a few times before coming to rest with all of the occupants now hanging upside down underwater, with only their seat belts holding them in place. 'The people in the middle seats must wait until those either side of them have unbuckled and exited by the windows before they move' had been the final instruction given to them. She waited. The man on the left was slow but managed to get out, and after his legs left the window opening, she unbuckled her seat belt, grabbing hold of the window frame with her free hand, before letting go of the seat with the other. As she fell off the seat she pulled towards the window, her lungs drawing heavily from the re-breather bag. The second man was now being assisted by one of the divers as he struggled through the opposite window. She pulled with all her strength as her head went through the opening, and her body followed through in a perfect glide. She broke the surface of the environmental pool and spat out the re-breather mouthpiece; the feeling of the fresh air rushing into her lungs was glorious.

"Okay," the instructor shouted, "everyone out of the pool. Line up on the side, and then jump in from the left in order. Swim on your backs to the middle of the pool, and then link up to form a human raft. C'mon, fast! There's a lot more to get through this morning."

The remainder of the three-day refresher survival course had raced by. So much information and practical work had been crammed into the time that she was now pleased to sit back on the short flight from Manchester to Aberdeen, enjoying the large gin and tonic she richly deserved. The course at the Nautical College in Fleetwood had been the only one she had been able to get on at short notice, and that was only due to a cancellation. Still, National Petroleum had insisted she take the refresher and it was now over. Tomorrow morning she could present her certificate in person at the briefing for the forthcoming work. She would now have two days to familiarise herself with the project before flying to Bergen on Friday evening to join the ship. It was anticipated that the survey vessel *Odin* would actually sail to the survey area late on Saturday, after completing the mobilisation trials in the sheltered waters of the Norwegian fjords.

Morgan took another long drink, and leaned back in her seat, closing her eyes. She thought of her dead brother and the work ahead.

CHAPTER 17

Atlantic Frontiers, West of Shetland.

Waking up on the third day was something Morgan did not want to do. She wanted to sleep forever, not caring if she ever got out of bed again. The merciless daylight brought with it the prospect of another day of dizziness and vomiting, and try as she might, her body simply would not give up and die. She longed to sit under the boughs of a tree, knowing in her heart that this would be the only cure for her seasickness. Either that or death! She didn't mind which.

She could imagine how the survey crew were talking about her, but quite frankly she was long past caring. How could she have forgotten how rough the sea really was? Why was memory such a poor slave? As she lay there she tried to remember when she had become so immune to the reality of the offshore environment. Somewhere along the way she had become office bound, and from that point on she had no longer appreciated the hardships, and what it took to work at the thin end of the exploration wedge.

Her few trips offshore with Delta Mex Oil during the summer surveys had really been jollies, a few days away collecting the offshore allowance to boost the monthly pay cheque, then going back to the office feeling that life offshore was easy. She had felt that she could hack it, and there had been no one in Delta Mex to disagree with her, because if they criticised her attitude, they would be criticising themselves. All of them felt that they could hack it! How wrong she had been, they all were, and now she was bitterly regretting ever joining

Oceansearch, cursing herself for her arrogance and her desire for revenge, wishing dearly that she were back in her old office, nursing the new Team Leader. Would it really have been so bad? It certainly couldn't be worse than this!

Morgan had to get up. Not because of putting on a show, but because her bladder felt like it would burst if she didn't make the effort to get to the toilet soon. She had put it off as long as possible, knowing that as soon as she was upright, her head would start to spin again. She swung her legs over the side of the bunk and sat up. The light-headedness hit her immediately, but the extra pressure on her stomach now forced her to move quickly to the en-suite shower and toilet. Thank God there was a handrail next to the seat. She grabbed it tightly as she sat down, certain in the knowledge that she would fall off the toilet if she let go.

Long after she had finished, she remained seated, waiting for the spinning in her head to slow down. The rolling of the ship didn't seem as violent today, and she stood slowly, her legs weak from inactivity, gradually standing upright and swaying slightly with the motion of the ship. She moved over to the mirrored cabinet on the wall, stared into her green eyes and had to smile. Her hair was stuck to her head on one side, and sticking out wildly on the other, a result of lying in the coma position for the last two days as she fought to keep still in the rocking and rolling bunk. The spinning slowly changed to a dull headache, a bit like a hangover but without the enjoyment of alcohol to remember. In fact the more she stood, the easier it became. She decided to risk having a shower.

Washing her hair one-handed was quite challenging, but she dared not let go of the handrail in the shower for fear of falling as the ship continued to roll. The water felt good on her skin, taking away the itchy feeling that always comes with long periods of sleep and extended rest. She promised herself she would lie down after she was dry, a kind of reward to look forward to, but later as she sat on her day bed and towelled her hair dry, she realised that she did not feel like throwing up. Apart from the headache and a slight dizziness, she was almost a different person from the puking specimen of the past forty-eight hours.

Morgan dressed slowly, wearing loose training pants and a sweater that would not put pressure on her delicate stomach, and then decided to venture outside her cabin for the first time since the ship sailed.

"Hi, Morgan. How're things?" The voice was matter of fact, no mocking tone, and no familiarity.

"A damn sight better than yesterday, but not as good as I'm hoping for tomorrow," she said looking through the open doorway into the adjacent cabin.

"Fancy a coffee or something?" Gary Myers asked as he walked to the door.

"Something, but I'm not sure what yet," she said. "It really depends on what my stomach says I can have."

"I know what you mean. C'mon, lets go to the mess."

"Actually, I'd rather go to the dayroom. I'm sure the smell of cooking won't be good for me just yet."

"Okay," he laughed, "you go on ahead, and I'll bring two coffees. Black, white, with, without? How do you take it?"

"Black without would be best for today, I think."

The three others sitting in the dayroom merely nodded as she walked in, then two carried on with their conversation, whilst the third returned to his book. She had expected all the survey crew to be in here, and had been sure that her absence would have been the topic of conversation.

“Black without,” Gary said, placing the coffee on the table in front of her and taking the armchair opposite. “You look much better than yesterday, I must admit.”

She was surprised. “I didn’t come out of my cabin yesterday. How do you know?”

“I came in to see if you were all right. When people don’t emerge for twenty-four hours, we have to inspect the cabin, and as the Party Chief on this trip, it was my responsibility.”

“Oh, God! I must have looked awful!”

“Don’t worry. Seasickness affects everyone in different ways. At least you weren’t throwing-up in your sleep, which is the main danger. You were just sweating a lot and your arms and legs were clammy, that’s all.”

“Really!” she said, a little disturbed that someone had been looking at her while she was asleep, especially as she always slept naked. It made her feel vulnerable.

“Believe me, compared to our regular crew, you are doing very well,” Gary added, giving nothing away as to how long he had spent staring at her nakedness.

“You mean I’m not the only one to be ill?” she asked, hardly containing her surprise.

“Certainly not,” he laughed. “On the first day at sea, Darren provided a waterfall of puke down the stairs to the lab, and he still hasn’t kept any food down.”

“You’re joking? Is it his first trip?”

“Good God, no! He’s always sick for the first few days.”

“Why doesn’t he quit? Surely he can’t enjoy it?”

“No, but he knows that it always wears off, and then he is fine for the rest of the survey.”

"I shouldn't have worried. I thought everyone would have been laughing at me! The woman client representative who is sick as a dog the first day out. You know what I mean."

"Listen, no-one will ever take the piss because you're sea-sick. It can affect anybody, at anytime. No-one can ever say that they are totally immune to it."

"Even you?"

"Even me, and I work month on and month off. Forget about it. You had a baptism of fire, anyway. Working west of Shetland on the Atlantic Frontiers programme is about as bad as it gets, and we were heading into a gale all the way from Norway. It'll get easier from now on."

"I'll take your word for it, and remember you if it doesn't!"

"All you have to worry about is being a good rep. Most people don't like women offshore. I personally don't mind as long as they're good and know what they're doing."

"That's very magnanimous of you," she said sarcastically, surprised by his sudden change of tone.

"That's the way it is. We work hard and we play hard. There's no room for pushovers."

"I'll remember that, as long as you remember that I'm not one of your men," she said putting her cup down and standing, already tiring of his macho stance.

"I saw that you weren't like the rest of my men yesterday," he replied grinning, wanting her to know that he had seen her naked.

It's going to be a pleasure bringing this job down she thought as she walked out of the dayroom, deciding there and then that the Party Chief would be her target, purely because of his display of arrogance just now. She left in the nick of time, and just made it to her cabin as the coffee started to erupt.

It was day five at sea before the digital equipment could be streamed ready to extend the data coverage over the massive new oilfields, which had always been suspected, but only recently proven. National Petroleum owned the bulk of the oil concessions for these blocks on the U.K. continental shelf, with only a small percentage owned by other oil companies as minor partners near to the block boundaries. N.P. did not choose to have partners, but it was unavoidable due entirely to the way the area around the U.K. is divided up into segments that have thirty smaller blocks. When the British government puts up new acreage for exploration, oil companies bid for the operating concessions on each block. National Petroleum had really done its homework for the Atlantic Frontiers acreage and had bought the concessions on large numbers of blocks, but even they had not realised the full extent of the oilfields. So it had turned out that where the edges of the oilfields crossed into another oil company's block, that company had become a minor partner in that particular oilfield. The two fields of Uther and Mordred had sent N.P. share prices soaring to their highest point for years, but the real value lay in the undisclosed discoveries, the other fields whose very names were a closely guarded secret. In time the Arthurian characters from which these fields took their names would be remembered as the largest oilfields ever found in British waters.

The schedule for the surveys was tight. Norquest, the Norwegian surveying company, had a maximum of four weeks to land the digital data, coupled with a fourteen-day processing deadline. In eight weeks' time, the next phase of well locations had to be finalised in terms of hazard assessments. If they were late, the standby time of the rigs alone would cost N.P. drilling departments millions. In particular the first well had to be spudded before January, otherwise one of the block concessions would be lost. The wells for Block 214/15 had been put on hold because of more urgent work to the south in Block 214/28 where the oilfields were known to extend, but now it was suspected that additional reserves might lie to the north. There would not have been any urgency had it not been for the British Government's clause stating that if a certain number of exploration wells were not drilled in a given time period, block concessions would be lost, and made available to other operators. N.P. was now a potential victim of its own success. Additional wells in the south had proved good, but had meant that the northern wells had been put on hold. Now they found that additional hazard surveys were required over the area before the Government would give permission for the wells to be drilled. If N.P. didn't drill the well they would lose the concession, but they couldn't drill without permission! The surveys were crucial.

On the morning of day five, the long, rolling North Atlantic swell was gradually decreasing, bringing down the noise levels on the streamer to within the operating specifications of eight microbars. Occasional swell bursts of twenty microbars were acceptable because the processing onshore could easily take out these random bursts. Morale onboard the *Odin* was now considerably higher, always being inversely proportional to the sea state. Everyone was looking more human, and decidedly friendlier, inactivity being the greatest depressant in the offshore world.

Morgan's seasickness had finally disappeared, and even the light headache was a thing of the past. Perhaps she had never really been as sick as she remembered. The other members of the crew looked smarter too, if only because they had had their first shave in five days.

"Most of them are Neanderthals, only one step away from the cave," said Gary, the Party Chief, "how else do you explain the scruffy habit of not shaving? And don't give me that old shit about designer stubble."

"Does it bother you so much?" asked Morgan.

"It's the attitude I find hard to grasp. At home they shower and shave every day, but as soon as they come offshore, their habits change, and if it's blowing more than a force four, they reckon it's too dangerous for a wet shave. Too dangerous? Fuck off! Lazy slobs, that's all they are, and I have to see their scruffy faces every day on top of that!"

"Why not say what you think?" she said sarcastically, then smiling. "Are you very popular?"

"Ah, it's always the same. For the next few days they'll look quite human again, but when the weather breaks, they'll all go back to their cave mentality, and will look rougher than a bear's arse."

She laughed at the comparison.

"Yeah, it does sound funny doesn't it, but it's all a matter of self-discipline. Pride in ourselves shouldn't fade away just because of the environment we are working in."

"I'm afraid I can't really comment on that, because the way I felt the other day I didn't really care how I looked, I must admit."

"I told you, you looked just fine, it's obvious you take care of yourself," he said smiling as he walked off the bridge.

So he *had* done more than glance when he had come into her cabin to check on her a few days ago, she thought. Was she bothered? No, not now that she was able to think clearly again. Perhaps this accidental voyeurism was not quite so innocent, and if not, it could lead to a way of completing this assignment.

On day six, the digital survey was in full swing and the quality of the data was good. The vessel was working a twenty-four hour system and things were going like clockwork. All that was needed was twelve full days for the surveys to be in the bag.

The small gym on the vessel was adequate for general keep fit, although the room was only large enough for two people to train at any one time. Today was the first day she had felt like training, and she went in to find Gary just finishing off his workout. He was stripped to the waist, and she stared longer than she should have done at his well-defined chest and stomach muscles, surprised that he was in such good condition.

"Why the look?" he asked. "I told you that we are not all slobs."

She blushed at being caught staring, and was momentarily at a loss for words.

"Well, how about that! A client's representative stuck for something to say. I never thought I would see that!" he laughed, to help her out of her embarrassment.

"Very funny. We're human too, you know! You look good and I was surprised, that's all," she said, deciding that the truth would appeal to his ego and win him round. It did.

"Thanks. Your compliment is accepted." He wiped the sweat off the bench with his shirt and moved to the dumbbells. "I'll be finished soon, and then you can have it all to yourself. Tell me what time you will be training each day and then we can work round each other. Steve, one of the engineers, is the only other crewmember who trains, so it should be easy to have the room to ourselves. The space isn't brilliant, but at least it's something."

"I don't mind," Morgan replied, "as long as I can keep things firm. Anything is better than going to seed."

"Couldn't agree more," Gary replied, glancing sideways to see her shapely legs as she started stretching.

For the next two days the survey progressed smoothly with only minor delays due to problems with the gun array. Gun 4 had been firing 0.6 milliseconds too late, but the problem was soon traced to the firing line, and production had quickly resumed. It looked as though National Petroleum was going to be lucky and complete the job ahead of schedule, until the five-day weather forecast was received on day nine. Gale force winds from the north-west were predicted later, which meant within twelve to twenty-four hours, but the forecast should have said imminent, because the winds came with a vengeance and within six hours the sea had changed to a rapidly increasing gale force eight. The crew moved swiftly to recover the equipment without damage, but the back deck was awash from the waves as the last section of the streamer, and finally the guns, came onboard.

The seas continued to build from the northwest, being pushed by the winds that had now increased to severe gale nine. There was nowhere to shelter, and the decision was taken to run for cover in the Shetland Islands. Morgan's seasickness hit her worse than ever, just when she thought she had conquered it, and she only just made the toilet when her enforced diet resumed.

The early Monday morning forecast had seriously underestimated the severity of the bad weather, and as the vessel finally rounded Muckle Flugga to the north of Unst, the winds were blowing severe storm force eleven, only one notch short of a hurricane. The weather centre in Aberdeen had now updated their predictions, and although the worst of the blow would be over in the next twenty-four hours, they showed no sign of workable conditions for at least three days. In the absence of Morgan, the Party Chief instructed the captain to take the vessel into Lerwick and tie up for two days. They might as well take the opportunity to offload the data already collected while they were waiting for the storm to subside. It would also give the crew a chance to relax. This was the second storm in less than eight days, and it would do everyone good to have a couple of nights on the town, himself included.

Gary knocked on Morgan's door and walked into her cabin to tell her the plans. She was lying on her bunk, eyes slightly glassy after obviously being sick, and feeling hot and clammy again. Her shirt was unbuttoned to the waist to help her to cool down and he couldn't help but stare at her exposed cleavage as he spoke to her. It was the second time this trip he had been in this position, and he just hoped that if it happened again she wouldn't be feeling sick. She had briefly opened her eyes when he spoke to her, saw where his eyes were focussed, but had made no attempt to cover herself. All she cared about was getting off this damn boat. When the *Odin* docked in Lerwick she swore it would leave port without her.

———

CHAPTER 18

Block 210/12, Northern North Sea.

The survey vessel *Odin* was not the only thing afloat having problems in the severe storm. The same northwesterly winds were now pushing enormous waves into the northern North Sea, affecting everything in their path, causing drilling to be suspended at the new 210/12-f well for Delta Mex Oil. The semi-submersible drilling rig, *Ronin Samurai*, strained against the eight anchors holding her in position as the forty-foot waves pounded her relentlessly. She sat like a giant crab clutching onto the seabed, determined not to be washed away. In the control room, Dave Tulloch, the Offshore Installation Manager, paced nervously as one of the worst storms he had experienced continued its twenty-four hour blow.

"Fucking forecasters! Bollocks to the lot of them," Tulloch cursed as he once again grabbed the five-day forecast from Searoutes in Aberdeen. "Force nine, my arse! We've a good fucking eleven blowing out there!" The piggy-back anchors tensioned one kilometre from the rig would hold if the wind blew steadily, but he knew it was the violent gusts, where the wind speed could rise from 50 to 70 knots, that would make the anchors slip, and if that happened the derrick would move away from the centre of the hole.

All along, his gut feeling had been to pull the drill string, bringing back on deck all the pipes before the storm closed in, but Wes Kerrison, his drilling manager, had persuaded him to leave it down. "The force nine forecast isn't bad enough to retract," he said, "we'll lose too much time re-entering the hole when it blows over. Anyway, we set the thirty-two inch casing in concrete yesterday, so we shouldn't have any problems."

Tulloch had gone along with it, the first time in ten years as an O.I.M. he hadn't gone by his instinct, and he had been wrong! Please God, let the anchors hold! He should have turned in two hours ago, but he had placed the *Ronin Samurai* on standby alert. There would be no sleep for him tonight.

And neither would Wes. If they lost the drill pipe, he would lose his job. There would be no let-off, and at 3 a.m. when he felt the first judder as the rig slipped, he mentally made a note of other drilling companies he would be contacting very shortly.

"WES! Control room now," the voice on the intercom shouted.

"On my way."

Within minutes Wes was with Tulloch, who was already giving advance warning to the standby vessel that the rig might have to be evacuated.

"No. 7 anchor has slipped," Tulloch said to Wes, "take three men and inspect the drilling platform. We need to know how much movement there is. The satellite DGPS shows a shift of 1.5 metres for the derrick, and if this buffeting continues for much longer, the drill pipe will be rattling about in the hole like a kid's dick in a whore's fanny. It will only be a matter of time before the casing and the concrete are damaged. What are the chances of pulling the string now?"

"Zero. Too dangerous. It's best to ride it out now."

"Okay, but the rig goes on full alert. The drilling hazard report expected gas, that's why we set the casing at that depth. If the hole is damaged, we are in deep shit!"

Twenty minutes later the inspection crew were back, reporting only slight movement, and it didn't appear to be getting any worse. The rig should be all right.

But the tiny bubbles had already started rising, expanding as they crept up the side of the casing. Occasional bubbles at first, but changing to a stream as the seepage became easier through the damaged concrete. The stream remained steady for over an hour, rising unnoticed to the surface of the storm-tossed sea, silently venting into the atmosphere.

Wes didn't believe everything would be all right at all, and every hour or so he went back to check, unaware that the bubbles were now rising in steady streams, larger and faster than before, the pressure in the hole building as the gas sought to escape from its underground tomb. It was on Wes' third visit, when the winds were finally beginning to subside that he heard the high-pitched squeal. It was eerie, a sound to make your blood run cold, like the cry of a banshee coming for the soul of a person about to die. Wes ran for his life, not because he feared a banshee, but because he had heard the sound before.

The squeal became louder and louder as the pressure of the pent-up gas became too much for both itself and the casing to remain in the hole. Something had to give, and with a mighty eruption, the well casing and the drill pipe was blown upwards out of the hole, straight through the drill floor of the rig and up into the derrick tower. Wes made it through the hatch door seconds before a thirty-foot section of steel pipe sliced across the deck where he had been standing. The twisting and tearing of the derrick continued as the casing was forced out of the hole, the metal screeching as the tower buckled, unable to resist the blow back.

The evacuation alarm was sounded and the crew made their way to the lifeboat stations, waiting for the final command to abandon the rig. The first to arrive at the muster points could see the shattering force of nature, as section after section of pipe was thrust upwards into the tower. The standby vessel kept at a safe distance until all the casing and pipe had been blown out. To the east side of the rig the sea was alive with gas bubbles, and the signal to abandon was given. The men entered the enclosed lifeboats on the south and west sides and were quickly lowered to the sea, desperate to evacuate the area in case of an explosion. Fortunately it never came, and one by one the standby vessel took the men from the lifeboats.

By dawn, the winds had dropped to force eight and the huge swell was beginning to decrease. Much of the bubbling beneath the rig had subsided and the *Ronin Samurai* looked like a stricken warrior in the distance, with its tower a mangled, twisted reminder that nature has a power that cannot be resisted. The back-up supply ship that had left Lerwick when the alarm was sounded had radioed to say that she was only a couple of hours away, and that she would be taking all non-essential personnel back to Shetland.

The first directive from Delta Mex Oil was for the O.I.M. to prepare an inspection and maintenance crew for re-boarding to see if the rig could be saved. Tulloch and Wes Kerrison were not to go back onboard, instead a helicopter would be coming to take them directly to Aberdeen, to attend an emergency meeting at the Central Business Unit scheduled for 14:00 hrs, where full details of the incident would be reported prior to the external HSE inspectors taking up the case.

CHAPTER 19

Great Yarmouth, Norfolk.

In stark contrast to the violent storms offshore, the weather was bright and sunny for Alex and his family as they headed across country that same Monday. The traffic had been surprisingly kind during the five-hour drive from Cheshire to Norfolk, and despite minor hold-ups near to Leicester, they were pulling into Great Yarmouth just before one in the afternoon, allowing enough time to check into their hotel and have some lunch before Alex's two o'clock meeting with the chief geophysicist at Britannia Surveys. The Cliff Hotel at Gorleston was quiet, well run, and had good food, plus it also had family suites. The children couldn't wait to check out their room, and unpack their clothes. Within minutes of opening the door they had picked their beds and were flicking through the channels to see what was on Sky TV.

"Will we have to have the joining door open?" asked Carrie.

"No, not if you don't want to," her mum answered, "but the door to the corridor must stay locked."

"Great. Did you hear that Andrew? We can close the door and watch what we like. This is brilliant. We won't have to watch the news!"

Alex smiled to his wife and put his arm round her. "I don't want the door open either, but I'm not going to watch the television."

"I should think not!" she said, giving him a quick hug.

"Okay, you two," Alex called into the next room. "Let's get some lunch, and then I'll drop you off at the town centre on my way to the meeting."

Phil Walton, PhD., had been the Chief Geophysicist at Britannia Surveys for over eight years now, and he showed no sign of ever wanting to move on, or up. He loved his work, thriving on the challenge of high resolution seismic processing. He had done well with the Delta Mex data from Africa, and Alex knew the project was in professional hands as soon as he saw the first stacks. They were excellent, far better than the Danes had produced in recent years, and proof that Britannia could handle such projects.

"It looks very good for the future, Phil. The new processing system you installed has paid off."

"Not yet, it hasn't. We have gambled an awful lot of money on my recommendations, and things have been tight where winning work has been concerned."

"But with data of this quality, you're bound to come through."

"Given time, yes, but we don't have much time left. We're running right next to the line, we can't cut things any finer."

"You'll win the Delta Mex contract with this, I can almost guarantee it."

"Almost isn't enough. We have to have it. I don't think you realise how bad things have been, Alex."

"Just stay in there, and keep producing data like this. Off the record Delta Mex International re-locates to London next year, to be run by Lawrence Taylor. When I put my report in from today, I'll be very surprised if your name is not at the top of the list of preferred contractors."

"The same way yours is, eh Alex?" Phil said.

"You've heard then?"

"We heard on Friday. News travels fast, especially when Carl was on to the old man saying how you had gone behind his back, no loyalty, biting the hand that feeds you; you know the score," Phil said smiling.

"And what was his response?" asked Alex.

"I said 'business is business' and that he'd had a good run out of you," Aldred said as he walked through the open door into the interpretation room. He extended his hand to Alex. "Aldred Grayson."

"Alex Haines. We meet at last," Alex replied, shaking hands.

"Sorry, Alex, I didn't realise you two had never met," Phil said.

"Oh, we've spoken over the 'phone many times, isn't that right? But this is the first time face to face." From that point on, Phil took a step back in Aldred's presence, allowing the old man to steer the conversation. "What do you think?" Aldred asked, sweeping his hand over the sample paper sections.

"Excellent. A first class piece of work."

"Good. I needed to hear that." He turned to Phil. "Are you all finished here?"

"Yes, just about. For today, anyway," he added.

"Let's go to my office, Alex. You've time for a quick chat, haven't you?" The invitation was made in such a way as to make it impossible to refuse.

"You're branching out, I hear, forming your own company," Aldred asked in the privacy of his office.

"It's already formed," Alex replied.

"So how many have you taken with you?"

"It's not just consultancy work, you know."

"So I hear, but it's the consultancy part that has irritated a certain *Associate* of ours. He believes you're the one doing all the pushing."

"Let me guess. Carl?"

Aldred nodded.

"He just wants someone to blame for something that was bound to happen sooner or later."

"Is it wise to have him blaming you though, Alex? He isn't the friendliest of people, you know," said Aldred, concerned that Alex was not considering just how badly Carl might take it.

"What can he do? We've already won the Delta Mex contract for the next two years; in fact, we're trading on it right now, because they can't do without certain individuals. Carl has been losing touch with the office side of the industry, he still thinks the real power is offshore, but he's wrong. He's welcome to the boat rider reps, I want the office side, because whoever gets in now, controls the show."

"You seem very certain, Alex," Aldred said, always ready to listen when information was on offer.

"It's been coming for a while, riding like an invisible horseman on the back of Total Quality Management, and now that TQM is failing, being seen as the flawed monster it always was, the oil companies are now without experienced personnel in their offices. All they have are shelves of paperwork, quality assured working practices that don't work, because they don't allow for real events which only experience can deal with. The oil companies have departments on the verge of collapse, held together only by freelance consultants."

"Your Deva freelance consultants!"

"That's right. Within eighteen months, maybe two years, we will have people in all the main oil companies. We will be almost driving the shallow seismic industry. Outsiders within!"

"You surprise me, Alex, I had never thought of you as being so ambitious. You always struck me as being content at Oceansearch."

"It's time to move on," said a slightly embarrassed Alex, now conscious of the depth of feeling in his voice, "it's just that I see so much stupidity in the oil companies these days, and I know that they are wide open to such opportunities. All the freelancers will benefit when it happens, it's not just for me. Of course we charge good rates for our services, but the oil companies gain too. At least they have their departments running efficiently again!"

"Does that mean you would award contracts for site surveys, as well as dealing with the reports?" Aldred asked, knowing that this would directly affect him.

"Pre-qualification, tender bids, awards, project management, the lot! From start to finish, we would be involved in everything. Carl should have pushed Oceansearch that way, but he didn't. He was content with the offshore side. He is an eighties man, a cowboy who likes riding boats. He still thinks that all outcomes are determined offshore. Anyway, that's his loss, not mine."

"So it would seem. But the consultants are only a part of your new business, aren't they?"

"That's right. We're specialising in coastal surveys as well."

"And encroaching on my domain?"

"No, Aldred, you know very well that you do not have inshore survey capability. Whenever you get to the coastal work, you sub-contract that part, and I expect you end up with any little fishing boat kitted out with a side scan sonar and a boomer."

"You're not far out with that."

"I know that I am exactly right with that! I have seen so many jobs suffer when it comes to the inshore part. Look at the Channel Islands fiasco a few years ago. It all but fell to pieces because the main contractor wasn't geared up for inshore working. It was after that job that I started looking into the market more, and there is a very big opening. But I'm not in this alone. The company I have become a partner in has the right idea, but lacks expertise and contacts. You and I both know about oil and gas coastal engineering work, but we live on the largest island in Europe, and the numbers of harbour extensions and marina developments are soaring. All of them need inshore surveys."

"Yes, but the profit margins have always been too low on these jobs."

"Only for someone with overheads like yours; and your reporting charges! A small, specialised company can make a tidy sum on these projects. Especially when they have equipment permanently installed on identical survey boats."

"Okay, I'm intrigued. What did you go for?"

"Sixteen-metre Auztec catamarans. The first is up and running and the second will be delivered in four weeks."

"That is a lot of investment so soon. I hope you can carry it. Are you certain the market is there?"

"Positive. Our nearest competitor is just using small catamarans with outboards, totally unsuited to twelve-hour operations; we beat them hands down on specifications. We are combining inshore geophysical surveys with environmental monitoring, but the icing on the cake is the renewables market. The Round One and Round Two UK offshore windfarm developments are providing a lot of work, and it will only increase with Round Three. That market alone cannot even be covered by existing companies. No, we are definitely in at the right time."

Aldred remained silent, watching Alex, sensing there was more.

"It doesn't stop there. How much have you looked at the windfarms, Aldred?"

"Very little; they just seemed too much trouble. Land engineers thinking they can work offshore because the water is only shallow, with budgets to match. Recipe for disaster."

"I agree, but they are not going away, and the installation problems are only the beginning. Reliability is a key issue. When you look out at the windfarm on Scroby Sands, how many turbines are inactive at any one time? I bet it's three or four every time."

"You have plans to move into maintenance?"

"Yes, service contracts, amongst other things."

"And all supported by freelance reps in the beginning," Aldred said, smiling at the plans.

"Yes, it will be supported that way, and why not? As you say, it is a risk, but one worth taking. The consultancy work will carry on while the coastal work builds up, and then we will have to see which way to go."

"But what of running the oil companies from without?"

"I can't see an end to it, and it will provide regular work until existing reps retire. Regular and boring, that is. But it's clear that environmental management is becoming more and more important. I don't just mean the occasional sampling and monitoring of conditions, but full environmental impact assessment, and systemic environmental decision making. Mark my words, Aldred, the big companies, and the not so big, will have to have environmental management systems in place very soon, otherwise they will not even be allowed to bid for work in an area, or country, for that matter. And if they don't issue annual environmental statements about their operations, they can forget about future work. That is where I want the repping to expand."

"And I would need such a system in place?"

"You will eventually, Aldred. For European work first of all, but it will come for everywhere else eventually. The Earth Summit in Rio set that ball rolling, and believe me, it won't stop. And neither should it."

"Maybe I should form a company like yours, just in case. Or maybe I should buy you out when the time is right!" Aldred said, half smiling.

Alex ignored the joke, realising that he had been talking long enough. "Look, Aldred, I'm boring you with my talk. You've been running a large company for years, and I'm talking about my first business venture," he said, adjusting his tie in embarrassment at his own excitement. It was then that Aldred noticed the tie pin. Small, flower-shaped, almost hidden in the pattern of the tie. A Forget-Me-Not. Aldred realised immediately the significance of the pin. Why had he not made the connection before? He should have guessed when people had talked of Alex and his family.

"Alex, would you like to join me for a meal tonight? There is an excellent Thai restaurant just off the sea front," Aldred asked, eager to dig deeper about Alex's plans now that he realised they had more in common than he first thought.

"I would love to, but I'm afraid I can't. I have brought my wife and children down for a few days' holiday, and I couldn't leave them to eat alone."

"But that's splendid! They can come as well, and I'm sure my wife would love to come along. Let's make a social evening of it, instead of a business dinner. Would your wife mind?"

"Not at all. Are you sure about the children though?"

"I'm sure that your children will be a credit to you, and unlike many old people, I actually love to see children in restaurants with their parents. We don't have any grandchildren and it would be a very pleasant change for my wife and I to have the company of a young family."

"You've persuaded me. It would be a pleasure."

"Good. Now, where are you staying, so that I can send my driver for you?"

"No, that's not necessary, we're staying at the Cliff in Gorleston, and it's no distance away for us to drive."

"I insist. He will be round for you at eight."

"Shouldn't you book first?"

"Don't worry, there will be a table for six of us. I can assure you of that."

The old man rose first, and walked round to shake hands with Alex. This time the handshake was altogether different from their earlier strong, businesslike approach. This time it conveyed a greeting, and the response from Alex told Aldred that the Forget-Me-Not had been purposely worn as a sign to other brothers that he was on the square.

The XJ6 pulled into the Cliff Hotel car park at exactly 8 p.m. and the driver walked into the foyer to be met by Alex and his family.

"Mr. and Mrs. Haines?"

"That's right."

"I'm Dave, Aldred sent me. Are you ready to leave?"

Fifteen minutes later they were entering the Sawadee Thai restaurant. The waiter showed them through to the lounge bar where Aldred, and his wife Ivy, were already waiting. Alex could see that Aldred was genuinely pleased to see them, and he stood to welcome them around the ornately carved low table.

"Alex, I would like you to meet my wife, Ivy."

"Pleased to meet you, Ivy," Alex said, gently shaking her hand. The elderly lady smiled and looked to Sarah and the children. "And allow me to introduce my family. My wife, Sarah, son Andrew, and daughter Carrie." They each shook hands with Aldred and Ivy, and then sat round the table.

"We've just ordered two beers, Singha of course. Do you want the same?" Aldred asked.

"Definitely. It has to be Thai beer with a Thai meal."

"And I expect you two would like cokes, would you?" he asked the children.

"Yes, please," came the joint reply.

Aldred leaned across the table as if to conspire with them. "I'd help yourself to the prawn crackers if I were you, it'll be at least half an hour before we eat." He winked at them as he sat back. Andrew gave a quick glance at his dad who nodded, and then they both reached for the crackers.

"You have beautiful children, Sarah," Ivy said, looking at the ringlets in Carrie's blonde hair.

"Thank you, but they don't always look quite so tidy."

"I bet your dad spoils you," Ivy said to Carrie, unable to resist touching her hair. "Oh, he's going to have his work cut out for him when you are older."

"She obviously gets her looks from her mother's side," smiled Aldred, "and lucky for her too, I'd say."

"Thanks very much, Aldred. Up to now, I'd always thought that I was passable."

"And you are, Alex. You ignore my husband."

"How are the crackers, Andrew?"

"Just right, Mr. Grayson."

"Now you can stop that straight away. My name is Aldred, and I like to be called Aldred." Andrew looked quickly to his dad, surprised, because he felt he should say 'Mr'.

"If Aldred wants to be called Aldred, then you'd better do it," his dad said.

"And I'm Ivy, don't forget about me."

"Of course, dear," Aldred said patting her knee, "we won't forget you." He then turned to Sarah. "Well, your description of your wife was accurate, Alex. She certainly is beautiful."

"Oh, you old flirt!" said Ivy. "You're embarrassing Sarah."

"No I'm not, she should know what he says about her. Andrew, I bet you think your mum's good looking as well, don't you?"

"Mm… mh," he offered through a mouth full of prawn crackers.

"Would you like to take the beers to the table," the waiter asked, "we shall be serving the mixed starters in ten minutes."

"I took the liberty of ordering the set meal for six before you came. It has a very good variety, and we can both recommend them," Aldred said, looking to Ivy for her agreement.

“That’s right, you won’t be disappointed. Would you like to sit next to me, Carrie?” Ivy asked, and was quietly pleased when the young girl said yes.

As they stood to follow the waiter through to the restaurant, Aldred placed his hands on Andrew’s shoulders. “And tell me, young man, where did you get such solid shoulders? School sports?”

“Rugby.”

“And are you in the team yet?”

“Reserves, but I only started at the big school this year.”

Whatever reservations Alex and Sarah might have had about sharing their evening with Aldred and Ivy were rapidly disappearing. They couldn’t get over how the man who had such a hard reputation for business could be such a family man.

The mixed starters were every bit as good as predicted, and the children ate their fair share as well, only leaving out the very hot chilli rolls. All the carved animals around the restaurant fascinated Carrie, and when Ivy asked if they should have a closer look at them, she quickly agreed. Hand in hand they slowly made their way round the large wooden figures before the next courses were served.

“You’ll have to excuse my wife, Sarah. Ivy loves children, and it is seldom we have the chance to mix like this.”

“Alex said you don’t have any grandchildren.”

“I’m afraid not. Our only son died some years ago.”

“Oh. I’m very sorry, I had no idea. Alex, why didn’t you say?”

“How did your son die?” asked Andrew, before anyone could stop him.

“Andrew! You don’t ask that,” his dad said.

"No, he's all right. His question is quite innocent," Aldred said, smiling at Andrew. "He died in a fire."

"How old was he?" asked Andrew.

"He was only twenty-six, younger than your dad," Aldred replied, and as soon as he said it he realised he had made a mistake in linking death to Alex. Andrew's eyes became glassy, and he immediately looked at his dad.

"Don't worry," Aldred was quick to say, "your dad is very careful."

Sarah raised her eyebrows at Aldred to apologise, but he simply smiled. "Your dad is lucky to have a son who thinks so much about him. I thought the same of my dad when I was a boy." The timing of the return of Ivy and Carrie couldn't have been better, and the conversation quickly changed.

During the meal the only topic not to be discussed was work, and as the grown-ups finished their coffee, two children began silently yawning, signalling the end to a busy day.

"Do you have plans for tomorrow?" Ivy asked Sarah.

"I'm not sure about the afternoon yet, but tomorrow morning Andrew and Carrie want to go down to the river to see if any survey ships are in."

"We want to see where Dad works."

"And where he sleeps and eats," added Carrie.

"Actually they don't like me going offshore, but they have both decided that they still want to see a survey ship."

"Well, two of mine are tied up at the moment," said Aldred. "You're more than welcome to look around."

"Can we, Dad?" asked Andrew. "That would be brilliant."

"And can we see the *Golden Hind* after that?" said Carrie. "The poster said it would be here for another three days."

"Well, it looks like the morning is all arranged," said Sarah.

"What about the afternoon? Would you like to visit Norwich? It's a lovely city, and I could show you round. I can have the car and Dave, can't I, Aldred?" asked Ivy.

"How can I say no?"

"I'll make sure that we're back by six o'clock so that you can meet your dad," she said to the children.

It was obvious to Sarah that Ivy wanted to take them out. "We'd love to."

"Looks like we've drawn the short straw, Alex, we have to go to work," laughed Aldred.

After saying their goodbyes, the Jaguar dropped them off at the hotel, and within five minutes of brushing their teeth, the children were fast asleep in their room.

———

Alex quietly locked the joining door, took his wife in his arms, and kissed her. With practised ease, his hands moved over her back and unzipped her dress, allowing the soft material to slip over her shoulders and fall to the floor. He took her over to the double bed and turned the lights low.

———

At nine the next morning, Alex parked his car outside the Britannia Surveys offices and walked the short distance to the river's edge with his family.

"Which do you want to go on? The *North Sea Tiger* or the *Arctic Challenger*?" he asked, pointing to the two ships.

"Which one was your favourite, Dad?" asked Andrew.

"I didn't know you had any favourites, Alex," his wife said smiling.

“I don’t, but the most comfortable was the *North Sea Tiger*.”

“Okay, I want to see that one,” Andrew said, already making his way to the gangway.

“Good morning,” the voice shouted from the bridge. They all looked up to see Aldred standing in the open doorway. “Welcome aboard.” Aldred made his way to the main deck while the four carefully walked up the gangway.

“Is it always this steep, Dad?” asked Carrie.

“It’s because the tide is in and the ship is higher. Later on, the tide will go out and the ship will go down. So will the gangway,” said Andrew, proud to show off his knowledge of the effects of the tides.

“Thought I would show you round myself,” said Aldred, once they were all safely onboard. “This old lady has always been my favourite. I started off with her, you know,” he said to Sarah, “she’s almost like a second wife. Now, where shall we go first?”

“The bridge,” said Andrew.

“And then my dad’s cabin,” Carrie added. Aldred smiled at their enthusiasm, and led them up the stairs to the bridge. The old brasses on the controls still shone bright, and Sarah was amazed at the four officers cabins, with the three-quarter beds and the walnut panelled walls.

“I didn’t realise that survey boats were so well fitted out,” she said. “Alex never described them like this.”

“That’s because most of them aren’t like this. This old lady used to be called the *Hesperus*. She was a lights-ship, built to take the watchkeepers to the lighthouses around the northern isles. That was in the days when most lighthouses were manned all the time, and the tradition was for officers to run them. As you would expect, officers demanded good conditions and that was how she was built. Let me take you to the officers' dining room, it's still beautiful even after all these years."

"How did you come by her?" Sarah asked.

"When most of the lighthouses became automated there was no longer a need for her, and she was set aside to be scrapped. I had a scrap metal business by the river and I bought her to break up, along with two other, poorer specimens. But when I saw how beautiful she was, I hadn't the heart to break her. So we reconditioned her engines, renovated her as best we could by taking parts from one of the other boats, and hired her out for survey work. That's basically how Britannia Surveys began from a scrap yard."

"And still ruling the waves?"

"Almost," Aldred laughed, "almost. But I'm afraid it really is the end of the line for her this time. We cannot justify the expense of replacing the port engine, so she is finally off to the breaker's yard."

"Oh no, she's too grand for that. She deserves better," Sarah said. "Shouldn't you set her alight and let her drift out to sea? That's far more romantic."

"Trust you to think of something like that, Sarah," Alex said, laughing at his wife's suggestion.

"It would be a fitting end for her," Aldred agreed, and the thought raced through his mind about fire damaged equipment being replaced on the company insurance. "Maybe I should give it some thought, Sarah."

"It would be like in *The Vikings*, Dad, where Kirk Douglas is burnt at sea."

"Now see what you've started!"

"C'mon, let's look at the instrument room, and then I'll show you round the decks. You can see all the pieces of equipment we tow over the side."

Three-quarters of an hour later, the tour was over. "Well, I'm afraid I must get back to work," said Aldred as they came to the gangway again.

"And so should I," agreed Alex. "I want to finish inspecting the rest of the data today."

"Are you staying again tonight?"

"Yes. We drive back to Cheshire tomorrow."

"Come on, you two, we've got another ship to see before we meet Ivy. Let these two men get off to work," Sarah said as she helped Carrie down the gangway.

"Thanks for showing us round, Aldred," said Andrew, holding out his hand to thank him.

"You're very welcome, young man."

"Do you want a lift into town, Sarah?"

"No thanks, Alex, I'll let these two walk. It'll help burn off some of their excess energy. See you later," she said as they turned to head up the river to the town bridge.

"You have a lovely family, Alex. You are a lucky man."

"I know," was the simple reply.

Alex had no sooner walked into the office he had been allocated at Britannia Surveys, when the receptionist phoned through with a message for him to call Lawrence Taylor at Delta Mex Oil as soon as possible.

"Alex, thank God you got the message! How soon can you get down here?" Lawrence asked, the urgency in his voice all too clear.

"Well, I won't finish here until about six tonight, and I will be driving back across country tomorrow. Why the panic?"

"Then it will have to be Thursday. You obviously haven't seen the news."

"No, we were out all last night, and I didn't catch the breakfast news this morning."

"And no-one has mentioned it today?"

"Mentioned what, Lawrence?"

"The 210/12-f well blew back last night during the bad storms, the rig was evacuated, and we lost the hole."

"Everyone safe?"

"Thankfully, yes. A few cuts and scrapes, that's all."

"Who is being blamed?"

"No-one, yet. But they're looking for someone."

"I'll bet they are. Are you in the clear?" asked Alex.

"That's for you to tell me. I need you to look at the hazard warning report that Chris Fletcher produced last week. They are looking to pin the blame on this department, and they have already requested that the new Team Leader be at the Central Business Unit in Aberdeen on Friday, to answer for the report. He signed and approved it!"

"Will he cope?"

"Not a chance in hell! I want you to go with him. I need you here on Thursday to prepare him, and on Friday you will have to present the argument for our findings."

"What about Chris Fletcher, he wrote the hazard report? Surely he should be the one briefing the Team Leader?"

"Not possible, he's in Brazil. I already spoke to Carl this morning to check."

"What if the report is wrong?"

"That's too serious to even contemplate, Alex. It has to be right. I'll see you on Thursday morning, okay? Oh, and one last thing Alex, Carl will also be at the meeting at the Central Business Unit. They insisted that there was a representative from Oceansearch present to witness the proceedings."

"Sounds like a witch hunt!"

"That's exactly what it is."

"I'll see you on Thursday, Lawrence." Alex replaced the receiver, feeling sorry for the man. Well, there goes the last two days of half term, he thought. Still, at least they had tonight to look forward to. He decided he wouldn't tell the children about work on Thursday and Friday until they got home tomorrow.

After Ivy returned with Sarah and the children at six o'clock, she stood arm in arm with Aldred as she waved goodbye to them. "It's hard not to think how things might have turned out if Edward had lived. Maybe we would have had a family like that to visit us."

"I know, Ivy, the same thoughts went through my mind last night. It was a lovely evening, and I couldn't help wishing they were my grandchildren." Aldred pulled her close to him as he saw the tears start to flow silently down her cheeks.

"We're welcome to stay with them in Cheshire anytime," Ivy said, "Sarah said so today."

"Then we won't have to leave it too long before we go, will we?"

"No, I'd love to visit them." She paused before speaking again. He read the signs and waited for her to continue. "Aldred…"

"Yes?"

"Would you have tomorrow morning off work?"

"Why, what do you have in mind?"

"I want to put some flowers on Edward's grave, and I don't want to go alone."

"Of course, I'll come with you," he said as they held hands and walked into the building.

———

CHAPTER 20

Lerwick, Shetland Isles

On the same morning that Alex and his family were being shown around the *North Sea Tiger,* Morgan wandered into Lerwick and it felt wonderful. Any port in a storm is like paradise, but the first half hour or so of the walk had been really odd; she had actually felt landsick. Her brain had been expecting the pavement to move just as the ship had been rolling, and now she was experiencing seasickness in reverse! Oh my God, is there no escape, she thought? But there was, and it came quickly, courtesy of the two shorts in the Thule dockside bar in the centre of town.

As one of the uninitiated she had heard many tales about the bar; how rough it was, the types that got in there, and the legendary fights. The description she had always liked the best was that it was like the bar at the edge of the universe in the film *Star Wars*, where all the alien outcasts meet for a drink, a sort of Last Chance saloon. When she walked inside, she realised it was true, and at any moment she expected to see Darth Vader walk by. Just like in the film, all eyes near the door turned to look at her. Even at ten in the morning, the bar was busy, full of fishermen, sheltering ships' crews, and island dossers. She felt conspicuous, but needn't have worried. Her red hair and green eyes were perfect Celtic colouring, and she was immediately accepted and ignored. She didn't know how to feel. The roughest bar in the universe had just accepted her as one of its own!

"Hey, Morgan! Over here."

She looked over to her right, in the direction of the pool tables, and saw the head of Dave the gun mechanic, who, at six-five, always stood out in a crowd. Four others from the survey crew were standing near the corner table, watching a pair of drunken locals trying to play pool despite not being able to focus on the balls.

“What’re you having?” Dave asked, already moving to the bar.

“It’ll have to be a short. Anything gassy will only make me throw up again,” Morgan replied.

“Vodka rocks?”

“Okay, but make it double.”

“Coming up.”

“Hi, Morgan,” said Gary, “good to be on terra firma, or Ultima Thule, as the Romans use to call this place?”

“You bet it is, but I still feel dizzy, almost like I’m swaying.”

“You are,” laughed Bob, “you definitely need some alcohol to even the balance.”

“Don’t worry, land-sickness quickly wears off, and if it doesn’t, you won’t notice after a few drinks anyway,” added Gary.

Two rounds later she found he was right, she was beginning to feel like a human being again, and not some desperately ill refugee from civilisation.

“My round. Same again?” asked Bob. They all nodded except Morgan. “Why not?”

“No, that’s enough for this morning. The last thing I want to do is get drunk and feel sick. I’ll catch you later.”

“Hey, we’re going out for a Chinese meal tonight, want to come? We need an injection of tasty food. The place is good; a hell of an improvement on the Norwegian food on the ship,” Gary asked.

“I could certainly do with something inside me, and fiskebals with mashed potato is not what I had in mind.”

“It’s the Party Chief’s treat,” he said.

“Really?”

“Well, I can claim it all back on expenses as client entertainment if you come; it means we all eat free.”

“And for one moment there I thought you were just being friendly,” she laughed. “Okay, it sounds good. Where is it, and what time?”

“Eight o’clock, above the Viking Bus Station on Commercial Road. No jeans or trainers.”

“Don’t worry, I feel like smartening myself up tonight, to remind me that there is still a real world to enjoy. Eight o’clock it is.” She turned and left.

“She looks okay to me as she is. I wish my missus’ T-shirts were stretched like that,” sighed Dave, “and look at the arse in those jeans. Why did you say no jeans with a rear like that?”

“You haven’t seen her legs yet, have you?” grinned Gary.

“And I suppose you have,” said Dave sarcastically.

“You bet I have, and they’re as good as the rest of her.”

“What’s that supposed to mean? Are you saying that you’ve fucked her already? Lying bastard.”

“Not yet, I haven’t,” Gary said, taking another long drink of his pint.

“Not yet! Save me from it, you bigheaded sod! Move over Ben Affleck, the Party Chief is here!” Ian scoffed.

“One hundred pounds says I fuck her tonight,” bragged Gary, pulling out his wallet.

“You’re definitely on. You’ve got no chance,” said Bob.

“Money up front now. Give it to Ian, he can be the judge.”

“Does that mean I get to watch, and verify penetration?”

“Fuck off, weirdo.”

“Money on the table, now. The bet’s on until midday tomorrow,” said Ian, taking the cash for safekeeping. “Shake on it.”

“You’ll never make it,” Bob said, squeezing Gary’s hand.

“This will be the easiest, and most enjoyable, £100 I’ve ever earned, plus it will pay for my wife’s birthday present.”

“How do you feel now?” Gary asked as he took Morgan’s coat.

“Absolutely ravenous. Have you been waiting long?”

“Five minutes.”

“What about the others, not here yet?”

“I’ve just left them in Captain Flint’s Bar having a quick one before eating! They said to wait until a quarter past eight, and if they hadn’t arrived by then, we were to start without them. Anyway they’ll join us at the Grand Hotel later if they don’t make the meal.”

“Why, what’s at the Grand Hotel?” asked Morgan.

“A small nightclub called Posers. Nothing much, but it’s a damn sight smarter than the Thule bar, that’s all.” He knew full well that the others would not turn up at the restaurant because he had told them not to, and at eight-fifteen Morgan and Gary were shown to a table for two, to enjoy a meal which would be the first part of his play for her. Had he known that Morgan had anxiously watched the door as they waited, hoping the others would not arrive, Gary would probably have been more on his guard, but as it was, he thought he had to do all the running to make the night a success.

She had dressed well for the evening, purely with the intention of showing that she was an attractive woman, and not just some puking girlie. Her outfit had the desired effect on Gary, because although she suspected he'd already had an eyeful of her curves without her permission, she wanted him to see her dressed well, her curves now accentuated but covered, adding to the allure. It was obvious that Gary was attracted to her, and his conversation was flattering, flirtatious and amusing. They both enjoyed the meal and when they finally left the restaurant and headed down the main street to the Grand Hotel, they appeared to any passers-by to be a couple whose final destination that evening was the bedroom.

Posers nightclub was basically a bar and small dancefloor in a large room at the back of the hotel; it could hardly be called a club or disco, but it was the best that Lerwick had to offer. After a couple of drinks at the bar, Morgan and Gary took to the floor for a slow dance.

"Your £100 doesn't look quite so safe now, eh Bob?" nudged Ian, looking across the room.

"Up yours. It's only a dance, he's got a long way to go yet."

"Well, from the way he's kissing her, it looks like his tongue is almost there, and I can't see much light between their hips either," laughed Dave, slapping Bob on the shoulder, causing him to spill beer on his shirt.

“Thanks, Kong, that’s just what I need,” he said, trying to wipe the stain away.

“Touchy, touchy!” Dave mocked, “You shouldn’t gamble if you don’t want to lose.”

“I haven’t lost, yet.”

“Gary was right about those legs though. I wouldn’t mind having those wrapped around me,” said Ian, dreaming again.

“Wouldn’t we all,” Dave said, “even poor old Bob here, who is now crying in his beer. Cheer up, Bob, what’s £100 anyway? Maybe when you’re a party chief, you’ll get to pull the rep.”

“Knowing my luck, she’ll be an old boot. That’s if its a woman at all!”

“From what I’ve seen, you’re never really all that fussy where you put it anyway. You’ve pulled some right slappers in your time.”

“Thanks very much, Dave! Are you trying to cheer me up, or what? I’m watching £100 rapidly slip away and all I’m getting is abuse.” Bob finished his pint in one lift. “I’m ready for another. Your round, Ian, and don’t argue.”

“Now you’re not going to go all moody on us, are you Bob?” Dave said, mimicking a mother telling off a petulant son.

“Oh, fuck off and get some drinks!” Bob said, unable to stop laughing as he looked at the stupid, puckered-lip face Dave was pulling at him.

“I know that you’re married,” Morgan said.

“I know you do, and I know that you’re not.”

“So?”

“It has nothing to do with tonight. You’re here, I’m here, and my wife is at home. Simple as that.”

"How can it be as simple as that?" she asked, still dancing close to him, enjoying the feel of his hard muscles.

"Because I have two lives. One when I am at home, and one when I am at work. It's the only way to handle being away."

"And is that how your wife deals with it?"

"She'd better bloody not! Anyway, why are you interested in her? You don't even know her."

"So it's okay for you to play around, but not for her? It's a bit one-sided, don't you think?"

"No, I don't. I'm the one who has to do the work, not her. She doesn't have to be away, missing everything that happens in a normal home life. I do, and this is how I cope with it. Two lives keeps me sane."

"Other people get by."

"Do they? Are you so sure? I've seen men who are torn apart by being away. They don't know how to deal with the loneliness, and eventually it gets to them. Before you know it they've split up with their wives, or had a breakdown. I love my family, but I have to do this work, and I'm here with you enjoying myself. Does that surprise you?"

"No. Many things about this industry are different. It's very much a live for today attitude, which suits me fine. I take things as they come," she said, pushing her hips against him. "We're very much alike you know, maybe it's time for us to go back to the ship."

Gary locked the door to his cabin and walked over to the leather sofa where Morgan lay. In the dimmed light she looked stunning. He knelt at her feet and ran his hands up her shapely legs, lifting her dress to reveal the beautiful firm white skin at the top of her stockings. Her arms moved out to him to draw his face to hers, but he resisted, and as his fingers curled round her lace thong, pulling it to one side to expose the triangle of fiery red hair, his head went down to kiss the prize. She gasped as his tongue began its lustful hunt, slowly at first, gently licking her most sensitive spot. Her response was immediate, and her breathing became heavier as she readily succumbed to his movements, easing her hips upwards as he slipped his hands beneath her thighs and guided them round his neck until her ankles crossed behind him. She was completely under his control, her whole body subservient to the movements of his tongue. As her breathing grew heavier, he licked faster, and she moaned, squeezing her thighs to feel him hard against her. She began to moan, finally holding her breath as her face and neck turned bright red with the intensity of the orgasm that overtook her.

The few seconds seemed like an eternity, and then her breath came in urgent gasps as her body continued to shake. His clothes were off in seconds, allowing her no rest as he quickly spread her legs wide to accept him. He pushed hard and fast into her wetness with no regard for her, his own desire for fulfilment now paramount. She took him easily, wanting it hard, her physical urges matching him thrust for thrust. He came quickly, and at the point of no return, she raked her fingernails down his back, the mixture of pleasure and pain causing him to cry out. Sweat and blood mingled on his back as they lay there, hearts pounding, unable to move while their passion subsided.

Then, without a word to each other, they stood up, her clothes creased but still on, his thrown to the floor. She walked to the door and in a moment was gone. They had both had what they wanted, and there was nothing more to it. Why spoil it with words?

In her cabin she took a shower, then dressed in training pants and sweater. After waiting half an hour, she stepped outside, and headed for the radio room at the back of the bridge.

Amanda Myers gave one final look in on the children, and went into her bedroom. The king size bed, a place of nightly sex when her husband was at home, seemed so big and lonely during his month away. She undressed slowly, there was no reason to rush when he wasn't here, and slid naked beneath the duvet, moving to his side of the bed to feel closer to him. The dreams had just begun when the phone rang, and at first it seemed part of her dream. But it didn't stop even when she knew she was awake. Reaching out in the dark, she lifted the handset.

"Mrs. Myers?" the woman's voice said.

"Yes? Who is this?"

"I'm Morgan O'Neil, the client representative on the *Odin*."

"Oh my God! There's been an accident, hasn't there? It's Gary. Oh no. Oh no!" Amanda's heart pounded at the thought. The dreaded midnight call.

"Relax, relax. It's not an accident. Gary's fine. Well, he's not too bad, but there are two things I must say to you."

Amanda sat up and clicked on the light; a puzzled look on her face. "What is this?"

"He's very good with his tongue, isn't he? It's perhaps the best oral sex anyone has ever given me, but he does come rather quickly, don't you think? Much too quick for me, I prefer a longer fuck than that. Don't you find it frustrating?"

"Get off the line," Amanda screamed, "I don't believe you!"

"Oh, it's true. Just check the scratch marks on his back."

Amanda slammed the phone down and Morgan replaced the handset, her heart pounding. She quickly went to the galley, poured some coffee and took it to the dayroom, where, thankfully, some of the others had returned from the bar and were sitting talking before turning in.

"Is the Party Chief there?" the voice said over the intercom, "there's a call from his wife."

"Try his cabin," Dave shouted to the speaker on the wall.

Morgan's pulse was racing, and her legs were shaking slightly as fear took a firm hold on her. She said nothing as she stared at her coffee, and the others continued talking. It was the scream from the corridor that made them all turn round.

"I'll kill the fucking bitch! Where is she? Where is she…?" The sound of running feet came closer and suddenly Gary burst into the dayroom, his eyes wild with anger, scanning the room and then stopping dead, locked on Morgan. He charged at her, and the wild punch that split the side of her mouth would have broken her jaw had she not instinctively turned. Her head rocked backwards with the force, and the resounding slap that quickly followed across the left side of her face knocked her sideways out of the chair.

After the shock of the punch, Dave was the first to move, and he caught Morgan as she fell to the floor, his body shielding her from the kick aimed at her groin. Bob hurled himself at Gary, the two of them falling backwards over the coffee table.

"I'll kill her," Gary screamed again. "Get off me, or I'll have you as well." In his rage he threw Bob off him and was back on his feet in seconds, charging once again at Morgan.

"Get out of my way, Dave. I'm going to make her so fucking sorry for tonight."

His eyes were still wild, unfocussed, as he charged at Dave. Perhaps if they had been focussed he would have seen the enormous fist on its way to his head. But he didn't. The attack was over as quickly as it started, and the aftermath was only just beginning.

CHAPTER 21

Dyce, Aberdeen.

At seven a.m. the next morning, when the bedside phone in his room at the Marriott Hotel rang, Geoff Platt merely picked up the receiver and put it down again, not bothering to speak. After all, it was only his wake up call. Twenty seconds later, the phone rang again. This time he put the handset to his ear.

"There is an urgent call for you, Mr. Platt," the receptionist said.

Within five minutes of taking the call from the director of seismic operations at National Petroleum, Geoff was out of the shower and having a rapid shave, wondering what on earth the incident in Lerwick was all about.

Now, after a morning of hectic meetings, he had time to reflect before he made his next call. Geoff had hoped that the survey would have run smoothly because he already had enough work on his plate. He accepted that minor problems were inevitable, but to beat up a rep! Christ, what had happened? His phone had started to ring as soon as the senior managers at National Petroleum had been made aware of the incident, and they had had no qualms about the instant removal of the Norwegian company from the contract. Even the prompt sacking of Gary Myers by the Managing Director of Norquest, as a damage limitation exercise, had been to no avail. To rub his nose in it even further, the N.P. management had insisted that the Norquest M.D. come round personally to their offices in Dyce to be informed of the removal of his company from the list of approved contractors forthwith. And now it was left to Geoff to mobilise another survey ship just like that! On the advice of Alex Haines, who knew that two survey ships were alongside in Great Yarmouth, Geoff contacted Britannia Surveys, which meant that Aldred Grayson became one of the first people outside of N.P. to know of the incident.

"We can mobilise the *Arctic Challenger* for a 1600hrs sailing today," Aldred said, "which would have her in Lerwick in approximately forty-eight hours. The survey crew would be flown to Sumburgh to meet the vessel when your representative goes onboard. That's the earliest we can have her ready for you."

"Then that will have to be good enough," replied Geoff.

"All I can say is that perhaps you should have considered us first, you know that we can meet all of your specifications."

"Hindsight is once again perfect, Aldred, but I believe that this time it has really worked in your favour. Up until yesterday, you were number two for the service contract, but now that Norquest are out for at least two years, due entirely to unprofessional conduct, the contract is yours. Unofficially, of course, but you will be informed within a matter of days."

Aldred couldn't help but be pleased. "Tell me, what exactly happened to cause the attack?"

"I'm afraid I can't say, it's all being investigated internally, and formal charges are likely to be brought against the Party Chief by Shetland police. He is still being held on the island for questioning. To attack a representative is bad enough, but the fact that it is a woman has turned it into a much bigger issue. Her own conduct is being investigated too, and, again unofficially, Oceansearch Associates are now seen in a bad light by National Petroleum."

"But that's good for you, isn't it?" Aldred asked. "I hear you're going along with Alex Haines."

“Well I have to say that news travels fast, but yes, it is good. In fact, it couldn’t be better, if the truth be known,” he agreed.

“One final thing, Geoff, how did you know the *Arctic Challenger* was available?”

“I spoke to Alex ten minutes before I phoned you. Anyway, must go, it seems I have another call holding for me. Speak to you later, Aldred.”

It was done, the old man thought. He had pulled it off. Next year he would have both the Delta Mex Oil and the National Petroleum contracts! Less than three months after Dog’s funeral, he had done it! Dr. Morgan O’Neil had certainly proved herself capable of destroying a survey, and he had no doubts that she would be equally capable of handling Carl when the time came for her to take revenge for her brother. When that was done the Oceansearch inner circle would be a thing of the past and could not present problems for Britannia Surveys.

———

CHAPTER 22

Guildford, Surrey.

Carl was tired. His eyes ached, and he gently massaged his temples in an attempt to ease away the strain of a day full of hectic phone calls, which was now taking its toll. The door to his office was open, awaiting the arrival of Mick Jones, his Operations Manager. Today had started off with the good news that the Norwegians had lost the National Petroleum contract, courtesy of Morgan, but the repercussions for Oceansearch seemed all out of proportion; unless of course Alex Haines and his new group were taken into account.

Carl now had to brief Mick on the fall-out, without being able to tell him the full story. He also wanted to say how he would get even with Alex, but that, too, was not possible. Each new development seemed to compound the last.

"Ah, Mick, come in, take a seat." Mick closed the door, sat and waited, subservient as ever. "Basically, Mick, we are in the shit! Full stop."

"Because of the attack on Morgan? I really don't see how we can be at fault because a woman is attacked!"

And there it was. Perfect reasoning, until you knew all the facts. Had it been any other company in this mess, Carl would have laughed. But it was his company, so he didn't.

"Let me give you the basic details, Mick," Carl said, his voice heavy with sarcasm. "After the attack, the ship's captain called the police and Gary Myers, the Party Chief, was arrested. Morgan was taken to hospital for x-rays, and kept in overnight for observation. She couldn't have guaranteed any more publicity if she had tried. The local papers got to hear about the attack on her, and then it all came out about what she had done as well. Her reputation is in tatters, and because we supplied her, some of the flack is hitting us. The reaction to it, and to us in particular, is all out of proportion, and it all points to Alex Haines."

"How can he be involved? He's nothing to do with National Petroleum. Don't you think that this 'Alex' thing is clouding your thoughts?"

"No, I don't," Carl snapped. "Alex may not be in with National Petroleum, but Geoff Platt is."

"But he's one of us," said Mick, not following Carl at all.

"Not any longer! He's in with Alex and James in this new company, I found out today! Tell me, Mick, why didn't you know about this?"

No reply.

"Anytime today will do," Carl continued.

Mick could feel the burden of blame sliding across the table and about to fall at his feet. "I probably didn't know about it for the same reason as you," he replied, determined not to be put into a corner.

"Really," asked a surprised Carl, "and what might that reason be?"

"It might be because they kept it a pretty good secret, wouldn't you agree?" The blame eased back to the centre of the table.

"You are my Operations Manager. You are supposed to know these things and advise me. How many more 'defectors' are there likely to be?" Blame back to Mick.

“Well, maybe as the Operations Manager, I should have had some say in the hiring of Morgan.” Blame centre table, plus immediate follow-up. “Because without her, there would be no situation to answer to!” Perfect delivery; blame slides relentlessly into Carl’s court.

“That wasn’t possible.”

Game over. Match to Mick, as the blame falls firmly into Carl’s lap. Carl looked down, almost as if he felt the weight, but when he looked up he saw Alex Haines. Then the face quickly changed back to Mick. Damn! Even his Operations Manager was getting the better of him now!

“Look, as I was saying,” Carl said, conceding defeat, “Geoff Platt is now one of them and it appears he’s milking this Morgan affair for all it’s worth. There was never any chance of Norquest staying on the project after the rep was assaulted, National Petroleum would never stand for that, whatever the circumstances, but they also believe that the actions of Morgan were indefensible. She’s out, and her chances of repping again in the North Sea will be zero when the other oil companies hear the full details. And our name is being dragged along with it in N.P. at every opportunity, thanks to Geoff. He is making as much capital out of it for Alex and his new company as possible; all at the expense of the reputation of Oceansearch.”

“Then we need to visit National Petroleum as soon as possible. We have to save our contract with them, especially now that the Delta Mex contract has been lost.” The concern in Mick’s voice was firmly linked to the loss of chargeable man-days to his operations.

“I’m going this week,” said Carl.

“Wouldn’t it be better if I go, as the resident Operations Manager?”

"No. As you so clearly put it, I hired Morgan, I'll deal with it. Which brings me to the second item. Delta Mex Oil lost the new 210/12-f well on Monday night."

"Not Chris Fletcher's work?"

"The same."

"And?" Mick asked, fearing the worst.

"There is a meeting on Friday to find the culprit."

"But Chris is in Brazil."

"I know, that's why I've been summoned. Still, at least Alex Haines won't have anything to do with it."

"You're obsessive about him."

"He's taking our clients and our business! I have every right to be obsessive," Carl shouted, causing Mick to flinch. "Anyway, you're in the hot seat for the rest of the week because on Thursday I'll be at National Petroleum, and Friday will be spent at the Central Business Unit for the Delta Mex inquiry."

CHAPTER 23

The Strand, London.

"Here's the contractor's report from Norquest, complete with all the paper seismic sections," Lawrence Taylor said to Alex, pointing to the three volumes laid out on the chart table. "The data is also loaded on the workstation; I want you to check both sets of data, belt and braces approach. Leave nothing to chance."

"Chris Fletcher did the same, so you should come up with the same findings," added Thomas Brooker, the new Team Leader of Seabed Services, trying to sound as knowledgeable as possible, but it was obvious to both Alex and Lawrence that the man was seriously out of his depth, and dreading tomorrow's meeting at the Delta Mex Central Business Unit in Aberdeen.

"Did you agree with the levels at which Chris predicted gas, and the depths where he advised caution?" asked Alex. Lawrence studied Thomas's face as they waited for the reply.

"I'm afraid I didn't check it at all," was the answer neither of them wanted to hear. "I assumed that as a consultant, his work would be perfectly acceptable, and I signed it off. In any case, he only presented it to me for signing at 4 p.m. on Thursday, and I had to send out an all-in-one notice to the various departments within the hour. There wasn't time for any checks to be made."

"Why did he take over three days to produce the report?" asked Lawrence.

"I've no idea," said Alex. "I know he doesn't do much office work, but it shouldn't have taken that long."

"Well, let's hope he was right with his interpretation. We'll all meet at five this afternoon to discuss how you should tackle tomorrow's meeting. For your information, the O.I.M. and the Drilling Superintendent from the *Ronin Samurai* are at the C.B.U. again today, and I know they intend to lay the blame firmly on my department. You have to show that they are wrong!"

Alex started with the contractor's summary of the expected drilling conditions, and from there worked back through their interpretation, checking the depths and lateral extent of any gas-charged layers. He could find no fault with the overall interpretation, and apart from the position of a couple of minor boundary limits that did not go near to the proposed drilling location, he accepted their report as being correct.

He then moved on to the drilling hazard summary report produced by Chris Fletcher two weeks ago, when Alex and James had been temporarily unemployable by Delta Mex Oil. Chris had advised care at two levels, one shallow and one deep, but had advised extreme caution at an intermediate level. The wording extreme caution was in-house terminology that told the drillers there was a high risk of gas, and that well casing should be set in the hole before reaching this depth. The drillers had obviously done that, as their operational record showed, which meant that other factors had affected the integrity of the hole.

Alex then looked at the deeper anomaly where care had been advised, but could find nothing wrong with the interpretation and recommendations put forward by Chris Fletcher. All in all, the report was looking good, and after plotting the shallow anomaly, he tended to agree with Chris that it was right to advise care at that level. Things were certainly pointing to it being the fault of the drillers for not withdrawing the drill string. It now seemed that the rattling drill must have damaged the cement and casing, causing the gas to seep from the intermediate level.

Only one thing puzzled Alex, and that was why was there no reference to other wells in the area. He was certain at least two other wells had been drilled close by, but there was no mention of any correlation in the Norquest report, or in the hazard report written by Chris. Alex felt he must be wrong about the wells being nearby, but for the sake of completeness, he went to the well log library on the fourth floor, and took out the previous well charts to check. His eyes immediately settled on well 210/12-3, lying less than 5 kilometres to the south east of the new well 210/12-f. His heart started to beat faster as he searched for the report, hoping that if a correlation existed, it would have the same warnings posted against it.

He quickly took the paper seismic sections from the plastic wallets at the back of volume two, and looked at the lines through the centre of location. Immediately he could see the same three levels, clearly anomalous, with the intermediate level easily the brightest, but this time with the upper level showing up much more readily. As soon as he saw it, Alex knew without looking that the associated drilling hazard report would have advised extreme caution at two levels and care at the third. Two minutes later, he had the hazard file in his hand and was staring at the words *extreme caution* against the shallow and intermediate levels!

"So he didn't check for other wells," said Lawrence, "is that what you're saying?"

"Couldn't have done," was all Alex could reply.

"What did the well log say?"

"No problems encountered, but they had already set the casing above the shallow level."

"What would you have done?"

"After seeing the 210/12-3 report, I would have had to advise extreme caution. It would have to be reported."

"Then basically, Chris screwed up!"

"Yes, but so did Norquest. They didn't refer to the well either," Alex said.

"Who checked their report when it came to us for approval?"

"Morgan O'Neil signed it off two weeks before she left."

"Great! Well, it looks like we are well and truly stuffed this time," Lawrence said throwing his hands up in the air, and looking across at his next-to-useless Team Leader, who had not said a word all the while Alex had been speaking.

"No, Lawrence, there is a way out where you won't take all the blame."

"Really? Then tell me, because I'm damned if I can see a way out if this mess," he said, eyes glaring at the still silent Team Leader.

CHAPTER 24

Bridge of Don, Aberdeen

"All set, Thomas? Alex asked the new Team Leader, who was looking most un-leader-like as they walked into the foyer of the Central Business Unit of Delta Mex Oil.

"No, but let's get it over with," he replied nervously.

"Just stay quiet on the interpretation side, and then you take over if the talk moves onto contracts. We'll come out of it okay, you'll see."

"I wish your confidence was infectious," Thomas said, trying to raise a smile.

They signed the visitors' book at the reception desk, and were asked to take a seat until the last person arrived. When they were all together they would be escorted to the inquiry conference room.

Carl Moston didn't really take much notice of the other people in the foyer when he approached the reception desk, and it was only when he was directed to the same seating area that he saw the impassive look on Alex's face.

"What the fuck? What are you doing here, you two-faced bastard?"

"Good to see you, Carl," Alex cut back. "Did Lawrence forget to tell you that I would be here?"

Thomas the Team Leader seemed to shrivel between the two men, but decided he had to intervene. "I thought it best that we have someone representing the department who is totally familiar with our operations, especially since Mr. Haines here reviewed Mr. Fletcher's hazard note."

"You did what?" hissed Carl, barely keeping his voice down.

"Someone had to, seeing as your ape-man is not here to speak for himself."

"Chris Fletcher is one of our best men, and unlike some weak shits, he still works offshore, Brazil in fact. But don't worry about him, I'll back him up 100%."

"That's good to hear, Mr. Moston," Thomas said, "because you may have a great deal to back up."

Alex was actually impressed by Thomas, because although he appeared to be a bag of nerves, his voice was completely controlled, without the slightest trace of emotion, as he completely shot down Carl.

"You've done a fucking job on us, haven't you, Alex? Just like the one I spent hearing about yesterday at National Petroleum," Carl said, his eyes blazing as he desperately tried to control his urge to swing at him.

"If you make the move, make it count," warned Alex, reading the situation perfectly.

"Gentlemen, I suggest this ends now because it looks like we are about to be escorted to the meeting," Thomas said, looking at the man walking directly towards them.

"Pray you are doing the right thing, Alex."

"Oh, I am, Carl, I am," he replied as their eye contact was broken by Thomas standing to meet the escort.

The faces of the four members of the inquiry panel were impassive while Thomas introduced Alex as the consultant brought in to evaluate the contractor's report and Seabed

Services' drilling hazard report. They then listened without comment until Alex had finished, never once baulking at the technical language or needing the methods explained. Alex knew he was talking to specialists and they expected nothing less of him.

"In summary then, Mr. Haines, am I right in believing that you think there was an error made in the contractor's report initially? An error of omission?" asked the eldest of the panel.

"Yes, that's correct."

"And that this error was compounded by Mr. Fletcher of Oceansearch Associates in the production of his drilling hazard report for the same reason, i.e. that he failed to check for other wells close by, and the recommendations raised for those wells?"

"That's correct, also."

"In your professional opinion, is this acceptable?"

"No, it isn't, but I can see why the advice of care was given. Taken alone, the interpretation in the 210/12-f report was correct because the level of amplitude of the shallow anomaly was not high enough to justify advising extreme caution. Only by referring to the 210/12-3 well would the level of warning be upgraded because of prior knowledge."

"I see. And what would you have advised, Mr. Haines?" asked the tall, thin man.

"Extreme caution."

"Because you thought to check?"

"That's correct."

"Are you convinced that the gas came from the top level," came the question from the youngest member of the group, who up until now had seemed remote from the discussions.

"No, I'm not. Because of the damage caused by the drill string not being withdrawn from the hole, it is impossible to say whether the gas came from the middle level or the top level."

"Are you then blaming the drillers?" the same man asked, and judging from the tone of his voice, Alex would place bets he was from the drilling department.

"I am not here to apportion blame. I believe the casing should have been set higher in the first instance, but I also firmly believe that the drill string should have been withdrawn. Either, or both, of these factors could be responsible for losing the hole."

"And hundreds of thousands of pounds worth of equipment," the old man added. "Thank you, Mr. Haines, you may sit down. Mr. Brooker, I believe you are the Team Leader responsible for running Seabed Services," he continued.

"Yes, sir."

"Then can you tell me why you did not employ Mr. Haines in the first place to write the hazard report, when it is apparent to us all that he is the only one seemingly capable of a professional appraisal?"

"We were unable to employ Mr. Haines at that time because of the contractual agreements entered into by Delta Mex Oil, which could not be resolved until Monday of this week," Thomas Brooker replied.

"I was under the impression that he had been working for us for some years?"

"That's correct. However Mr. Haines was no longer available to us under the Oceansearch Associates contract, and his own company, Deva, was not allowed to supply personnel, including himself, to us until Monday of this week. I have here all the relevant documentation for your inspection, which show this to be the case," Brooker said, passing them over the table.

“So we are victims of ourselves? Is that what you are saying?” the old man asked.

Thomas Brooker thought it best not to answer.

“Very well. Mr. Moston, in the absence of Mr. Fletcher to defend his hazard analysis, it falls on you, as the chosen representative of Oceansearch Associates, to speak on his behalf. Your comments, please.”

Carl cleared his throat as he studied his interlocking fingers, the knuckles turning white with the force of his grip. His voice was controlled, but the anger he was suppressing was almost tangible. “Gentlemen, there are many things I would like to say regarding this hatchet attack on my company, and particularly on the good name of a well-respected representative.”

“I advise you to proceed with care, Mr. Moston,” the old man said.

“Really? How odd! Because it seems to me that Chris Fletcher advised you to proceed with care, and you didn’t take a blind bit of notice! You know damn well the drill string should have been pulled. All you want is a hanging party, and that snake,” pointing at Alex, “is swinging the rope at Oceansearch.”

“You are strongly advised to control your emotions, Mr. Moston,” the thin man said. “Mr. Haines has been thoroughly objective in his appraisal.”

“Objective! That’s rich. Let me tell you how objective he has been. He has taken some of my best representatives and set up in competition to me. This is all part of his plan to win your contracts.”

“That is incorrect,” interrupted Thomas Brooker. “Mr. Haines’ company was awarded the contract before this incident occurred.”

"What the fuck do you know?" Carl shouted. "You need him to hold your hand! This man," he motioned dismissively to Brooker, "is a fool, and should never have been placed as a Team Leader."

"Mr. Moston, you are seriously out of order," said the old man, now standing. "I must remind you of the seriousness of this inquiry. We are discussing a rig blowing up, and we are not interested in your character assassinations. In fact, you would do well to copy the actions of Mr. Haines at this time, and adopt a more professional approach. Leave the room now, and compose yourself before we call you back."

Carl had no option but to leave. He pointed at Alex, "You will regret this, believe me!" The door slammed behind him.

"Would you gentlemen also please leave the room for ten minutes whilst we talk amongst ourselves?" was the politely phrased command from the tall, thin man.

Less than five minutes later they were summoned back inside the room. They were not invited to sit, which meant it was verdict time! It was the old man who spoke.

"Gentlemen, in the absence of Mr. Moston, who has chosen not to reappear, I can tell you the findings of this internal inquiry. It is the opinion of this panel that the fault can be apportioned in two parts. The first part regarding the drilling hazard report is the direct result of Mr. Fletcher's incompetence, and he will never work for Delta Mex Oil again. Also, in this respect, Mr. Brooker, as the Team Leader, you are to be severely reprimanded and this will be entered on your service record. In the second part regarding the drill string, we find the Drilling Superintendent of the *Ronin Samurai* to have been negligent in the extreme, and his employment has now been terminated."

"With regard to Mr. Carl Moston, his conduct was totally unbecoming of a professional in this industry and his company,

Oceansearch Associates, will not be invited to tender for future contracts whilst he is head of the company."

"Finally, Mr. Haines, we would like to thank you for your impartial assessment of the situation, and trust that you will continue to work in Seabed Services for some considerable time to come. It is our recommendation that all future drilling hazard reports pass over your desk for approval." The old man gave a curt nod. "Good day, gentlemen."

Within twenty minutes of leaving the meeting, Carl was back at his hotel bar with a large whiskey in one hand, and his mobile phone in the other. He had already made the first of two planned calls, and was now waiting for the reply. It came quickly, as expected. He knew full well that his secretary wouldn't dare keep him waiting, knowing the foul mood he was in.

"When?"

"She will be on the last flight from Sumburgh. It arrives at Aberdeen Airport at 1800hrs," the nervous voice said.

"Thanks," was all she got in reply, but it was more than she expected. He clicked the phone off and downed his whiskey in one shot. The next call he would make would be from the privacy of his room before he checked out.

The call was answered at the second ring.

"Mr. Grayson is on one of the ships at the moment. You may be able to reach him on his mobile if it is urgent," the receptionist said.

"Thank you. Could you connect me please.?"

"I'm sorry, that's not possible. If you don't already have the number, I'm afraid you are not meant to. Who should I say called?"

Carl pressed 'End Call'. "Officious bitch! It was to save me time," he said out loud, as he clicked his mobile to find Aldred's number.

The sudden intrusion of the sound of his phone caught Aldred unawares, breaking the peaceful silence in the officers' stateroom onboard the *North Sea Tiger*. Over the years, Aldred had often sought peace and quiet in this beautiful room, reflecting on the quality of the workmanship and the days when craftsmen worked in wood instead of chipboard and plastic. His orders had always been strict and fiercely obeyed, ensuring that this room never lost it's elegance, much to the chagrin of the ship's crew who spent hour upon hour waxing and polishing the panelled walls and carved table. Aldred sat in the admiral's chair at the head of the table admiring the beauty, and was more than a little saddened that within less than two weeks this ship would finally be scrapped.

He begrudgingly took the phone out of his pocket and answered with more than a hint of irritation in his voice. "Yes?"

"Bad timing, obviously," said Carl.

"Too late now. What do you want?" Aldred asked, immediately recognising the voice.

"A small matter of settling outstanding debts. I believe I have completed my side of the deal. Both jobs executed to perfection, and you benefiting already," he replied, trying to sound upbeat to counteract Aldred's bad mood.

"I would hardly describe them as being 'executed to perfection' as you put it; the first one was seen, and the second one, well, just about everyone in the industry knows about it because of the way the woman acted. It was a disgrace and I'm not surprised it backfired on you."

"It worked, that's all that matters."

“She acted like a whore, and then told the man’s wife. We always agreed to leave families out of it. This has turned bad because the wife became involved.”

“You’re out of touch, Aldred. Morgan got the job done for you, and she took a beating because of it. As far as I am concerned, anything goes, and Morgan is no whore, so before you think of saying that again, hold your tongue, otherwise I will personally rip it out! Do you understand?”

This was an excellent development as far as Aldred was concerned; Carl was being protective.

“I understand, but for you it’s over, Carl. That was the last time. You’re losing your grip on the whole industry. You’ve become reckless on the special jobs, and you can’t even hold the ordinary repping jobs, from what I hear.”

“That will change on Monday. You see if it doesn’t.”

“Really? And just how will it change?” Aldred asked.

“You don’t want to know. It won’t fit in with your ‘family loyalty’ bullshit. Suffice to say that when I have finished my business trip deep in the heart of Cheshire, Oceansearch Associates will be back in the driving seat, and Alex Haines will be a name of the past.”

Aldred remained silent at the mention of Alex’s name, seeing if Carl would say more about him. He didn’t.

“Aldred, my old friend, payment is now due in full, and I will be coming to Great Yarmouth next week to collect. Have it ready in cash by Friday.” The line went dead.

Aldred tapped the ‘Call End’ button on his phone, concern now etched into his face as he realised just how unbalanced Carl had become. There was a knock on the door, and Melvyn, the base engineer, walked in.

“I’m sorry to disturb you, but we’re ready for the demonstration now, Mr. Grayson. The second Strataview system has been linked up and we believe the system will work.”

“I’ll be right along, Melvyn,” Aldred said, pushing the chair backwards. He stood slowly, then walked beside the table, idly drawing his fingers over the curved edges as he thought about what Carl had just said.

When her flight arrived at Aberdeen Airport, Carl was waiting. He walked to meet her and her eyes immediately filled with tears at the sight of him. She readily accepted his arm around her and leaned her head against his shoulder as they walked through the arrivals hall. His was the first friendly face she had seen since the story of her phone call had broken.

“Why are you here?” Morgan asked between sobs.

“To meet you and to take you away for the weekend.”

“Why?”

“Because I want to.”

“No, Carl. It won’t work. We can’t just start again.”

“No strings attached. Cross my heart,” he promised. “Separate rooms. Just a weekend away. Look at you. Do you really want to spend the weekend alone? Come with me. Three nights away. My week has been bad and I need a break as well.”

“Where to?” she said, softening.

“Cheshire.”

“What?”

“I have business there on Monday, and I am flying to Manchester tonight. You too, if you want to.” Carl held up the two tickets he had already bought for the seven o’clock flight.

“No strings?”

“No strings. Promise.”

“Okay.”

“Good. Wait here while I get your bag from the carousel. We just have time to make the flight.”

She watched him walk away, pleased with this unexpected development. She had wanted a special job to get close to Carl, and it was working. A weekend away would bring them even closer together, and the closer they were, the easier it would be for her to find a way of taking her revenge on him for his part in Sean’s death. She hadn’t meant to cry when she first saw Carl, but the ferocity of the attack by the Party Chief had scared her, and it was impossible to forget how she once felt for Carl. She would never let such feelings develop again, but she still needed affection and reassurance. Who wouldn’t? Let Carl chase after me all he wants, she thought, because the more he chases, the less chance he will realise he is being hunted.

At nine-thirty Morgan and Carl checked into the Hilton Hotel at Manchester Airport. They took separate rooms as Carl had promised, and after a quiet meal together, he escorted her to her room and said goodnight. The perfect gentleman. He had different plans for tomorrow night.

———

CHAPTER 25

Beeston, Cheshire

Carl's hire car was delivered to the hotel at 11 a.m., and after ten hours of undisturbed sleep both Morgan and Carl looked and felt remarkably refreshed. The swelling from Morgan's lips and cheek had all but disappeared, and even the darkness and tension previously evident around Carl's eyes had started to fade.

Neither spoke much during the journey south through the Cheshire countryside. At Sandiway, Carl turned left off the old Chester road, and headed for Tarporley. The village was small, with one main street, and when they appeared to be passing right through, Morgan began to wonder just how far they would be driving.

"Do I get to know where we are going, or is it a surprise?" asked Morgan.

"We are going to stay at the Wild Boar Hotel at Beeston. It's not far now."

"And what kind of hotel is that? Small, cosy, family-run type?"

"Oh no, this is really beautiful. It's a large, black and white timbered building near to the ruins of Beeston Castle, and the standard is as good, if not better, than anything in the south. Plus tonight there is a dinner dance. I've already checked."

She laughed. "What good is that to you? You could never dance at all. In fact, you wouldn't even try!"

"Yes, but that was before I met Marianne."

“Oh, I see,” Morgan replied with a knowing tone in her voice, which she hoped disguised the faint tinge of jealousy that just came over her unexpectedly.

“Marianne was Spanish, and introduced me to the delights of Latin American dancing, amongst other things, and now I’m quite addicted to it. What about you, did you ever find a dancing partner?”

“I’m afraid not. Looks like I’ll be the wallflower tonight.”

“I doubt it very much.”

“Anyway, I don’t have a dress for a dinner dance.”

“No problem, you can get one in Chester after we’ve had lunch. It’s only ten miles from the hotel. I’ll take you. Look!” he pointed, “there’s the hotel up there on the left.”

“I see what you mean; very impressive. What a location!” But the car turned right off the main road, before reaching the drive, following a narrow lane leading to the castle. “Aren’t we checking in?”

“No need to yet. They’re not expecting us until later.”

“Where to now?” she asked, looking straight ahead to the imposing ruins of the thirteenth century castle standing high on the sandstone outcrop.

“Let’s find a pub and have some lunch. Then I’ll take you to Chester for that dress.”

They sat in the conservatory of the Shady Oak, which looked across open fields to the rear of the castle, for well over an hour, enjoying a leisurely lunch talking of inconsequential things.

“It really is peaceful here. How did you get to know about these places?” Morgan asked.

"From an old business associate who lives near to here."

Morgan immediately thought of Alex Haines. Was he in some way involved with Carl's business trip to Cheshire? She didn't know. Nothing more was said, and she let it go. Yet her innocent question had somehow changed the atmosphere. She needed to know more. At two o'clock they left the Shady Oak for Chester, where Morgan purposely chose a dress to kill.

At six o'clock they checked into the Wild Boar Hotel. Morgan took the double room with a view to the castle, while Carl took the single room, two doors down the corridor.

"I insist," said Carl. "I know how impressed you were with the castle this afternoon. I really don't mind."

"Okay, as long as you are sure," she replied, carrying her bag into the room.

"I'm sure. I'll see you in the lounge bar at seven-thirty. Don't be late."

"I won't be."

Carl smiled as he caught a glimpse of the king size bed before Morgan closed the door, the four corner posts perfect for his plans tonight. He hoped her tastes hadn't changed too much since they were last lovers.

Morgan luxuriated in the herbal bath, only her head visible above the layer of foam. She lay back with her eyes closed, allowing her body to relax completely while her mind remained as clear as ever. Her plan was simple. Use the lure of sex to ensnare him. It had worked before and it would work again, she just needed to be more careful this time. She would lead him along, waiting for an opportunity to take her revenge for her brother's death, starting with tonight.

She quickly showered and washed her hair as the bath water drained away. The new dress was laid out on the bed, with the matching shoes by the kidney-shaped dressing table. After drying her hair she slipped on the shoes and looked at herself in the full-length dress mirror, sideways first of all to see the lift of her bust and the flatness of her stomach, then turning on her heels, head over her right shoulder to inspect the well-muscled legs and high rounded buttocks. She loved her body and the effect it had on men.

Within fifteen minutes her make-up was complete, and she carefully lifted the fawn coloured dress over her head, allowing the sheer material to slide over her arms and her shoulders. It fitted tight to her bust and waist and flared over her hips to mid-calf length. The wearing of underwear was impossible without ruining the fall of the dress. As she walked a few paces towards the mirror, the dress clung to her like a second skin with one sway of her hips, then fell away with the next, as if to tantalise the observer.

She wanted to know what Carl was up to, and if wearing a dress like this loosened his tongue, then she didn't mind at all!

Carl put down his drink and couldn't help but stare, along with the three other men, when Morgan walked in the lounge bar. He stood to greet her, and gave her a gentle kiss on the cheek as she took the adjoining seat.

"You look stunning, absolutely stunning."

"Thank you," she nodded, whilst quickly smiling to the three women who were glaring at her, "but I'm not sure that they would agree with you."

Carl glanced across to the table. "Oh, they know how good you look all right, and so do their husbands. Let me get you a drink." He went to the bar without asking what she would prefer, and came back with identical drinks.

“*Kir normal*,” she nodded at his choice. “So you still persist?”

“Old habits die hard,” he replied, while his hand inadvertently moved to the inside pocket of his dinner jacket, checking once more that the contents were still there.

The talk between them was good, never once flagging nor touching on the subject of work, and after the third drink Morgan was having to remind herself she was not on a date but here to get information. She suggested they eat, hoping a change of atmosphere and room would focus her mind.

After reading the menu, any thoughts of a light meal disappeared, the choice was too good to ignore. They decided on lobster thermidor, the house speciality, as recommended by the waiter, and Carl chose one Chilean and one South African wine to accompany the meal.

There were no other tables between them and the dance floor, their position having been purposely requested by Carl, and only occasional early diners were taking to the floor while most other couples were still eating. The four-piece band played a wide variety of music, alternating approximately every thirty minutes to more modern styles.

“Now this is more to my liking,” said Morgan after the second change of music.

“I hope you are not going to back out on me,” Carl chided in a friendly manner. “I’ve been looking forward to showing off my new skills.”

“Really, it would be pointless,” she argued, “I honestly have no idea how to dance, apart from casually. I would be embarrassed.”

“Nonsense. It’s easy. We’ll start off with the first dance I ever learned. The steps are simple but it looks good.”

"Please, Carl, no. We just watched that other couple do the…? See! I don't even know the name of it."

"It was a rumba, but forget about that. We'll start off with an easy dance. Believe me, you'll enjoy it." His eyes were almost pleading with her. She relented.

"Okay, but not just yet. I feel like I have eaten enough food for three people. It will take weeks to work off the extra pounds I will have put on tonight," she said, trying to find some fat to pinch.

"I really don't think you have a problem, do you? Anyhow, dancing is very good for losing weight, and when the place livens up a little, with more dancers on the floor, we will begin to hone your body to perfection once again."

"Well, it will have to wait a while for the food to find somewhere to settle, before I do any honing, as you put it."

"Okay. A digestif while we wait?"

"Only a small one," Morgan said, "the wine has already gone to my head a little," which wasn't a lie. She would have to watch her intake of alcohol carefully from now on because Carl hardly appeared to be affected by the drink.

After half an hour, he could wait no longer, and insisted that they dance. It was towards the end of the casual music, and he took her hand and led her to the dance floor. About ten couples were dancing and he agreed to dance slowly until some of the drink began to wear off. He had a much better sense of rhythm than she remembered. He was actually quite good. After a few dances of standing apart, the music changed and he took her in his arms in a cross between a Latin American and a ballroom hold.

"I can't do any dances like this," she reminded him.

"Don't worry," Carl said, "it's easy. We're going to start off with a social foxtrot, and then make it sexier."

"Are we indeed? And why do you think I will want that?" Morgan asked, raising her eyebrows flirtingly.

"I think you will when we start. It's good and it feels really nice, plus it will certainly bring us closer together," he laughed. "Ready? One-two, one-two-one…two, one-two-one…two, one-two-one…two. Just follow me. Two steps back, two to the side and two steps forward. It's easy, follow my count." He was right, it was easy. It took Morgan about thirty seconds to pick up the beat.

"Now for the enjoyable part," he said pulling her tight to him, feeling her bust against his chest, as his hand pressed into the small of her back.

"Are we close enough?" she asked, smiling.

"Nearly. Now push the front of your thighs against mine, and don't let them come away." She pushed, and realised that their hips were also rubbing together in this position.

"Now, you have to feel for any movements with your thighs, and follow them. If I move forwards, you move back, and if I move backwards, you move forwards. Always keep our thighs touching." He then moved through the basic steps again, but also started to turn and weave around the dance floor. Their bodies were locked together, feeling every rubbing movement. He was hard within seconds, and she didn't mind. His stiffness felt good against her as they danced, and she was enjoying being held so tight.

"You're an absolute natural," Carl said.

"I'm only doing what you told me."

"Yes, but it's the way you move. It's perfect." They danced the same way for the next two numbers, which coincidentally had foxtrot beats that Carl put down to the band avidly watching Morgan dance, and then returned to their seats. "I need another drink to cool off," he said, "same again for you?"

"Only mineral water. I couldn't take any more alcohol," Morgan replied, turning to watch some of the other couples now jiving. Had she continued to watch Carl she would have seen the large vodka go into the Perrier water, but with the generous slice of lemon promptly dropped in afterwards, she never tasted the difference.

After the drink and four more dances, Morgan had to stop. Her guard was lowering by the minute and Carl was making the most of it. His movements became more suggestive as they danced, and she couldn't help herself as her body started to react to his swaying and pressing. His erection was pushing against her and his hand pressed into her back, forcing her hard against him, the dress offering no barrier to his ardour. She felt herself becoming aroused in response to his movements, and knew she had to stop now while she still could. She had to make him wait, she hadn't found out a thing about his meeting next week, but her body was letting her down.

"I don't want it to go further, it's too soon," she said as she broke away from him and left the dance floor, collecting her bag from the table. He followed her through to reception and up the stairs to her room.

"Why do you want it to stop? You were enjoying it as much as I was."

"I don't want anymore," she said, turning the key in the door.

He roughly grabbed hold of her and turned her to face him, his right hand darting up the front of her dress, fingers touching her wetness. She gasped.

"It doesn't feel that way to me," he said pushing her backwards into the room, "don't you play the innocent little girl with me, Morgan, I know you better. This has been coming all night, and you have played up to it."

“Get out!” she said unconvincingly.

“Not a chance,” he said as he grabbed her left arm and pushed the door closed behind them. “I’m having you before I leave, just like you want me to.” He forced her back against the wall and lifted both her arms above her head, holding them tight with his left arm while his right hand moved up her naked thigh. He stood between her open legs and when his fingers reached their target they started their rapid movements that made her shudder. He kissed her hard to stop her protesting, only stopping as her breathing became so heavy she was almost gasping from the feeling. She pushed her hips forward and he felt her lips swell and open. And then she stopped breathing! Her body tensed and he felt the wetness run over his fingers as she came. His fingers stopped their rapid movements and she hung limply from his firm grip.

He easily swept her into his arms and carried her to the bed, laying her spread-eagled in the centre. He kissed her softly as he took out the lengths of silk cord from his jacket pocket, and proceeded to tie her arms and legs to the four posts. She pleaded with him to hurry and undress, lifting her hips as he placed the pillow beneath her buttocks. Morgan strained against the cords as he pushed deep into her, and was unable to hold back the moans as his thrusts became harder and more urgent. Carl brought her to orgasm twice more before allowing her to relax and fall asleep in his arms.

The next morning they had sex again. It could hardly be called lovemaking because of the almost violent nature of their passion, both hurting each other in their urgency. Finally they pulled their sweat-soaked bodies apart and lay side by side, breathing heavily, unable to speak as their heartbeats slowly returned to normal. It was Morgan who moved first, stretching her leg over his thigh, her hand gently toying with the thick dark hairs on his chest.

"Surely not again?" Carl sighed.

"Why can't we stay here all day, and tomorrow? In fact why do we have to leave?" she asked, moving her hand teasingly down his stomach.

He lifted his head and smiled at her in disbelief. "You really are insatiable."

"Do you mind?" she purred.

"We can stay all day and tonight, but tomorrow it's business."

She pulled her face in mock annoyance. "And what could be so important that it would take you away from this?" Her hips pushed against his thigh, while her hand squeezed his rapidly hardening manhood.

"I'm going to persuade Alex Haines to quit the industry." She eased herself over him, guiding him between her legs, determined to keep him talking.

"Impossible," she said seductively, whilst pushing down on him.

"Oh no, it will be very easy," he groaned, "in fact, I won't even have to speak to Alex at all." She smiled, took his length easily, and slowly started to ride him. "You see," Carl continued, "after I have raped his wife, Alex will never be able to leave her alone again."

"So why Monday morning?" asked Morgan after they had passed through the gatehouse to the castle, and were walking towards the middle battlements, careful to be out of earshot of other people.

"Because Alex will be getting the early train to London, just like most Mondays, and his family will be alone."

"Why not go for Alex? Why hurt his wife?"

"No! He's trying to ruin my business, so I am going to ruin his family life. I'm going to teach him a lesson that his wife will never forget. When I have finished with her, Alex's days in this industry will be over. She'll never be able to stay by herself again."

"But his children will be there."

"So what? That will make her shame even worse."

Morgan said nothing more, but her stomach was churning. She felt sick at the thought of it. All her childhood memories came flooding back; how she had been repeatedly raped, her own guilt, and her nightmare recollection of the very first time it happened, which even now turned her cold at the thought of it. She would never wish it on another woman, and somehow she had to find a way of preventing Carl carrying out his plan.

They walked up the hill in silence, through the ruined battlements to the middle keep, and finally over the new bridge across the moat, a moat which had never seen water due to it being hundreds of feet above the surrounding countryside. From the inner keep the view across the Cheshire plain was magnificent, and to the south, just a short distance away was the neighbouring castle of Peckforton, nestling in the trees on the sandstone ridge. The day was cool and the air crystal clear, and the brisk wind made people's eyes water, but Morgan's eyes carried tears. She simply couldn't shake the picture from her mind of Alex's wife and what was going to happen to her; the thought of the little girl possibly seeing it happen filled her with dread. She knew she could never erase her own memories, but perhaps if she helped someone else then she might at last find some peace from the demons that haunted her…

———

CHAPTER 26

Tarporley, Cheshire.

At 5:25 in the morning Carl was already covering the short distance from the hotel to Alex's house. Morgan had watched from the bedroom window as his car had pulled away, and had dressed immediately and gone into Carl's room. She was looking for his address book. He hadn't been carrying his briefcase and she prayed that it would be unlocked in his room. It was. She carefully opened the case, not wanting to disturb anything that would make Carl later suspect she had been there. She found the book and now quickly flipped through the pages, desperate in her search for the name. It was there! Alex Haines. Last night Carl had not left her side, making any contact impossible. She now ran back to her room, hoping she would be in time.

Alex glanced in on his son, whose head was just visible above the duvet, then walked to his daughter's bedroom. She looked like an angel sleeping, her beautiful blonde curls spread over the pillow, surrounding her head like a halo. He gently kissed her forehead so as not to waken her, and took one last look at her as he walked out of the door. Finally, he went to his own bedroom where his wife was waiting for him.

"See you tonight," he said, as he leaned over to kiss her.

"I love you, Alex. Ring me when you get to the office."

"I'm only going to London, you know," he said smiling.

"I know, but I just want to know that you got there safely. Silly, isn't it?"

"Yes, get back to sleep, it's really early."

"Bye," came the sleepy reply.

Aldred suddenly sat bolt upright in bed. He hadn't been able to get the thoughts out of his head all evening, and now he was even dreaming about it! His mind had been constantly going over what Carl had said to him about business in Cheshire, wondering what on earth could happen today that would change things. He looked at the clock on the bedside table; 5:25. It felt like he had never slept. And now why did the conversation he had with Alex keep running through his mind as well? They had spoken last night for about half an hour, but nothing had come up about business. Aldred had rung Alex to invite him to his installation as Master of the lodge next Saturday, suggesting he bring his family down for the weekend again. Alex had been delighted to accept the invitation, but that was really all they had talked about.

And then like a shot, it hit him! At the end of the call, Alex had said about catching the six o'clock train to London in the morning! Ye gods, Aldred thought, that mad bastard Carl is going for Alex's family! He grabbed for the phone, hoping he was not too late.

Alex stepped out of his front door into the cool morning air. Out of habit he turned on his mobile phone, then quietly reversed the car down the drive and left for the station.

The knock on the door drew Sarah out of her sleep. Clicking on the bedside lamp she glanced at the clock; 5:30. Alex must have forgotten something and left his door key inside, she thought, as she stepped naked out of the bed, and pulled on her Saigon robe. She shivered slightly at the cold feel of the silk, and sleepily she walked down the stairs.

"Is it Dad?" Andrew called out.

"Yes, go back to sleep before you wake Carrie up."

"I'm already awake," said a soft voice.

Sarah slipped the Yale catch to open the door, and realised the dead bolt was still on. Without thinking that it must have been put on from the outside after Alex left, she picked up the key and unlocked the door. It immediately burst open, slamming into her shoulder and knocking her backwards onto the carpet as Carl pushed his way into the house. Sarah screamed when she saw his face.

"Shut up, bitch!" ordered Carl, as he reached down and dragged her to her feet. She screamed again, only to be stopped by the heavy slap across her face. "Well, well, well," he said seeing her nakedness as the robe came open. "This is going to make it very easy for me. Doesn't look too bad either!"

The phone in the hall suddenly rang, but before the third ring had finished Carl ripped it from its socket without even loosening his grip on Sarah.

———

Morgan wept as the phone went dead, knowing she was too late. She replaced the handset and within seconds was in the bathroom, her stomach heaving at the thought of what was about to happen.

———

Five minutes into his car journey to the station, Alex's mobile phone rang. At first he thought it must be Sarah, calling to say that he had forgotten something, but a man's voice started to speak.

"Alex, where are you?"

" Aldred? Is that you?" Alex asked in puzzlement.

"Where are you, Alex, godammit!"

"I'm on my way to the station," he said surprised at Aldred's tone.

"Turn round now, and go back home."

"What on earth for? What…"

"For Christ's sake, and the sake of your family, do as I say. Do it now, as fast as you can! Carl is going to do something to your family as a warning to you not to go ahead with your new company! It must be happening now, Alex, because your house phone is dead! I've just tried it."

The tyres screeched as Alex spun the car round. He cut Aldred off and immediately called the police.

"What do you mean it will be fifteen minutes before you can get a car there?" he shouted. "My family is probably being attacked right now!" He threw the phone to the floor and drove, realising he was their only chance.

"What do you want?" Sarah said, the fear causing her voice to tremble.

"This," Carl replied, roughly grabbing one of her breasts and squeezing hard.

"Mum!" came the shout from the top of the stairs.

"No, Andrew, get back to your room!" a terrified Sarah shouted. "Now! Get back."

Andrew ran into the spare bedroom, and came out holding his dad's rattan canes. "Leave my Mum alone!" he shouted as he ran down the stairs.

"Go back, go back," Sarah cried, but the boy had only one thought, and that was to protect his mother.

Carl started up the stairs, half-carrying, half-dragging Sarah with him. "Come on, little tiger, show me what you can do."

The boy lashed out with both canes.

"Not bad!" Carl taunted as both swings missed. "Try again."

He did, very quickly, and this time the second cane stung Carl across the cheek. "You little bastard!" he yelled, raising his arm. Carl's hand slapped hard against the boy's face. Sarah screamed as Andrew's head hit the wall and he slumped unconscious down the stairs.

In the few seconds it took for this to happen, the soft, swift movement of tiny feet went unheard.

"There's another brat somewhere," shouted Carl, "where is she? I want her locked in her room, so that I can enjoy you without interruptions." Sarah screamed for Carrie to stay in her room, now that she realised what was going to happen to her. Please God, don't let her see, was all she could think.

He stood at the top of the stairs, his arm tightly round Sarah's waist, and saw the door with the sign *Carrie's Room*. He looked inside at the empty bed. "She's not in her room, she must be hiding. Where would she hide?" Carl said, his voice heavy with menace.

"I don't know, anywhere! She's probably terrified."

"Pray she doesn't interrupt us." Sarah almost broke free, but the second slap to her face sent her dizzy.

The angel's breathing was so shallow it was almost non-existent as she watched the man walk into the master bedroom half-carrying, half-dragging her mum under his arm. She could see her mum kicking and flinging her arms, but every time her mum shouted, the man slapped her. She closed her eyes, remembering that her mum had once told her that when a little girl prays, the devil trembles. Well this man was a devil, and she prayed for her dad.

"Hey, how about that; a brass bedstead," Carl said as he kicked the bedroom door closed behind them. "I'm glad I brought these with me." He pulled the silk cords from his pocket and threw her on the bed. "When I've finished you won't walk for weeks." He tied her right wrist to the rail.

The angel's eyes opened wide as she heard the squeal of car tyres, followed by the sound of running feet. It had to be her dad! She opened the top of the Ali Baba washing basket and climbed out, running quickly across the landing and down the stairs. She saw her dad standing over her brother, feeling for his pulse. When he saw her, he put his finger to his lips to signal quiet.

"How many?" Alex asked softly.

She raised her finger.

"One?"

She nodded.

"Sit here with Andrew. Don't move until I tell you. He will be all right." The little girl cradled her brother's head, tears running silently down her cheeks, as her dad raced up the stairs, the rattan canes in either hand.

"Hold still," shouted Carl, as he tied Sarah's other wrist to the rail. She kicked out. "Fucking bitch!" Slap.

The noise as the bedroom door burst open made him freeze. He looked round to see Alex.

"How the…?" but Carl never finished his sentence. Within two strides Alex was in striking distance, and the blow from the cane in Alex's left hand split Carl's forehead open, and the cross from the right cane struck horizontally across his throat, choking off the words. Carl's hands shot to his neck as he fought for air. Alex flashed a look to his wife.

"I'm all right," she cried, "you're in time."

Alex heard his son moan. He shouted, "Andrew, Dad's here. Stay where you are. Mum's safe."

And in that instant, Alex turned his head slightly to see the blur of Carl's shuffle, and the snap kick aimed to his knee. His right cane instinctively swept down in an arc, the tip catching the instep of Carl's left foot. The high pitched snap of a small bone was barely audible, but the searing pain told Carl of the damage that had been done. The left cane whirled to strike the right side of Carl's face, only to be blocked as an arm flicked out in a block-punch movement that broke through Alex's guard to hit him in the chest.

Carl followed through immediately with a second strike to the head, knocking Alex sideways. Carl tried to spring forward off his left foot to follow up the attack, but the injured foot collapsed beneath him, and as he fell to his knee Alex delivered five rapid percussion strikes to his head, face and neck, stopping only when the sound of his wife screaming finally registered. Two more cracks of the rattan canes echoed through the room as Alex broke both of Carl's wrists with deadly accuracy. The man collapsed choking on the bedroom carpet.

"For God's sake, stop! Stop before you kill him!"

"I want to kill him!"

"No you don't! Think about us. Where would that leave us? It would be worse than if you hadn't come back. A murder charge would take you away forever."

He struck once more, shattering the fingers on the hand he saw hit his wife when he first entered the bedroom.

"Enough, Alex!" Sarah screamed.

The sound of his daughter crying on the stairs made him drop the canes, and he went to his wife, stepping over the still gasping Carl as he did so. He untied her wrists and they ran to the children on the stairs.

Through the open front door could be heard the sound of distant police sirens.

"Ivy, pack a few things quickly! We're going to Cheshire."

"What on earth for, Aldred? What's happened?"

"There's been a break-in at Alex's house. Sarah and the boy were attacked!"

"Oh God, no!" Ivy said, her voice immediately breaking and a lump rising in her throat. "Are they all right?"

"They're at the hospital now."

"And the little girl, Carrie? Oh, please say that she's all right."

"Don't worry, Ivy," Aldred said, putting his arms round his now tearful wife, "she wasn't hurt. She's sitting with her dad as we talk."

"What happened to Sarah? She wasn't…?" but the word wouldn't come out, in case it made it true.

"No, she wasn't. Alex got back in time. She's badly shaken, that's all, but Andrew was hurt."

"Not badly? Why hurt the boy?" she asked, incomprehension written on her face.

"He tried to protect his mother, and was hit. He's got mild concussion. The bastard hit a little boy!" Aldred shouted as he thumped the table. "Come on, the sooner we leave, the sooner we get there. Just get enough things for a couple of nights."

"Did Alex call to tell you?"

"No, I called him."

"But, how did you know?"

"We've a long journey ahead of us, and I'll tell you everything on the way."

It was late in the afternoon when Aldred and Ivy arrived at the hospital on the outskirts of Crewe. They were directed to the children's ward where Andrew had been placed in a private room. Ivy couldn't hold back the tears when she saw the little boy. The left side of his face was swollen from where he had been hit by Carl, and the rapidly discolouring lump on the right side of his forehead showed exactly where he had hit the wall. Andrew's eyes were open, but he looked very tired. His mother was sitting next to him, holding his hand, and Carrie was sitting on her knee. When Sarah looked up to see Ivy, her own tears began again.

Alex stood at the foot of the bed, his hands gripping the metal frame. "Look at my little boy, Aldred, he was trying to protect his mother, and look what Carl did." His voice quivered with emotion. Aldred walked over and placed a hand on Alex's shoulder, squeezing gently.

"What kind of man could do that to an eleven-year-old boy? I wanted to kill him!"

"You did enough," Aldred said.

"I don't think so. He doesn't deserve to live."

Ivy walked round to sit next to Sarah. "What about you, love? Were you hurt?"

"No, I was slapped a few times, but Alex saved me from anything else. I don't understand, why would he do it? Why?"

Her tears changed to heart-breaking sobs, unable to hold it in anymore.

"You let it go, I'm here for you," Ivy said, putting her arms around Sarah and the little girl. Alex and Aldred walked out into the corridor to leave them alone for a few minutes.

"You didn't have to come all this way, Aldred."

"Do you think Ivy would have forgiven me if we hadn't?"

"Will you be staying over?" Alex asked.

"Yes, for a couple of nights. We'll find a hotel easily enough."

"Not at all. You can stay with us."

"No, we couldn't put on you," Aldred said.

"Look, Sarah will be staying at the hospital with Andrew, and I know Carrie would like having Ivy around for a while. Our spare room is always ready for guests. I'll be offended if you say no."

"As long as you are sure that we are not intruding."

"I'm positive."

That night, long after Sarah and Andrew were asleep at the hospital, and Carrie had listened to Ivy read her a third story, Aldred and Alex continued their conversation in the subdued light of the living room.

"It isn't enough, Aldred. He will only be charged with GBH, and Christ knows I will be charged with that as well; and I was only protecting my family! He will get a fine, and be free to do it all again if I don't quit. It's over Aldred," Alex said, shaking his head slowly, "he's done what he set out to do, he's frightened me off."

"I fear you're right, that he will try again if you don't give in. But, it's not just you that has problems with him. I know Carl far better than you realise, Alex, and I think I should tell you a story which goes back to my son Edward in Malta, part of which I expect you know, but what it all lead to, only a few of us really know. You came too close to finding out what happened in Vietnam, and when you started to link different events, and threatened Carl over them, I'm afraid he realised that he would have to do something to keep you quiet. Unfortunately, forming a new company came entirely at the wrong time as far as Carl was concerned. I will tell you what I know, which isn't the full extent of his operations remember, and when I have finished, you will know what you are truly up against, and why Carl must be dealt with once and for all."

Alex listened to the story that described the birth of Oceansearch Associates, and how it took its full shape when Carl became Dog's partner. Even Alex in the field in Sicily had influenced the beginning of what was ultimately to become a cover for industrial sabotage. But the thing that shocked Alex the most was the vast amounts of cash involved. For a while after Aldred had finished, Alex said nothing, breaking the stillness of the room only to pour two more drinks.

"I would never have realised how much Oceansearch made that way," said Alex. "I always thought everything had been above board. The profits to Carl and Dog were enormous."

"Still are! And now that Carl has complete control, all the profit is his, with payments in cash. He will never allow you to take away his cover of legitimate representatives."

"I'm out of my depth, Aldred. I have to quit."

"And what of me? Wasn't I one of those using the services? I thought I was controlling the industry, but if I don't do something soon I will become a victim as well. You opened my eyes only a few days ago with some of the things you said.

My methods are antiquated, and I can see now that the real control will soon be in the hands of people like yourself. Thugs like Carl, with their ideas of tough guys and sabotage, have had their day, but they won't want to give it up. I don't like how things have become, and now Carl wants revenge. He won't stop if you don't quit, and I also know that he will come for me next because of our recent meeting at his offices. Eventually he will work it out that it must have been me who warned you today. I only wish that I had warned you sooner, but it didn't occur to me how he would do it until minutes before I phoned you. If I had been quicker, you wouldn't have left the house, and Sarah and Andrew would not have been hurt. I was slow and stupid."

"You stopped it from being worse, for that I will always be grateful," said Alex, "and thank God you thought to phone my mobile when your call to the house was cut off."

"No, Alex, I said the phone was dead, I couldn't get through."

"That's odd, Sarah said the phone rang twice and Carl ripped it from the wall on the third ring," Alex frowned. "I thought you meant the phone had gone dead on you."

"No, definitely not."

"Then who…?"

"We'll probably never know, but what is important is Carl, and what to do about him. At the hospital you said that you wanted to kill him, but stopped. Why did you stop?"

"Because Sarah was begging me to."

"And you know that he will be back if you don't quit?"

"Yes, that's why I said he's won. I can't take the chance of a return visit," Alex said, wondering why Aldred was going over the same ground again.

"There *is* a way to deal with him. I wasn't sure before today how to do it, but now I know how to take out Carl and make it look like an accident. With your help it will be easier, because I need someone who will guarantee absolute silence. It would be on my territory and there would be no risk for you. It's up to you. Will you help?"

"No comebacks? If that's what you're offering, I'm in," Alex said, downing the scotch.

"Good, because it has to be this Friday!"

———

CHAPTER 27

Guildford, Surrey

Morgan's wish to stay in Cheshire longer had been granted, but only for one extra night. After Carl had been x-rayed and treated at the hospital, he had promptly been taken in for questioning, held overnight and charged on the Tuesday morning. She had stayed on at the hotel and eventually collected him from the Cheshire Constabulary Headquarters in Winsford later the same day.

He looked a mess. The cane strike to his forehead had left a nasty weal, and the bruising had produced two beautiful black eyes as the blood had drained to the skin beneath. His wrists were both encased in short plaster-of-Paris casts to give support and ease the pain from the multiple fractures received from the rattan canes.

Just as he had met her in Aberdeen, she looked after him. She carried his bags, opened railway carriage doors and eventually got him back to his flat in Guildford. But during the journey Carl had told Morgan exactly what had happened, swearing he would find out who alerted Alex. He didn't believe in coincidences, and when he knew, that person would suffer just like Alex would do in the very near future. He was going to pull in some favours. Next time he would go with help, next time Alex and Sarah would not be so lucky!

As she had listened, all thoughts of taking revenge for her brother had left her. Morgan was terrified that he might find out about her call, because even though it had failed, she knew he would get even with her for simply trying to warn Alex. Carl was unbalanced and she had to get away from him, but when? He clearly thought they were an item again. She needed to bide her time, then run. On Friday she would be paid her £30,000 for the National Petroleum 'special'; after that she had to make a break. Overseas somewhere, start again. That's what she would do, just disappear!

Three days later, Morgan left Carl's flat for the last time.

———

CHAPTER 28

Central London

"Are you sure it's a good idea me coming with you?" Morgan asked. "Aldred seemed adamant that there should only be the three of you at the meeting."

"I really don't care about the meeting Aldred has set up. All I'm interested in is collecting the money he owes me, and I want you with me so you can carry the damned briefcase!" replied Carl, looking at his wrists. "Besides, you want your money as well, don't you?"

Of course I want my money, you dumb bastard, why do you think I'm sticking around you, she thought. One more day! That's all she had to endure before her flight out of the country tomorrow. Everything had been planned so well, until Carl had told her she had to accompany him to Great Yarmouth on Friday. When she had objected, he merely pointed out that she wouldn't get her money if she didn't. Simple as that. But she was worried. The idea of having to sit through a meeting where Carl and Alex were together filled her with dread. What was Aldred thinking of? He would never reconcile Carl with Alex; she knew that because taking revenge on Alex had been all he had talked about for the past three days.

"Why do you think Alex will be there?"

"To make some sort of deal, I expect."

"I don't like the thought of it."

"Look, it was Aldred's idea. Alex is down on business anyway, and Aldred wants us to patch things up, otherwise he sees us all losing out. My main concern is to get the payment from Aldred for the two specials we have just done, and if it keeps him happy by me meeting Alex, then I'm prepared to go along with it. Once we have the money, it will be open hunting season on Alex, and his wife," said Carl, now glaring at the man he had just seen staring at his bruised eyes.

"But don't you think you achieved what you set out to do? Don't you think he's already been frightened off? Surely his wife will be petrified of staying by herself if he carries on with his plans of going up against you from now on anyway?"

Just then the underground train lurched to a halt at Liverpool Street Station, and Carl winced in pain as he grabbed the handrail, momentarily forgetting about his broken wrists. It was a stinging reminder of how easily Alex had beaten him. Carl needed revenge!

"I really don't care, because I will visit again!" he answered dismissively as they left the carriage and headed for the main line station, hurrying to catch the three o'clock train to Lowestoft.

CHAPTER 29

Great Yarmouth, Norfolk.

"Has the *North Sea Tiger* moved to the bunker's berth yet?" Aldred asked the marine superintendent.

"She goes alongside at five o'clock," said George, Aldred's cousin on his father's side. "Are you sure we need the starboard tank full? If she's only doing two days of trials, it seems a waste of money. You won't get the value of the fuel back when she goes for scrap next week."

"It's best to. We have to prove the twin Strataview system set-up is viable, and who really knows how long that will take? It's the old girl's last job, so I don't want her running out of fuel!"

"I suppose you're right," George said.

"And she still has to sail to the breaker's yard after that as well. Don't forget that!" Aldred reminded him.

"Okay, but make sure the engineer only uses the starboard tank. The port tank has cracks along the old welds. It definitely can't be used. Poor old girl, she's in a bad way all round."

"Soon be over for her," Aldred said, as if an old member of the family was about to die.

The shorter of the two men nudged his companion as Morgan stepped off the train at Lowestoft station, and both watched as she walked past them towards the taxi rank, her appearance a welcome diversion to the monotony of waiting. They both grinned as the man with the battered face gave them a hard look, someone had certainly seen to him, and, unmoved, they continued to stare at his partner's legs until she disappeared. Their train to London was not for another half hour, and after the brief 'pretty woman' interlude, they turned back to their newspapers. Just ordinary businessmen in dark suits admiring an attractive woman. Only the grime beneath their fingernails gave any indication of their true occupation.

Aldred put away his book of ceremonies. That was his final revision before tomorrow's ceremony, and although he was already word perfect, so much had happened in the past few weeks that at the moment he didn't feel as confident as he would have liked. His mind was cluttered with business arrangements, and until all accounts had been settled this evening, he knew he would not be able to relax.

Alex and his family would be arriving shortly, and Aldred had booked them into the largest suite at the Cliff Hotel, the one at the front with the balcony overlooking the river. When Alex had accepted his invitation to the installation, he had wanted them to stay with himself and Ivy all weekend, but the children had asked for at least one night in the hotel again. So they had come to a compromise, the Cliff Hotel tonight, Aldred's home tomorrow. It would actually work out very well that way, because it allowed Aldred and Alex to complete their business tonight, while Alex's family was safely in the hotel.

Aldred called the *North Sea Tiger* and asked to speak to the third engineer, who, apart from the watchkeeper, was the only person on the vessel now that she was on the bunker's berth, the remainder of the crew having been stood down for the night.

"Yes, Mr. Grayson?" the engineer said.

"I have just been informed that the vessel may have to go to Aberdeen, instead of Grimsby, after the trials have been completed. We will have to take on more fuel to cater for this, so fill the port tank as well."

"Are you sure, Mr. Grayson? I was told only to fill the starboard tank."

Aldred had transferred the third engineer to the vessel yesterday after only having been with the company for two weeks for this very reason.

"I'm positive, Andy. They have to be full. Go ahead with it and put the watchkeeper back on." He heard the muffled sound of the phone changing hands.

"What can I do for you, Mr. Grayson?" the watchkeeper asked.

"I want you to ensure that the officers' stateroom is absolutely spotless for this evening. I have two very special guests coming onboard for an important business meeting. I want the spirits cabinet to be fully stocked when they arrive at seven o'clock. The gentleman from London will arrive first, and I want you to show him to the stateroom and offer him drinks. Myself and the other guest will arrive shortly afterwards, and then I want you and the engineer to disappear for a couple of hours while we have our meeting. Go to the pub or something. Understand?"

"Perfectly, Mr. Grayson," he said, smiling to himself at the thought of having a few hours off at the old man's expense.

"Good, see to the drinks now," and he put the phone down. All Aldred needed now was to wait for the call from Alex to say that he had arrived safely at the hotel.

CHAPTER 30

Guildford, Surrey

When the two men with dirty fingernails arrived at Liverpool Street station it was already dark, the autumn evening having already drawn in. They took the underground across London to Waterloo station, and then joined the remainder of the Network SouthEast commuters making their way out of the city. Neither spoke during the thirty-minute journey to Guildford, determined not to draw attention to themselves by letting anyone hear their broad Norfolk accents.

At Guildford they checked the times of the returning trains, and then waited for forty-five minutes in the coffee bar. The taller man made two calls to the same number while they sat drinking coffee, and was pleased when, on both occasions, the calls went unanswered. After the second call they walked the short distance to the Oceansearch Associates offices. From the car park the security lighting inside the building made it look as though people were working late, but they both knew that was not the case.

When the tall one knocked at the door in full view of the passers-by, he attracted little attention. After all, he was a businessman with a briefcase outside some offices, perhaps working late, or had maybe forgotten something. Who would know and who cared? The people walking from the station certainly didn't, they simply wanted to get home. He knocked a few more times and then passed his briefcase to his partner, while he fumbled in his pockets as if looking for keys. And then he was alone. The smaller one now quickly and quietly walked round the side of the building to the back entrance.

From his own briefcase he took the tin of black treacle, and deftly spread it over the glass in the top half of the door. He then opened the cardboard roll, pressed it against the sticky surface, and banged hard against it with his elbow, smashing the glass quietly, then pushing it through and onto the floor. He was quickly inside and now had thirty seconds to turn off the old infrared alarm. He did better than that. Within fifteen seconds he had turned all the power off. Unless a battery back up had been installed he would be okay. He stood and waited.

The tall man at the front took a step back when the lights went off, as if looking for signs of activity, and then walked away, heading to the station, appearing to be, if anyone was watching, a man who had been locked out and had finally given up.

The man inside now reached for the two briefcases through the broken window and went quickly to the computer room in the back office. From the cases he took six soft plastic bags, similar to those used to carry blood except that these were filled with paraffin, and placed them by each computer terminal and by the disc storage systems. Taking the knife from his breast pocket, he stabbed each of the bags, allowing the paraffin to leak slowly. The seventh bag he stabbed was used to make a trail linking all the leaking bags, and ending at the back door. After passing the two briefcases back through the window, he climbed out, and his final act was to drop the match onto the carpet. He watched the blue flame snake across the carpet, through the doorway, and into the other room before walking to the front of the building. He resisted the temptation to turn to look at the windows as he crossed the car park, but even if he had, he would have seen nothing. The fire was in the back room, and not yet visible from the street.

He walked calmly to the station in time to join his colleague who was waiting on the platform for the return train. Within five minutes they were heading towards London, and the fire was out of control. Tomorrow they would be able to tell Aldred that their visit to Surrey had been productive, but dull. And also that they didn't like the crowded underground.

CHAPTER 31

Great Yarmouth, Norfolk

"The meeting won't take long. I will be back at nine o'clock and then we will eat in the restaurant," Alex said, "and you two make sure that you are good for your mum. I don't want any bad reports when I get back." The children looked at him and nodded. "Look, it's a full moon tonight, so you can watch some of the ships going up and down the river from the balcony if you want to."

"See you later, Alex, and don't be too long," Sarah said as she kissed him on the cheek.

"I won't," he answered, hoping he covered the unease he felt at what he was about to do.

———

The taxi dropped off Carl and Morgan at the *North Sea Tiger*, and they made their way up the steep gangway with some difficulty. The spring tide was just turning in the river and the boat was at its highest. Soon the ship would be lower in the water as the flow of the ebbing tide would begin to surge down the river, but for now Carl cursed as he struggled to hold on to the ropes with broken wrists, wincing with the pain of every change of grip.

The ship's watchkeeper was waiting for them to board the vessel. He stared at the woman in high heels. "I was told to expect one man, that's all," he said, delighting in her every awkward step.

"This is my fiancée, and she doesn't like to be stared at," warned Carl.

"Suit yourself. All I know is that Mr. Grayson isn't going to like this. He doesn't like changes to his plans." Morgan finally made it to the top and the muttering watchkeeper begrudgingly took them to the officers' stateroom.

"He will be here shortly, please help yourselves to brandy or whiskey. The cabinet is well stocked. I shall tell Mr. Grayson about the extra guest," the watchkeeper said, looking once more at Morgan's legs before leaving.

"Sod off," Carl said as the door closed. "What a prat!"

"Maybe he's right. Aldred won't be happy when he sees me."

"Stuff him! Come on, do the honours and pour a couple of drinks. We might as well relax until the old bastard gets here with the money. If he turns up that is."

Morgan looked round from the drinks cabinet. "Why? Do you think he might not come?" Her voice was trembling as she said it.

"Relax, I'm joking. Listen, Aldred is capable of anything, but I doubt if he would have invited me here to his favourite old ship if he wasn't going to come." She passed his drink. "Thanks." He raised his glass to her. "I think you should knock that straight back and pour a second. You sound as nervous as hell."

"I am. I'm scared of what will happen when Alex walks in." She turned her head to the door at the sound of the watchkeeper talking to someone in the corridor outside.

"Sounds like he could be here," Carl said, "so watch what you say." They sat down and waited.

Outside the room it was the third engineer now talking to the watchkeeper in a hushed voice. "I tell you, the smell in the hold is terrible. I'm sure there's a leak somewhere. I think we should stop taking on fuel now. We already have one full tank and the other half full as it is."

"Did the old man tell you to fill both?"

"Yes."

"He won't like it if its only half full," the watchkeeper said. "One thing you will learn about this company is that his word goes, and if he says to do something, then do it."

"But the tank must be leaking! It should already be full by now with the rate I'm pumping fuel in."

"Well maybe the gauge is wrong. Anyway we were told to leave when this bloke arrived and I don't like the look of him. Did you see how bruised his face was? Plus he's got his fancy piece with him. Mr. Grayson won't like that, and I'm not going to be the messenger who tells him. I'm off, and you'd better go as well. Check on the tank in an hour or so, and I bet you find it full. Come on, let's have a couple of pints in the Rumbold."

Alex had stayed quiet in the lab knowing the two crewmen would not go there. When he heard them leave, he began to turn on all the pieces of equipment that drew heavy power loads, but he shut down the main generator and let the equipment pull all their power from the old back-up generator in the hold; the very generator that now had fuel slopping around its base.

Morgan was passing Carl his second brandy, when the door suddenly opened and in walked Aldred Grayson. "Glad you could make it, Carl, I see you have made yourself at home." His eyes flashed at the woman and back to Carl.

"The brandy is excellent, Aldred, I must congratulate you on your choice, but that is not what I came here for. Is it here?"

"Why be so rude? Is it too much to expect people to be polite these days, and at least extend a courteous greeting? And who is my unexpected guest?"

"Sorry!" came the offhanded reply. "Aldred Grayson meet Morgan O'Neil, Morgan O'Neil meet Aldred Grayson. Satisfied?"

"Well, we meet at last, my dear," Aldred said extending his hand to greet her. "Believe me, I've heard so much about you, I feel I know you already."

Morgan was about to reply, but Carl cut her off. "Cut the crap, Aldred. Listen Morgan, he said you were a whore for the way you fucked the Party Chief in Lerwick and then called his wife. Don't be fooled by this charming pretence."

Morgan stiffened at being called a whore, but could see from the look on the old man's face that Carl was not lying.

"I simply did not agree with you involving the man's wife."

"But it did the job for you, didn't it?" Morgan said, finally finding her tongue, her eyes cold as ice as she watched Aldred's face.

Carl put his drink down and stood next to Morgan. "That's right. Now you've delayed long enough, and I'm not happy at having to come down here to this God-forsaken part of the country to collect. Tell me it's here."

"It's here," Aldred lied.

"And where's that shit, Haines? I thought he was going to be here to talk business?"

"He'll arrive shortly."

"I'll look forward to it. You say the money is here, well let's get on with it. I'll explain how life will be for Alex when he shows up. *If* he shows up!"

"Very well. Shall we go," Aldred said, opening the door.

"To where? Why haven't you brought it with you?" demanded Carl.

"Don't worry. It's on the ship, but you don't think I'm going to leave £400,000 out in the open, do you? It's in the ship's safe in the hold." Aldred saw the look on Morgan's face at the mention of the amount of money. "I see from your surprise, my dear, that you were not aware of the price Carl charged for your services. I do hope you are getting a fair price for your body."

"Knock it off, Aldred, before you get hurt."

"Is it true?" she asked.

"Of course it is," Aldred replied, "you really have been used, haven't you?" The slap across his face took Aldred by surprise. For a second he stood there stunned.

"I am not a whore!" She turned to follow Carl through the door.

Aldred watched her walk in front of him, and wondered to himself how such an attractive woman could have turned into such a heartless bitch. To phone the man's wife like she had done had revealed a heart of stone, with not a drop of emotion to spare for the woman or her children. Whatever the Party Chief had done was wrong, but the bitch had no right to take it out on his family. She couldn't be trusted, and now that she could link him to Oceansearch, he realised she would have to share the same fate as Carl.

Aldred led them down two levels to the ship's hold, then through the watertight door into the storeroom with the safe. The safe was just like everything else on this ship, old-fashioned and big. He turned the dial on the old combination lock and stood back to allow Carl to open the door.

"It's all in there," Aldred said, walking back towards the door. He stopped and picked up the canvas holdall he had left there earlier. "You'll need this as well," he said, throwing the bag to Morgan.

The safe door swung open and Carl was sure that the safe was completely empty in the brief glimpse he caught of it before all the lights abruptly went out. Aldred, who had stood holding the edge of the hatchway, immediately stepped out in the complete blackness and pushed the door to, quickly turning the three levers to the locked position, heaving on the centre one with all his weight. In the few seconds between the lights going off and Aldred closing the door, the first explosion rocked the vessel.

"What the fuck?" shouted Carl. And then he realised. "The bastard, the old bastard!" He turned quickly and bumped into Morgan in the darkness. "Get out of my way, bitch, and find the fucking door!" He knocked her to the floor in his panic.

Aldred didn't need to follow the fluorescent arrows to find his way around, he knew the old lady like the back of his hand, but the force of the second explosion as he went up the first flight of stairs had him worried. Had they allowed enough time? He just hoped that Alex was clear of the lab.

"Here's the door! I've got it!" shouted Carl. "Christ! All the fucking levers are on!" He tried to turn the top lever but he couldn't move it, his damaged wrists too weak to grip tight enough. "Morgan, come here you stupid tart, you'll have to help; I can't move the fucking things! I'll kill that old bastard when I get hold of him, and that fucking Alex! I bet he's on the ship somewhere; he's in on this. I just know he is!"

"Shut up and move," she screamed, pulling him out of the way. She felt for the levers, finding the top one first. With one violent push, the top lever turned upwards. When the second explosion rocked the boat, it sent her backwards to the floor.

"Get off me, bitch!" Carl shouted, kicking out at her. She crawled away, quickly finding the door again, her mind now much clearer than the rage-crazed Carl's. She grabbed the bottom lever and with one heave turned it upwards. One to go.

Aldred was now at the end of the second corridor and his hand touched the stair rail. He held it tight as he fought to catch his breath before climbing the steep stairs.

The third lever wouldn't move! Morgan strained at the jammed lever as Carl yelled insults at her. She felt like her heart would burst under the pressure, but her muscles, built from years of training, were now fuelled by a desire to live that was overwhelming, and slowly the lever started to turn.

"Faster, you dumb slut," Carl yelled. The door swung open and in that instant Morgan kicked backwards with her heeled shoe catching Carl directly in the stomach, pushing him away from the doorway. She scrambled through and swung the door closed behind her, rapidly turning the levers tight before Carl could push at the door.

"Bitch am I? Tart? Dumb slut? Die slowly, Carl!" Then she ran, following the shining arrows. She kicked off her high heels at the first flight of steps and climbed.

Aldred walked quickly down the last corridor. Steps slowly became visible in the dim light from the stairwell and he gave a sigh of relief as he heard Alex shouting from the main deck to the men on the dockside. Just one more flight of stairs and he would be out. He was halfway up when the ship's main tank exploded and the vessel rocked from the force. He slipped and lost his footing but hung on to the rails for dear life. He called out to Alex, and as he scrambled to the top of the stairs, he felt a hand grab the back of his jacket collar, roughly pulling him up and out onto the deck, then pushing him towards the gangway.

Morgan was half-way up the first flight of stairs when the final explosion occurred. The panic that rose in her chest as she scrambled to the top and burst out into the last corridor gave way to a scream as she became aware of the orange glow behind her.

Alex immediately turned to Aldred.

"Ignore it, Alex," Aldred begged, "get off the ship now!"

Another scream.

"But it's a woman. You said only Carl!" Alex shouted.

"He brought Morgan with him. I shut them both in, I had to. Let her die."

Morgan was now at the bottom of the final stairs and the orange glow had turned to bright red as the wall of flame raced towards her. "Alex!" she cried out in desperation, hoping he was there. "It was me who phoned! I tried to warn your wife." She reached the fourth stair and could hear the roar behind her. "The phone rang twice. Help me! Please! Oh God, someone help, just once in my life!"

In that instant Alex knew it was the truth, and her plea for help was chilling, like a cry of the soul. He turned and raced to the stairwell, reached down and caught her outstretched arm. With one heave she was on the deck, and he dragged her away from the huge tongue of flame that now roared out of the stairwell. They quickly followed Aldred down the gangway as flames erupted from every opening on the ship, and the windows and portholes all glowed bright orange before exploding outwards.

"Shut the valves and cut the fuel hoses. We need to stop the flow before the fire races back to the bunker tanks!" screamed the engineer who had run back from the pub when he had heard the first explosion. Quickly the stop valves were shut, and the fireman's axe made short work of the hoses, but the heat from the ship was tremendous and the danger was not past.

"She'll have to be cut loose," a voice shouted, "otherwise the heat from the fire could cause the main storage tanks to explode."

"But she'll be adrift in the river, God knows what she'll hit. And what if she sinks in the river?"

"She won't," the old docker said. "She's facing downriver and if we cut her ropes, she'll drift on the tide. We're at top springs now, and the flow will take her out of the river mouth and out to sea. It's the safest way to deal with her."

"Do it!" Aldred shouted.

The two axes sliced through the air, cutting the bow and stern ropes, the men shielding their faces from the heat. The ship moved slowly at first, but soon picked up speed as the river took her. If anyone had looked at Aldred they would have seen the tears in his eyes as the old lady floated away on her final voyage.

"Mum! Carrie! Look!" Andrew shouted from the balcony. "There's a ship on fire, and it's floating down the river! Mum, it's just like the Vikings, like you said to Aldred." All three of them watched the ship burn bright as she floated out of the harbour mouth and into the sea. It was a beautiful, moving sight.

CHAPTER 32

The Lodge.

At 15:45, Alex fastened the apron around his waist and put on the white gloves. One last check in the mirror to see his black tie was straight, and he was ready to join the other brothers in the temple. At exactly 16:00, the Great Yarmouth Lodge was tyled and all those now present for the installation were asked to rise and greet the outgoing Master and officers of the lodge.

Alex sat with the visitors from other lodges and watched as Aldred Grayson was once again installed into the chair as the Worshipful Master of the Lodge, and the humble representative of King Solomon. The ceremony was flawless with not a single prompt required as the officers and outgoing Master performed the set rituals.

After the ceremony was over, and the lodge closed, all the brethren lined up to congratulate Aldred and his new officers before removing their aprons and gloves and retiring to the bar. In all, over eighty people attended the installation, a mark of Aldred's popularity in the area. As they had drinks before the meal was served, the Chief Superintendent of Norfolk police expressed his regret at the loss of Aldred's ship last night.

"It seemed like we expected one voyage too many out of the old lady. All we can think is that the fuel line ruptured."

"Well, I tell you, Aldred, we were lucky not to have a major incident on our hands. The quick thinking of the old docker saved us. If the bunker berth had gone up, God knows how many people would have been injured."

"Was the man found?" Aldred asked.

"Yes, well, what was left of him, that is. I was radioed just an hour before we started. Seems they found his badly charred body on one of the lower decks. He stood no chance. You three were incredibly lucky to survive."

"I put that down to Alex, he pulled me clear and then went back for the woman."

"Brave man! He'll certainly be recognised for this. It's not every day that someone rescues the Worshipful Master, Aldred!" The old man nodded and smiled.

"Gentlemen, would you please take your seats so that dinner may be served," called out the Master of Ceremonies.

"We'll talk later, Reg," Aldred said to his old friend, leaving him to mix with the other members of the Norfolk Constabulary.

The wine flowed thick and fast during the four-course meal, and spirits were high when it came to the ritual toasts, a custom at every lodge dinner. As was also the custom, a visitor was always invited to take the floor to thank the lodge members for their hospitality. When the MC stood to announce the toast to visiting brethren, Alex could have dropped through the floor when his name was called out to reply to the toast. He looked to Aldred, and saw the mischievous smile on the old man's face. Alex had no choice but to respond.

He walked to the end of the tables and turned to face the Officers of the Lodge.

"Worshipful Master, past Masters, officers of the lodge, brethren all," pause, "this comes as a great surprise to me, but not to all of you, as I can see from the look on a number of faces." He looked to Aldred, who merely sat there with a grin from ear to ear.

"Sink or swim, Alex," Aldred called out.

"I'm swimming the best I can."

"That's fine by us," the MC said, playing along with the ritual of putting off the guest speaker, "but remember, we will fine you for every stutter, or silence of more than two seconds. Proceeds to charity, of course."

"Gentlemen, then allow me to proceed with all haste," Alex said, his nerves now beginning to subside. "First of all, I must congratulate the officers of the lodge for a ceremony which I am sure we will all remember as being word perfect. A truly excellent example of how a lodge should be run."

A loud round of applause, and agreements of 'Hear, Hear', filled the room.

"Secondly, I must pay tribute to the caterers for the excellent table this evening." More applause. "But most of all, I must thank the Worshipful Master for inviting me to his installation. Aldred is a dear friend of our family, and with his good wife, Ivy, has provided much reassurance to my family during a recent difficult time. For that, Aldred, I thank you." Serious applause now followed.

"And finally, in the time-honoured tradition of all after-dinner speakers, I must tell a joke. As you all know, I had the time it takes to walk from the table to here to think of one, and I make no excuses for it."

"This sounds ominous," a voice shouted, and was followed by loud laughter.

"As masons, we all know that the right attitude is important to progress up the ladder, just as it is important to progress in life. The right attitude to family, to work, to our colleagues, and I remember the advice once given to my older brother by his wife on their wedding night. It was advice he never forgot, and I believe we can all learn from his experience. They had left the wedding party and were alone in the bridal suite, and Terry, for whatever reason I cannot imagine, decided that he must start married life as he intended to go on. He took off his trousers, threw them on the bed, and then said to his wife 'Put them on'. She looked at him strangely, but slipped them on over her panties and fastened the belt. 'Now take your hands away' he said to her. She did and the trousers fell down. 'They're too big for me' she said. 'Yes, and don't ever forget that!' he said triumphantly." The room filled with laughter, but Alex continued.

"His wife merely smiled at her new husband, and then slid off her silk panties. She threw them on the bed saying 'now you put those on'. Well, my brother thought that this was going to be a good game, and eagerly stepped into them, pulling them up to his thighs where they became stuck. 'I can't get into them' he cried. 'No, and you never will unless you change your attitude' she said."

The place erupted in laughter, and Aldred clapped along with the rest. As he watched Alex return to his seat, he saw a man with the right attitude, a man who could take over Britannia Surveys when Aldred retired, a man who had a son who could carry on after him. Aldred saw in Alex the future of his company; together they would control the industry. He would just have to pick the right time to tell Alex!
